CATCH THE MAGPIE

Cristina Pisco

CATCH THE MAGPIE

Published 1999 by
Poolbeg Press Ltd
123 Baldoyle Industrial Estate
Dublin 13, Ireland

Web page www.poolbeg.com

A catalogue record for this book is available from the British Library.

ISBN 1 85371 901 3

Cover design by Vivid
Set by Rowland Phototypesetting Ltd, in 10.5/14.5 Garamond
Printed and bound in Great Britain by
Cox & Wyman Ltd, Reading, Berkshire.

About the Author

Cristina Pisco was born in Spain of a Spanish-Filipino mother and an Italian-American father. She was raised in seven different countries, speaking three languages. Her family eventually settled in Brussels where she married a Belgian, and built a career as a freelance journalist and television producer.

In 1992 she quit her job and moved to Ireland with her family. She is now separated and lives with her four daughters in a small village in West Cork.

Catch the Magpie is her second novel. *Only a Paper Moon*, her first novel, is also published by Poolbeg.

Acknowledgement

One of the perks of being an author is writing an acknowledgement. To do so one has to take the time to reflect on the year gone by, which is in itself a blessing. Then one has the privilege of thanking people publicly. So indulge me in my ramblings.

This year has been one of the most fulfilling in my life. A real rollercoaster of a year. Not only did I manage to get my life and family together after the pain and dislocation of a marriage breakup, I finally achieved the life long ambition of being a full time author, despite the loss of my mentor and editor, Kate Cruise O'Brien.

Being a full time author is tough. Being a mother of four is tough. Being a single parent is tough. It was a case of REALLY bad timing to try and do it all at once. For those who would be quick to congratulate me I have just one thing to say: it is impossible to do it alone. So thanks to all those who through their hard work, kindness, friendship, love and support helped me to get through such a great year.

First and foremost are my family who are the bedrock of my life. My family is a source of unconditional love. So thanks to my parents, particularly for a wonderful break in New York when I finished this novel; to my sister who searched until she found a really cheap long distance phone company; and to my wonderful, extraordinary daughters without whom none of this is worth it. They are my *raison d'etre*, my barometer of wellbeing, and their happiness is the top prize against which the merits of everything else is measured.

My thanks to everyone at Poolbeg Press: to Philip, Kieran, Paula and Nicole for all their hard work, and to Val for coming on board. And especially big thanks to my editor Gaye Shortland for stepping into Kate's shoes and making time in her desperately busy schedule to offer her advice and encouragement, while still writing her own magnificent novels. Gaye, more than anyone else, understands the challenges of being a single parent AND an author. A true Superwoman. I would also like to thank Ros Edwards of Edwards and Fuglewicz, who have successfully sold the rights to my first novel "Only a Paper Moon" to various foreign countries, thus ensuring that I will now be published in French, German, Dutch, and Polish. Most of all I would like to thank Ros for coming to West Cork to visit me.

Thanks to Grainne O'Brien for her advice and spare room. To Eddie Twomey and John Hickey, a special thanks for their sound business sense and help at a time when I needed it most. Thanks also to the Bank of Ireland, Clonakilty for their continuing support.

CATCH THE MAGPIE

A big thanks to all my friends who are writers especially Judy McGinn (with a special thanks for Judy and Michael's amazing hospitality), Janet Sahafi and, of course, Neville Thompson and Conal Creedon. Friends who are also writers are the only ones who actually enjoy talking about writing for hours on end. Your company is priceless.

I apologise to the many, many friends and neighbors that I cannot thank personally for reasons of space (this thing is long enough as it is!). To start with, all those who live in our village. For someone who has never belonged to a community, your warm welcome has made me feel more at home than anywhere else I've lived in. Similarly, a big thank you to all in Clonakilty. Your support has been phenomenal, from giving me a job when I was broke to the hundreds of small acts of kindness which I have been blessed with in the last year.

For the record, here's a totally incomplete 'thank-you-to-my-friends' list: thanks to the Michigan farmboy, Brian Fox, for terrific conversations and for chopping up seven huge trees with a bowsaw; to Tony Dineen 'sempre fidelis'; to Martin Kelleher for always being there for me; to Dave Edmund – I wish you well, we will miss you; to Carolyn 'come-back-soon' O'Keefe; to Jenny Mac (lunch?); to Elaine Walsh and her children: Brendan, Sinead, Orla and Nicky, "Mi casa, tu casa" has never been so true; and to the dozens who have peopled my house on the weekends bringing much great chat and laughter and too many late nights. A special big *bualadh bos* to Mark Stewart and Niamh O'Reilly for deciding to move to West Cork and join the party.

Last, but far from least, my thanks to John Noonan for his patience and kindness, his lavish affection, and for making the day bright no matter how badly I wanted to make it grey.

Finaly a note to my readers. I had an extraordinary revelation with my first novel. After years of trying to get published one gets so involved in the process that one forgets the end result. Becoming an author means being read. You write the book. They read the book. The circle is complete. I know it sounds simple but it totally blew me away. I would like to thank all those who read 'Only a Paper Moon', who came to the signings, who wrote to me. Your support has changed my whole reason for writing. I hope you like this one as much.

Ramblings over. Talk to ya next book.

July 1999, West Cork

Dedication

Though every human receives half of their DNA from their father and the other half from their mother, the mitochondrial DNA passes intact from the mother to her offspring.

Thus every mother's daughter carries the same mitochondrial DNA as her mother's mother's mother's.

This book is dedicated to my mother, her mother, her mother's mothers and all their daughters.

Wildcats shall meet with hyenas,
Goat-demons shall call to each other;
There too Lilith shall repose,
And find a place to rest.
There shall the owl nest
And lay and hatch and brood in its shadow

Isaiah 34:14f

One . . .

Chapter One

•◦•

Kilkeambeg, West Cork:

I took the dogs for a walk this evening. We went to the top of her hill. At the very top I climbed the gate and the dogs jumped up on to the wall with me. The sun had just dipped below the horizon and the hills looked like they were on fire, glowing pink to blood red. I knew that to my left was the sea and to my right, far away, were the Kerry mountains, but I could see nothing through the scarlet glare except for the round flat disk of the new moon, like a black hole sucking in the landscape.

And somewhere, out there, thousands of miles away was New York. I heard a loud chattering coming from the copse of trees where I'd found the fairy fort. I looked over and saw a group of magpies take off and fly down

3

into the valley. I counted them under my breath: one, two, three, four, five, six, seven.

We must have looked like cut-out silhouettes up there on that wall, me and the dogs. I bet you could see us for miles around. The evening chill seeped in under what was left of the afternoon's warm breeze and I shivered under my thin T-shirt. By the time we got home the night had come, making shapes out of shadows.

What an odd way to start, thought Cat, laying down her pen and yawning. The fire crackled in the hearth. The dogs lay curled at the foot of the sofa.

But where should she start? How could she begin to tell what had taken her from the West Side of Manhattan to this tiny cottage perched high on a hill in West Cork? Cat looked at the collection of objects she had placed carefully on the table: an old necklace, a thimble, and a piece of mirror. What did she expect anyway? The candles she had lit flickered, throwing little pools of trembling light around the room. What did she think was going to happen?

The wind rose suddenly and started to whip the cottage. It screeched down the hill and through the sheds. It does sound like a wail, thought Cat. She reached over and put on some soft music to try and disguise it. But as her mind drifted off she could still hear its sad keen.

Two . . .

Chapter Two

·—◆—·

A bell was ringing somewhere. Cat struggled to block out the sound but it just kept on ringing. It was a phone. Why didn't someone pick up the goddamn phone?

Her hand snaked out from under the tangled sheet and searched blindly on her night table for the offending noise, knocking over an ashtray and a glass of water.

"Oh, shit!" she said, opening one eye and peering over the edge of the mattress. The water had soaked the pile of magazines lying on the carpet. Her new copy of *Vogue* was ruined. Linda Evangelista's face on the cover was puckering up already. And that damn bell was still ringing.

"Shit. Shit. Shit," murmured Cat as she dug her head

under the pillow. She could hear movement in the next room.

"I'm coming!" sang Fiona in her Julie Andrews voice. Fiona was a star. One thing about the British – they knew how to get up in the morning. Fiona was always instantly wide awake and cheerful, while it took Cat most of the morning to just get her normal voice back. Cat sunk gratefully back into bed, knowing that whatever it was, Fi would deal with it. Who in God's name would show up on a Saturday morning anyway? Probably some delivery guy.

Cat heard Fiona speak into the intercom and tell someone to come on up. She decided to stay in bed until they went away. A soft knock interrupted her cosy sink back into sleep.

"We have visitors!" Fiona cooed brightly as she came into the room. She was already dressed in a pair of slacks and one of those soft cashmere tops she seemed to own in every colour of the rainbow. "Rise and shine!"

"Who is it?" mumbled Cat, her head still under the pillow.

"It's Vaalerie," said Fiona exaggerating the "a" in an attempt at Valerie's California accent. Cat groaned loudly.

"But wait! The little princess comes bearing gifts. A man! She says we must meet him!"

"God, Fi. Can you imagine what he's like? I mean

we're talking Valerie here. He's probably another dud. Dull, ugly and dumb."

"And rich. In all fairness, Cat, he's probably rich."

"Who cares?" said Cat, propping herself up in bed. "He'll still be boring."

"I care, darling. Some of us still hope to marry money, you know," clipped Fiona, her eyebrows arching back at Cat. "Now get up, you lazy bugger. It's almost one o'clock."

"You know, Fi," said Cat as she swung her long legs out of bed, "one day you'll make some man very, very unhappy."

Fiona's clear sparkling laugh lit up her face. "Oh, I most certainly hope so, darling. Especially if he's very, very rich. I'll make the coffee, shall I?"

"You do that," laughed Cat as Fiona ran to answer the doorbell. Then she flopped back on the bed.

Cat closed her eyes and searched inside her head for any signs of a hangover. Nope. A little fuzzy in there, but otherwise fine. Not that she had overdone it last night, but you never know.

Cat could hear people moving into the living-room and Prince playing in the background. Fiona had, as usual, flicked on the TV even before she opened the door. They had two "tellies", as Fi called them. One that had MTV on all day and another for actually watching. The first one was like having a radio with pictures.

CRISTINA PISCO

If they wanted to watch a programme, or listen to something on the stereo, they'd just mute MTV and let the pictures dance around without the sound.

Cat hummed along with the Prince tune. It was some song about a one-night stand. Well, thank God she had resisted anything like that last night. Dinner was nice. The show was nice. The bar after was nice. But all through the evening Cat couldn't help thinking how much Bruce looked like Stockbroker Ken. She mentally patted herself on the back for having saved herself from listening to stories about pork-belly futures at breakfast.

When Ramon had walked through the double-glass doors it was like rain after a seven-year drought. Cat had jumped on him immediately and demanded to know where he was going. So they'd followed him to a club where Bruce bobbed up and down looking totally out of place in his Brooks Brothers suit. They'd ended up with a bunch of Ramon's friends, including a six-foot-tall drag queen called "Lolita". She'd teased Bruce unmercifully, singing the words to "Lola" until everyone joined in. Cat sang along, feeling only very vaguely guilty for Bruce's painful attempt at being a good sport. Hell, Bruce was a big boy. Still, she'd have to watch herself. She was turning into a fag hag.

Maybe she should just become celibate. She laughed, thinking of Ramon's reaction to that one. *"Estas loca? Are jew outta jure mind?"*

When Bruce had gone to the men's room, Ramon had slid across the velvet settee and whispered in her ear, "Good-looking, but *plastico*, honey. Plastic people don't know how to focka." Cat and her friends had a theory about some people being totally plastic. There were lots of different moulds but only the seamless were totally plastic. They had fun pointing at people and mouthing the "P" word.

It was really getting pathetic, she thought, as she pulled on a pair of black leggings off the floor and grabbed a clean white T-shirt from a drawer. For the last two years she seemed to have to go to another city to get laid. Manhattan was too small. She didn't know how to date anymore. Cat picked up a brush and ran it through her hair. It wasn't like there weren't any men out there. It was just that they were so predictable. The men were all the same – either they were pretentious and self-involved, or they were plain boring suits like Bruce.

Cat stuck her finger between the pencil-thin black Italian blinds and peered out. The sharp sunshine had been beating down on the concrete for hours and the sidewalks were starting to sweat. Cat was suddenly aware of the sounds of traffic which she had been filtering out. Cars honked. Buses belched. Trucks ground their gears, while somewhere in the distance an ambulance siren screamed. The avenue below looked jammed. From her window she could look straight over to the 59th Street Bridge. The traffic on it was at a standstill, a shiny red and chrome fire truck stopped halfway up the ramp.

God, I love the city, she thought. The city was her friend, keeping her constantly amused, constantly on the move. She loved the feeling of being on the pulse and yet being anonymous. The city was her refuge. Like a merry-go-round, the faster it spun the more everything seemed brighter and happier and less in focus, until all you could do was throw back your head and laugh at the fact that nothing made sense. Cat smiled.

"Hello, City," she said softly, and let the blind snap back into place.

Cat popped her head into the living-room en route to the kitchen. She definitely needed some caffeine if she was going to face perky Valerie and some strange man first thing in the morning.

"Cat! You must meet Trevor!" Valerie called after her. Valerie was wearing one of those ridiculous pink Chanel suits with the black trim. Valerie's role model seemed to be Ivana Trump. Unfortunately she had enough money to follow her idol. Cat waved her hand over her shoulder as she went into the kitchen.

"Hi, Trevor! Do you guys want coffee?"

"That would be great, thanks," said a deep voice behind her in a broad accent that made Cat stop and turn around.

"You're Australian?" she asked, coming in to get a good look at him. She was disappointed. His voice was warm and mellow. The accent was a turn-on too. But instead of the Aussie hunk she had expected, she found a pleasant-looking "Leave it to Beaver" sort of guy, with a broad grin, in a terrible shirt and chinos. His haircut was pretty awful too.

"Fair dinkum, sheila," he answered, laughing. "I guess the accent is pretty hard to miss."

"Pleased to meet you, Trevor. I'm Cat and I need some coffee," she answered bluntly.

"A fellow member of the Commonwealth!" exclaimed Fiona, coming in with the coffee all laid out on a proper tray, just like her Mummy had taught her. Cat mimed her thanks.

"Well, you know, some of us think it's time we severed our ties with the monarchy," said Trevor, accepting a coffee.

"What's this I hear? Treason before breakfast! You shall be deprived of milk and sugar and sent back to the penal colony."

"That's fine. I take it black," said Trevor, grinning.

"Trevor is a journalist," said Valerie. "I met him over at the magazine."

"Do you work for *People* as well?" asked Fiona. "Can you get us freebies like Val?"

Cat was only half listening. Her mind idly worked out what she was going to do with the day. The first thing was to get away from these people. She let Fiona do the hostessing, savouring her first cup of coffee in silence.

"Nah," said Trevor, settling his broad frame back into the armchair. "I was just over there sniffing around to see if I could get some freelance work. I've been here three weeks and my money is running out. I've got a string with a paper back in Adelaide but that doesn't pay the rent in New York. This is a really nice place you have here. It must cost a fortune."

"It's not mine," said Fiona. "It's Cat's."

"Wow. You rent this place on your own?" asked Trevor, turning to Cat.

"She owns it," said Fiona.

"Not technically," smirked Cat, bored with where this conversation was heading. She was not in the mood for the Little Orphan Annie routine, as she called it. That was when someone new discovered that she was immensely wealthy and an orphan, raised by her doting great-grandfather from the age of three. She rolled her eyes at her friend, who ignored her.

"I get to live here rent-free as long as I keep an eye on Cat," continued Fiona.

Cat threw a small silk pillow at her and missed. "Bitch!"

"Are you rich?" asked Trevor looking straight at Cat, his pale blue eyes perfectly guileless.

"No, not particularly," answered Cat. These Australians were incredible. They just came straight out and asked whatever it was they wanted to know! In anybody else she would have considered it rude, but there he was still looking at her inquisitively as if observing a really interesting new species of bush kangaroo. He had no hidden agenda. He just wanted to know.

"Not yet, anyway," she snapped. "Not, like, this very minute."

"Cat doesn't get her trust fund until she's thirty," Fiona contributed. "Which is rather a shame really, because I rather fancy setting up housekeeping with her in the Bahamas."

"Right! Gotcha!" said Trevor, snapping his fingers.

"*I* don't get my trust fund until I'm thirty. Unless I get married before that. That is like, so sexist," said Valerie with a pout.

"In case you're wondering. My name is Fiona and I don't have a trust fund," said Fiona. "I have to work for a living."

"Me too," said Trevor.

"Well then, we are totally unsuited to each other,"

said Fiona. "Get away from me, in case something dreadful happens like I fall in love with you."

"I think falling in love with me is a great idea!" said Trevor happily. The man was like a Labrador puppy, thought Cat.

"Fiona is determined to marry a rich American," she said. "So I'm afraid you don't qualify."

"Very well then," said Trevor, not the least bit ruffled. "I forbid you to fall in love with me!"

"I figure it's just as easy to fall in love with a mega-rich man as it is to fall in love with a pauper. It's good planning. You see, I am quite, quite, destitute," said Fiona holding her hands up to her heart like the heroine of a Victorian novel.

"Stop, Fi. You're going to make me cry," Cat said sarcastically. "You're not exactly impoverished. I mean you do have your Daddy's credit card for emergencies."

"Yes, but that is for real emergencies. Blood must be spilt. Not like your grandfather's credit cards."

"Granddad's credit cards are only meant for emergencies," said Cat haughtily.

"What about the Charles Jourdan shoes you bought last week?"

"Now that was a definite emergency!" Cat laughed. "They were on sale!"

Their conversation was interrupted by the inside doorbell. Cat jumped up to open it. As she put her eye up to the spy-hole she could hear someone thumping on the door singing *"Honey! I'm boooome!"* in a thick Spanish accent.

Through the peep-hole Cat saw Ramon standing with his arms spread out wide, his devastating Latin good looks grossly exaggerated by the fish-eye lens. A large expensive-looking paper bag was swinging in his right hand as he swayed his hips.

"It's Ramon!" yelled Cat, delighted. Finally, someone with a bit of pizzazz to liven up the two bores sitting drinking coffee. With Ramon's arrival, the interesting people now outnumbered the boring people three to two. The only thing worse than plastic people were bores. The worst of all, of course, being boring and plastic. Things were looking up.

Ramon swept into the room, stopping to air-kiss Cat. He smelt absolutely wonderful and looked drop-dead gorgeous as always.

"Hola, mi amorcito! Look what I am bringing to you!"

Ramon kissed Fiona and Valerie, commenting at how great Fi looked and what a wonderful suit Val was wearing. He bent down to peck Trevor's cheek, then stopped, changed his mind, and held out his hand. Trevor shook his hand enthusiastically, blushing slightly.

"Good to meet you, Ramon." He hung his head and

chuckled. "I guess we're not too used to kissing guys back home. Except at a rugby match. I guess I'll just have to get used to it." He threw Cat a goofy apologetic smile.

"So what's in the bag?" asked Cat. She smiled back at Trevor, clearly amused.

"You won't believe it! I couldn't believe it!" stated Ramon, standing dramatically in the middle of the room and commanding their attention. "Guess what just opened in the Village?"

They all looked at Ramon and made gestures indicating they hadn't the vaguest idea.

"Just around the corner from my place! Can you believe it?"

Everyone shook their heads in disbelief, enjoying getting caught in Ramon's little drama.

"Chocolate con churros!" he whispered in a hushed reverential tone.

"Chocolate con churros!" shrieked Cat. "Gimme, gimme, gimme."

"Chocolate – that's chocolate," said Valerie in her best California Spanish. "What's *churros* again?"

"They're those wonderful Spanish long doughnut-type things we had in Madrid, aren't they?" said Fiona.

"I have no idea what you people are talking about," said Trevor. "But they smell wonderful."

"They are Spanish pastries," said Ramon impatiently. "We better have them before they get cold."

"They are more than just a pastry," Cat explained as Ramon went off to the kitchen to get some plates. "They're a ritual. You go out to eat them especially. At *merienda* – sort of tea-time for you, I guess. Or really late at night after a club."

"You remember, honey?" asked Ramon coming back and laying everything out on the already cluttered bleached-wood coffee table. "That night after my cousin's party?"

"You mean the time you tried to get that terrible American girl to eat octopus?"

Trevor sat back and enjoyed the show.

"Midge Steinman!" they all cried out in chorus.

"She was a dog. What was she doing there anyway?" said Ramon, passing the platter of golden oblong pastries around. Trevor took one and was about to bite into it, when Ramon told him to wait for the hot chocolate he was pouring out of a large Styrofoam jug.

"She was Scott's brother's girlfriend, remember?" said Valerie. "He was doing an internship at Citibank in Madrid and she'd come over to visit him."

"She was so grossed out." Cat smiled remembering. "We were so mean. Especially you, Ramon. You don't even eat octopus."

"How can you eat something with so many tentacles and those horrible little eyes staring at you?" Ramon let an exaggerated shiver of disgust run up his spine. "Anyway, I'm a vegetarian."

"They aren't exactly looking at you off the plate," said Cat.

"I thought you eat chicken?" asked Valerie.

"They are stupid animals. That's different."

"Ramon doesn't eat anything that is scary or cute," Fiona said to Trevor.

"That could limit the menu," commented Trevor.

"I eat chicken and turkey," Ramon said, flicking his long black hair over his shoulder. "And fish. Fish are also stupid."

"So you only eat stupid animals?" asked Trevor with a twinkle in his eye.

"As long as they're not too cute or too scary," added Fiona.

"OK, everybody has their chocolate?" said Ramon clapping his hands. "We're ready!"

The steaming cups were so dark that they almost looked black, and the air was filled with the heady smell of strong cocoa. Trevor watched as Cat carefully dipped one of the *churros* about a third of the way in and covered it in chocolate.

"Oh yum!" she groaned. "This is *sooo* good."

"Not as fabulous as the ones in that place off the

Gran Via. But it comes close. It comes close," said Ramon closing his eyes and smacking his lips.

Trevor followed suit and was delighted. Those things were delicious. "If I understand correctly," said Trevor as they ate, "you all went to Madrid for a party?"

"Some of us did," answered Fiona. "Some of us just happened to be in Madrid at the time. I was lucky. I was living in London, so it was just a hop really."

Trevor didn't answer. He seemed to be digesting this bit of information along with his *churros*. Then he picked up a pile of paper that had been lying at his feet.

"I brought up the post for you," he said, smiling broadly as he handed it over to Cat.

He was a nice guy, she thought. She smiled back her thanks and let herself meet his clear, friendly gaze. He was probably one of those genuine straight-up, nice people. She wondered what the city would do to him.

Cat leafed through her mail, throwing the junk mail on the floor, and set the bills in a small clear space on the coffee table. There was very little else except an invite for a charity concert at the Lincoln Center and a large thick cream envelope addressed in beautiful handwriting and jet-black china ink. The stamp was from France.

"Looks like Phillipe's wedding invite," said Cat as she waved it at Fiona. "It's addressed to both of us."

"How cheap of them!" exclaimed Fiona coming over and sitting on the arm of the sofa. Her attention was caught by something on the floor. She picked up a flyer and read it out loud.

"Look at this: Madame Zora, the Fifth Avenue Fortune-teller. I've heard she's good. There's a free fifteen minutes, or a $10 discount on the full reading. That could be fun."

"I'd love to have my fortune told," said Valerie.

"I'll do it for free, honey. Save your money," said Ramon rolling his eyes. "You know I come from a long line of *brujos.*"

"Well, why don't you come with us and check if Madame Zora is for real?" asked Valerie. "We could go for lunch and maybe see her later this afternoon."

"I could meet you," said Cat, "But I want to check on my studio this afternoon, so I'll skip lunch. What about you, Ramon? Are you in the mood?"

"Darlings, I'd love to. But I have to get everything ready for tomorrow night," said Ramon, standing up and brushing the crumbs carefully from his impeccably white jeans and soft Gucci loafers. Cat and Fiona nodded.

"Scott is probably wondering where I am by now. He'll be locked in the kitchen for two days, I'm sure. I'll see you tomorrow at eight."

"Dressy or not dressy?" asked Fiona as Ramon headed towards the door. He stopped and considered the question for a minute.

"Oh, dressy, don't you think?" he said with a coy smile.

"Oh, goody!" said Fiona, "It's been a while since we've dressed up."

"Why don't you come along as well?" Ramon asked, pointing at Valerie.

"I'd love to," beamed Valerie.

"And bring your friend Ted. The more the merrier I always say."

"Trev. That's Trevor. I'd be delighted," said Trevor, blushing again.

"Whatever!" said Ramon blowing him a kiss. "See you all tomorrow at eight o'clock!" Then he blew another round of kisses and waltzed out the door.

"So where is this dinner?" asked Trevor.

"Down in the Village. Ramon lives with Scott," explained Cat. "He's a Wall Street broker, very straight-looking."

"And gorgeous," added Fiona. "Why are all the gay guys gorgeous?" she asked raising her eyes to the ceiling. "Or maybe that should be why are all the gorgeous guys gay?"

"Some of us gorgeous guys are straight," said Trevor, jumping up and doing a little Charles Atlas strut around the room. He looked so silly in his buttoned-down shirt and crumpled chinos that Cat started giggling. This encouraged him to pose some more. Catching sight of the TV, he made a lunge for the remote. "Turn it up! Turn it up! I love this song!"

Right Said Fred were filling the screen with their bald heads and gyrations. Trevor stood in front of the TV, blocking the screen, and mouthed the words:

"I'm too sexy for my shirt, too sexy for my shirt,
I'm too sexy for my shirt, too sexy for my shirt
So sexy it hurts."

The effect of the deep growly voice coming out of this ordinary-looking guy had Cat bent over double laughing. Trevor stood rod-straight like a six-year-old at his first grade Show and Tell, pointing at his shirt. The girls joined in, dancing around the coffee table.

"I'm too sexy for your party, too sexy for your
party
The way I'm disco dancing!
I'm a model and I do my little dance on the cat
walk."

He mimed every verse until the three of them had tears running down their faces. After it was over he took a bow and flopped back on the sofa.

"Oh my, that was an incredible performance!" said Fiona, still laughing. Cat had to admit that he wasn't half bad. Another couple of numbers like that and he might even be considered a candidate for one of the interesting people.

Chapter Three

·—◆—·

"So are all the men at this dinner going to be poofters?"
asked Trevor as they walked out of the air-conditioned
lobby into the heat of the city. It was like walking into
a furnace. Trevor had decided to accompany Cat to the
Village as he was heading that way.

"Don't tell me you're one of those sexually repressed,
homophobic, gay-bashing, Australian rugby players,"
said Cat as she raised herself on her toes, craning her
neck to look up 57th Street to try and catch a cab.

"Yes, No. No. And it's football. I'm too short for
rugby. Of course it was Australian football, not pussy-
footie like the Europeans play. Soccer is for girlies.
Australian football is a *real* man's game."

Cat whipped around to berate him for being so
macho, when she noticed that he had a huge grin on

his face. He was pulling her leg! She bit back her words, annoyed at having been such an easy target.

"So," he said pleasantly. "Which way are you walking?"

"Walking? You must be kidding. You'll melt before you walk a block." Cat had showered and changed into crisp linen cuffed shorts and a big baggy shirt, but she could already feel the sweat trickling down her back.

"It's a beautiful day!" Trevor protested. "Anyway, working up a sweat's good for you."

"Horses sweat. Men perspire. Ladies glow."

"Who's being sexist now? Come on. It's no more than two clicks." He started walking briskly up the street. Cat ran after him, catching up just as he stopped for the light on First Avenue.

"Slow down, you're going too fast," she gasped. God, it was hot. If they were going to walk all the way down to the Village she'd be glowing all right. She'd be lit up like the giant tree in Rockefeller Center at Christmas.

"*You've got to make the morning last,*" Trevor said, sounding serious.

Cat looked at him, not understanding. What was he talking about? Trevor looked as if he expected her to answer a riddle.

"Give up? OK, the next line is: "*Tripping down the cobblestones. Looking for fun and . . .*" he prompted.

"*Feelin' Groovy!*" sang Cat, catching on. "Simon and

Garfunkel. '59th Street Bridge'. A classic song. By the way, the bridge is back behind us. It's really called the Queensboro bridge though."

"You've got to know your classics," said Trevor, walking down First Avenue in big long strides. Cat tugged at his sleeve and he slowed down to a more leisurely pace.

"You really had me worried back there. For a minute I thought you were a rabid male chauvinist pig."

"Nah. I have impeccable credentials in that department. Very caring sharing sort of "new man" kind of guy. I was raised on a sort of commune in the outback. Very touchy-feelie. I learnt to comb my aura before I knew how to brush my hair."

Now that he had slowed down Trevor took his time looking at everything he passed. He peered into the wood-panelled entrance halls of the luxury apartment buildings, said hello to the uniformed doormen, and exclaimed loudly when a giant limo pulled up in front of them.

"So what brings this Flower Child so far from home?" Cat asked amused.

"Well, I started Uni in Sydney, but I got bored really quickly. I was studying law. I thought that was the best way to attack the problems of society – study law. Then I took the job at the paper one summer, and it was so much more interesting, so much more alive, that I figured that being a journo was an even more effective way to save the planet. I plan to live in New York for about a year. I hope to get a string covering the UN to get to see how it works. Then maybe a year in Washington. Then I'll go home."

"And what do you plan to do then?" asked Cat

"Politics maybe. Or go back and complete my education. Ecology or economics. I can't decide which."

"And then you'll presumably be ready to change the planet?" Cat quipped.

"Save the planet," Trevor corrected. "I'm going to save the planet." Cat looked at him to see if he was pulling her leg again, but this time she thought he might actually be sincere.

"So you really are a Flower Child," exclaimed Cat. "You certainly don't look like one."

Trevor laughed. "You should see my Dad. He's got long hair and a beard and beads. He's always studying something. He's got more degrees than I've had hot dinners. But enough about me. What do you do when you're not shopping, or going to dinner, or jetting off to Madrid for a party?"

Cat didn't like the sound of that. This guy was a real smartass.

"I paint," she declared, regretting it the minute the words were out of her mouth. Why the hell did she say that? She never mentioned her painting, except in an offhand manner. It sounded so pompous. Why did she feel she had to justify herself to this rude individual? She hadn't even set foot in her studio for weeks. She'd been too busy. "Doing what?" asked a little voice inside her head. "Shopping and going to dinner parties," replied another little voice in an Australian accent. Damn him. At least she didn't go around declaring she was going to save the planet.

"I wondered what you did in your studio," Trevor continued pleasantly. Either he was ignoring her discomfort or he was totally oblivious to it. "You know there's a magnificent exhibition of Aboriginal Art at the Met. Maybe we could go and check it out sometime."

"Maybe," mumbled Cat. She was hot. They'd walked at least ten blocks and her feet were swelling in her uncomfortable new mules. She wanted to sit down and drink something very cold and wet. As if reading her thoughts, Trevor pointed to a sidewalk cafe with a large awning.

"Come on, girl. You look like one horse that needs watering!"

They didn't talk as they waited to be served. Cat fanned herself with the menu while Trevor sat and watched the city go by, grinning from ear to ear when anything caught his eye. A cop on a horse made him positively beam and he waved as the cop rode by. Cat felt much better once she'd taken a long swig of her iced tea. She was just about to mention that she really had to get a move on when Trevor turned his attention to her again.

"So is that Cat as in Kathleen or Catherine?" he asked intensely.

"Catherine, as in Catherine Richardson."

"So tell me about yourself, Catherine Richardson," he demanded. He grabbed the salt-shaker from the table and held it tightly up against his mouth like a mike. Cat threw up her hands and shrugged her shoulders in disinterest.

"Catherine Richardson. This is your life," he said in a broad American accent. Cat was both amused and appalled. People at the next table were looking over. Trevor pointed the salt-shaker at her, but Cat shook her head.

"Where were you born?" he asked talking into the "mike".

"The city," Cat sighed into the salt-shaker.

"Speak up, please. Schooling?" asked Trevor, leaning over the table.

Cat giggled.

"Boarding-school in Maine, where I met Valerie and Scott who's giving the dinner party. Junior year abroad in England."

"Where you met Fiona," Trevor interjected, raising one eyebrow like a cartoon detective.

"Yes. Then college in Boston – Fine Art. A year in Madrid."

"Where you went to a party. Aha! Zee plot theeckens," he declared in an atrocious French accent.

"That is the worst French accent I've ever heard," laughed Cat.

"I know," said Trevor. "How do you feel about global warming?" he asked changing back to his serious American voice. Looking down, he realised that he was still pointing the salt-shaker at Cat and broke into loud peals of laughter that was totally contagious.

"Scared. And I don't use any products containing CFC's," she guffawed into the "mike".

"How can you laugh about something so serious?" he asked trying hard to keep a straight face. "But seriously now, where do you stand on nuclear disarmament?"

"Get rid of them!" Cat declared. This guy was hilarious when he got going.

"Tabloid journalism?"

"Love it."

"Pantyhose?"

Cat burst out laughing. "Hate 'em."

"What's your favourite colour?" he asked in the rapid fire manner of a game-show host. "Quickly!"

"Black," Cat blurted out.

"Black isn't a colour! Fine Arts my arse."

"Blue! Blue," Cat answered laughing.

"*Blue is the colour of the sky above,*" Trevor said intensely.

Cat grinned back at him. He wouldn't get her this time.

"*In the morning, when she rise,*" she declared proudly.

"Absolutely!" said Trevor snapping his fingers and jumping up. "Donovan. Shall we go?"

"Sure," said Cat still smiling. "But there is no way I'm walking."

The loft smelt stuffy. Cat went around opening windows while Trevor poked around looking at everything, picking up paint brushes, and sniffing pots. Her grandfather owned the building and was presumably waiting for some trend in the market, or some tax incentive to sell it. Cat was the only occupant once the shop on the ground floor shut for the day. Trevor went over and sat on the large windowsill and stuck his head right out the window.

"You know, when I first got here, I kept looking up to try and see the sky. It felt so strange not having a great big sky over my head. Back home the sky is massive. This city is mad. I've crossed tens of thousands of people in the last two weeks but I've been drinking with the flies since I got here."

"Come again?" asked Cat confused.

"I've been alone all the time," Trevor translated. "You lot are the first people I've actually met."

"New York grows on you, believe me. But if you want to see really big skies go West," said Cat rummaging around in the little refrigerator she kept in the studio. The soda was flat, but she spied a couple of frozen daiquiris.

"Lemon or strawberry daiquiri?" she asked.

"Strawberry, definitely. Though I'm more of a gin and tonic man myself."

"I thought real men drank beer," teased Cat.

"Beer is beer," Trevor said solemnly. "It's not a drink so much as our life-blood. To Oz," he added, lifting his glass. "Where the men are men and the sheep are nervous."

The afternoon flew by as they talked about everything and nothing. Aided by the Daiquiris, Trevor's flow of ideas became even more erratic. He jumped from the importance of waste management to surfing to television sitcoms. Cat was having such a good time that she totally forgot about meeting the girls at Madame Zora's.

"Jesus Christ!" she said looking at her watch. "I was meant to meet them now!"

"Were you going to have your fortune told?" asked Trevor.

"I don't know. If she's any good I might though I'm not into that stuff really," said Cat picking up her bag and closing the windows.

"Don't you believe in the paranormal?" Trevor asked, helping her with a window that was stuck. Cat couldn't help noticing how nice he smelt. Like soap, even after their walk in the blazing heat.

She paused, thinking about the question. She felt something stirring, just out of reach and then it was gone. She shook her head, flicking the long black pony tail over her back.

"Sure. Well, I don't really know. There's definitely something more, but I'm not sure what. Do you believe in it?"

"I was raised in the outback. The line between reality and dreams, or magic and science, isn't as strictly drawn as over here. You'll see when we go see that show at the Met." Trevor looked once around the room again. "This is really a great building. I can't believe it's empty."

"I know. There's even a caretaker's apartment," said Cat, pointing to the door behind her.

"An apartment!" said Trevor leaping up. "Can I see it?"

"It's really gross. You'd have to do a lot of work to actually live in it," Cat said, but Trevor was already through the door.

"It's great," he enthused as he came back in. "The water works, and so does the cooker and the fridge. The bed's a bit dodgy but I was going to buy a futon anyway. How much do you want for it?"

"I don't want any rent. You can stay here for a while if it helps you out, but I don't want to rent it," said Cat, taken aback at how fast the negotiations had proceeded.

"No. I'd have to pay rent, otherwise that causes problems," said Trevor shaking his head. Then he snapped his fingers. "I've got it. How about this? I pay rent, which I deposit every month to your favourite charity. Like that everybody is happy and we get to do a good deed as well."

"But I don't think I want to rent it," Cat said slowly, though now that she thought of it, there was no real reason not to.

Trevor deflated into an abject picture of misery. Then he raised his pale blue eyes at her and smiled his best first-grader smile. "Please? You would really be helping me out."

He reminded her of her beloved pet Lab when he was a puppy. Cat shrugged her shoulders and sighed. What the hell, he was a nice guy. Definitely not a psycho, and it would be good to know he was around when she came over. She'd always felt a bit unsafe in the building on her own.

"OK. Deal," she said, shaking Trevor's hand.

"So what charity would you like to designate?" he asked, delighted with himself.

"I guess a charity that helps the homeless would be most appropriate," Cat said.

"Excellent choice," whooped Trevor. "The homeless it is!"

They made up a contract there and then to "make it more real" as Trevor said, and toasted it with another round of frozen daiquiris. It allowed Trevor Manning to occupy the apartment for as long as he liked, on the condition that he pay his rent to a charity that helped the homeless.

Chapter Four

◆━◆

Cat and Fiona stood in front of the full-length mirror in Cat's bedroom. All the doors of her wall-to-wall closets were open. They'd been trying on outfits for an hour for the dinner party that night. Shoes spilt onto the floor and the bed was strewn with various items of clothing which they had tried on and discarded.

"Why did you have to say 'dressy'?" moaned Cat. She'd come home the night before at five o'clock in the morning after spending the night clubbing and had stayed the entire day either in bed or lounging on the sofa watching TV. She didn't feel the least bit inclined to change out of her comfortable track-suit bottoms. In fact she'd much rather stay home and order Chinese.

"It wasn't me," whined Fiona. "All I did was ask. It was Ramon who chose dressy. Valerie bought this amazing Dolce Gabbana top yesterday. You know, one of those brocade bustier things. It would look so much better on me. It's not fair. Oh God, I can't be bothered. I'll just have to wear my little black dress!"

"No, you can't," said Cat. "I was just about to say that *I* was going to wear my little black dress." Half her body was in the closet as she rummaged around. Then again, she thought, if she wore the dress that meant wearing high heels. She would look great but she knew she would be squirming around feeling uncomfortable within the hour.

"But I don't have anything to wear!" moaned Fiona. "We can't very well show up looking like the bloody Bobbsy twins, can we?"

"That's OK, Fi. You can wear your little black dress. I don't think I'm in the mood for a tight dress and heels tonight. Not to mention that Scott's a great cook and I intend to pig out."

"Wonderful! Though it's only fair. I deserve it after you went and abandoned me yesterday afternoon," said Fiona flopping back onto the bed. "You know, that was really rotten leaving me all alone with the dreaded Valerie while you went off and had interesting conversations with that Australian bloke."

"Well, I did come in and save you eventually," said Cat, trying on a pair of black silk flowing pants and a matching tank top. She'd rushed into Madame Zora's tiny studio just as they were finishing their reading.

"Thank God for that!" exclaimed Fiona, looking at Cat critically. "That looks comfortable. Why don't you wear that fabulous short kimono top with it. It'll give you a bit of colour. It's on the top shelf in a garment bag."

Fiona sat up and reached for a cigarette. Cat smiled back at her friend. She was the most organised person Cat had ever met, keeping track not only of her things and appointments but Cat's as well.

"Actually I've been meaning to ask you," Fiona said, lighting up. "How did you know Madame Zora was from Hoboken? She was totally blown away by you. Valerie was most impressed."

"Oh, it was just a fluke really. I just said the first thing that came into my mind. Silly really," said Cat absentmindedly as she tried on the kimono. As always she only gave a passing glance at the mirror. Fi was right – it was perfect, very dramatic: gold and red silk, with a stylised dragon up one side. Most of all it was really comfortable. A bit of chunky jewellery and she'd look great.

"Talking about Valerie," said Cat. "Has she had something new done to her face? She looks different. Then again every time she comes back from LA she looks different."

Fiona laughed. Valerie's father was a prominent

plastic surgeon in California. Cat and Fiona used to say that he became so successful because he had so much practice on his family. When Valerie had arrived in boarding-school out East, she was thirteen, overweight, with a large nose and a mouth full of metal. By sixteen she'd had her nose done, and for her eighteenth birthday, Daddy had given her new boobs. Her mousy brown hair was windswept and blonde these days and she'd lost a ton of weight after various stays on a fat farm in Arizona.

"It's nothing drastic,' said Fiona." She just got some new coloured contact lenses. I think she called them 'sapphire'. But she *was* talking about having her lips injected. "

Cat groaned. "God forbid. That always looks like you've been stung by a bee. I tried coloured contacts once, but I couldn't wear them. Though I must admit I looked terrific with green eyes!"

"You'd look terrific in anything, Cat," Fiona sighed. "Poor Val, she works so hard at it and she only manages to look like an over-groomed, slightly pretty, Barbie doll."

"I'm not sure she even qualifies," snickered Cat meanly. "She's more of a Sindy doll really. Come on, we better get our make-up on or we'll be late."

"So tell me about this Trevor bloke," said Fiona as she followed Cat into the bathroom. In her bare feet she was a good head taller than Cat. Fiona was not a beautiful woman but she was striking, with fine patrician lines and long limbs. She was what you would call a handsome woman. "I still can't believe you gave him the flat for free!!"

"It's not really for free," said Cat, her face jammed up to the mirror as she applied her mascara to her bottom lashes. "He's donating the rent to the homeless. It was kinda his idea, but I thought 'what the hell!'"

"My, my, we are being very Lady Bountiful, aren't we? Honestly, Cat, sometimes you have more money than sense. You don't know anything about him."

"I know he's OK. I can feel these things, you know. I've always been pretty good at judging people. He's a really nice guy. That's all I can say – he's really nice. I know that sounds awful."

"You're trying to say he's common, aren't you? NOKD?" laughed Fiona.

"Well, he's definitely 'Not Our Kind, Dear', but I wouldn't call him common. He's interesting and kinda goofy. He knows a lot of stuff. And he can be very funny. I'm almost considering making him a friend. You can tell me what you think tonight."

"I shall indeed," said Fiona. "Actually it will be interesting to see how the young man performs when thrown in with that crowd. It could be like a lamb to the slaughter."

Cat paused and thought about it. "Well, if they don't hate him on sight, I think he'll be fine. Like I said , he's very funny, and very smart."

"Then again, if they don't like him," said Fiona, checking her face in the mirror, "they'll tear him to shreds and serve him up for dessert!"

Both girls laughed as they finished getting ready, but Cat couldn't help feeling a twinge at the thought of Trevor being humiliated by the pack of bitchy people that would be there tonight.

Cat and Fiona were the last to arrive. You could hear the buzz of people and the clinking of glasses as they waited for Ramon to undo the various locks he had on his door.

Ramon and Scott's apartment was a war-zone of competing styles. Scott liked clean uncluttered lines, while Ramon was more of a paisley print sort of person. The spectacular result was that the small apartment was crammed with a collection of severe classical pieces in black leather and chrome draped in wild colourful throws and pillows.

Tonight Ramon had outdone himself on the decorating. Scott was probably too busy in the kitchen to stop him, thought Cat, as she surveyed the dozens of candles and night-lights that dotted the room. The table looked gorgeous. Ramon had managed to restrain himself and had set a large square glass vase with long-stemmed white lilies as a simple centrepiece. The table was lit by long tapered thin white candles.

Cat accepted a glass of champagne and stood back to survey the room as Fiona followed Ramon to the kitchen to help Scott. If she had counted correctly they were ten for dinner. Valerie was talking to a six-foot-tall, very skinny, but extremely beautiful girl. Cat recognised her from the summer Calvin Klein show but she couldn't remember her name. She caught sight of Trevor sitting on the big black sofa, deep in conversation with that awful German guy. She made a bet with herself that the German had brought the model. Trevor looked up and saw her standing there. He waved a big hello.

He didn't look too bad, thought Cat, as he walked up – though she could have given the white shirt and tie a miss.

"That's a fantastic kimono," he said. "You look stunning."

"Thank you. It was a present from a Japanese business associate of my granddad." Cat leaned closer. "I see you've met Helmut the Hun," she whispered.

"Who is that guy? Is he for real?" Trevor whispered back. Cat started giggling under her breath.

"He started in on me as soon as we were introduced. The lack of existentialism in contemporary Australia and how could anyone pretend to have a film industry without it! Is he a poofter as well?"

"No. I think he's with her," she said cocking her head towards the model at the window. "Though he likes to tell people that he swings both ways."

"God, she's amazing. How did that git ever get a girl like her?" Trevor gawked openly. "She looks like a model."

"She *is* a model," said Cat adding, "a minor model."

"That's fine with me," said Trevor, still gawking.

"Close your mouth, Trevor," said Cat in an upper-class British accent. "We are not a codfish!"

"Mary Poppins!" answered Trevor picking up the reference. "*Practically perfect in every way*. I'll say she is!" he added still gawking.

Scott breezed in and stared to lay platters on the table. He looked wonderful in a thin black turtle-neck and tailored black pants. Ramon and Fiona followed him carrying bowls of salads.

"OK. I'm afraid we're going buffet tonight. Ramon always insists on inviting more people than we can fit around the table," declared Scott. "But I am delighted you could all make it. So just come right up and get some goodies to start with."

"So what do you think of my table?" asked Ramon with a dramatic sweep of his arms. Everyone cooed and told him how wonderful it looked.

"He's quite the diva," said Trevor as Ramon began to tell those serving themselves that he was thinking of starting up a dinner-party-setting business. "But I like him."

"He comes from a very old, very aristocratic Spanish family. I'm afraid he's a bit of a disgrace to them. Ramon has a dream of being a Broadway star, which is not really what his father had in mind," explained Cat.

"What about the others?" Trevor asked.

"Well, you've met Val and Fiona. Val works at *People* though we haven't really figured out what she does there. Fiona works in PR. Scott was in boarding-school with us. His family made a fortune with a chain of discount stores in the Midwest. He's down in Wall Street and doing really well."

"And has his family objected to his lifestyle?" asked Trevor.

"No. They pretend he isn't gay. And he pretends they know, and everyone gets on just fine. Very civilised."

"What about Helmut the Hun?" asked, Trevor watching as the large German pointed at everything on the table and demanded explanations from Scott who patiently obliged.

"He's a set designer or something like that. Which is why Ramon keeps inviting him. He thinks he can get him an audition. I can't remember the model's name and the other couple are a fashion photographer and his wife. She works with Scott. Not a very interesting bunch, I'm afraid," sighed Cat.

"On the contrary, my dear Watson," said Trevor. "It is a perfect opportunity to observe how the other half lives."

"No shit, Sherlock?" said Cat. "How about you find out how the other half eats? I'm starving!"

Once everyone was served they all found seats around the living-room which was dominated by a low glass table. A naked figure of a man on all fours held the large oval table on his back. Cat avoided the shiny leather sofa. She chose one of Ramon's massive pillows and sat on the floor instead. Trevor seemed to have made fast friends with Scott and they were busy discussing sushi recipes. Trevor had obviously scored major brownie points by commenting favourably on Scott's home-made varieties. Scott had made up three different platters along with a large tray of smoked salmon. The salads were fresh and green with a light vinaigrette and Cat was enjoying it all immensely. Especially when Scott remembered that he had put a bottle of Russian vodka in the freezer to go with the salmon.

"So how was your reading yesterday?" asked Ramon. "Did you ask about me?"

"It was rather predictable really," Fiona answered in a bored voice. "Except that Valerie is definitely not getting married this year and I have to watch out for stomach problems."

"I thought she was really good," said Valerie. She was dressed to the nines in the brocade bustier and thin black toreador satin pants. Valerie had obviously also been to the hairdresser. Why did the woman insist on having such big hair? thought Cat. Her own black hair was slicked back and tied in a soft bun at the nape of her neck.

"Oh!" shrieked Valerie, waving her long red fingernails in front of her face. "Fiona! Tell them about what Cat did!"

"Don't," ordered Cat severely.

"Do!" chorused the dinner-party guests.

"Well," said Fiona, gesturing Cat to keep quiet. "Cat came in late and Madame Zora asked her if she wanted a reading. She went on to say that she could feel that Cat had great insight, spiritual powers, what have you . . ."

"And then Cat turns around, says that she can tell that Madame Zora comes from Hoboken, has a son, and is a widow!" gushed Valerie. "And she was right! Can you believe it!"

"How did you know?" Trevor asked.

"It was a fluke. I'd had a couple of afternoon

Daiquiris!" said Cat, throwing her hands up in exas-
peration. "I saw a graduation picture of a pimply kid,
another old one of the same kid as a baby with a
younger Madame Zora and a proud Daddy person, but
no other pictures of the guy. I figured he must be dead.
You don't keep pictures of your husband out when
you're divorced."

"But what about Hoboken?" Fiona enquired.

"I don't know," said Cat laughing. "She just looked
like she came from New Jersey!" Everyone laughed and
demanded to have Cat tell their fortune. Cat declined,
saying it was all a rip-off anyway.

"Fortune-tellers are just a scam, especially in
America," pronounced Helmut emptying the bottle of
vodka without serving anyone else. "You cannot have
magic in a spiritual desert like New York."

"That's not true," said Ramon shaking his head. "We
even have a ghost in the building. And across the street
are two lesbian witches. They are very good. Especially
for back problems."

Helmut was about to start pontificating again, when
Scott interrupted him by declaring that they were all
ready for the main course. All thoughts of ghosts and
witches were forgotten as they tucked into delicately
flavoured *"poussins au peches"* served with fresh
mangetouts and tiny roast potatoes. Trevor leaned over
and whispered in Cat's ear.

"What are these little birds I'm eating?" he asked.

"*Poussins*," said Cat smiling. "They're delicious, aren't they?"

Trevor shrugged his shoulders. "Translation, please."

"Ah. I guess they would be called chicks over here," Cat said hesitantly. "Very young chickens in any case."

"Oh my god!" Trevor whispered in mock horror. "I'm eating a baby bird! That's almost as bad as eating Bambi!"

"Who, might I add," said Cat wickedly, "is absolutely delicious with plum sauce."

They all agreed that a pause was required before dessert. Ramon put some Latin music on while Scott busied himself clearing away the dishes and making sure that everyone had enough wine. Miss Model got up and started swinging her skinny hips around the room and was soon joined by her large German escort who was a surprisingly good dancer. Ramon was high as a kite and started dancing wildly in the small hall-way, having decided the living-room was too cramped for his fancy footwork. He signalled Cat to join him. Cat got up with difficulty. She'd stuffed herself and the combination of vodka and wine was going to her head. Dancing was probably a good way to wake up again. Trevor and Fiona followed and Ramon and Cat made fun at their attempts to samba. Trevor was like a wooden puppet. Cat couldn't stop laughing as he did his version of a Latin Lover to the equally wooden Fiona.

Soon they were all dancing around the apartment, banging pots in the kitchen, whooping with laughter, and gyrating to the rapid salsa. Finally, after three wild numbers the album eased into a slow ballad and they all flopped back around the coffee table, gasping for breath.

Miss Model returned from the toilet and slid languorously down the arm of the leather sofa. Cat observed that it was her third trip that night – that was probably once to throw up and twice to do a line of coke.

"You know, every time I go to the little girls' room I can hear someone walking around above me. I hope we haven't disturbed your neighbours," she said in a surprising Southern accent.

"Don't worry," said Scott. "The people below us are on holiday. And we're at the top of the building. There's no one above us. That's the attic."

"You must have some big rats crawling around up there!" declared the model, reaching for another glass of wine.

"No, honey! We don't have rats! *Aqui no hay ratas!*" said Ramon, horrified.

"New York is plagued with them," said Helmut solemnly.

"No, no, no. No rats!" insisted Ramon. "That's just

the ghost," he concluded as if it was a much more plausible answer than rodents.

"Maybe we should summon him and ask him if we're being too noisy!" giggled Miss Model, slurring her words slightly. "Maybe he wants to join the party!"

She was getting plastered, thought Cat. They all were. Then again, everyone was becoming so much more fun and interesting. Even Helmut had made her laugh, doing the tango with her down the hall. Trevor kept looking at her pointedly with wet, glassy eyes. Oh my God, thought Cat. He's going to come on to me. She rejected the prospect instantly. This guy was great as a friend. But he wasn't her type at all. He was too short. His shirts were terrible. She hoped he'd either change his mind or get it over with quickly. Scott came in with the coffee and liqeurs and asked if anyone was ready for dessert yet. They all groaned and decided on later.

"Calling the ghost could be fun," said Ramon. "But we have no jeejee board."

"That's an ouija board," corrected Scott rolling his eyes heavenward. Scott got more camp the more he drank.

"We can make one," said Fiona. "It's easy. All you need are pieces of paper and a pen. You write out the twenty-six letters of the alphabet, one for 'no' and one for 'yes', and you use a small shot glass for a pointer."

They all got busy clearing the glass table and laying out the alphabet in a large circle. Halfway on the left-hand side they inserted the word "no", while on the right-hand side they slid in the word "yes". Cat stretched out and propped herself up against the big pillow.

"OK. Now everybody hold hands and concentrate," said Fiona in her schoolmistress voice.

"Aren't you summoning with us?" asked Trevor, holding out his hand.

Cat declined. She was feeling quite merry and was happier just to sit back and watch. She'd done this sort of thing quite a few times in boarding-school but had soon tired of it. There was no ghost involved. Anybody could do it. It was so easy to make the glass move. All you needed was to get in the right mood. She had no idea how it worked but she knew the people themselves were the ones moving the glass. Even if they weren't touching it. It was the will of the many, or something like that. Cat giggled to herself. Not that these guys looked like they had much of a collective will. Most of them were trying hard to keep a straight face, while the others made ghost noises.

"Come on, you lot. Cop on! Now I want you to concentrate. And no more laughing!" Fiona was losing patience.

Everyone shut up and closed their eyes, though you could still hear a few stifled snickers. Cat watched as the little shot glass slowly started moving under their collectively pointed fingers.

"It's moving!" said Valerie excitedly.

Of course it is, thought Cat. It always does. It just never goes anywhere until you tell it to. She sat up and stared at the glass.

"Spirit, are you with us?" asked Fiona solemnly.

The glass started moving in short erratic jumps that began to form a circle. Valerie let out a tiny mouse shriek of excitement. The people around the table stretched their arms to follow the glass.

"Spirit, are you there?" asked Fiona again. Miss Model giggled loudly and was silenced by a dirty look from Fiona. The glass stopped moving.

"Come on. Let's try again. Remember, concentrate," Fiona ordered.

Cat was getting bored. She couldn't believe Trevor was being so serious. And she thought he was an intellectual! Slowly the glass started moving again.

"Spirit, are you with us?" Fiona intoned.

Oh, for Christ's sake, thought Cat, will they just get on with it and push the glass over to "yes"? The thought of dessert suddenly made her want to get this silly stuff over and done with. She watched the glass moving in a small circle, staring at it intensely. It started to describe a fuller circle. That's right, thought Cat, now inch it to the right, you guys. I want some of that marvellous fluffy concoction I saw in the kitchen. The glass swung to the right and stopped above the word "yes".

"He's answered!" said Fiona. "He is with us!"

Everyone instantly took their hands away as if they had been burnt and started talking excitedly.

"You pushed it!" said Helmut.

"The glass was definitely moving by itself," declared Valerie.

"It always does," sighed Cat in a bored voice. "Now why don't we just have dessert?"

Dessert was accompanied by more wine and liqueur. Helmut was getting boisterously verbose. He was still maintaining that New York had no magic left. That it was buried deep below the concrete and couldn't get out. For some reason, the brandy probably, Ramon decided to take him on.

"There are no spirits left in New York – dead or alive!" declared Helmut looking into his brandy snifter as if one might be lurking there.

"That is not true. There is magic in New York. And I don't mean the Madame Zora. Or even our two lesbian *brujas* across the street. If you want real magic, you go to Brooklyn. Go see the *Santeros*."

Everyone at the table looked blank and shook their heads. Scott intervened to explain.

"*Santería* is a religion created long ago by West Africans enslaved in colonial Cuba and imported to New York City and other places in America with a large community of Caribbeans and Latinos. They have secret rites and do things like sacrifice chickens. Very messy, I'd say."

"So it's a kind of voodoo, is it?" asked Trevor, slurring his words. He turned and gave Cat another of his longing looks. Though she felt she should be annoyed she couldn't help giggling. He looked such a fool, with his tie undone, and one white shirt tail hanging out.

"It has very similar elements," continued Scott, waving his hand lazily over the table. "A magic mix of African and Christian deities and secret stuff."

"But it is very chic now," added Ramon. "It is coming out of the ghetto and into Manhattan. Maria told me all about it."

"Maria? Our hairdresser?" asked Cat, surprised. Maria was a boisterous, zany, Cuban girl who worked at the unisex salon they all attended.

"*Si*. She's from Brooklyn, remember?" said Ramon "And I have to go and see her soon. My split ends are atrocious!" he added flinging his shoulder-length black locks over his shoulder.

"You all go to the same hairdresser!" Trevor

whooped with laughter. "Well, there's one for the books!"

"Listen, little *hombre*," said Ramon. "You are in New York now. And a visit to Maria would be a good idea – I hate to tell you but your haircut is terrible!"

Everyone exploded into laughter and the talk moved from magic to hairdressers until the last bottle of wine was empty and someone suggested they go to a club.

Cat and Trevor sat in the back of a cab. Cat was too tired to go clubbing. She wasn't surprised when Trevor announced that he would share a cab home with her, to make sure she got back safely. He was definitely going to make a pass at her. She hoped she was sober enough to reject his advances gracefully. There was nothing worse than fumbling around trying to get some guy's hands off you, she thought with a giggle as they walked arm in arm down the stairs, bumping into the wall and each other. She had expected him to try and kiss her in the doorway, but she had managed to avoid it by slipping out from under his arms and scooting into the waiting cab.

Cat sat at the window watching the city drift by. Trevor was stretched out on the other side, his arm along the back of the seat. Cat was drunk enough to want a friendly cuddle, but she figured it might encourage him, and so she kept to her side. Out of the corner of one eye she saw what looked like a drunken fight in progress. Trevor nodded towards it.

"It's nice to see that some things never change no matter what part of the world you're from. People get drunk on a night out and then they have a bash at each other. It makes me feel right at home!"

"If you're into that sort of thing, you'll blend right in," she said.

"This city is so diverse I bet you could blend right in no matter what you were into," he said softly as if to himself.

"I guess you're right. They say it only takes six months to become a New Yorker."

"Is it true that the city never sleeps? Is there any time when there is absolutely no movement?" he asked, his face pressed up to the glass as he peered out the window.

"I think there is, but it's really short. I came home after four one morning and sat looking out the window. I started counting the cars on the bridge. I was timing how long an interval there was between cars and it was never more than a minute and a half. Then the weirdest thing happened," Cat said remembering. "At around four-thirty there was a twenty-minute interval when *not one* car went up or down the ramp. The city felt absolutely still. It was really weird. Then they started up again, and by quarter to five, the cars were flowing one after the other."

"That reminds me of being up near Darwin. Up there, it's not dry like the outback, more tropical jungle. Stuff growing everywhere. Everything is lush, green, noisy. The bugs never stop. Especially the cicadas. They drone all evening and night and you end up not hearing them. They're like crickets, only cicadas are a lot louder." Trevor paused and Cat looked at him quizzically, not understanding the connection. He raised his hand. "Hang on. I'm getting to it," he said laughing. "You see, during the monsoons, the cicadas are particularly loud but at certain times in the evening they get really loud. Then they get louder. You can't keep up a conversation. Then they get even louder!"

Cat laughed and shook her head. "And?"

"And then they all stop! The silence is absolutely deafening!" He threw his hands up in the air and then shrugged. "I don't know why but it reminds me of your bridge."

The cab was slowing down and pulling over. The short trip midtown was over too soon. Cat was really enjoying his company.

"Do you want to come up for a coffee?" she asked.

"No thanks, I've got to get up early," he said as she slipped out of the cab.

It was only when she was back in the apartment

curled up on the sofa, eating a bowl of cereal and watching MTV, that she realised that he hadn't made a pass at her. And she was annoyed to admit that she was more miffed than relieved.

Chapter Five

◆—◆

Cat didn't see Trevor again for a week. She'd been down to the loft twice, but he was always out. The first time there was clear evidence that he had started to move in. The second time she had found a huge potted sunflower in the middle of her studio. Attached to the enormous big red bow was a note: *Thanks. T.*

Then he just popped up the following Sunday morning with a bag full of bagels, cream-cheese and lox. Fiona had left for brunch with some friends and Cat was alone. She had vaguely planned to spend most of the day lounging around, maybe taking a jog in the park, and then going to visit Ramon.

"You've certainly caught on fast," she said as they settled into eating. "Bagels and lox! And I see you're wearing shades now."

"Well, you said it only takes six months to become a real New Yorker. I've been here a month so it's about time I started blending in a bit more. By the way, did you like the pressy?"

"I loved it. I've never seen a potted sunflower that tall. You must have paid a bomb for it!"

Trevor grinned. "You're right there. It cost big bikkies, all right. But I got two new strings this week so my finances have improved dramatically. Which is why we're going to celebrate. So, are you ready?" He jumped up and put his shades back on.

"Ready to go where?"

"To the Met. Aboriginal art – remember? I thought we had a date."

"We most certainly did not," said Cat indignantly. "I haven't even seen you for over a week."

"Well, maybe I dreamed it. You'll understand when you see the exhibit," he said, wiggling his eyebrows and making her laugh. "Come on! It's summer in the city."

Cat looked down at her baggy shorts and T-shirt, "I'm not in the mood to get changed."

"You look great," countered Trevor. "Anyway, what do you care – the museum's gonna be full of fat women in tank tops with curlers in their hair!"

"At the Met?" said Cat. "I don't think so." But she got

up and grabbed a pair of Nikes anyway. If she knew Trevor, he probably wanted to walk there.

The weather had cooled down a bit. The sky was slightly overcast and a breeze was blowing through the city, blowing their hair at each street corner. The streets had that slow-walking Sunday feel about them, with people strolling slowly past shop windows, eating ice creams, pushing toddlers in buggies, or being dragged along by leash-tugging dogs eager to get to the park.

They hit the crowds at 57th and Fifth where throngs of tourists and day-trippers were enjoying the sights. Cat and Trevor joined them, taking a detour over to Rockefeller Center and then across the street to Saint Patrick's Cathedral, where groups of people dressed in their Sunday finery were just coming out of Mass. Backtracking into the park, they stopped to inspect the various stalls set up to sell everything from souvenirs to watercolours of the Manhattan skyline. Trevor bought a cheap plastic toy camera that showed old views of New York when you looked through the lens. He was delighted with himself, and kept clicking to another view and passing it over to Cat.

"Look! It's the Empire State building," he said, clicking the little plastic button. "And here's the Statue of Liberty. I've never been to either."

"Neither have I," said Cat as they walked into Central Park.

"Can we go?" he asked, sounding like an over-excited six-year-old.

"I don't see why not," Cat laughed.

They got hot dogs and pretzels from a street vendor and walked past the Zoo to sit on a bench and watch the crowds drift by.

"We could even go to the zoo," said Cat, pointing at the tall fence in front of them.

"Nah," said Trevor shaking his head. "Zoos are full of ankle-biters."

"Come again?" asked Cat.

"Children. Well, smallies, you know – the ones that are only about so high," Trevor explained, holding his hot dog about one foot off the ground.

"Don't you like kids?" asked Cat.

"Love 'em!" declared Trevor. "Especially with relish. What about you?"

"I've never eaten any," said Cat laughing. "I'm not really sure if I even want to have any."

"Me, I want a load of 'em. All boys. Then we can start our own football team," said Trevor as they watched a mother struggling with two small children and a buggy as she tried to get her money out at the Zoo's entrance. Cat pointed to them. One of the children was wailing and the other kept trying to run into the zoo on his own.

"I don't know. It's an awesome responsibility. Anyway, I'm too young to have children."

"How old are you?"

"I'll be twenty-five in September," said Cat. "I'm still a kid."

"And at what age do you expect to officially become an adult?" asked Trevor. "Do they hand out diplomas over here or something?"

Cat was stung by the sharpness in his voice, but when she looked over he was busy trying to finish his hot dog without spilling ketchup down his front. Trevor looked up at her and smiled.

"You have mustard on your nose," he mumbled, still chewing. He reached out a finger and gently wiped her nose and Cat found herself smiling back. This guy was something else, she thought.

Without losing a beat Trevor leaned forward and looked up and down the path as if checking to see if anyone was coming their way. "Coast is clear," he whispered. "Look what Uncle Trevor has for you." He pulled two cigarettes from his pocket and straightened them out.

"I thought you didn't smoke?" Cat enquired, taking one.

"Not tobacco, my dear. Great mull – grass in your language. To get us into the mood for some Australian dreaming."

Cat lit up and let the sweet smoke fill her lungs, careful to blow it out behind her. It was definitely fine grass. She giggled, thinking what a ludicrous pair they made sitting there on the bench in their baggy clothes and shades. Trevor was taking long, obvious tokes on his joint, with the precision of the non-smoker. She looked around to make sure they were alone. From the zoo she could hear the roar of the sea lions and the high-pitched shrieks of small children. Ankle-biters! That was a good description, she thought, leaning back with her eyes closed.

"So did you really grow up in the outback?" she asked as the sun peeped out from under the grey clouds, bathing the bench in heat.

"Until I was about eleven years old, yeah. My oldies were real died-in-the-wool hippies. Went off on a self-sufficiency, save-the-world, sort of trip after they finished Uni. Which was a bit of a joke really, as my mother was a terrible cook, and Dad has two left hands. We lived near a small outpost in the middle of nowhere. My parents both taught in the aboriginal primary school. I went to school there. There were only six other whitefellas out of two hundreds kids, and three of them were my sisters."

"So you lived among the Aborigines?"

"Well, they were our neighbours. I kinda stuck out like a sore thumb really. I certainly felt different," he answered pensively. Then he pointed his finger at Cat and winked. "But I know how to skin a kangaroo!"

"That should come in handy in New York," said Cat, scrunching up her nose. "And no, I don't want to hear how you do it."

"You hang the roo from a tree," he continued, disregarding her completely. "Then you slice the belly open and you take all the guts out."

"I said I didn't want to hear!" insisted Cat. She hit him on the arm. He shoved her back.

"They made a great dish called 'pudding' with all the guts," he teased laughing.

"I said stop!" Cat shoved him back so hard that he slipped half off the bench, laughing and trying to protect himself from her blows with his arms.

"It tastes delicious!" he yelled, stumbling to a stand. "Then again, I did say Mum was a terrible cook!" He started shadow-boxing her.

She got up and boxed him back. He was weaving back and forth so fast that between the effects of grass and the fits of giggles she failed to land even one blow.

"Girlie! Girlie!" he taunted.

"Take that back!" She danced in front of him trying to punch his shoulder. People walked around them and smiled, giving them a wide berth.

"You fight like a girlie!" Trevor sang, fending off each of her attempts easily. Then he darted away and started to sprint up the path. Under the arch with the bronze statues of animals on top, he turned and put his hands on his hips. He batted his eyelashes provocatively and stuck his tongue out at her.

"Girlie! Betcha can't catch me!" he yelled in a shrill voice. Then he ran through the arch and disappeared down the path.

Cat yelled and took off after him. She was laughing so hard, and running so fast, that she was getting a stitch in her side. But she didn't care. She ran, whooping and laughing, as she caught sight of Trevor jumping over a small fence and heading off the path. As she raced down a little hill after him, she wondered why it had been so long since she'd played catch with anyone.

The exhibition was really fabulous. Cat had a vague idea about Aboriginal Art before, but seeing the real McCoy was something else. At first the paintings looked really simple, but the more she looked at them the more she was blown away by the brilliance of the colours and the complexity of the patterns. She felt instantly connected to it.

Trevor knew a lot about the paintings: what the symbols meant, how the artists had mixed the colours from natural pigments, what tree they got the bark from which they used as a canvas. One of the rooms was dimly lit with only stark spotlights on the art work.

Piped music and sounds of the bush created a spooky yet lulling atmosphere. Cat and Trevor sat together on a bench, gazing at a large canvas depicting a lizard surrounded by spirals, stripes and dots that swirled into patterns. Trevor's low voice talked softly in her ear as she swayed to the beat of the drums. After a few minutes, she found that though she was still looking at the painting, she was not seeing it. She knew that somewhere someone was talking to her, but she wasn't listening. Instead she looked in her mind's eye, and felt herself mixing colours, heard the paint splash on snow-white canvas, smelt the sharp bite of turpentine. Time was suspended as she sat in perfect peace, watching. A gentle shake on her shoulder made her blink and remember where she was.

"Cat? Are you all right?" asked Trevor, looking at her intensely.

"I'm fine," she said, shaking her head. "I was kinda gone for a minute there. I guess that grass was stronger than I thought."

"Well, you've got to watch it with these paintings. They can put you in a trance." Cat looked sceptical. "Seriously," continued Trevor. "In fact they were never meant to be permanent. Putting them on canvas isn't how it used to be done. They're too powerful to leave lying about. These were patterns you made in the dirt or scratched on a rock, to be blown away or washed out by the rain."

"That's marvellous," said Cat beaming. She felt incredibly refreshed and filled with a sense of purpose. She took one last look at the painting and grinned.

"Are you sure you're all right?" asked Trevor again.

"I'm great," said Cat, standing up. "But we've got to go, because right now I've got to paint."

"Suits me," said Trevor following her out of the museum, "how about you paint and I cook?"

Trevor wouldn't hear of calling a delivery service. He was determined to cook and went out to do some shopping. By the time he came back to the loft, Cat had hammered three two-foot-long canvases together and was mixing paint. He didn't disturb her. He just scooted straight into the adjoining apartment. Cat could hear him opening cupboards, banging pots around. Every once in a while she could sense that he was at the door looking at her, but still he did not disturb her. The sound of chopping and the smell of something sizzling in a pan made her look up. Trevor was standing in the doorway, holding a bottle of gin. He smiled his wide bright smile as he caught her eye.

"Drink?" he said. Cat nodded. "I'm afraid I forgot to get ice but I have tonic."

"There's ice in the little refrigerator in the studio,"

she said clearing her throat, not having spoken in a while. "A drink would be wonderful," she added, getting up and stretching. She had laid the now huge canvas on the floor and surrounded it with opened pots of brightly coloured paint, putting all the blues, yellows and greens in little groups. She stood back and looked at the blank canvas. The light was starting to fade. Cat stood in the shaft of brightness from the tall windows and watched the dust motes dancing in the beams. The potted sunflower was framed by the big window. Its leaves were like outstretched arms as if the big yellow flower reached for the light.

Trevor silently handed her a drink and started back into the apartment.

"Thanks," said Cat softly. "And thanks for leaving me alone."

"Where I come from, it would be really rude not to," said Trevor turning back to her and leaning in the door frame. "An Aborigine would never disturb anyone who is doing something. You just sit to one side and wait for the person to be ready to talk to you. It's very civilised, don't you think?"

"Damn civilised," she said, taking a long pull on the G&T. The bitter taste of the tonic was wonderful. She hadn't realised how thirsty she was. Cat finished the drink in two gulps, still looking down on the canvas.

CRISTINA PISCO

"Would you like another one?" asked Trevor. She nodded.

When he came back he said, "Just tell me when you're hungry. I'm doing a stir-fry so it'll be ready in minutes. It's getting a bit dark in here. Do you want me to turn on a light?" He handed her another drink.

Cat sipped it more slowly, thinking hard. She looked at the canvas, the pots of paint, the sunflower framed in the window, and then slowly shook her head.

"No. Don't turn on the light. I think I want a lot of candles. Let's light a ton of candles. And let's eat. I'm starving and stir-fry sounds great!"

She stood there smiling, covered in splashes of paint, holding the G&T in one hand and brushing her black hair away from her face, letting the cool glass rub along her forehead. She could feel Trevor watching her, as if a beam connected them. But when she turned to see him, she found that his face was in the shadows and she could only make out a dark silhouette in the doorway.

They lit every candle they could find and still Cat was not satisfied. So she ran down to the corner and bought some more while Trevor cooked. They ate sitting on the floor of the loft, surrounded by the flickering candles. The shaft of light at the window was replaced by the sharp beam of the streetlamps outside. The sunflower danced between it and soft yellow glow of the room. They shared a bottle of wine and another smoke, but spoke little, each of them comfortable in the silence that was sometimes broken by a wailing siren or the sounds of traffic from nearby Washington Square. Cat vaguely thought about going home. But the idea of breaking the mood and walking out into the dark, dangerous streets did not appeal to her. She leaned against Trevor. She could feel the muscles of his broad shoulders against her arm. He felt warm and safe, and when his arm went around her she nestled in closer and lay her cheek against his chest. He stroked her hair and then bent down and softly kissed the top of her head. Cat sighed in contentment.

"I'll let you get back to it then," he said abruptly, standing up.

Then he was gone.

Cat spent most of the night hovering over the canvas. Instead of sketching an outline she carefully divided the long white rectangle into small squares and tri-angles like a grid, starting with a border and working inwards until she had a large blank space surrounded by little symmetrical patterns. Trevor came in as she worked, silently handing her another drink or another smoke. Each time her mind was pulled away from the canvas by the memory of that fleeting chaste kiss, and she felt confused. She shoved the memory aside as she grabbed a paint-brush and started dipping into the colours, following the grid, filling it with little blobs of colour. *"Que sera, sera. Whatever will be, will be,"* she thought trying hard not to imagine herself wrapped up in his arms. Wait and see.

Trevor walked into the room and sat on the windowsill.

Cat looked up and smiled. She grimaced as she tried to stand up.

"I have a terrible crick in my neck," she said, slowly moving her head in a circle to try and ease the cramp.

"Come here," said Trevor softly. Cat sat in front of him on the floor and leaned back. He started massaging her shoulders and neck. His fingers were remarkably strong yet gentle. She felt her whole body relax as she closed her eyes. The mix of alcohol and grass and intense concentration made her delightfully woozy and she let herself go with the feeling. What a perfect day, she thought and silently groaned with pleasure as Trevor's fingers instinctively found the knotted muscles and eased them.

"You're very good at this," she murmured.

"I'm good at lots of things," he said, placing both hands gently on her head. He slowly massaged her temples, her eyebrows and her head. She felt wonderful.

"I'm going to have to call it a day. I have to get up early," he said. His hands were back on her shoulders, just resting. Cat leaned back and felt his strong thighs and chest behind her. *Que sera sera*, she thought suppressing a giggle.

"I have to get up early too," she said. "I'm having breakfast with my grandfather. He's actually my great-grandfather but that always seemed too long, so I just call him granddad."

"What about your real granddad?"

"He died before I was born," Cat said sighing to herself. She decided to answer his next question before he asked. "He was in an accident. My father and grandmother were killed as well. I barely knew my mother. I was three when she died but I still remember her, sort of."

She was surprised at how easily she spoke of it. As if she had just informed him of a shopping trip. Trevor wrapped his arms around her and gave her a big bear hug.

"It's all right," said Cat. "It was a long time ago."

"I know. My mum died when I was ten. She . . ." he said softly, leaving the sentence unfinished. Cat felt his pain and reached her arms above her head to cradle him as he leaned his cheek against hers. They sat like that, Cat, Trevor and the sunflower, silently looking at the flickering candles and the long canvas in the middle of the floor.

It came as a shock when he straightened up and disengaged himself from her embrace.

"Do you want the sofa or the futon? I'm easy either way," he said, not looking at her.

Cat was so shocked at his sudden absence that she was instantly snapped into sobriety. "The sofa would be fine," she answered, hoping that in the dim light he would not see her blushing.

Chapter Six

.**-**.

Cat straightened out her skirt and glanced quickly at her reflection in the big revolving doors as she walked up the wide marble steps. Her head was pounding with a god-awful hangover. She wondered how Trevor was getting on at work. The thought of being in an office made her head hurt even more. She wished she could keep her shades on through breakfast, but she knew she would never get away with it. Her great-grandfather was a stickler for tradition.

Though she had woken early, Trevor was already gone. She felt a twinge of regret mixed with relief that they had not slept together. Her sleep had been filled with vivid dreams of walking naked through red caked arid plains where sunflowers grew in rows between stunted trees. Cat still felt the strangeness of the dream, and the intensity of the night before as she tried to shake herself awake.

She had just enough time to go home to shower and change before meeting with her granddad. He was a traditionalist and liked to see his women in skirts. Trousers or shorts were only acceptable out in the Hamptons, and never for dinner. To please him Cat had chosen a blue teal washed-silk dress with a flowing skirt and long line of little buttons. At her neck she wore the thick strand of pearls he had given her for her eighteenth birthday.

She waved to the uniformed doorman, who tipped his hat to her, and walked into the cool lobby. It was a huge round hall, big enough to park a helicopter in. A long row of red marble columns went right around the room, stretching up to the first floor gallery. The hall was dominated by a majestic staircase that wound gracefully around the wrought-iron cage of the elevator shaft.

Hearing her heels clicking across the marble always reminded her of the patter of her black patent-leather shoes as she crossed the hall to go to school as a child. She used to love the sound her shoes made and she often walked in different ways just to hear it. The limo and driver would be outside waiting but she always lingered a while. If no one was around she would stand right in the middle of the hall and shout up to the first-floor gallery and listen as her voice echoed back. She used to pretend she had a magic twin who lived up there and called back down to her. It was the same twin who lived in the mirrors and only came out when Cat was alone. Cat would look at her reflection, look deep into her own eyes, and pretend she was talking to her twin. She kept playing the game long after she knew that she was too old for it.

She didn't recognise the uniformed young man seated behind the massive oak reception desk. Cat thought he must be new. He rushed to pull back the grill of the elevator.

"Good morning, Miss Richardson," he said flashing a row of bright white teeth.

"Thank you," said Cat. "I'll see myself up." She closed the inner grill as he closed the outer one and the elevator slowly creaked up. There was a more modern high-speed one tucked behind a marble column, but Cat always preferred the old creaky elevator.

The building was on the West side of the park. It was an imposing dark edifice with high windows and little turrets. Her great-grandfather had bought it to please his new bride Martha. She had loved the social swirl of New York's first nights and charity balls, and they had lived through the Season in the city, returning out to the Hamptons for the summer months. Though she had died thirty years before, it was as if she had just stepped out to do some shopping. Her favourite fresh flowers decorated every room and her ball-gowns were still hanging in the closet of her dressing-room.

Cat had grown up in this apartment and knew its every nook and cranny. She'd spent most summer holidays in the Hamptons but she preferred the city, always begging to return before school started. She loved the buzz of traffic, the crowded streets that beckoned below.

Nowadays her granddad preferred to live out in the Hamptons the whole year around. Thanks to modern telecommunications, he rarely had to actually be in the city, and his personal helicopter could whisk him in and out without ever having to fight the traffic. But every time he came into the city he took time to meet with his beloved Cat.

The inside grille was already open when Cat reached the top floor. The elevator opened directly into the apartment's main hall. Victor, her grandfather's Filipino butler was waiting to welcome her. Victor and his wife had been in service to the Richardsons forever. They doted on Cat, or Miss Catherine as they called her, and travelled with her grandfather wherever he went. Margarita would cook for him even when they stayed in the finest hotels. Her grandfather said he couldn't be bothered to suit himself to new tastes. "You can't teach an old dog new tricks," he always said with a twinkle in his eye.

"Good morning, Miss Catherine. Your grandfather is waiting for you in the dining-room," Victor said in his heavy Filipino accent that was flavoured by over twenty years of service in New York.

"How is he?" asked Cat.

"Thanks be to God, he is very well. He will outlive us all," laughed Victor as he led her down the long hall and held the door of the dining-room open for her.

It was a beautifully proportioned room with big French doors that were open onto the rooftop garden. Cat knew that if you leaned over the parapet you could see the tops of the trees in Central Park swaying below.

"Margarita thought it too windy to eat outside," said her grandfather, rising to greet her as she entered the room. She gave him a big hug and a kiss, smelling the familiar men's cologne he bought in that tiny shop on Jermyn Street in London. He was dressed, as always, in a starched white shirt and a dark suit. His trademark bow tie was a dark red paisley print today. Cat knew it had been hand-knotted by Victor that morning. Gold cuff links sparkled at his cuffs but he wore no other jewellery except for his class ring. Harvard Class of '28.

"You're looking well, my dear," he said, motioning her to the long table as Victor pulled out a chair for her.

"Not as good as you," Cat answered. Her grandfather was eighty-five years old but could easily pass for a man twenty years younger.

The table was set for two up at one end though it could sit fourteen. Fresh papaya and mango slivers glistened in silver fruit bowls. The middle of the polished table was a riot of flowers in a huge centre-piece. Cat knew they came from the garden in the Hamptons and promised herself to go spend a few days there before the summer was over. Margarita came in just as Victor whisked away the empty fruit bowls. She teased Cat for being too skinny and proudly produced perfect Eggs Benedict, which she knew were Cat's favourite breakfast. Her grandfather had only toasted brown bread and tea. Cat watched as he selected a series of pills from a silver tray that held a wide range of vitamins and supplements. She knew he had already had a swim and done thirty minutes on the stairmaster, before he had showered and changed.

"I wanted to talk to you, my dear," he said once the breakfast things had been cleared away. Cat knew that tone. It was the tone he used when she didn't get the grades he thought she should have, or when he decided to comment on her credit-card bill. Cat had always managed to cajole him in the past, but she knew her time was running out. Cat had been back in New York over a year and she knew the lecture that was coming to her was long overdue. She had finished her "studies" with a year in Brussels learning specialised paint techniques while Fiona did a stint at the European Commission. They'd had a ball. Cat wished he'd picked a morning when she didn't have a hangover.

"I started a fabulous painting last night," she said, trying for a pre-emptive strike. "It's this massive sunflower on a huge canvas."

"I'm sure I'll love it, my dear, but we have more important things to discuss," he said sharply.

Cat shut up. She knew when it was wise just to listen.

"You will be twenty-five in September." He began slowly pacing the room.

A bad sign, thought Cat. This could get pretty heavy.

"And I'm not getting any younger." Cat started to protest, but her granddad held up his hand to silence her.

"Don't feed my vanity, my dear. I have people I pay for that privilege. I know who I am, and how old I am. And frankly, I'm getting tired. Business does not excite me the way it still did only a few years ago," he continued pensively. "One starts to think of one's legacy. I never thought I'd be speaking like this to a woman. No offence to your gender, my dear, but women were different in my days. Then again, I never met a man who could better my Martha." Her grandfather stood with his back to her, looking out through the French doors. "I know I've mollycoddled you and I make no excuses for it. You are my only family, my only descendant and it was my prerogative to spoil you. But I believe that you are made from the same mettle as your great-grandmother."

Cat said nothing. She knew there was more to come. Though her face held a pleasant interested look, her mind was whirring. What was he up to? What did he have planned for her? She knew her family had business interests in many different areas, but she was unclear about what exactly her grandfather did.

Invoking the dearly departed Martha was a sure sign that the subject was serious. Throughout her childhood she had heard many stories about Martha, far more than about her grandparents who her granddad always dismissed as "social butterflies". She had heard even less about her own parents, gathering information mainly from domestics. As a child she'd hungered to know more, but instinctively knew that the subject was not to be broached. Her grandfather's eyes always clouded over if her father's name came up, the pain of losing him still fresh. Once Cat had asked him about her mother. Granddad had just smiled sadly and said, "She was a lovely lady. Very beautiful," and left it at that.

Her granddad turned and saw the small furrow on Cat's brow which she instantly smoothed out. "Don't worry, my dear. I'm going to start by spoiling you some more. I'm going to throw you a birthday party. A big one."

Cat's face lit up despite herself. That sounded more like it.

"You can invite as many people as you like. I will in turn invite some business people. People you've met and others you should meet. Apart from that, it is to be a surprise. Just send the guest list to my secretary and we'll send out the invitations. And I want you to get yourself the most beautiful ball-gown in Manhattan. Make me proud, Sugarplum."

Cat smiled at the nickname. He had taken her to see the Nutcracker Suite when she was six years old and she had spent the days that followed dancing around the house pretending to be the Sugarplum Fairy until her grandfather had agreed to let her take ballet lessons. Throughout her childhood he had taken her to every Radio City Music Hall Christmas spectacular, along with opening nights of Broadway musicals. Ballet lessons had been scheduled in with riding lessons, tennis lessons, private French tutorials, and of course Art lessons. He had refused her very little, thought Cat, looking down and catching sight of a dab of bright green paint she'd missed on her wrist. Mind you, he was a sly dog – he had something up his sleeve. She didn't want to think about it. Right now all she wanted to think about was finishing her painting.

"Come with me," said her grandfather ushering her into the adjoining library. It was oak-panelled from ceiling to floor. Cat knew it had been designed by a master-craftsman in England who had travelled for months just to find the wood. Rows of files were spread out on the large desk. A computer hummed discreetly in a corner as if trying to be as unobtrusive as possible in this nineteenth-century room.

"These files contain information on all the charities we are involved with. They are also on the computer, so you can view them on that if you prefer. With very few exceptions they are all New York based, so you wouldn't have to travel very far. You'll be pleased to see we have quite a lot of involvement in the Arts. You know how much Martha loved the Arts," he said with a sweep of his arm. Cat looked at him inquisitively.

"I want you to familiarise yourself with them. Pick a few you like. Get involved. Give me your thoughts. Your suggestions," he said, answering her unspoken question. "It's a way for you to ease into the family business. To start doing something useful. To make a name for yourself. Over the summer we can discuss your involvement and perhaps start looking into the more commercial aspects of what we do so that you will be better prepared when the time comes."

"When the time comes for what, granddad?" she asked, picking up a file. The title read *The Metropolitan Museum of Art.*

"When the time comes for me to go," he said softly.

Cat looked up sharply. In the dim light of the library she could see her grandfather's frailty more clearly and she felt a stab of panic. She loved the old codger. She'd be lost without him.

His eyes softened as he smiled. "Don't worry, Sugarplum. I'm not going anywhere just yet."

Cat beamed back at him. This wasn't too bad. It could have been a lot worse. She'd humour him and go through the files. She'd probably find something in there that would catch her interest. And it looked like she had the whole summer to think about it.

"I went to the Met yesterday to see a wonderful exhibition on Aboriginal Art," she said, tapping the file in her hand. "It was spectacular."

"You should have told me," said her granddad, clearly pleased. "We are important patrons. I'm sure the director would have loved to be your personal guide."

"Well, if we're giving them money, then I think it's better to see it as a member of the general public does – don't you think? To make sure they are spending it wisely." Anyway, I had my own private guide, thought Cat.

"Good point," he said as Cat sat down at the desk and started to read. "I must go to a series of meetings now, and I'll be back in the Hamptons for dinner. Stay as long as you like. I'm delighted you're taking to the task so well."

He bent down and kissed her quickly on the cheek. "By the way, my dear, you know I hate to pry, but I was wondering if you were seeing anyone special these days?"

"Special? You mean like a boyfriend? Granddad! You know you've always been the only one for me," she teased. "Anyway I'm too young to be thinking of getting married, or anything like that."

"Too young? Why, in my day an unmarried woman of twenty-five was an Old Maid."

"Old Maid? More like young, free, and single. And I intend to remain that way. I like being alone."

"God forbid you should end up alone," said her granddad, dropping his voice. "I just want to give you an old man's advice. Choose wisely. You are beautiful, charming, and very rich. These can be disadvantages as much as advantages. When the time comes for you to choose a life-mate I can only wish you the joy I knew with my dear Martha." Then he turned and left the room.

"What is with everybody?" thought Cat as she summoned Victor with the little silver bell on the desk. She needed more coffee and some painkillers if she was going to go through these files. Why did everybody seem to want her to grow up all of a sudden?

Chapter Seven

◆▬◆

For the next few days Cat spent every morning in the Central Park West apartment going through the files. Her granddad called in twice and they had lunch while he explained the finer points of tax deductions on registered charities and how one project could be financially linked to another, or broken up into separate entities, for maximum financial benefit to all those concerned. She found she had a real taste for it, and looked forward to taking a more active role. Her granddad was right. It was time she started doing something useful.

Every other available minute was spent either painting or with Trevor. The canvas was going really well. Cat had painted a big bright sunflower that snaked its way up the long canvas. It was surrounded by

multicoloured patterns with little flickering flames that
were repeated within the sunflower's centre.

Trevor cooked as she painted, or they called for a
delivery service. Her little refrigerator was covered in
take-away menus. Sometimes they went out to eat in
little restaurants in the Village, or went late-night bar-
hopping through the Irish pubs down on Second
Avenue. They'd also become quite the New York tourists, visiting landmarks and museums at every opportunity. Cat was discovering a whole new side to the city
she had lived in most of her life. Trevor could not
believe she had never ridden the subway and insisted
they do so immediately. After the smelly, jolting ride,
in a cramped rush-hour train, Cat decided that she
hadn't been missing much.

More often than not they talked late into the night
and she ended up sleeping on the sofa. Fiona would
not believe her when Cat insisted that nothing was
going on with Trevor. Cat didn't really understand it
herself. They were friends and nothing more. Except it
was a lot more. She just didn't know what that might
be. All she knew was that she had never met anyone
more fun, more witty, and more intelligent than Trevor.

The only shadow was Trev's attitude to her family.
Or more specifically to her family's wealth. Or any
wealth for that matter. He lectured her on the struggle
of the working classes until she told him to shut up,

and often came up with stupid statements out of the blue about how it would cost six months wages for a worker from a Third World country to buy her shoes, or her bag, or whatever he objected to as being frivolous.

The issue had come to a head the morning before, when she asked him to meet her at the West Side apartment. He had been impressed by the luxurious surroundings but had hidden it behind sarcastic banter about all great wealth being tainted. He had dismissed Cat's pride over the Richardson charities as mere tax breaks, which really annoyed her. But that didn't annoy her as much as when she found him at the computer when she left him alone in the library for a few minutes. He had been upset when she walked back in and flicked off the machine.

"Hey!" he yelled. "I was just about to get in. Did you know you guys have your own network?"

"Didn't your parents teach you it was rude to pry into other people's affairs?" she snapped, angry at his lack of manners. He did not even seem ashamed at having been caught.

"Cat, I'm a journo. That's what I do."

"Not all journalists are like that," she said defensively.

"Oh yes we are," he countered. "All of us are."

The incident had cast a shadow on their friendship and it was a relief when he said he would be out of town for a few days. It was time she called up her old gang. She had been neglecting them.

Cat readily accepted Ramon's invitation for "a little *aventura*" on Saturday night. He had refused to tell her what was up, which was why she now found herself stuffed into a cab with no idea where she was going. They had first gone out for a boozy dinner with Fiona, Valerie and Miss Model whose name turned out to be "Sheri, with an S".

They were all in high spirits as they spilled onto the street and hailed a cab. The driver had at first refused to take them, complaining loudly that he was only insured for four. He was a tiny wizened old man. Despite the heat he wore a huge tweed cap. A Hebrew newspaper lay spread out on the front seat and there was much haggling going on as Ramon tried to convince him to let him sit up front. The cabby finally relented and they were on their way.

"I'm taking the Brooklyn Bridge," announced the cabby as if declaring war on the enemy.

"Brooklyn? We're going to Brooklyn?" asked Cat. Ramon nodded back and smiled slyly. "What the hell are we going to do in Brooklyn?"

"That's what I thought," said the cabby, talking to her in the rear-view mirror. "You look like nice kids. Rich kids. What are you doing going to Brooklyn?"

"We are going to visit an elderly aunt of mine who is not very well," said Ramon giggling.

"Family! That's what's most important in life," commented the cabby unperturbed.

Val and Sheri-with-an-S were having a fit of giggles, holding on to their sides, trying not laugh out loud. The two seemed to have become very palsy in the last few weeks. Cat gestured to Fi with a "What's up with them?" look. Fi motioned to her nose and sniffed loudly. Ah, thought Cat, we've been hitting the nose candy.

"So Cat," said Ramon turning all the way around to face the back seat, "you have been spending a lot of time with dis Trevor? Tell me everything."

"There's nothing to tell," said Cat. "We're just friends." She saw the old cabby look up at her in the mirror and smile for the first time.

"That's what she says," said Fiona haughtily. "But they've been to the museum, the top of the Empire State building, and the zoo."

"Sounds like they're in love to me," said the cabby with authority. "The zoo is a dead giveaway."

"No. No. No. We're just friends," said, Cat slapping her leg for emphasis.

"*Methinks the lady doth protest too much*," said Fiona.

"Ya know in my day we didn't have that. Men friends with women. Women friends with men," the cabby said into the mirror, shaking his head. "You mean to tell me he's never made a pass at you?"

"No."

"A pretty girl like you? I don't believe it!"

"Well, he hasn't."

"Maybe he's gay," giggled Valerie. The cabby lifted both hands towards the heavens as if agreeing and stole a glance at Ramon.

"No. I don't think so," said Cat. "He talks about women a lot. He looks at women a lot. In fact he gawks!" She laughed, remembering Trev sitting in a bar commenting on every woman that came in and not daring to talk to them until he'd consumed a large quantity of beer. It was one of his more endearing qualities. A lot more endearing than his rabid left-wing politics.

"Look. Look! There's Maria!" said Ramon, waving wildly. He turned to the cabby. "This is it. Here we are."

Cat looked out and saw Maria standing beneath a streetlamp, her wild mane of hair backlit so it seemed to be giving off sparks. Maria was jumping up and down welcoming them in rapid-fire Spanish. She looked very different without the upper East Side work clothes she wore in the salon. She was dressed for the neighbourhood in red spike heels, tight jeans, and a low-cut top.

The street looked dirty and deserted until you noticed

how many people were hanging out in the shadows. Heavy iron mesh covered the shop windows and Cat could see that the groups of people sitting on the stoops were staring at them. She felt overdressed in her cream linen pant suit. The cabby wasn't impressed either.

"You sure you're at the right place?" he asked, leaning out of the window. "You want I wait for you?"

"No. Everything is fine," laughed Ramon, paying him. "My aunt is looking better, no?"

Val and Sheri nearly fell out of the cab laughing. Cat thought they must be out of their minds. They must be doing more than just coke. She wandered over to Maria and gave her a hug.

"What are we doing?" she whispered in her ear.

"My uncle has agreed to meet with you. But first we must visit my *abuelita* – my grandma – and pick up some things. Come. You follow me." Before Cat could ask for more details, Maria waved them down the street as if she were corralling a group of rowdy schoolchildren. Her red heels clicked up the old stone steps of a building, stepping over the men sitting there and yelling abuse at anyone who did not get out of her way fast enough.

They followed her into a dimly lit hall. In the floors above Cat could hear the sounds of televisions blaring, music being played, a baby wailing. At the end of the hall Maria knocked and then turned to face them.

"You will meet my *abuelita* now. I live with her,"
she said, hushing Val and Sheri who were still giggling.
"We will get some things and then we go. OK?"

The apartment was tiny and every available space
was crammed with furniture. Red and pink were the
dominant colours. Several large plaster statues of
garishly painted saints were dotted around the room.
Each was surrounded with flowers and candles. A huge
old woman in a flowered house-dress was wedged in
a large armchair by the open window. She held a cigar
in one hand and a large fan in the other which she
waved lazily back and forth catching the breeze. She
sat in front of an old black and white television set that
was tuned to a Latino channel.

"*Abuelita, estos son mis amigos*," said Maria, softly
tapping the old woman on the shoulder.

Ramon strode up and bent down to kiss the little
dark-brown hand. "*Mucho gusto, senora*," he said
formally.

The old woman smiled broadly and stroked his
cheek. Maria was delighted. They each went up to greet
the woman. When it was Cat's turn the old lady put
her cigar down and took Cat's hand in both of hers as
if weighing it. Then she looked Cat straight in the eyes.

"*Si, si*," she said, still holding on to her hand and
patting it. "*Muy guapa. Muy guapa.*"

"Abuelita says you are beautiful," said Maria, who

CRISTINA PISCO

had returned from the tiny kitchen with two big shopping bags. "I think she likes you." Maria held up the bags to them. "I got everything we need. You guys owe me a hundred bucks."

"One hundred dollars?" asked Fiona surprised. "What is in there?"

"Gifts. You have to give gifts. Cigars, *aguardiente* – that's like a really strong rum – cake, all sorts of stuff. I went all the way to the South Bronx to a special "*botanica*" to buy everything." She put the bags down as her grandmother called her over and whispered in her ear.

"*Abuelita* says you must have a drink before you leave. I'll be right back. Oh, yeah and it's twenty-five bucks each to get in."

"Where the hell are we going? The Brooklyn Ritz?" Cat whispered through a forced smile. The old lady was still holding on to her hand and smiling at her.

"Maria's uncle is a famous high priest. A very important *Babalawo*. He has agreed to see us," said Valerie excitedly.

"For an extra one hundred and twenty-five bucks, I'm sure he has," said Cat under her breath. The old lady gave her hand one last pat and let go. She was still staring at Cat. She took a long pull at her cigar and let the smoke out slowly. Maria came in with a little tray that held five shot glasses filled with a golden liquid and the old lady gestured to them to have a drink. The alcohol hit Cat's stomach like a bomb and she found herself coughing loudly. The old woman laughed as they all bent over, tears streaming from the strong drink. Her eyes danced merrily but never left Cat's face.

"*Lukumi*," she said beaming, letting each vowel trip slowly out of her mouth. "*Muy bueno para ti.*" Cat looked at Maria for a translation.

"That's the African name for *Santería*," said Maria picking up the shopping bags again. "She says it's good for you. We gotta go now or we'll be late."

Ramon explained they were going to a *toque*, a sort of celebration ceremony. It was being held in a large building in a neighbourhood that must have been used for warehousing. Cat had no idea where they were, only that they were back on Manhattan Island some-where downtown.

The others were all chattering happily as Maria led them down a long large alley, occasionally breaking into a song in Spanish and doing little dance steps. Fiona tried to imitate her to the general amusement of the others. Sheri-with-an-S was visibly staggering as she balanced on her high heels and straight skirt, looking even more out of place than Cat in this dark, empty place. Cat wanted to get into the mood and dance around with them but she couldn't shake a sense of brooding that seemed to get worse as the night progressed.

"You OK, darling?" asked Fiona, sensing Cat's mood. "You look slightly stressed. Missing someone, perchance?"

"No. I'm fine. Just a little tired," said Cat.

Valerie came up to her and held out a tiny gold box. "Here have one of these. You'll feel much better," she giggled, flipping the top open. Inside were a half a dozen little white pills that looked like breath mints.

"They're wonderful," said Fiona, reaching in and taking two. She gave one to Cat and swallowed the other. "I had one earlier and I feel like I'm walking on a little cloud. It'll cheer you up immensely."

Cat swallowed it down. She could use some cheering up. Maybe it was the little pills that made the others seem so carefree and silly. At the end of the alley light spilled out from big double doors. A hand-written sign said *This way to Toque*. Cat could hear the noise of people chatting in Spanish and laughing softly.

Inside, the air was heavy with cigar smoke and the smell of something Cat couldn't place – something sweet and spicy. About a dozen people dressed in white stood around chatting, some of them holding bags similar to Maria's. The atmosphere was relaxed as more people came in and greeted those already there. Everyone was smiling and fanning themselves with big

leaf-shaped fans. Cat noticed that they had heavy necklaces made of shells and beads. Maria excused herself,
leaving the group to mingle. Ramon was off talking to
some men with drums, while the girls chatted away to
a group of women. The place had the feel of a Sunday
afternoon picnic and Cat found herself relaxing. Maria
came back dressed in white with a large necklace
dangling around her neck.

"We will all go in soon," she said, her eyes sparkling.
"Stay in the back of the room and just watch. Don't
be scared. It can be very exciting. Just remember you
are not alone. We are all watching, no matter what
happens."

People were slowly drifting out through an open
door and Cat could hear the drummers getting ready
inside. Ramon had already entered and she saw Fiona
go in with Val and Sheri.

The room was large and clean, but had no windows.
Ramon was sitting to one side with the drummers, deep
in conversation, while most of the other people
grouped themselves around the room, leaving a space
in the middle. Cat peered over the shoulders in front
of her and saw what looked like an altar at the far end,
flanked on one side with a large statue of Christ and
on the other with a woman saint. What looked like a
large soup tureen was placed before each statue on big
colourful mats. The air was thick with cigar smoke and

the heat began to rise as more people crowded in. There was a palpable sense of anticipation as people slowly filed up to the mats and placed their offerings in front of the altar. Bottles lined up alongside fruit, vegetables and platters of cooked food, filling the room with exotic smells. Maria went up, followed by Val and Sheri. They lay the contents of the shopping bags among the other "gifts" as Cat and Fiona looked on.

The drums started a slow beat, picking up speed every bar or so. The crowd pressed in closer, swaying to the beat, and Cat moved off to a corner to get a better view. She found herself standing next to a tall black woman who smiled at her warmly and moved to make some space for her.

The crowd parted as an elderly man made his way to the altar, stopping to talk and smile with people as he passed. He was accompanied by two women who danced alongside him. As they reached the top of the room a singer started chanting in a language Cat did not recognise.

"He is calling the *Orishas* to come," said the woman next to Cat. She was smiling broadly and swaying her hips to the drums. Cat found that she too was dancing. She looked across the room at Ramon who was happily banging on a drum someone must have lent him. Fiona was on her own, eyes half closed, moving in her wooden fashion to the beat. Cat heard a stifled giggle.

Looking over she saw Val and Sheri dancing and giggling as the singer rose and started strutting in the middle of the room yelling what sounded like insults at the crowd, who responded by jeering and laughing.

"He is insulting the Gods," said the woman, enjoying the performance.

"He is trying to make them angry so the *Santos* will appear."

The drums started pounding in earnest as the man continued to yell. The older man reached down, picked up a bottle and filled his mouth. He then turned on the crowd and sprayed them with a fine jet, his eyes bulging out, his feet stomping the beat loudly. His two assistants circled around with two other bottles.

"The *Babalawo* is blessing us," explained the woman.

Cat felt her heart pounding with the drums. It was impossible not to get caught up in the dance. One of the assistants put a bottle to her mouth and Cat sputtered as the strong *aguardiente* was poured down her throat.

The drums died down at a signal from the *Babalawo*. Everyone settled in front of the altar as he held up a small container.

"That is *Omiero*. It is a mixture of rainwater, riverwater, seawater and holy water with *aguardiente* and other things," the woman whispered. Cat noticed that the drums had started up again, more languorously, as the *Babalawo* passed the container over the people, stopping at each of the four corners of the room before facing back to the altar. He started calling out names of Saints, inviting them to join them, circling the room and spilling a little of the *Omeiro* as he went. The drums picked up the beat of his chant as the people rose. Each one took the container, drinking from it and passing it on.

The room was getting really hot. Cat was thirsty. When the container reached her she drank a big gulp, tasting coconut and fruit and the kick of strong alcohol. The chanting started up again and Cat let herself go with the music. She felt really relaxed and at one with these smiling people.

The drums beat even faster and Cat felt a delicious tremble rise up from her belly. Colours exploded in front of her, making her gasp. Oh man, she thought, opening her eyes in shock as her heart raced. She was tripping! She remembered the little white pill and wondered what was in it. She looked over at Val and Sheri, trying hard to focus. They were dancing seductively with Maria and a skinny young man, but they seemed fine. Looking through half-closed eyes she could see Ramon drumming wildly, his long black hair falling like a curtain around his face. Fiona was on her own. Her eyes were closed and a serene smile played on her lips as she swayed.

Cat took a few deep breaths to calm herself. She was OK. Everything was OK. All she had to do was sit back and enjoy the ride like everybody else. After all, she felt absolutely wonderful. Her body was like a warm pulsating membrane that vibrated with each drumbeat. It was like the afterglow of sex.

Her gaze kept going back to the two girls dancing. Val's hair had come undone and her blouse was open. Her hips were thrusting to the beat. Cat watched in fascination as Valerie started to shake. The room was tilting slightly and Cat reached deep inside herself to try and straighten it out. Valerie was shaking more violently. People moved away to give her space. Cat reached out to try and push her way through the crowd to her but was stopped by a strong black hand on her arm.

"She will be all right," said the woman next to her. She pointed to Maria who was standing over Valerie. "She is with Maria."

Of course she'll be all right, thought Cat. They were all right.

The room was swirling. Cat found she could stand back and just watch it. She knew her body was dancing but she felt completely disconnected from it, as if she danced only in the quiet space inside her head while the drums echoed far away in the room.

Across the room a woman shuddered violently and

dropped to the floor. The *Babalawo* went to her immediately and sprayed her with the bottle. The woman's eyes glazed over and then rolled back into her head. Another started twirling low to the ground, round and round, touching her forehead as if to soothe it while her fingers massaged the intricate rhythms of the drums. Out of the corner of her eye Cat saw Valerie fall to the floor and start to tremble from head to toe.

I should be worried, she thought. But they were all so far away and she felt so wonderful, her whole being filled with a tickling sensation. Her vision was slightly distorted as well. Like she was standing behind her own eyeballs looking out through her pupils.

Suddenly her view was obstructed by the large black face of the woman beside her. She was peering at Cat, bringing her face up close. Cat could feel the woman's breath, warm and sweet and smelling of the *aguardiente.*

"Who are you? What are you doing here?" the woman asked in a rough voice. Cat started to answer but found she could not move. The woman was bending down as if peering through a keyhole. Cat tried to turn her head, to see the rest of the room but could not see past the tall woman towering over her, asking her who she was. The heat felt oppressive, the drums pounded in her temples. She closed her eyes and gasped as a strong wind lifted her off her feet.

Cat opened her eyes and looked down on the swaying crowd. It was as if she was watching from somewhere up near the ceiling. *How can I be floating up on the ceiling?* She could see the crowd dancing below her. Valerie was still lying on the floor, her eyes glazed over as her hips thrust up and down. The *Babalawo* was spraying her with *aguardiente*. His assistants danced around clapping their hands. A small goat stood in the middle of the room surrounded by small cages. Through the bars, Cat could see the fluttering of wings. She saw everything in sharp detail but she could not hear above the sound of raging wind. She could not feel her body at all.

Cat searched the crowd. There, in a corner, she saw the tall black woman. Her heart jumped as she realised that she was looking down on herself. She was standing rod-straight, looking blankly back into the woman's face. *That can't be me!*

The wind howled in her ears. Her stomach churned as she heard a soft whisper, like a caress close to her neck:

"Who are you? How did you come here?"

Cat felt as if something had thumped her in the belly, forcing her to battle for breath. She struggled for air. A sharp slap stung her cheek and she opened her mouth to scream, feeling a rush of air, gulping it down. The hair on her head stood on end as something lifted out of her, making her stagger back.

Cat was back in her body. *I'm OK. It's just a bad trip*. The woman was still looking at her. Then she passed her hand over Cat's brow and bowed. Over her shoulder a figure caught Cat's eye. It was a woman with long black hair. She was dancing, though her steps were different from everyone else.

Cat felt the panic rise. *Was she looking at herself again?* Then the woman turned and smiled at Cat as if she knew her. She waved, beckoning her to join her. She was barefoot and dressed in drab rags. She seemed vaguely familiar to Cat. No one else seemed to notice her, though she danced right in front of the altar. The dark-haired woman smiled sweetly. Her eyes sparkled brightly catching the glint of a knife the *Babalawo* was waving. Cat felt a cold river of fear run through her. *She had to get out.*

Willing her legs and feet to move, Cat shoved her way to the door. She passed Fiona who tried to stop her. Cat pushed on, mumbling. *I have to get out. I have to get home*. Before Fiona could follow her, she was running down the alley.

Cat's heels echoed as she ran, trying to get out of the dark alley, heading for the dim lamplight on the street. She was scared shitless.

Everything was slightly out of kilter. The angles were

all wrong. Her heart was racing. It skipped a beat as she slipped on a pool of something oily, catching herself on the grimy wall just before she fell. She thought she heard someone behind her, but she was too frightened to look over her shoulder. Rounding the corner Cat slowed down.

Look normal. Look normal, and find a cab.

The street was pretty much deserted. Down about a block or so, a group of men were standing under a streetlamp. They stopped talking and watched her walk down the street. Cat needed to stop and catch her breath. She longed to lean against a stoop and try and get a hold of her senses. But she knew the city. She had to keep walking. She had to look as if she had somewhere to go. As if someone was waiting for her.

Don't look lost. Don't look lost. Don't look weak and lost.

The men all smiled appreciatively as she approached. Cat looked back at them and lowered her head but did not smile.

"*Hola, chica,*" said one of them through his teeth. A low whistle followed.

Cat straightened up, determined to pass them by.

"Hey baby! Come with me. I show you a good time," said the man, stepping out in front of her.

Cat heard the others chuckling softly.

This is it. This is where it all ends. Headlines

screamed through her mind: *Woman Raped! Woman found dead! Brutal killing!*

What the fuck was she doing? Anger mixed in with her fear as she felt a tug on her sleeve.

"You have a cigarette? You give me a cigarette?" said the man tugging at her sleeve.

Cat stood very still, sobering up her senses.

Then she faced the man and looked into his eyes. She gazed straight into his pupils and felt him let go of her. She willed her beating heart to slow down. He was just a man. She could see him clearly on the edges of her vision. Small but very compact, with dark olive skin and black shiny hair. His eyes wavered for an instant but Cat caught them again. Slowly she looked at all four of them standing there under the lamp. They were all poised, held by her gaze. She turned back to the first one and let a slow smile spread across her face. Cat caught the reaction in his eyes. A lightness which she egged on with her own eyes. She smiled and watched as the men relaxed.

"Sure," she said, holding them with her smile. "I have some cigarettes. Have you got a light?"

Cat opened the flip top and passed the pack around. The men all took a cigarette and fumbled in their pockets. As she took one herself, three lighters flicked at the same time. Cat laughed, letting her voice ring clearly, like a bell. The men all laughed with her, enjoying this game of courtly manners. But Cat knew it was a dangerous game. She could feel the tension like separate strings pulled taut between her and each of the four men. She had to play them right or they could snap.

"So what you doing around here?" asked the first man, his voice taking on the soft tones of seduction as he moved closer.

Cat didn't flinch. She tossed her hair and blew the smoke up over her head where it hung in the lamplight like a halo.

"I'm going to see a friend. I'm late," she answered lightly, knowing just how hollow that sounded.

"Ah, women! They are always late!" laughed the man. His companions leaned back to watch.

"That's what men say," said Cat and winked. "But then again you guys seem to think we're worth waiting for."

She was scaring herself. The men all tossed their heads back and laughed too loudly at her feeble joke. Cat heard the grinding of gears in the distance. "Please let it be a bus," she prayed. Across the street a door opened and an older woman came out, locking the door behind her.

"So? You want to come dancing?" said the man executing a twirl. "You want to party?" The others were egging him on, whistling and hooting. The sound of the engine was getting nearer. The woman across the street walked up to the corner and stopped, putting her heavy bags down beside her.

"I'd love to," said Cat, reaching out and touching the man's arm. She felt his muscle twitch. "But I have to go. Keep the cigarettes. I have lots more." Then she turned on her heel and ran across the street just as a bus pulled up in front of the woman standing there. She felt the panic rise again in her throat as she fumbled in her bag for the exact change. Her hands were trembling, and she dropped the coins twice as the driver looked on impassively.

Cat could hear the men still calling to her as the bus pulled out. She had no idea where it was going. She could be on her way to New Jersey for all she knew. Cat's stomach was churning. She could taste the acid burn of nausea rising in her throat. Her hands were shaking as she gripped the seat. Everything was swirling again, now that she had lost the focus that had kept her alert back there with the men.

The bus swayed sickeningly as it bumped down the street picking up speed. She tried closing her eyes but it only got worse. Her mind was filled with images and sounds that confused her. Across from Cat sat an old transvestite, his lipstick smeared across his face, his pancake makeup a ghostly white against his dark skin. He turned and smiled hideously at Cat. Looking down to avoid him, Cat spotted a damp patch on the floor. Blood? There was blood on the floor? Cat felt the bile rise in her throat again. She stood up and peered out the window as the bus passed a street corner. Broome Street? That wasn't far from the loft. The thought of Trevor filled her with relief. Maybe he was back. She couldn't bear to be on the bus another minute. Cat rang the bell and jumped off the minute it stopped.

A light was on in the kitchen window. Thank God! Trevor was home. Cat fumbled with the locks, hearing her breath come in jagged gulps. Once off the bus she had lost her last shred of calm as the paranoia grasped her again. She took no comfort from the street. Faces peered out of the dark at her and she did not know if they were real or not. She ran all the way up the stairs, too scared to call his name.

The place was empty. She couldn't tell if Trevor was back or not.

She had to call Fiona and reassure her she was all right. She must have looked crazy bolting out like that. Cat felt faint as she dialled the number and listened to the familiar message:

"Hi. We're not home right now, but if you leave your name and credit-card details, we'll be happy to go out and spend all your money as soon as we get back!"

"Hi, Fiona. It's Cat. Jesus, I hope you're all right. I

kinda freaked. I think I had a bad trip. I'm fine now. I'm at the loft. Talk to you later."

Cat felt very tired. She switched on the little table lamp and slumped on the sofa. What would the others think? What the hell had happened to her? She felt heavy, letting all her weight sink into the velvet upholstery. Something caught her eye, but she could not move.

The door was open. She had left the door open as she ran in! She listened, holding her breath. Soft steps were coming up the stairs. Cat was paralysed. She remembered the alleyway. Someone had been following her back there. Maybe they'd found her. How could they have followed her on the bus? She willed herself to jump up and lock the door but she could not move. She watched as the door swung open and felt a scream catch in her throat as the familiar figure of Trevor filled the doorway.

"Cat? Are you all right?" Trevor said as he walked in and saw her crouched in the corner of the sofa.

Cat flew into his arms. She was crying and shaking, her words caught in a torrent of shuddering sobs. He led her gently back to the sofa. He cradled her like a baby as she sobbed, stroking her hair.

"Are you hurt?" he asked softly, holding her at arms' length so he could get a good look at her.

"I'm fine," Cat managed to blurt out. She buried her

head in his shoulder. "I'm just scared, and drunk, and stoned, and I thought someone was following me."

Cat felt a torrent of emotion as she clung to him. She knew he was speaking softly to her but she could not hear what he was saying. She could only feel his warm breath in her ear, smell the hot city off his neck. Her mouth searched hungrily along his jaw until it connected with the soft flesh of his lips. She saw his eyes flash open as she kissed him. Her hands fumbled with the buttons of his shirt, feeling the smooth skin of his chest under her fingers. She kissed him again. This time he kissed her back and she felt a thrill that took her breath away.

"I want you," she whispered into his neck, her lips tracing his pulse. "I want you now."

He started to speak, but she stopped him, kissing him hard, feeling him respond with his whole body. Her hands worked swiftly, pulling at his clothes, tearing off her own, stroking him as he lay back and groaned. She couldn't get enough of him. His warm smell enveloped her, pulling her down towards him until she felt she was falling slowly, whirling like a feather as she fell. He grabbed her hips, guiding her to him. Every cell in her body exploded as she straddled him. The drums pounded in her head. Her mind filled with images – of white-robed dancers, of blood and feathers, and of a lone woman twirling round and round the room, her black hair flying – until she fell shuddering on top of him and everything melted into darkness.

Chapter Eight

Cat woke to the smell of bacon and coffee. She lifted her head and winced. Where was she? She sat up and rubbed her eyes as the crazy events of the night before came slowly back to her. What the hell was that about? She didn't remember much, but she definitely remembered having amazing sex. She looked around and realised with a jolt that she was in Trevor's apartment. She was naked in his futon on the floor! She could hear him singing in the kitchen. She'd had sex with Trevor? Cat's hand flew up and covered her mouth. "Oh my God!" she thought. "I jumped Trevor last night."

"I see the princess has finally risen," said Trevor, popping his head in the doorway. "Breakfast will be ready in a minute if you think you're up to it."

Cat mumbled something as she tried to pull the sheet up over her shoulders. She felt a blush rising up her neck. Damn! She hated blushing.

"So get your arse out of bed. Tucker's on!" he sang from the kitchen.

She scrambled to put some clothes on. That was a close call. She had no idea what to say. She hadn't had the time to let it all sink in. She pushed the thought of the two of them entwined on the sofa way back to where she hoped it would disappear into oblivion. She'd stick it with the rest of the "Stupid Things I've Done (and would rather forget)". Like the time she got drunk, climbed up and danced on the table and fell off, or the time she kissed the gardener's son behind the potting shed, or the time she *refused* to think about in the back seat of Joe Hansen's parents' Mercedes. Cat splashed some water on her face and looked in the mirror. Man, she looked like shit.

"You've been a very naughty girl," she told her reflection. Wiping her face, she caught a whiff of Trevor and fought the urge to breathe it in, feeling a tingle run up her spine. No way, she thought, throwing the towel on the bathroom floor. No way was she going to get turned on by him, even if he did have a really cute butt. She was going in there, to face him, and get this over with once and for all.

"Trevor, I don't know what to say. About last night,

I mean," she stammered as she walked into the kitchen. He was serving up big plates of bacon and eggs and pouring coffee as if nothing had happened.

"Ah! You've remembered," said Trevor, smirking. "Don't worry yourself about it. Like the song says: *It was just of those things.*"

"I was out of my head. It was a really weird night," Cat continued searching for the right words. "I don't want it to change things."

"Nothing's changed. We're still mates, aren't we?"

"Sure. Sure we are," she agreed.

"I know I should have put up more of a fight, but what can I say? It's not every night I come home to a very beautiful, very horny, woman who is intent on ripping my clothes off."

Cat felt herself blushing again. He was going to make her suffer. She looked up expecting to see him laughing at her but his eyes were soft and full of concern.

"No sweat, sailor. We're fine," he said softly. "It never happened."

Cat ate in silence as Trevor chatted about anything and everything. She relaxed as she listened to him. He told her that Fiona had called several times but that he had reassured her that Cat was fine.

"You scared her last night," said Trevor. "She said you ran out into the street alone."

"I scared myself. I can't remember much. I just had to get out of there."

"Was it the voodoo thing?"

"No. It was something else. Like I had a really bad trip or something. It scared me shitless."

"Fiona said you flew out the door."

"You didn't tell her?" Cat asked softly. "About, you know?"

"Naw! Anyway, it never happened, remember?"

Cat smiled gratefully, and pushed her plate away. Trevor stood, hurriedly washing the dishes, his broad back hunched over the sink, his floppy hair drooping over his eyes. Friends. They were just friends. Cat felt the relief well up inside her. She would just totally forget the entire night ever happened. All of it. And no more little white pills, she promised herself.

"I've gotta go," said Trevor, grabbing his jacket. "I'm meeting an old mate of mine who's over from Sydney. I thought I might come round to your place and visit later on. Maybe we could go out and have a few drinks."

"Great," said Cat smiling at her friend. "Great, bring your mate. I look forward to meeting him."

"Right!" answered Trevor. He stopped as if to say something, then looked quickly at his watch. "Gotta fly. See you later!"

Cat stood at the window and watched him stride

down the street, his arms swinging. He glanced up and waved, beaming that goofy smile that scrunched up his face. Cat waved back and smiled fondly. She really had to take the guy shopping. That was one horrendous jacket.

By the time Cat got back to her place, Fiona was in full Mary Poppins mode. She was vacuuming with a vengeance. Hoovering, she called it. It was her rather eccentric way of dealing with a hangover.

"I see you exaggerated again last night," said Cat, flopping on the sofa. Ever since they had shared a room in boarding-school it was the same tableau: Cat lounging somewhere and Fiona bustling around her. Cat had given up long ago getting the woman to sit down when she was in one of her busy-bumble-bee phases.

"*Moi?* What about you? Don't ever run out on me like that again! Anyway, you missed a great night. We had a ball."

Cat cocked her head pensively. "I wouldn't have called that having a ball. It was pretty weird."

"You were out of your head. You must have had a bad trip all right – all I felt was wonderful. Granted the bit with the chicken was a bit gruesome, but the music was fabulous. Ramon was drumming like a man possessed," said Fiona, mercifully unplugging the vacuum.

She flopped down next to Cat and lit a cigarette. Cat took one as well, leaning back and closing her eyes as she smoked.

"Talking of possession, I think I remember some of that going on. What was with Valerie? She looked pretty possessed to me."

"Doesn't she always! You know our Val. Always overly enthusiastic. I think she went off with one of the drummers – lucky lass. She's quite taken with all this mumbo-jumbo stuff at the moment with her new friend Sheri. I really don't see what Val sees in her. She has the IQ of an aubergine. Then again I suppose our Valerie isn't exactly a genius either. Still, you should have stuck around. The *Babalawo*, that's Maria's uncle, gave us each a reading. He wanted to know where you'd gone."

"So what did he have to say?" Cat asked.

"I shall not marry until I'm in my late thirties, and Ramon is going to be rich – but in some sort of restaurant trade. Forget Broadway. Ramon is a bit disappointed, but he thinks his dinner-party business might be his destiny. I, however, am devastated." Fiona stretched herself out to her full six feet and then jumped up again with a snap.

Cat smiled up at her. "Well, I'm going to forget about the whole thing. It was like, too weird," she said, inwardly reminding herself to forget the end of the night in particular. "Trevor said he might stop by later," she added casually.

"I know, he called to arrange the time just before you got back." Fiona was at it again, emptying the ashtrays and putting all the magazines in a neat pile under the coffee table. "He wanted to know if we wanted to go out for drinks. He's bringing a friend."

"Some guy flew in this afternoon," explained Cat taking advantage of the full length of the sofa now that Fiona was doing the Domestic Goddess thing again. "Some schoolfriend. He's probably another rugby-playing Aussie."

"Methinks not," said Fiona arching her eyebrows. "Her name is Kylie. It seems they used to live together in Sydney," she added in a conspirational tone. "The 'ex-love of my life', he called her. And, I could hear her giggling in the background."

"Kylie?" echoed Cat. She felt a nasty stab just below her breastbone. Hadn't he said it was some guy he'd known in Sydney? "I didn't think there were people who are actually called Kylie. That's like meeting someone who was born in Las Vegas." Cat said with a mixture of disgust and disbelief. So his "mate" was a girlfriend, was she?

"Indeed!" laughed Fiona. "It's almost as bad as Norelle. Very *Home and Away*. Actually, I believe it was *Neighbours*."

"Kylie, huh?" she repeated, smirking. "She's probably a blonde bimbo lifeguard with big boobs."

Kylie turned out to be blonde all right, but she was no bimbo. She was tall and willowy with almond-shaped eyes that flirted with Trevor at every opportunity. Her boobs were perfect along with the rest of her figure. She had, in fact, been a lifeguard. That was when they were both students and madly in love. Back in the days when she lived with Trevor in a communal house near Bondi beach where everybody was smart and funny, and wanted to change the world, as Kylie and Trevor fondly remembered ad nauseam. Kylie now worked as a wildlife photographer, travelling around the world taking pictures of endangered species. Worst of all, she was classy. Cat hated her on sight.

Excusing herself, Cat left the table and walked up to the crowded bar to buy some cigarettes. All around her people sparkled. Their laughter echoed around the room with its ceiling-to-floor mirrors.

What the fuck were they all so happy about? thought Cat. Or more to the point: what was she so grumpy about? She'd been like a prickly cactus ever since Trevor and Kylie had come in. She had hardly spoken through dinner except to throw in some nasty off-handed comments with a smirk. She'd even felt the need to excuse her lack of socialising, blaming it on the excesses of the night before. But she felt perfectly fine. Pissed off, but fine.

Cat leaned against the bar and looked at the band. They were singing some stupid song about somebody missing somebody. Why was the world populated with lovesick songwriters? Why don't they try and write about something else for a change?

She could see her table reflected in the mirror behind the musicians. Kylie was leaning in close to Trevor, chuckling at some private joke. The little lamp on the table cast a halo around the two of them. Cat thought that she'd never really noticed how strong Trevor's jaw-line was. He reached up and tucked a lock of Kylie's blonde hair back into place. It made Cat cringe.

I can't be jealous, she thought. This is stupid. I have no reason to be jealous. She's a perfectly wonderful person and Trevor is perfectly entitled to her. In fact, she was exactly the type of woman Cat really liked. She was beautiful and intelligent and witty. She was the type of person Cat loved to have as a friend. Except that she hated her on sight.

She wasn't jealous – it just felt like jealousy. That nauseating pull somewhere around the solar plexus that made you want to be able to spit venom. Or strike someone down with a blink of your eyes.

After all, it was perfectly normal to feel that way. It was weird to know that they had slept together the night before, and here he was, not even twenty-four hours later, clearly infatuated with this other woman. Cat decided it was one of those hormonal things. A kind of primitive instinct of territoriality that her body was throwing at her. It didn't mean a thing, so why should she care. In a few days, it would pass.

Cat caught Trevor looking at her. She smiled a little too brightly. His eyes asked if she was all right. She waved back cheerily and pointed to the band as if to explain her prolonged absence from the table.

She sat herself back down, determined to shake off her lousy mood. She avoided looking at Trevor and was extremely friendly to Kylie. She turned the full glare of her charm on the evening, going from her previous grouchy state to being the life and soul of the party. She made Trevor laugh. She made Kylie laugh. She made Fiona howl. She got the people at the next table to join in and flirted outrageously with a guy called Brett. She didn't see the nuzzling going on between the two supposedly ex-lovers. She didn't care. She was on a roll.

Cat was so busy having fun at the table beside them that at first she did not notice that Trevor and Kylie were leaving. She looked up to see Trevor with his arm around Kylie who was leaning heavily into his shoulder.

"We're going to call it a night. Kylie is jet-lagged and I'm really tired. I'm falling asleep on my feet."

"Hey, lover boy," Kylie teased, "I hope you're not gonna fall asleep too soon?" She nuzzled his neck.

"Well!" said Trevor with a mix of embarrassment and delight. "It looks like tonight's my lucky night!"

"You betcha," growled Kylie.

They all laughed, Cat more raunchily than the rest, as they said their goodbyes and watched the couple walk out of the bar.

"What is it with Australians?" asked Fiona, sipping her Stoly and tonic. "They have such a jolly-hockey-sticks attitude to sex. It must be something we left behind. It's very British really."

Cat nodded, staring at Kylie walking out. She hated her. It was unreal, but she detested her. Cat was blown away by the intensity of her feelings. It was like a mountain shuddering inside her. Cat felt that if she focused she could shatter the mirrors around her into a thousand pieces. She watched Trevor holding the door open, caught Kylie's laugh echoing above the noise of the crowd, saw her long legs as she walked out the door.

"Eat shit and *die*, you bitch," she whispered to herself.

She spent the rest of the night being her most scintillating, swatting men away like flies. She drank way too much vodka, convinced herself that she was having a great time, crawled drunkenly under her duvet and cried herself to sleep.

Cat didn't have much time to think about it all before she met Trevor again. At ten o'clock the next morning he was buzzing her doorbell.

She let him in, secretly glad that she felt like shit, looked worse, and was ready to snap the head off anyone who didn't immediately pass her a cup of coffee.

He bounced into the room with a box of doughnuts. She felt her stomach heave at the sweet smell of them.

"You look terrible," laughed Trevor.

"Coffee," Cat muttered from under her hair.

He respected her head and was soon back with a steaming cup of coffee, a large glass of water and two aspirin.

"Looks like you had a better time than I did after I left last night."

Cat looked up to see if he was kidding. He seemed perfectly delighted with himself but was clearly not messing with her.

"What happened to the hot and heavy Kylie?" she said, trying to take the acid out of her voice and failing miserably. "Sorry, I didn't mean it that way. She's beautiful and very charming," she added lamely.

Trevor waved her comment away. He stood as if trying to figure out what he was going to say.

"Kylie and I. We . . . I mean *I* . . . thought that maybe . . . you know, maybe, we could have another bash at it. We were really good together, you know."

"No, I don't actually," said Cat bluntly. Where the hell was this leading to? The last thing she needed right now was being an Agony Aunt to Trevor's love life.

"Well, I really thought, especially last night. I was sure, but it just didn't," he stammered, getting visibly frustrated. "Oh fuck it!" he finally exclaimed, throwing his hands up in defeat.

"What?" said Cat, snapping to attention.

He was standing there looking down at her, blushing beetroot from the neck up.

"This is probably the stupidest thing I'll ever say but, ever since the other night with you – OK, I know I promised not to mention it, but what the hell! Ever since the other night I can think of nothing else but you. You've got me bloody well bewitched. In fact, I'm lying. It's not since the other night, it's since the first time I saw you," he blurted out in one breath.

Cat was stymied. Her hangover was slowing her responses to the swirl of emotions growing inside her.

"I thought when I saw Kylie – well it was great! I forgot about you," he continued. "And then when I saw you – and you were so miserable."

"I was not!" she countered defensively.

"OK, you *looked* so miserable. I wanted you to look miserable. I think I was rather chuffed. And Kylie was being a darling. So I thought: what the hell? Here's Kylie – a beautiful woman who wants me." Trevor pointed to Cat on the sofa. "And over there is a beautiful woman who I want, but who doesn't want me. Where's the problem? Except that when we were alone together, I don't know why, it just didn't happen!"

"What do mean it didn't happen?" Cat tried to suppress a smile. She was starting to enjoy Trevor's discomfort.

"We were just getting friendly and she got sick."

"How friendly?"

"Friendly enough to know it as a sure thing, mate." He shook his head. "As I was saying, we were just getting friendly and she got sick."

"Really?" said Cat trying not to sound too delighted.

"She couldn't breathe," said Trevor. "It was weird. Uncanny. She had a full-blown asthma attack. She hasn't had one in five years."

Cat suppressed a giggle. "Gee, I'm sorry, Trev." Her eyes were dancing up at him.

He looked at her and caught her merriment. His eyes sparkled back at her as he sat down next to her and pulled her into his arms.

"I had to take her to Casualty. They had to give her

a shot to get her breathing properly again. She left this morning. She thinks it's the pollution in the city or something," he said, his voice getting deeper still.

"Poor baby!" she laughed, snuggled up in his arms.

Trevor started to say something but she stopped him, putting her hand gently over his lips.

"Shut up and kiss me," she ordered, smiling broadly.

They didn't leave the apartment for the next three days. They didn't even get out of bed except to go to the bathroom, and occasionally to open the door to a delivery man. Fiona had left to Boston for the week and the apartment was theirs. They lay around naked watching day-time chat shows and laughing. They ate pizza for breakfast and chocolate pudding in the middle of the night. They switched on the answering machine and turned down the volume on the speaker. They read papers and magazines that the doorman deposited in the hall, spreading them out over the bed and pointing out articles or photographs that took their fancy. They even went through the LL Bean catalogue, choosing the gear they would buy for a trek up the Himalayas. But most of all they made love.

They made love and fell asleep and woke up and made love again. They took a shower and came back to make love. They didn't even call out for food for the first twelve hours, waking up after the second nap of the day to find that they were ravenous. It was wild and passionate and sweet and soft. And it was nothing like anything Cat had ever experienced with a man before.

By the time Trevor decided it was time for him to get back to a pending deadline for his newspaper, Cat was caught, hook, line, and sinker.

"I'll be pulling an all-nighter to catch up," said Trevor, picking up the phone. He held the receiver to his ear, checking the messages on his machine. "I have to fax the piece for the morning edition. Too bad Sydney is bloody six hours ahead."

He put down the telephone and smiled at Cat. She was wrapped in a crimson velour dressing-gown. It had been horrendously expensive but she had been unable to resist its sensual folds and deep colour when she saw it hanging in the window of Saks Fifth Avenue. She frowned at the thought of him leaving and reached out to pull him down for a last kiss.

"There was a message from Kylie," he said smiling. "She's flying back home today. She says she was sorry it didn't work out."

"I'm not," Cat chuckled as she nibbled his ear. Trevor laughed with her.

"We shouldn't joke, you know," he said still laughing. "She was really ill. I could hear her lungs rattling as I was taking her to the hospital. They had to put her on a respirator."

"Oops!" Cat giggled. "I just wanted to get rid of her. Not send her to hospital."

Trevor pulled away from her embrace and pointed a finger at her. "I knew it! You did this to her. It was you," he said laughing.

"Nonsense. No way. I never wished her to have an asthma attack or anything like that. In fact, I specifically remember thinking 'Eat shit and die'. Nothing about respiratory illness at all." Cat was trying to kiss him, but he kept laughing and pulling away from her.

"You see, you *are* a witch! I can tell."

"Bull shit!"

"Really, you are one. Back home it's accepted that some people are more witchy than others. And you are a prime example."

"You'd better watch out then," said Cat, narrowing her eyes.

"No. I mean it," said Trevor, putting on his serious voice. "Why do you think we call certain people charming instead of just plain attractive? It's because they can charm, that's why. They cast a spell and charm you! Like you did to me."

"And how, pray tell, did I do that?" asked Cat.

"Look into my eyes." Cat looked up at him. "What do you see?"

"They're blue," she said. "With little yellow specks."

"Right," agreed Trevor looking at her. "Do you see anything else? Look only at my eyes now."

Cat watched and saw his pupils change size and a sparkle appear.

"You're smiling!" she exclaimed, delighted. Trevor lowered his eyes for a second and took a deep breath, before looking into her eyes again, this time more deeply. She was momentarily caught. She felt as if something was flowing from his pupils and tugging at her heart. She let a sigh escape from her lips.

"Let me in, Cat," she heard him whisper gruffly. She could feel the link between them as their eyes locked. But she could also feel a invisible wall pushing him away. Cat looked deeper still into Trevor's eyes and willed the wall to dissolve. They sat, wrapped in and around each other, unable to break away.

"Why didn't you tell me you wanted me? Why did you wait for weeks?" she asked softly, still not breaking her gaze. She saw the faintest flicker cloud his soul.

"Because I knew that I would get caught in your spell," Trevor answered, his voice deep and husky. Then he leaned over her and kissed her, slipping his hand inside the robe. Cat pulled at the belt and let the robe fall open.

"What about the deadline?" she asked.

"I'll write double time," he answered as he lifted her off the sofa, letting the robe fall on the floor, and led her back into the bedroom.

Chapter Nine

◆

They spent the next three weeks totally engrossed in each other. Three glorious weeks of filling every available minute with each other. They laughed at stupid jokes. They ran around the city like demented schoolchildren. New York was her playground and it had never been sunnier, or funkier, or more fun than when she shared it with Trevor.

When they weren't together they called each other on the phone, or left messages on their answering machines. They slept together every night, either in the loft or in Cat's apartment, and went into spasms of agony if Trevor was called out of town. Cat had even flown to Chicago to be with him when he left to cover a story there, justifying the trip to Fiona by saying that the airfare was what they'd be spending on telephone calls anyway.

If the city was their playground, then making love was their favourite game. Cat could not believe she could want a man that much, nor that often. It was the high point of the day, or morning or night, and many a time they both rushed to the loft at lunch-time to make love, before going back to work. When they were together they could barely keep their hands off each other, as if the physical connection had to be maintained. In fact, Cat's friends had teased them so much that they had to vow to cut down on the public displays of affection, or PDA as Ramon called it. This made things even more fun, as they secretly held hands under the table, or excused themselves to make out in a hallway, or found ways to be alone together.

Cat was sublimely happy. There were no yesterdays and no tomorrows, only the thrill of being together now. When Trevor was working she spent most of her time painting. Her work was going so well that she was even thinking of trying for an exhibition sometime in the Fall. Trevor was a wonderful critic, both discerning and encouraging. He saw her as a serious artist and for the first time in her life she thought that might be a path she could follow. She knew that in the back of her mind a picture was forming of a life she might lead. It was life full of painting and laughing and doing great things, and she knew that Trevor was there in the corner smiling his goofy grin. But she did not look at it too closely. She did not want reality to rear its ugly head and spoil the picture.

Cat had not been in the West Side apartment for over two weeks now. She'd spoken to her granddad several times, assuring him that she was getting on with the charities review. Every day she promised herself to go over the next day. Except that the next day there was always something else to do with Trevor.

"How goes the whirlwind of romance?" Fiona asked one morning. Trevor had left for work after spending the night at their place.

"Wonderful," sighed Cat.

"I must say falling in love suits you. You are positively glowing."

"I am not falling in love," said Cat defensively. "And Trevor most certainly isn't. We are far too busy having fun."

"Well, you could have both fooled me," said Fiona.

"Oh, I admit we are totally infatuated, but that's all. We are free spirits roaming the Universe together for a glorious while," Cat said loftily.

"I guess what you are really saying is that you are not ready to bring him home to granddad yet."

"Heaven forbid!" laughed Cat. "Actually, I'm not sure I want to bring granddad home to Trevor! He does go on about the oppression of the working classes."

Fiona raised an eyebrow and then smiled fondly at Cat. "Well, whatever it is, I'm really happy for you. Long may it last. I have to admit, I like him."

To Cat's delight, Fiona's feeling were echoed by most of her friends. Despite his politics, he fitted right in. He had found his niche in the group. He discussed economics with Scott, food with Ramon, and had an ongoing colonial feud with Fiona to their mutual delight. He even managed to get Valerie thinking about whether great wealth came with its own burden of responsibility to the world at large. Valerie had listened intensely at the last dinner they'd had, her face scrunching up as she tried to grapple with the ideas Trevor was throwing around the table. Sheri had giggled, saying that being raised dirt poor she was thankful not to have to worry about those things, and Cat had been surprised to see a flash of steel under the perfectly made-up face. There was more there than met the eye, she thought. Val and Sheri had taken to wearing only white as part of some sort of initiation process they were hoping to undertake. Valerie explained that it was to cleanse their souls of the material world – though, as Fiona pointed out, wearing white Versace somehow didn't seem to be much of a sacrifice.

Life was fun, and the summer stretched in front of Cat like a long sunny afternoon with nothing to do but enjoy it. Her birthday was three weeks away. All the invitations had been sent out. Cat knew that the party marked some sort of end, or beginning in her grandfather's mind, but she was damned if she was going to let that spoil anything. She had loads of time to worry about it come September.

Cat sat on the steps of the New York Public Library waiting for Trevor to show up for lunch. He was half a block away when she caught sight of him striding down Fifth Avenue with that long swinging walk of his. He waved enthusiastically, making others in the crowd turn to look at her. Cat laughed and waved back, not giving a damn that they were making a spectacle of themselves. Trevor ran across the street and swept her right off her feet, before giving her a big sloppy kiss. Over his shoulder Cat saw a man feeding the pigeons look up at them and smile.

"So where are we going for lunch?" asked Cat when he finally put her down.

"Right here," he said, pointing to the little kiosk at the side of the building. "I thought a sandwich al fresco was just the ticket!" He wanted to sit on the big stone lions, but finally relented and sat with Cat at one of the little wrought-iron tables in front of the kiosk.

"So what are you doing today?" he asked, biting into a huge ham and Swiss cheese.

"Well, I went to the gym and worked out. And I've

been thinking I might go over to my granddad's. He's bound to find out that I've been doing fuck-all about those charities he wanted me to look through."

"Scared the old geezer's going to get stroppy?" he asked with a wicked smile. "Send you off to bed with no dinner?"

"Don't be stupid," she said laughing. "I keep telling you he's a real softie."

"Well, you know, Cat, I'm not sure I can think of the Master of the Universe as a softie. Most of the time I just try and forget that side of you."

"Like what?"

"Like your personal trainer, and your three-hundred-dollar shoes," he said.

Cat looked up at him, stung by the sharpness in his voice.

Trevor smiled and softened his tone. "Though I have to admit, they both suit you." He finished off the sandwich in one last big bite.

Cat wasn't going to let him off that lightly. "What difference does it make?" she said. "I'm still me. Would I be a better person if I was poor? What do you want me to do? Shop at K Mart? Would that make you happy? And by the way, you can make me walk all over Manhattan for the greater good of mankind, but I draw the line at my personal trainer. No way I'm giving him up."

"Come with me," Trevor said suddenly jumping up. "I want to show you something."

He pulled her by the hand up the long line of stone steps and through the revolving doors. They stood together in the great white marble hall. Though she had passed the library countless times, she had never been inside. It was a majestic building with two magnificent staircases flanking both sides of the great hall. Trevor let go of her hand and opened his arms wide.

"Can you feel it?" he said.

"Feel what?" asked Cat.

"The books. We are surrounded by books. We are encased in knowledge. But that's not the best bit," he added and grabbed her hand again. They ran up the stairs and entered a hushed wood-panelled room. Long tables ran the length of the room. All around them were shelves stacked with leather-bound reference books. People sat at almost every chair leafing through books and periodicals. Trevor pointed to a corner where a young boy in a Mets sweatshirt was intently working on a computer. Next to him sat an old unshaven man in faded crumpled clothes. He was peering through a magnifying glass as he read a copy of the *New York Times*.

"The best bit," Trevor whispered into her ear, "is that all this knowledge, all these books, and newspapers, and computers are free. It belongs to everyone. Anyone can walk right in and help themselves."

They wandered through the library until it was time for Trevor to catch a cab over to the UN. The Australian Prime Minister was coming to town and Trevor would have to follow him around for the next two days. Cat walked around the building to Bryant Park and sat down on a bench. The trees were lush and green, dwarfed by the tall buildings surrounding them. Cat recognised the man who had been feeding the pigeons earlier. People strolled down the paths. Tourists took pictures, children played in the dappled shadows as their mothers looked on, while on her left a woman lay asleep on a bench, wrapped in a dirty blanket. Cat looked up to the square chunk of sky over her head. The day was getting overcast, the grey clouds hanging low over the rooftops.

Lunch with Trevor had rankled her. His holier-than-thou attitude could sometimes be a pain in the neck. So what if her shoes cost three hundred dollars? Big deal! What did he want her to do? Give it all up and go live in a tent somewhere? And who the hell was he to brag about the New York Public Library? Who did he think built it in the first place? It was the wealthy people of New York, that's who. Maybe she should ease up seeing him, thought Cat. They were too different.

Cat got up as she felt the first drop of rain hit her nose. She would grab a cab over to the West Side before it really started raining. She was looking forward to starting on the charities again. In fact she knew the first thing she was going to look up was the New York Public Library. She'd show that snooty Australian! Wouldn't he be surprised if her family had donated millions to the library? As she passed the woman on the bench, Cat reached into her pocket and pulled out a ten-dollar bill. Then she smugly deposited it into the little Styrofoam cup at the woman's feet before running to hail a cab that was just coming up to the corner.

By the time she got across town it was raining hard. The doorman scurried out with an oversize umbrella as Cat stepped out of the cab, but she waved him away, enjoying the cool feel of the rain as she ran up the steps.

Once inside she went around switching on lights. The live-in maid was out on an errand, so Cat went into the kitchen and fixed herself a cup of coffee. She loved the kitchen. Though it had every modern appliance the furnishings were still those of a kitchen in the twenties. She sat on the straight-backed chair remembering how she used to sit and watch the staff at work. Cook would let her peel and chop on her own little chopping-board. And if she were baking Cat always got to make her very own roll, or bun, or cake. It would be served up at dinner on a little silver platter with great pomp and circumstance, and her grandfather always made a fuss, declaring Cat was a better cook than many "high-falutin chefs" he knew.

Now that she was actually in the apartment, she found that she had no desire to do any work whatsoever, preferring to wander around. As a little girl she had spent many an afternoon virtually alone in this place. She had many imaginary friends and would spend days making up elaborate adventures down one long corridor and up another.

She stopped at a polished oak door. Stepping inside, she felt a thrill of the forbidden. When she was about ten, she liked nothing more than to step into this, her great-grandmother's, room. It was more of a suite really, with a large bedroom, a sitting-room alcove overlooking the park, a huge pink marble bathroom, and, best of all, a dressing-room.

The dressing-room was small and square, like a little bonbon box. Three walls were taken up by open closets. The fourth wall was a full-length mirror. Shoe racks were stacked about a foot off the ground and countless little drawers held treasures such as evening gloves, costume jewellery, and silk scarves. The ball-gowns still hung there, the beading glittering in the light from the small crystal chandelier which hung overhead. In the corner was a tiny little gilt stool, with a red velvet seat which matched the thick dark red carpet. She used to love that stool. When she wanted to hide she would pull it in behind the dresses and sit, quiet as a mouse, feeling her breath softly rustle the silks, and organza, and satins.

Cat sat on the little stool and let her face brush the soft fabric of the ball-gowns. Even after all these years a faint smell of perfume still lingered. Her eye was caught by a colour. She reached in and pulled out a long peach chiffon gown. It had an empire waist and a delicately beaded top. Loops of diamante sparkled around tear-drop pearls. Swirls of tiny glass beads curled into intricate patterns that were interwoven with the larger loops. A faint smell of lavender filled the tiny room.

Cat held it up and looked at herself in the mirror.

"Gorgeous!" she whispered, waltzing slowly as she held the dress like a partner. She laughed as the fabric floated and twirled. She smiled and saw herself smile back. Her mouth was pursed in amusement. Her eyes sparkled. The gold flecks were startling as they flickered in the bright blue that surrounded the black pools of her eyes.

Something stirred inside her. Something just beyond her thoughts, like a dream. Cat held the dress and heard echoes of voices, feet running swiftly down carpeted halls, doors banging shut, and the muffled sound of crying. She was aware of the front hall door clicking shut and thought to herself that the maid must have returned. Still she did not move, intent on the other sounds just outside her range. Knuckles rapped politely on locked doors. Soft voices called urgently in concerned tones. She heard the maid calling to her and had to resist the urge to crawl into the closet as she had done so many times as a child.

A soft knock on the door made Cat snap her head up. She was sitting on the stool clutching the dress. Tears streaked down her cheeks, which she quickly brushed away with the back of her hand.

"Miss Catherine? Are you there? Your grandfather is on the phone for you," the maid called through the door.

"I'll be right out," Cat said brightly. As she rose to leave, she folded the gown and stuffed it into her oversized Vuitton bag.

She took the call in the library.

"I'm glad to see you're hard at work." Her grandfather never said hello or goodbye on the phone. He just said what he had to say as quickly as possible.

"I have some catching up to do," said Cat feeling guilty.

"That's fine. Just keep working at it. I wanted to ask

you down this weekend. Can you make room in your busy schedule for a senile old man?"

"Oh granddad, you know you're far from senile!" answered Cat. Her mind was racing to try and find an excuse not to go. She didn't want to stay away from Trevor all weekend. So much for easing off, she thought with a grin, remembering her earlier resolution.

"Good. I'm looking forward to seeing you," he said, taking Cat's acceptance for granted. James Richardson III was not a man who was used to not having his wishes granted. "By the by, a little bird told me you've been seeing quite a lot of one particular young man. I'd like to meet him. Bring him down with you. I'll expect you Saturday for lunch."

Then he hung up.

"Can you believe it!" yelled Cat as she stormed around the living-room. "How did he find out about Trevor? I swear that old man has spies! When I was a kid, half of the time I was sure there was someone up a tree checking out what I was doing and reporting back to him!"

"Don't be ridiculous," snapped Fiona in a bored voice.

"Did I ever tell you about the time we were in the South of France? I was fifteen and spending the summer in Antibes. One day I went down to the public beach on my own. I got friendly with some really cute French guys, and we were splashing each other and having a good time. I kept looking over at the villa to see if anyone was on the balcony, I was so paranoid. And then at lunch my grandfather said 'I almost got very angry this morning. I was doing some bird-watching and I saw a girl that looked just like you fooling around with some rough-looking local boys. I was just about to send Victor down to fetch you when I realised that it was not you. Thank goodness.' Bird-watching, my ass! It was like this little game he was playing."

"He probably heard it from someone. It's not like you haven't been seen throwing yourself at Trevor all over Manhattan." Fiona blew her nose noisily. She stubbed out her cigarette and lit another one.

"That's it! You are *so* right! It's that nosy O'Connor woman! The one who lives in East Hampton. We were having an intimate dinner in that little French bistro on Lexington and 80th. You know the one that has the great dessert trolley. And that O'Connor woman popped out of nowhere and wanted me to introduce her to Trevor, and *then* she went on and on about her son in graduate school. I swear the woman practically wanted to arrange a marriage there and then. I bet she was on the phone to granddad from the Ladies' Room!"

"Will you sit down, Cat! You're ranting like a lunatic.

Have a drink. Have a joint. Take some Valium, but please stop babbling!" Fiona said wearily.

"But I don't want to bring Trevor for the weekend!" Cat wailed, throwing her arms up. "I don't want them to meet. They'll hate each other on sight. Or worse, maybe they'll get on. God! I don't know what to do."

"So bloody well don't go!" Fiona yelled harshly and blew her nose again.

Cat was surprised by the anger in Fiona's voice. She took a good look at her friend. She was in an old grey track suit that had shrunk in the wash. Her eyes were red and the ashtray in front of her was filled to overflowing. Cat also noticed that the apartment was impeccably clean. She was confused.

"You shouldn't smoke if you have a cold," Cat said lamely. "And, by the way, the place looks great. You shouldn't have cleaned if you're feeling sick."

"I don't have a cold," said Fiona sniffling. "And I didn't clean. Margarita came over and I couldn't stop her. Not that I had any intention of doing so. I couldn't be bothered, frankly."

"Fi? Are you all right?"

"No, I am not all right!" said Fiona. "I am not at all right!"

Cat immediately forgot her worries as her friend broke down sobbing. Cat rushed to comfort her, but Fiona pushed her away. Her head hung low and her hands were shredding the tissues into little pieces which fluttered down onto the carpet.

"Mummy called," she began as soon as she had managed to compose herself. "She said that Daddy made some bad investments. Mummy was awfully jolly as always, but apparently she's been giving piano lessons in the village to help with bills. I didn't know it was that bad. She said they've had to put the house and the farm up for sale, to pay for my sisters' school bills and debts and such. The housing market is terrible at the moment. In fact, the only way they can survive is if they subdivide the whole place into seventeen lots!"

"What about your brother?" Cat asked softly.

"That bollocks is surfing somewhere in Australia. We don't even know how to contact him. He is so useless he might just as well be dead for all the help he's ever given me. I'll have to go home. But I can't even afford the ticket."

Fiona broke down crying again.

"I'll buy you a ticket," said Cat, passing her a fresh tissue.

"But I don't want to go home," sobbed Fiona. "I know it's awful of me, but I couldn't bear to go back and care for my parents in some pokey little house. I can't bear the thought of losing my home."

"Don't worry. We'll think of something," said Cat reassuringly. The best thing was to calm her down.

"Well, it would take a bloody miracle!"

"You've had a bad shock. There's nothing you can do right now so just take it easy. What was that you were saying about a drink or a joint?" Cat said cheerily. "Tell you what! We'll call for some Chinese, and some fudge ice-cream and veg out together. How's that?"

"What about Trevor?" sniffed Fiona.

"He's working. Let's have a girls night in. It's been a long time," said Cat.

"Oh, Cat. Thanks. I've missed you," said Fiona blowing her nose again and looking up, her bright blue eyes bloodshot and puffy.

"And I've missed you too, babe."

Later that evening, after they had gorged themselves on both Chinese spare ribs and Mexican fajitas, Fiona seemed much better. When the girls settled down in front of the TVs with three different pots of ice cream, Fiona brought up the subject of Trevor again:

"So what are you going to do, Cat? You can't hide him away for ever. Why don't you just dive in at the deep end and bring him along for the weekend?"

"I guess I will," mused Cat, licking a spoonful of double chocolate fudge. "I'd really rather not, but you know granddad – an invitation is more like an order."

"Talking of invitations," said Fiona, "I got my invite to your birthday bash today."

"Oh, let me see it! Let me see it! I still haven't the faintest idea what's happening,"

"Well, it's very grand. *Très, très chic.* But I'm not sure if I am allowed to divulge any more information. It *is* supposed to be a surprise, you know. Your grandfather would *not* be pleased with me," teased Fiona.

"Are you two in cahoots or something?" asked Cat.

Fiona frowned for a second and then laughed, shaking her head. "Don't be silly. You know I only report back the seedier side of your life: the drink, the drugs, the plethora of men."

"Come on, Fiona! Quit pulling my leg! At least tell me where it's being held. How will I know what to wear?" Cat pleaded.

Fiona pulled a large cream envelope from under the pile of magazines and waved it enticingly. Cat made a grab for it, but Fiona whisked it away.

"Well," she began, "let me see? I guess I can tell you it's being held on the 9th of September 1991. Which is no surprise since that is your birthday. It's black tie. And it starts with drinks at seven o'clock."

"More," demanded Cat.

"I'm sorry but I am not at liberty to divulge any further information."

"Fi!"

"All right. But only because it's you, my darling! It's

being held at the Top of the Sixes on Fifth Avenue. There! I shall say no more. My lips are sealed."

"Well, that doesn't really tell me much," said Cat, spooning out the last of the ice cream. "Except that we have to go shopping."

"When in doubt, go shopping I always say," echoed Fiona. "Though in my present circumstances I shall have to wear a bin-liner. It's about the only thing I can afford."

"Don't be stupid. It's my treat." said Cat, getting into the idea. "We'll go the whole hog. We'll even call Valerie to come with us. She knows all the personal shoppers in New York. For a rich bitch, she's really good at getting discounts. We'll do them all: Bendels, Saks, Bergdofs, Barneys, you name it!"

"Can we have our own private changing-room, with chocolates and fruit baskets?" asked Fiona, clapping her hands.

"Absolutely. Hell, we'll get them to send up champagne! Let's go this Saturday."

"Haven't you forgotten? You're going away for the weekend."

"Oh fuck!" said Cat, her enthusiasm momentarily dampened by the thought of Trevor in the Hamptons. "Tell you what. Why don't you 'chuck a sickie', as Trevor says, next week?"

"Sounds wonderful" said Fiona. "I feel a wicked tummy bug coming on."

"Yeah, you look a bit pale," Cat contributed, giggling. "I'd say you'll be out for at least twenty-four hours. Maybe more."

"Possibly a forty-eight-hour bug? In fact, as I can only possibly be ill on Wednesday that only leaves Friday before the weekend, I'd say it's best to take the rest of the week off so as to be really sure that I am totally well on Monday."

"Excellent! It's going to be great. Shop till you drop!" said Cat, adding, "Actually, why don't you join us in the Hamptons? It would make my life that much easier."

"Sorry darling, but I promised Valerie to go out with her on Saturday night," Fiona answered vaguely.

"What am I missing?" asked Cat.

"Oh nothing really. She wants me to come to another of those magical mystical things she's going to these days. She's found another group in the Bronx that will initiate her. That's why she's wearing white all the time. Valerie says that the high priest is very powerful. He could help me."

Cat looked at her friend and shook her head disapprovingly.

"Listen, Cat," Fiona said, her eyes glistening again. "I'm desperate. I know it won't do any good, but you never know. I'll light a candle in St Patrick's, and dance naked in the moonlight if it can help my family. It can't hurt."

Cat put her arm around Fiona and gave her a hug.

"OK. Just be careful. That stuff isn't as harmless as it seems. But you're right. You might as well hit all the bases – light a candle and do a little dance. And don't forget me. If there's anything I can do – just ask."

"Thanks, Cat," said Fiona hugging her back. "But you've done so much already."

Chapter Ten

◆◆◆

To Cat's relief Trevor had thought that a weekend in the Hamptons was a great idea and made no nasty comments about meeting the Master of the Universe. He had been all sweetness and light since they'd woken up early to beat the traffic and sleepily made love that morning. He held her hand all the way up, kissing it frequently. He massaged her neck as she drove, and even lit cigarettes for her though he hated smoking with a passion. The sun was shining, the traffic was light. It should have been perfect – except that it wasn't. As she got further from the city, Cat felt a familiar knot grow and tighten in her stomach.

"You really are freaked about me meeting the old man, aren't you?" said Trevor, catching her mood. "Don't worry. I promise to behave."

"No. It's not that," said Cat. "It's something about the Hamptons. It's so . . . I don't know. The house always feels weird to me. I guess that's why I don't go out there as often as I should. It's so big and empty. I don't know, I always feel lost there. I can't explain it."

"It's not that difficult to explain," Trevor said gently. He brushed her hand against his cheek and kissed her fingers gently. Cat shot him a sharp glance. His eyes were misty and he looked like he was going to burst with love. Cat bit her lip.

"It's OK, darling. Your mum died in that house, didn't she?"

"She drowned. She swam out off the dock without telling anyone. They never found her body," Cat said matter of factly.

"You must have felt very lost. I know I did when my mum died, and I was a lot older."

"I don't remember a thing about it. In fact, I don't remember her at all. I was only three."

Cat kept her eyes on the road, holding back the tears that were threatening to cloud her vision. She took a deep breath and turned off the tap of emotions welling up inside her. She wasn't going to think about that now. In fact, if she could help it, she wasn't ever going to think about that.

"You probably repressed whatever memories you had. But they linger in your feelings towards the place."

Trevor paused, lost in his thoughts. "It could be a blessing – not remembering," he added pensively.

"What do you remember? About your Mom?" Cat asked, relieved to change the focus of the conversation. Trevor let go of her hand and crossed his arms over his chest, looking straight in front of him. Cat thought he was sulking, but after a moment he spoke.

"I was ten years old. Mum had been very unhappy. She was always unhappy I guess. She'd had a screaming row with Dad earlier that evening. She said he'd accused her of drinking on the sly. He said he trusted her and tried to calm her down but she just got angrier and angrier, until she stormed out of the house and drove out down the road like a lunatic."

"Where did she go?" asked Cat her eyes wide.

"Oh, I don't know. Some bar. She stormed back a couple of hours later, brakes screeching, dust flying in the moonlight. She missed the turn into the drive and ran straight into a tree."

Cat gulped. She didn't know what to say.

"I watched them cut her out of the car. I kept my sisters inside, but I watched from the window."

Cat reached out and lay her hand along his thigh. Trevor took it and held it against his chest. He looked over at her and smiled.

"Enough of the past. Let's get on with the future."

* * *

CRISTINA PISCO

They were met at the door by Victor who led them through the great hall, past the main reception rooms, and into the small cosy sitting-room overlooking the pool. Cat was grateful he had not shown them into the main living-room with its French tapestries and original Chippendale. Trevor had grown quiet as they drove up through the main gates, a low whistle his only comment as the massive house came into view.

Fresh lemonade and thin sugar cookies were laid out on the table and Cat thankfully accepted a large crystal tumbler as she sank into the comfy wicker armchair.

"Your grandfather will be busy until lunch-time," said Victor. "Perhaps you would like a swim to cool off. Or I could show you to your rooms if you would like to freshen up."

"Thanks, Victor," said Cat waving him away. "We can manage. What time is lunch?"

"One o'clock," said Victor, leaving them.

Trevor was stalking the room having finished his lemonade in one long gulp. Cat watched him as he picked up trinkets, stared at the paintings, and looked at every photograph. He didn't exactly fit in, but he didn't look wildly out of place either, she thought, feeling her heart lift. This wasn't going to be so bad after all.

"Great bikkies!" he said, stuffing two cookies into his mouth and grinning. "It looks like it took some serious bikkies to build this place as well. It certainly is big. How many rooms does it have?"

"God. I don't know," laughed Cat. "I think there were originally twenty-three bedrooms, plus reception rooms, the dinning-room, the ball-room, the billiards-room. Most of them aren't used anymore. In fact the entire east wing has been closed off since I was a kid."

"And all this will be yours. How do you feel about that?" asked Trevor.

"I never really thought about it," she answered pensively. "Sad I guess. It's kinda sad really. This house was built for a big and boisterous family and now it's just Granddad and me."

"That could be easily sorted," said Trevor, sitting down next to her and leering at her. "I feel in the mood to found a dynasty. Seven sons and seven daughters should just about do it, don't you think? Lead me to the billiards-room, wench!" he added grabbing her by the shoulders and tipping her over the arm-rest. Cat laughed, trying to avoid his kisses and failing miserably.

"Why the billiards-room?" she managed to gasp.

"I dunno. It kinda turns me on. I like the idea of having you on the billiards-table," he explained in a muffled voice as he nibbled at her neck, his hands pushing up her T-shirt.

Cat pushed him away in mock horror. "Trevor! What do you think you are doing?"

He laughed loudly and grabbed her again. "I can't believe it! You're worried about what the servants might think!"

"I don't care what they think. But I don't particularly want to be interrupted," she said, standing up arranging her clothes. Trevor followed her over to the big French doors that opened out to the pool area. A path led down from the little pool-house through a row of bleached sand-dunes and then beyond to the Atlantic Ocean, glaring frothy and white in the sharp summer sun. Trevor stood behind her, slipping his arms around her waist and leaning his chin on her shoulder.

"We've still got a couple of hours until we have to change for lunch. Do you want to have a swim?" she asked leaning back into his arms.

"I'd much rather have you," he said, hugging her tightly. "Surely we can find some privacy in a mansion this size?"

Cat giggled. "Well actually, I lost my virginity down in the pool-house the summer of my senior year. Not that it was anything that special, mind you."

"Well then, it is my duty to erase that memory right away and replace it with mind-boggling cosmic sex. I'll go get my togs!" said Trevor, releasing her.

"There's no need." Cat stepped out on to the patio.

"If I know Victor, the pool-house will have everything we need for a swim."

"Then what are we waiting for?" Then he grabbed her hand and they ran all the way down to the pool-house, laughing.

Cat and Trevor met up in the big hall after changing. He was wearing a pair of summer pleated trousers and a white button-down shirt. With his hair wet and slicked down he looked like a naughty schoolboy on his best behaviour. Cat smiled at him fondly and wondered how he'd managed to get such a sharp pleat into the pants. Trevor took her by the hand and led her into the main reception room.

"I was having a bit of a snoop around and I found this," he said stopping in front of a polished side table and picking up a silver framed photograph.

It was a portrait of a black-haired woman with very light eyes. She was elegantly dressed and held a small child on her lap. Her eyes looked defiantly into the camera with a hint of a smile in the jet-black pupils. Cat nodded, answering the question which hung unasked between them.

"You look exactly like her," Trevor said, putting the picture back carefully. "Are you the baby she's holding?"

Cat was about to answer when they were interrupted

by the sound of feet crossing the big marble hall. Cat turned to the door and smiled as her grandfather walked in. He was looking dapper and fresh in a pin-striped seersucker suit and white shirt, his bow tie today a navy and white polka dot. He kissed Cat warmly before turning to Trevor.

"I'm very pleased to meet you," he said, extending his hand. "I hear you are an up and coming journalist."

"Well, I'm not sure if I can qualify yet, but I'm trying," answered Trevor, taking his hand and shaking it a bit too enthusiastically.

"I must give my friends down at *Time* a call. They're always looking for new talent."

"That would be great!" said Trevor blushing slightly.

Cat stood back and watched them. Her grandfather looked relaxed and pleasant, the perfect host. But she knew he was circling like a tiger. He turned and smiled benevolently at her.

"I thought we might have lunch outside. Shall we?" Then, without waiting for an answer, he took her arm and led them out to the terrace overlooking the ocean where a beautiful table was set for four, its crisp white linen tablecloth rustling softly in the breeze. Cat asked her grandfather teasingly if he'd invited a girlfriend as Victor pulled out a chair for her.

"Thank God I'm too old for all that malarky," he answered chuckling. "No. Bob Stigemann will be joining us for lunch. I'd like you to meet him. He's our youngest VP, and I have to say that he has managed, in a very short while, to make himself indispensable."

As if on cue the purr of a motor heading up the beach cut through the sound of the surf and the squawk of the gulls. A bright red dune buggy appeared. It parked on a sand-dune and a really tall guy wearing shades got out. Even from a distance, Cat could tell that he was drop-dead gorgeous. He sauntered easily down the sand with a big friendly wave at the terrace. As he got closer, Cat could see that he was wearing impeccably cut navy pants, a faded blue Lacoste polo shirt and tasselled loafers. His blond hair was sun-bleached and he had the sort of tan you can only get from sailing. He strode up to the table, flashing a brilliant set of perfect teeth and shook hands all around before accepting a Bloody Mary from Victor who had materialised with a tray of drinks.

"Victor makes the best Bloody Marys east of the River Club," he said, easing his lanky frame into the seat between Cat and Trevor. Close up, he was even more good-looking than Cat had thought, with a strong masculine jaw and a body that clearly worked out several times a week.

Cat's grandfather beamed as he lifted his glass. Trevor smiled brightly, but Cat could tell he was feeling uneasy.

"Bottoms up!" said Trevor and swallowed half of his drink in one gulp. Cat flinched inside, but Bob laughed loudly.

"That's what I like about Australians!" he declared, lifting his glass to Trevor. "They sure know how to drink!" The men eyed each other and then finished off their drinks in one swallow.

Oh boy, thought Cat, they're getting competitive. Why did men always do that? They'll be arm-wrestling next.

"I asked Bob over because I've given him a very important job," said her grandfather as Margarita wheeled out a trolley and started serving small plates of fresh salad, helped by a young maid in a light cotton uniform.

"Bob's going to help you get to know the business better," he said casually. "Be your personal guide as it were."

"That's right!" said Bob, winking broadly at Cat.

Trevor flashed her a look, but was distracted by the plate being put in front of him.

Cat didn't know what to say. She was too busy trying to figure out what her grandfather had up his sleeve, but the subject was apparently closed. She nodded and pretended to be engrossed in her food as the men chatted. Trevor alternated between trying too hard and not trying hard enough. Bob played host while her grandfather sat back and seemed to enjoy himself. Lunch was tense though charming, with platitudes flying fast and furious around the table as the first course was replaced by a perfectly chargrilled tuna steak and baby potatoes. Cat did not speak again until coffee and a deliciously light lemon cheesecake had been served.

"I thought we might go for a drive this afternoon," she said to Trevor, intentionally cutting Bob out.

"Well actually," Bob said, flashing his perfect smile again, "I was hoping to steal him away for a round of golf." Bob cocked his head at Trevor. "You do play, don't you?"

"In fact, I do," said Trevor, smiling back but looking predatory. Cat looked at him in surprise but Trevor just nodded at her reassuringly.

"Golf it is," said her grandfather. "In fact, I might just join you. The exercise would do me good."

Cat was clearly not invited. She was starting to get annoyed with this Blond Wonderboy. He seemed much too at ease in the house and she had never seen her grandfather let someone take control like that.

Her grandfather reached out and gave her hand a gentle squeeze, as if appeasing a child. "I have a few surprises lined up for your birthday, my dear," he said, his eyes twinkling.

Cat tried to sulk but she was too intrigued. "Like what?"

"Well, it wouldn't be a surprise if we told you," said Bob beaming.

"We?" Cat snapped raising one eyebrow. Bob's smile did not falter one bit as he disregarded Cat's curtness.

"I've been helping your grandfather with a few things. He has some really special things planned for you. You're a very lucky girl."

"Well, she deserves it," declared her grandfather, rising from the table. He put his arm around Cat and gave her a quick hug. He pitched his voice so the others would not hear.

"There's something I've wanted you to have but I was waiting for the proper occasion," he said. "I've left it in the nursery – like when you were a little girl."

"Did you hide it?" Cat said smiling. She could never be angry with her grandfather for long, she thought, remembering how he used to buy her presents and hide them when she was a child. Sometimes looking for them was more fun than finding them.

"You'll find it easily," he said, straightening up and facing the two young men. "Now, I believe there is a game of golf waiting for us gentlemen."

Cat went straight to the nursery as soon as they left. It was in the central wing on the first floor. She opened the double doors and stood looking at the playroom. The middle of the room was filled with life-sized stuffed animals. She knew that to her left was her bedroom with its cheery chintz prints and to her right was the little box-room a succession of Nannies had slept in. The house was quiet around her, the only sounds filtering through from the outside. It occurred to her that she had not actually been in these rooms in years. After they had moved to Manhattan when she was seven, Cat had never felt right in the nursery when they came back for the holidays. When she went away to boarding school she had demanded a new room, saying that the nursery was too babyish. She'd had a large suite in the west wing ever since.

Mr Jiffy, her baby giraffe with the big sad eyes, was still there. And Lion, and Kanga and of course her two sheep, Mr Baa Baa and his wife Betty.

Cat walked in and sat on Lion looking up at Mr Jiffy towering above her. Two large windows facing the sea filled the room with light. Between them was a beautiful antique hobby-horse, his dapple-grey body still gleaming as if in full gallop, his mane and tail made out of real horse-hair. A slight breeze caught the white curtain and Cat saw a red round box with a gold tassel sitting on the ledge. A large card was propped up beside it. Cat recognised her grandfather's flowery handwriting with its loops and swirls.

"This is your mother's jewellery box," Cat read. *"I have never opened it as I thought that would be for you*

to do. Happy Birthday, my darling." It was unsigned, as were all the notes her grandfather wrote her. Inside the envelope was a tiny golden key.

Cat took the box and sat back down among the stuffed animals. It was made of red leather and looked like a little vanity case. It felt heavy and rattled when she shook it. A zipper went all the way around to the back where a tiny, gold, heart-shaped lock hung. Cat took the key and, after fiddling for a few minutes, opened the box.

It was filled with a jumble of jewellery: necklaces knotted up with rings, odd earrings tucked in amongst brooches. It seemed to be a mix of good pieces, expensive costume jewellery, and real junk. Cat untangled a fabulous diamond necklace with little sapphires from a cheap brass cuff. She rummaged around and gasped with delight when she found the matching diamond tear-drop earrings. A ring fell out and rolled on the floor. Cat was astounded to find that it was a plastic daisy ring – the kind you get in a gum-ball machine. Shaking her head at why anyone would want to keep such a thing, Cat spilled out the contents of the box onto the carpet at the foot of the stuffed sheep.

"I say we do this methodically, don't you think?" Cat said. Betty Baa Baa looked on approvingly.

Cat kicked off her shoes and started sorting through the stuff. She patiently undid all the knots and shook out all the smaller pieces. She lay each item in one of three little piles which she designated as: good stuff, nice stuff to wear, and trash. Surprisingly there was as much of the last pile as the first. Little plastic rings, cheap bangles, and earrings that went for a dollar a pair had presumably been kept by her mother with as much care as the diamonds and pearls.

When she had sorted the box out two items remained. One was a tarnished silver thimble with an intricate pattern etched into its rim. The other was an odd type of necklace. It was dull and brassy, and rather heavy. She turned it over and found a mark: 9 carat. So it was gold. The chain was like a twisted rope and in the middle hung a thin gold rod with a piece sticking out of it. It looked like a shortened T. Both the thimble and the necklace seemed very old, and Cat felt something stir inside her as she held them.

She was distracted by the sound of someone running in the hall. A gust of wind swept through the playroom and Cat heard doors slam further up the corridor and the sound of someone calling. Maybe Margarita was looking for her.

Cat jumped up and peered into the corridor. It was empty. She heard a dog bark and thought it odd. She was sure she could still hear someone calling. She walked into the corridor and listened, still holding the thimble and necklace. The blinds were down to protect the carpets from the harsh summer sun, and the place was in half darkness cut across with the occasional shaft of light. She thought she heard soft running down to her right and she followed it to where the corridor took a sharp turn and became the east wing. There was a definite rustling sound ahead of her but it was difficult to see in the shadows. Then she distinctly heard the sound of old hinges creaking. Cat stood dumbfounded as she saw a door opening halfway down the east wing.

Cat darted down the corridor just as the shadow of a woman slipped into the room. Her bare feet made no sound as she ran down the thick carpet. The door was still ajar. With a pounding heart she stepped into the room.

It was dark but the room was glowing. As she entered Cat realised that all the shutters were closed. The glow came from a fire burning brightly in the hearth. The room smelt closed in and slightly musky, but a distinct smell of lavender drifted past, making her swoon, leading her further in.

There was a change in the quality of the shadows at the head of the big four-poster bed. Someone was bending down, pulling up the carpet. Cat could hear her scratching. The person looked up quickly as if checking that she was alone, and Cat caught a glimpse of long black hair and a milky white skin. Then the figure disappeared.

Cat felt rather than saw a slight movement to her left. Turning her head, she caught her breath. A magpie was sitting on the mantle above the fireplace. It stopped preening itself to cock its head and look at Cat.

Cat was terrified. She was rooted to the spot, unable to move or speak. She heard a scream faraway and wondered if it was herself. But then the screams grew closer. There was a scuffle outside. A group of people were passing in the hall banging on the walls as they passed. A woman was screaming and other deeper voices were speaking, trying to calm her down.

"Get off me ye fecking cunts! Get off me! Leave me be, will ye just leave me be!" Cat heard the woman screech.

Then all she could hear were sobs and Cat realised her face was drenched with tears. Everything was dark. Dark and cold. She felt the sway of the sea, the cold slap of the waves. Her sobs were choking her. Cat tried to gasp for breath but could only taste the salt tears filling her mouth. She tried to open her eyes but everything was blurry. Someone reached out for her. Cat was sobbing and shaking. Someone was holding her. Shaking her. Cat was drowning. Water flooding.

"Senorita! Senorita!" Wake up. You must dress for dinner now."

Cat blinked. Margarita was standing next to her. She was in her bed in the west wing. A silver tray sat on her night table with a coffee and cookies laid out along with a crystal pitcher of ice water. Next to it sat the red jewellery box.

The evening went without a hitch. Trevor and Bob got on surprisingly well at dinner. Trevor was chuffed because Bob had promised to put in a good word for him with a friend at *Rolling Stone* magazine. Her grandfather had retired early and Cat followed shortly after. When she heard the door close in Trevor's bedroom she slipped out to join him. Servants be damned. She didn't care what Victor might think if he found her with Trevor in the morning. She didn't want to be alone.

Only after they had made love and she lay curled up in Trevor's sleeping arms, did Cat let herself think about the weird dream. But when she tried to figure it out it defeated her. It was just a weird dream.

Trevor stirred. Sensing she was awake, he kissed her forehead gently.

"You OK?" he whispered sleepily.

"I had weird dream today," Cat said. "More of a nightmare really."

Trevor kissed her again and shifted to hold her more tightly.

"Trev?" Cat whispered, feeling the warmth of his chest on her cheek. Trevor's breathing was slow and regular and lulling. He murmured. Cat felt herself relax.

"Magpies mean bad luck, don't they? Aren't they meant to mean something?"

"Bad luck? No. I think it depends how many there are," Trevor mumbled. "It's a rhyme. Can't remember. Too tired. *One for sorrow. Two for* . . . I forget. Something like that." He kissed her gently and sighed contentedly. "You know, I could get used to this."

"What this?" Cat asked, letting herself sink into a half-sleep.

"Sleeping with you," said Trevor giving her another squeeze. "It sure beats sleeping alone."

Cat murmured her approval. As she felt herself drift she wished that she could wake up in the loft, alone with Trevor. She wanted to get back to Manhattan and forget about this house with its weird dreams. Cat decided then and there to leave immediately after breakfast.

Chapter Eleven

Cat sat in the shade of a large green awning and nibbled on a bread-stick. She watched the traffic go by, thankful that she had arrived early to the Trattoria where she was having lunch with Fiona. It would give her some time to be alone and just enjoy doing nothing. God knows, she could use it. Cat remembered how she'd looked forward to the last lazy weeks of summer but it had been anything but lazy.

The weeks had flown by in a frenzied swirl of activity: countless afternoons shopping, Fiona frantically calling England practically all the time until she looked as if she had a phone surgically attached to her ear, an increasing number of lunches and meetings with Bob as he "guided" her through her family's business, and sweet nights with Trevor who was pulling at her heart in a way she had never felt before.

As if that wasn't enough, Cat was trying, and failing, to catch up on her painting. A small gallery owner had come over to have a look and seemed interested. His visit had resulted in a few days of bursting creativity which, with her birthday fast approaching, had now ground to a halt. Cat had hardly had a minute just to stop and chill. And under it all was the disturbing memory of the nightmare she'd had in the Hamptons, like a shadow walking behind her.

Cat checked her watch. Fiona would be along in a few minutes. She decided to order the wine while she waited. Calling the waiter over she chose a red spumanti and told him to make sure it was well chilled, which he seemed to take as a personal insult. Cat ate the last bread-stick and was annoyed that she hadn't asked the waiter to bring more. She looked around to make sure he wasn't watching and then swiped a fresh basket from an empty table. The sun was still streaking down on to the concrete, but it had lost the burning glare of high summer. Soon the first leaves would start to turn.

Cat thought to herself that she'd better be out of there by two o'clock if she wanted to make her last fitting. She had finally settled for a rather extravagant Versace number. She still wasn't sure if she liked it. The dress looked spectacular but did it look right? She wanted to have the right mix of sexy and conventional, classic and trendy, to make her look unique. It was her birthday after all, and as Bob had pointed out – Cat was the star of the show. He'd let it slip that the press would be there and her look had to be just right. She wasn't sure if the Versace fit the bill. There was something about the design, it was too in-your face, too much gold and flash. But after the third shopping trip, Cat just got fed up with dresses and caved in to Valerie's bullying. Fiona had offered no advice whatsoever. She was too engrossed in her parents' problems to be of any assistance. Her Dad had managed to put the banks off for a fortnight and, as Fiona quipped, the phone bill alone would have probably paid off the interest.

In fact, despite the personal shoppers, the fruit baskets and chilled white wine, the whole shopping thing had been stressful and annoying and not much fun at all. Fiona spent most of her time worrying out loud and only gave a passing glance as Cat paraded around in a succession of ball gowns, while Valerie alternated between Bitch Shopper of the Year and a voodoo princess spouting mumbo-jumbo to Fiona about how somebody was taking care of things in the spirit world for her.

Valerie was becoming increasingly weird, thought Cat, and she wished her friend would get through this new fad. Val had been quite taken by the *Santería* ceremony and had decided she wanted to join, but had been put off by the lengthy initiation process and insulted that no amount of money would speed things up. Being Valerie she would not take no for an answer – "I want it all and I want it now," must have been her first words.

So Val and Sheri had gone off to find a different church, one which allowed for fast initiation. Valerie went on about it being the real thing, but Cat couldn't help wondering how much it had cost to gain a speedy entrance.

Still, she wasn't unduly worried. Valerie had always been poised to jump on the newest, most expensive, magical-mystical bandwagon she could find. Another couple of months of mumbo-jumbo and wearing white, and she'd be off to get a decent tan and find her inner child on some island in the Caribbean.

The waiter came back with the wine and asked if she would like to go ahead and order. Cat shook her head and asked for some more bread-sticks, ignoring his pointed look at the two empty baskets as he deftly swept them up.

Cat remembered the snooty waiter from the first time she'd been here with Bob Stigeman. The service was borderline nasty but the food was terrific. She'd wanted to bring Fiona right away.

One thing about Bob – he certainly knew New York. Along with the Trattoria, he had introduced her to a great Lebanese restaurant and an Italian bakery that had pastries to die for. In fact, thought Cat, Bob knew a lot about a lot of things and managed to make them all interesting. Yet he was anything but flamboyant. With his perfect preppy looks and conventional clothes he was a pure deb's delight. Cat knew there was more to him than that, but the veneer was so perfect that it was impossible to see what was underneath.

He'd taken her grandfather's wishes very seriously and Cat had been spending a lot of time with him. He took her on visits to offices, introduced her to people and generally shepherded her around like a benevolent collie. Cat had tried not to like him. She tried to find him arrogant, or pushy, or sexist, but it just hadn't worked. She had to admit he was pleasant company but she wondered what made him tick. She'd teased him once, telling him to lighten up. "What do you mean?" he'd asked, seeming truly intrigued.

He called her Catherine and was almost a caricature of a gentleman, yet he always seemed to know when he was starting to bore her with explanations of how the business was interconnected. Then he'd take her to lunch, or out for a coffee and cake. And they'd talk. Inevitably the conversation would steer its way to what Cat would most like to do within the company. Bob talked of working a year in one of their foreign offices: Maybe Paris? Or Tokyo? Cat went along with the game, but she didn't really want to think about it right now. She didn't have the time. And she still hadn't even mentioned the possibility to Trevor. Cat wasn't looking forward to that. It would be pressure on their relationship. They'd have to make decisions, discuss commitments, and Cat had no idea where she stood on that front.

Bob was almost the direct opposite of Trevor. Trev's veneer was so thin it often shattered with the unrestrained passion he was capable of summoning up — whether it was about acid rain in Germany, or why *The Empire Strikes Back* was the best in the trilogy, or how much he loved Cat. He was openly jealous of Bob, and Cat rather enjoyed that. She felt a warm giggle of a glow as she thought about him.

Trevor was on her mind a lot of the time. Every time she stopped thinking about whatever she was doing — he seemed to pop up and wink at her. They had gone seamlessly from being friends to being joined at the hip and madly in love. They spent hours entwined in each others' arms trying to work out when it had happened: this "falling in love *thang*" as they called it, relishing reliving key moments. If anything their passion for each other had reached new peaks and they often made love several times a night. Cat laughed to

herself, remembering Trevor the night before, saunter-
ing around his apartment in his underpants brandishing
a long cardboard tube as a light sabre in a perfect
imitation of a Jedi Knight in training, complete with
sound effects. He made an intricate figure eight at her,
one hand on his hip.

"I, Trevor, Jedi Knight from Down Under, do solemnly swear to protect you from all carbon-based life
forms," he declared.

"Forever and ever?" asked Cat laughing. He really
looked ridiculous prancing around like that.

"Past, present and future lives included," he shot
back. "Though time, as you well know, Oh Great Mis-
tress of the Hourglass Figure, is an illusion. But I shall
slay them all. All the monstrous beasts your nightmares
may bring will quake in fear of the mighty Trevor!" He
sprang on to the futon, slicing the air with the cardboard
tube.

Cat shuddered slightly at the mention of nightmares
and as always Trevor picked up on it. That man could
read her like a book. "I've been meaning to ask you,"
he said, keeping his eyes on the end of his "light sabre".
"What was that thing about a nightmare that night in
the Hamptons?"

Marvelling at his instincts, for the first time Cat told
him about the weird dream and he listened, though he
seemed to be still engrossed in his game. She made it

brief, only really mentioning the magpie and the black-haired woman hiding something under the carpet. She also made it sound as if she had fallen asleep in her bed – which in a way was pretty much what she figured must have happened. That she didn't actually remember getting into bed was another thing she didn't want to think about.

"So who do you think it was?" Trevor asked, finally putting his toy down and coming to sit next to her. "And what was she doing?"

"I don't know. I guess the most obvious bet was that she was my mother, but I don't feel that at all. I feel like I know her, but I don't think it's my mother."

"Maybe that's because you didn't get much of a chance to know her? What do you know about her anyway?"

Cat looked blankly, shrugged her shoulders and shook her head.

"You know, come to think about it, there is very little I *do* know. My parents met when my father was doing a college year abroad – in England or somewhere. My mother was widowed very young. Younger than I am now, I guess. Her name was Kelly. Anne Kelly. I think she came from the Philadelphia branch of the Kellys – but I've never met any relatives on that side of the family. Granddad and I have always been, sort of self-contained, really. He doesn't like to talk about it. It must have been awful for him, losing his son, his daughter-in-law, and his grandson in the same accident and then having his grandson's wife drown just a few years later. He never really told me anything about her."

"Do you want to know more?"

"I guess so," Cat said hesitantly. Why shouldn't she want to know more? Maybe it would help sort out what was going on in her head. The feeling that someone was watching her. Cat thought about telling Trevor how she felt, but decided against it. He would probably blow it all out of proportion.

"Would you like me to snoop around a bit? See what I can find?" he asked, gently stroking her cheek.

"Yeah sure." She tried to sound casual and picked up a magazine to hide her confusion.

She hadn't told him that she'd seen that dark-haired woman before. She was sure it was the same woman she'd seen dancing that night at the *toque*. But the voodoo thing wasn't the first time. Even then she'd seemed familiar; Cat just couldn't remember from where. She could just as well have been from a book, or a movie. It could just be her mind playing tricks. Or just a coincidence.

Except that she'd seen the woman twice again: once as she looked out the window to the street below about a week after the dream, and again walking through the sliding doors of D'Agostino's supermarket just a few days ago. But it was just too weird to mention. She'd start sounding like Valerie if she didn't watch out.

She shook her head to try and chase the thought away, making her hair snap around her like a horse's mane. She checked her watch. Fiona was ten minutes late. The waiter had come over once again to ask if she wanted to order, and Cat had already devoured three baskets of bread-sticks and drunk two glasses of wine. She was just wondering what to do when a cab pulled up and Fiona got out. Cat was surprised to hear her friend tell the cabby to keep the motor running.

"Darling, I'm so sorry to have kept you waiting, but something's come up," Fiona said breathlessly, still standing. She had her Ray Bans on but Cat could tell by her bright red nose that she'd been crying. She motioned Fiona to sit down but Fi just waved her away. "Sorry, sweetie. I can't stay. I'm already packed. I have to catch the first plane to London. Oh, Cat, it's my bloody brother. It seems he missed a wave and got himself killed! Can you believe it?"

Cat reached out for Fiona's hand as a big fat tear rolled out from under her dark glasses and streaked down her cheek.

"Mummy is beside herself. She always spoiled him

rotten. I feel so bad. I never liked him. I was always jealous. It's all my fault!"

"What do mean? Your brother was in Australia. For God's sake, Fi!"

"But I wished him dead. I really did," Fiona whispered. "I was so angry that the stupid twat wasn't there and that I had to deal with everything, as usual. And now he's gone."

"You can't wish someone dead, Fiona," Cat said, keeping her voice calm.

"Valerie says you can."

Cat shook her head and was about to speak, but Fiona stooped her. "And that's not all. He took out an insurance policy. He's left a ton of money to Mum and Dad. It's – it's," Fiona continued searching for the right words, "it's just all too awful."

She bent down and gave Cat a peck on the cheek. Then she drew herself up to her full height and took a deep breath.

"Don't worry, Cat. I'm fine. Stiff upper lip and all that," she said with a wan smile. "I'm so sorry I'll have to miss your party. The funeral is the day after tomorrow. They're shipping his body home. I'll call you when I get to London."

"Do you need anything?" Cat asked as Fiona walked back to the waiting cab. "Do you need some money?"

"No, darling. I'm fine – really! You take care of yourself. Promise? And don't forget to pick up your dress!"

Cat watched the cab try to pull into the slow-moving flow of the traffic. A truck and a U-Haul van were blocking the intersection and there was a lot of honking and yelling out of windows going on. She waved at Fiona as the cab finally pulled away from the curb. Then her heart gave a lurch.

A magpie flew across the street, swooping low above the traffic. Cat watched it as it disappeared between the truck and the van. In the thin space between the two was the woman. She was standing as still as a statue looking straight at Cat. As the U-Haul moved Cat could see her clearly: the long black hair, the bright blue eyes. Cat peered to try and get a good look at her, but the traffic moved and her view was blocked by the truck. She had definitely caught a glimpse of brown. A long dress of some sort. Cat stood up to try and see over the top of the van, but the traffic was at a standstill. She could still see Fiona's cab a half a block away. The light changed and her view cleared, but the sidewalk was empty except for a dog-walker being pulled down the street by five different dogs.

Cat felt faint. She sat down again and poured herself another glass of wine. Maybe she was losing her mind. She had distinctly seen a woman with long black hair, dressed in a brown, drab dress, standing across the street, looking straight at her. But that was not what scared Cat the most. Her stomach lurched as she realised that the woman had clearly been barefoot.

What the fuck was going on?

Chapter Twelve

◆

The day of her birthday dawned grey and miserable. Though it was only six in the morning, Cat was wide awake. She lay staring at the ceiling, watching the faint rays of light seep through the blinds and make patterns on her bedroom wall. "Twenty-five today!" she sang to herself but she couldn't manage the elation the occasion called for. She should be tingling with excitement at the coming day and the big party that night, but instead she felt only a swirling emptiness inside her.

Twenty-five years ago a woman named Anne Kelly was giving birth to her. Or about to go into labour. Cat realised that she didn't even know at what time she was born, or where for that matter. She knew so very little about her mother. What was she feeling twenty-five years ago? Was she happy? Scared? She tried to imagine what might have been going through her mother's mind as her body took over the business of giving life, but it only made her feel a cold sick nausea that filled her mouth with a sour metallic taste.

A wave of sadness passed through her. Cat had always taken a twisted pride in being different, in being perfectly adjusted, perfectly whole, despite being raised by an old man and an army of servants. Now, for the first time, she acknowledged the pain of never having had her mother's love. Tears slowly crept down her cheeks as she cried silently, not wanting to wake Trevor. She cried for the little girl playing alone in the long lanes of the perfect gardens at the mansion. She cried for the woman she'd never known. How had she died? Had she just gone into the sea on a whim? Or had the despair of losing her husband finally made her decide to go and join him despite having a baby daughter? The image of the black-haired woman kept flitting through her mind. The magpie flew across the street, the woman stared, the van moved and she was gone. Cat curled up into a tiny ball on the edge of the mattress. Was she losing her mind or what?

Trevor lay next to her fast asleep. The alarm was going to go off any minute now, she thought. It was hardly worth trying to sleep. She watched Trevor as he slept. He looked like a little boy, all tousled and freckled, with his arms splayed out above his head. Cat wanted to light a cigarette but was afraid to wake him.

She'd tried to tell Trevor about seeing the woman again, but she never got around to it. He had a big day today. Bob's call to the guy at *Rolling Stone* had worked, and Trevor was going to meet him. He had been full of plans when they had met up last night. For once he didn't notice that Cat was only half listening as she listlessly pushed the sushi they had ordered around on her plate. She was trying to muster the courage to tell him about the woman. But he was brimming over with excitement at his first real break and she didn't have the heart to bring him down off his little pink cloud.

The alarm went off. Cat cringed. Trevor rolled over and took her in his arms. Cat let herself uncurl, seeking his warmth.

"Happy Birthday, my love," he whispered softly.

She sighed and snuggled closer. She could feel his body respond though he was still half asleep.

"Do you want your present now or later?" Trevor said huskily, pushing his hips against her.

"That's my present?" Cat said, resisting the desire to snap at him. Take it out on someone else, woman, she told herself. This guy is good for you.

"Na. That's *my* present," he laughed, raising himself on one arm and winking at her. Then he covered her with hungry kisses and Cat felt herself let go and give in to the moment as he made love to her.

When it was over Trevor did not linger in her arms as he usually did. Instead he gave her a quick kiss and headed for the shower. Cat could hear him singing at the top of his voice. He soon stood naked and dripping at the foot of the bed holding out two practically identical white shirts.

"The button-down, or the dress shirt?" he enquired intensely.

"Isn't white a little too conservative?" Cat answered, lighting a cigarette.

Trevor frowned. "Hey! I'm a conservative kind of guy."

"You are not."

"I am, compared to some of the fruitcakes living in this city," he said, still frowning. He chose the button down and started searching the floor for his pants, mumbling to himself. "I should have pressed these last night."

He turned to Cat and gave her a long look. "I wish you wouldn't smoke in bed," he said, shaking his head.

"It's my bed and I'll smoke in it if I want to," Cat said coldly.

"Fair enough," said Trevor, looking hurt. He sat on the edge of the bed and got dressed. Cat stared at his back, feeling cold, and alone, and miserable.

"Baby, I need to talk," she said softly.

"Now?" asked Trevor, putting on his socks.

"No, I guess not. It's pretty important, but it can wait," said Cat, her voice trailing off as she tried to stop herself from crying again. Trevor turned and looked at her intensely. Then he reached across the bed and pulled her into his arms, cradling her like a baby.

"I'm so sorry, Cat. It's your big day and I've been so wrapped up in myself I haven't given you the attention you deserve. But believe me, if I'm so worked up about today it's because of you."

Cat looked up at him, not understanding.

Trevor was blushing. He buried his face in her hair to hide his embarrassment. "You see. I was thinking. This could be a real break for me. I could be on my way. You have all that money and I couldn't ask you to, you know, be with me forever and ever until I know I can stand on my own two feet at least."

"Forever and ever?" echoed Cat.

"Yeah. Forever, you know? You could paint, I could write and we could have seven girls and seven boys and teach them all to play football. I can't do that until I feel I've sorted myself out."

"Why not?" Cat said, forcing him to look at her. "I love you anyway. I'd love you whatever you do."

"Really?" he said, blushing again. "Would you still love me if I were an impoverished psychopathic serial killer with a predilection for wearing ladies' frocks?"

"I draw the line at cross-dressing. I can't stand a man who looks better than I do in a dress," Cat joked, feeling herself relax into his arms. He glanced at his watch and let out a yelp.

"Look, sorry. I've gotta go," he said and kissed her one last time. He stopped at the door and looked back smiling. "I love you. What did you want to talk to me about?"

"Don't worry. It'll keep," said Cat smiling back.

"Great. I'll call you if I'm late, but I should be back by five. And then we'll talk. I promise."

The day went from bad to worse. Cat had fallen asleep after Trevor left. She was jolted awake by the phone. Cat checked the alarm clock before picking up. It was nine. It was her grandfather.

"Happy birthday, darling!" he said cheerily. "Twenty-five! Bright-eyed and bushy-tailed and roaring to go!"

"Thanks, Granddad," said Cat, feeling anything but that, as she tried not to sound as if she had just woken up. Her grandfather thought anyone who slept in past eight-thirty was wasting their life away.

"Sorry I couldn't get a better deal on the weather," he chuckled down the line. "Good thing we're not having a garden party! See you tonight, sweetheart!" Then he hung up.

The phone rang almost immediately after Cat put the receiver back. It was Bob. He too wished her a happy birthday and then quickly ran down the schedule of the evening.

"The limo will be there at six-thirty, but don't worry – there's no rush. We want to be sure that everyone else has arrived before the guest of honour. Just take your time and check in with the desk downstairs so that they can call ahead and tell us you've arrived."

"No problem," said Cat, wondering what sort of surprise they had planned for her.

"I hope you don't mind but I've arranged a little photo op. Your grandfather will be announcing a new merger tomorrow and a nice picture of the two of you together with the bigwigs will be great. It won't take more than five minutes, I promise."

"That's fine."

"Good. Now spend the rest of the day pampering yourself. And if you need anything just give me a call," he said jovially.

"I'll do that."

She might as well start with a long bath, she thought, as she crossed the living-room and flicked on the TV. First coffee, a croissant, and then a really long bath before her hair and nail appointment at two. She still had to pick up her dress. If the traffic wasn't too bad she might even get time for a short nap before starting to get dressed. Trevor should be back, complete with rented tux by five. The limo was due at six thirty. She should call Ramon and see if they wanted to travel with her.

The doorbell rang before she had poured herself a cup of coffee. It was the doorman with an enormous bouquet of flowers. They were from her grandfather. Two more huge bouquets arrived before she had managed to find a vase for the first bunch. One was from Bob, the other smaller one was from the house staff. The next time she answered the door, the doorman and the super were both holding a large bouquet each. They were from people she didn't know. The next lot was a fruit basket with a bottle of champagne from Fiona, an exotic plant from Ramon and Scott, and another bouquet from someone Cat presumed was another business associate of her grandfather's. The flowers and gifts just kept arriving, so Cat left the door ajar. Trevor called twice: once to say he loved her, and once to tell her that he'd be late, but not to worry. And still the flowers kept arriving. She stopped reading the cards. She ran out of vases, ice buckets, or any other thing to put them into. The super kindly brought her up a couple of large buckets and she shoved them in there. "I can get ya a couple of garbage cans if this keeps up," he joked.

The place was starting to look like a flower shop.

The air was sick and muggy with the smell of them. Cat opened the window and a hot blast of sticky heat rushed in. She turned the air conditioning on full blast and went back to help the doorman who was struggling with what looked like a large wicker hamper filled with gourmet food. Cat told him to keep anything else downstairs. He could bring them all up later when she had left.

It was still only eleven. Cat sat on the sofa wondering what to do. The apartment felt oppressive. Where was Fiona when she really needed her? Why wasn't Trevor here with her? What was she doing all alone on her birthday in what looked like a funeral parlour? Maybe she should have a joint? Or go back to sleep?

Cat picked up the phone and called Ramon. Scott would be working. Maybe Ramon could come over and keep her company. There was no answer and Cat hung up without leaving a message. Cat tried Val. What the hell, she thought, it was better than being alone. There was no answer and no message. Maybe Valerie was with Sheri, who had recently decided to change her name to Sheree and had dropped her last name altogether. She thought it was a wise career move. There was no answer but a long breathy message explained that Sheree was flying off to Paris on an assignment and wouldn't be back for two weeks. The bitch! She didn't even have the decency to call and say she wouldn't make the party.

Cat ran a bath and was about to undress when the phone rang. She jumped for it. It was Ramon. Great!

"Hey baby, where have you been?" said Cat delighted. "I'm going crazy all alone here. How about meeting me for lunch? I have a two o'clock hair appointment. It's my birthday, remember?"

"I'm so sorry. Happy Birthday, honey," said Ramon. Cat didn't like the sound of his voice. It was tired and tense, his accent even heavier than usual.

"Listen, Cat," he continued. "There's been some *problema*. Trouble. It's Valerie. You have to come."

"Is she all right?"

"She's all right. She's not hurt. But she is pretty shook up."

"Was there an accident? What happened?"

"No. Not exactly. Look I'm on a pay phone. I can't explain now. She wants to see you. Can you come right away?"

"Sure," said Cat, mentally calculating that she still had two hours to get to the hairdresser's. Maybe she could have a bath when she got back. Ramon was giving her the address: 27th and First. Cat could hear the sound of people and traffic in the background. As she ran out the door she wondered what Ramon and Valerie were doing down in that part of town.

*   *   *

Cat let herself back into her apartment five hours later. Her hands were shaking so badly that she dropped the key three times before she found the lock. The smell hit her as the door opened. An ice-cold, sickly sweetness overpowered her nostrils, making her take a step back into the hallway. The flowers! She had forgotten all about the flowers. Cat shivered as she walked around the apartment turning on the lights. The air-con had been left on full blast and the place was as cold as a meat freezer. The heavy perfume hung in the air, strangling her. Her neck felt tight. Her stomach shrank. She couldn't breathe. Cat ran to her bedroom to escape the stench. She walked around in a daze. The alarm clock read half past five. The traffic had been horrendous – a combination of Friday rush and rain had brought most of midtown to a halt. It had taken her an hour to get back home. An hour of sitting in the back of the cab, her head reeling, biting her nails and trying not to scream.

She shut the bedroom door and sat down. Trevor would be home soon. Shouldn't he already be home? Maybe he'd got stuck in the traffic as well. With a sinking feeling Cat remembered that he was going to be late. How late? How late did he say he would be? She tried to remember their conversation that morning but she couldn't. The answering machine was blinking at her. Cat hit play and listened as Trevor apologised, explaining that he'd accepted to go for a drink with some of the staff at the magazine. He would meet her at the party. He had his tux. He sounded happy. He said he loved her. Cat slid off the bed and onto the carpet. She hung her head between her knees and sobbed.

The cabby had known exactly where she was going.

"27th and First? That's Bellevue Hospital. Emergency or the main entrance? Guess it's not for you. You look pretty sane to me." The skies were low and black. The rain would not be long coming.

It took Cat a half an hour to find out where they had brought Valerie, and another ten minutes to find the psychiatric emergency ward. People walked past Cat not noticing her. Some looked busy. Some looked lost. Bedlam. The word drifted into Cat's mind. That's what they called it. Bedlam. Loony-bin. This was where they put the crazy people. She saw a nurses' station and willed herself towards it. Everything about the place made her want to bolt and run: the sting of disinfectant, the glare of the neon lights, the man crying silently in the corner. A woman shrieked hysterically somewhere behind a curtained cubicle and then stopped in mid-scream. Cat stared at the cheerful flower print wondering what had cut her off so abruptly. Up ahead an older woman was rocking back and forth on a chair, praying aloud in Spanish: "*Madre de Dios ayudame. Mamacita.*

Ayudame. Padre nuestro que estas en el cielo . . ."

She wanted to run – back into the light, the air, the wind and the rain. Every nerve in her body was wired, hating this place.

A tap on her shoulder made her jump. She looked around wildly, taking a few seconds to recognise Ramon.

"Cat. Thank goodness you're here. Thank you for coming down so quickly."

"I got stuck in traffic and then I didn't know where to find you," said Cat, feeling her pulse calm down, thankful for a familiar face. "Where is she?"

Ramon took her by the hand and led her to a curtained cubicle in the corner. "She looks worse than she is. She is not hurt at all, in fact," he said before pulling back the curtain. "She's been asking for you. She won't talk to anyone else."

Ramon was visibly shaken and wanted to get to the point as fast as possible. He looked ashen under his tan. Before Cat had a chance to ask exactly what had happened, he whipped back the curtain.

Valerie was strapped down to the bed. She was roughly covered by a blanket. Cat was shocked to see that she was naked underneath. Her hair was spread wildly around her face. Dried blood was smeared across her arms and she had an ugly bruise across her temple.

"Oh my God, Valerie!" she said, unable to hide her horror. "What happened?"

Cat's head was spinning with questions as she reached out and touched Valerie's arm. It must be a rape, she thought. Where did it happen? Why was there all that blood? Why had Ramon said that she wasn't hurt? The woman was covered in blood, for Christ's sake. Cat could see that it was even smeared down her perfectly tanned, waxed, calves. Cat forced herself to take a good look at her friend. Valerie looked terrible, but she did not seem to be in pain. She was smiling. Had she been doped up? She looked different, almost blank and Cat realised that it was the first time she'd seen Valerie without make-up in years.

Valerie looked at her and smiled again. Cat reached out and smoothed the hair out of her eyes.

"Tell those fuckers to let me go," Valerie hissed. "They forced me down. They tied me to the fucking bed. There's nothing wrong with me. I want to go home." Valerie's smile faded and she became agitated. Her shoulders strained against the wide straps as she tried to lift herself up.

"I'll get you out," said Cat, feeling her anger rise. She turned and faced Ramon, her eyes flashing. He flinched as she pushed him back out of the cubicle.

"Why the fuck is she strapped down?" Cat demanded. "Why did you let them do this to her?"

"It's for her own protection," said a small black man in a white coat as he walked up to them. He spoke quietly in a soft African accent.

"Though we were also thinking of ourselves," he continued chuckling. "She landed a few punches before the police arrived. We were lucky no one got hurt. I hear she was brandishing a rather large knife. Are you a relation?"

"Yes," Cat answered, lying automatically, "I'm her sister, who are you? What knife? Who called the cops? What the hell is going on? Was she raped? Who did this to her?"

"She mainly did it to herself, Miss," the man explained slowly as if making sure she would understand. "Except for the smack across the face. Unfortunately they had to use some force to subdue her. It looks like your sister had a full-blown psychotic episode. I'm very sorry. I am running some tests on her before we can be sure what is going on."

"That's not possible," Cat blurted. "I saw her a few days ago. She was fine."

Ramon took her arm and squeezed it. "He is telling the truth, Cat. I was there. I saw her." Ramon closed his eyes as if trying to erase the memory. "I was meeting her at eleven. I was a little late, as usual. There was an ambulance and a cop car outside. People looking into the building. The super found her naked in her hallway.

She was covered in blood." Ramon stopped and took a deep breath before continuing. "Cat, she was trying to nail a chicken to her neighbour's door. Valerie said he was spying on her. The super went up because he heard the banging. She attacked him with a knife so he called 999. The ambulance men could not catch her so they called the cops. It took five of them to strap her down."

Cat looked from Ramon to the small doctor and back again. She wondered where in Africa he came from. Apart from that thought, her mind was numb.

"Is she on any medication?" asked the doctor. "Could she have taken drugs?"

"I don't know." Cat shook her head, feeling it clear as the awful reality sank in. "But I don't think so. She's been going through a sort of initiation. It's drug and alcohol free. Do you think that could have something to do with it? She was getting into some weird voodoo stuff."

"Frankly I do not think so," said the doctor, writing something down on his clipboard. "It could be the event that tipped the balance, but it could just as well have been Mr Magoo on TV. It would have happened anyway. Your sister was a time-bomb waiting to go off. She has all the classic signs. I'm sure that if you trace the family history you will find other cases of this sort," he added, eyeing Cat.

She felt violated, as if he was trying to get inside her head. She turned her back on him and went back inside the cubicle. Valerie was calm. She gave a little wave as Cat stepped in.

"I'm going to get you out of here as soon as I can, sweetie," said Cat, trying to sound reassuring. "They have to run some tests. Then you'll be fine. I'll get you a private room. I'll take care of you. Don't worry."

"You've been in my dreams," Valerie said as pleasantly as if they'd just met for a coffee. Cat nodded, feeling her throat tighten as she tried to smile.

"But why the birds? Why do you keep sending me birds? Stop crying, Cat. I can fix things for you. Didn't I fix things for Fiona? And Sheree?"

"I'm not crying, Valerie," Cat said, feeling the tears smart her eyes.

"You're crying inside. Tell me why you're crying inside. I can fix it for you. First I have to do something about Mr Finkelstein, but that won't take a minute once I'm out of here."

"Mr Finkelstein?"

"The toad next door. I'm gonna fix it for him too." Valerie chuckled and dropped her voice. "I have to. He's spying on me. He has really big ears. He sticks them up against the wall at night and he listens to me. And then he files a report."

"Who does he file the report to, Val?" Cat asked, her voice dropping.

"The FBI. The CIA don't care but the FBI want my ass. They think they'll get to my parents that way. They want to get Daddy but they can't catch him. Are they still in the Bahamas?"

"I guess so," Cat said in a cracked whisper.

"Good. Tell them to stay there. It's safer."

Cat could not listen to another word.

It took two hours to wait for the tests and arrange for Valerie to be transferred to a private room. There were forms to fill and papers to sign. The little doctor came back and told them that he would put her under sedation and keep her overnight. Ramon insisted Cat go and get ready for her party. He promised to stay with Valerie until she was settled and asleep. Cat did not protest as Ramon led her outside and bundled her into a cab.

Cat lifted her head and stared at her reflection in the closet mirror. She looked a real mess. Her nose was red from crying. Her eyes were puffy and swollen. She quickly shifted her glance and avoided looking into their despair. She had to get herself together. Cat checked the alarm. Six! In a half an hour the limo would arrive and she would have to face hundreds of people. She'd never made it to the hairdresser's. She would have to slick her hair back into a chignon. As she reached for the brush Cat's heart skipped a beat. The dress! She had forgotten to pick up the dress!

Cat stood up and flung open the closet doors. Her eyes scanned the hangers, past the suits and shirts, the cocktail dresses and jackets. She reached out and touched peach chiffon, feeling the fabric slide over her fingers. On the shelf above sat the red leather jewellery case. Cat grabbed it and put it on the bed. Then she shucked off her jeans and shirt and threw them on the floor.

The receptionist recognised Cat as soon as she walked into the Tishman building. From the outside the building was just another shiny New York tower, distinct only because of the large red row of three sixes on the very top floor. The lobby was spectacular, however, with its black and white patterned ceiling and cascading waterfall. Cat walked slowly, feeling as if she was being sucked into an abstract perspective. The receptionist smiled broadly, stepping out from his station to accompany her to the bank of elevators. He ushered her past the massive waterfall with its stainless-steel strips that reflected her in rippling waves of peach.

She was calm now. Her composure had returned as she carefully made up her face and dressed. She had gone through the motions, blanking out the afternoon

CRISTINA PISCO

from her memory, steeling herself to be the star of the show. Opening the jewellery box she had dumped the contents on the bed and selected the diamond necklace and drop earrings. The doorbell rang just as she finished adjusting the clasp. On impulse she grabbed the funny-looking gold braid with the strange T and put it on as well.

The elevator doors closed and Cat felt her heart lurch as the speed picked up, shooting her straight to the top floor. Why was she alone? She should have walked in on someone's arm, no matter what Bob thought. The acceleration was making her light-headed. The elevator was completely mirrored and her reflection was multiplied all around her. She turned and checked the back of her dress, catching sight of her profile as she looked over her shoulder. Her face was drawn, her brow furrowed with worry. She forced herself to relax and watched as the frown lines disappeared. An infinity of reflected smiles acknowledged the improvement. She turned to face her full reflection and nodded. Cat felt the rate of her ascent slow down. She took a slow, deep breath and set her smile in place as the elevator door opened.

The sound of a party in full swing made her look to the right. People were milling around a huge floral arch which framed the double doors into the ballroom. Beyond Cat could see tables, waiters, men in tuxedos, and women in colourful gowns. Someone was speaking on the PA. Cat thought she recognised Bob's voice. A bell-boy in a bright red jacket and shiny buttons saw her standing there and ran into the ballroom, probably to alert them. Cat closed her eyes and took a final deep breath before stepping out of the elevator.

Something flashed at her feet. It was a small black kitten. It darted past her and ran around the corner to her left. Cat followed it as its thin black tail disappeared. The kitten was strolling down a small corridor leading to an emergency exit. It stopped and looked back at her. The black-haired woman was standing at the fire door. The kitten mewed and ran into her arms as the woman bent down to pick it up. Her bare feet were caked with dirt. She stroked the kitten and looked up at Cat, her piercing blue eyes flashing under long black lashes. Cat gasped. Her hand flew to her throat and instinctively clutched the gold T necklace. The woman smiled, still stroking the kitten. Then she held out her right index finger and pointed at Cat before bringing it up to her lips in a silent warning.

Cat heard footsteps behind her. They were calling her. She turned around and saw a man in a tux rounding the corner followed by the bell-boy. When she turned back the woman had gone. The kitten sat licking its front paw. The bell-boy ran up and got it as the man in the tux took Cat by the elbow and led her away.

Cat followed them back to the floral arch. Here eyes had trouble adjusting. She was aware of someone holding her by the elbow, guiding her into the room. She heard a voice ask her if she was ready. Cat heard herself answer but could not feel her lips move.

She was moving through the crowd. Up ahead was an elevated podium. Her grandfather stood in the spotlight looking dapper in his tuxedo and red bow tie. Bob stood next to him flanked by five Japanese men. They were considerably shorter than both Bob and her grandfather. They looked like five little penguins and two big ones. Cat heard herself giggle. Bob was pointing to the door.

"I'd like you all to help me welcome the Birthday Girl!" Cat heard her grandfather's voice booming out. "My great-granddaughter. Miss Catherine Richardson!"

The spotlight swung off the podium, teasing the crowd as it swirled through the room before landing on Cat. She was caught in its glare, momentarily blinded. The band struck up "Happy Birthday to You" as she tried to focus. Cat willed her feet to move, her smile to beam. People were clapping. She could feel waves of them rising to their feet as she passed. The clapping was getting louder. A few people started singing and soon the whole room joined in. The noise was deafening. Cat caught sight of Trevor and hesitated. She thought she might faint. She couldn't faint. He was smiling so sweetly. She wanted to run the last few feet that separated them and fling herself into his arms. Trevor abruptly looked away. Then he spun around and faced the front of the room. Cat followed him with her eyes and saw a commotion up at the podium. The Japanese were yelling and waving their arms. Bob was grabbing the mike and calling for a doctor.

Cat broke into a run as she saw her grandfather slumped on the floor. Her head cleared instantly. In two seconds she was kneeling next to him, cradling him.

"Granddad!" she yelled. His eyes were closed and he grimaced as if in pain. His eyes fluttered open for a moment and stared blindly at Cat. One hand clutched at his chest while the other tried to grasp her own.

"Oh my God! Annie!" he gasped. Then his body was wracked with a spasm and he closed his eyes. A large man pushed her gently away and bent over the old man, quickly loosening his bow tie and belt.

Cat stood helplessly on the sidewalk as the medics lifted the stretcher into the ambulance. She was just about to climb in after it when someone caught her arm.

"You have to go back upstairs," said Bob. His voice was low but firm. "There are a lot of important people up there. You can't just leave them."

Cat felt the hysteria crawling up through her body. Trevor was standing at the building's entrance watching her anxiously.

"I have to stay with Granddad. He could die!" Her voice shook.

"Listen to me, Cat," Bob said grabbing her by the arm. "Those Japanese flew all the way from Tokyo to be here tonight and sign the merger tomorrow. If they think anything is wrong the deal is off. We're talking millions here. You have to go in there now, and so do I. And tomorrow you have to be at that meeting representing your grandfather."

"You're crazy," said Cat. "I'm not leaving him." They were closing the doors of the ambulance.

"Your grandfather is going to get the best medical care in the world. He's going to be fine. It's what he would want you to do. We've worked for three years putting this merger together and I'm not going to let his spoilt little great-granddaughter blow it for him!"

Cat's hand flew out before she realised what she was doing. She slapped him hard, the flat of her palm connecting with his cheek with a satisfying crack.

"Get out of my way," she said, pushing him aside.

Then she strode back up the stairs. She could hear

the siren wail as the ambulance drove off behind her. She walked straight into the building without giving Trevor a second glance.

Three . . .

Chapter Thirteen

✦

Catherine Richardson waited until all the other passengers had left before rising out of her seat and having a discreet stretch. The KLM flight from Tokyo to Amsterdam had been as pleasant and comfortable as First Class could muster, but the bottom line was that she had been cooped up in that plane for what felt like days. She had slept most of the way but the roar of the engines had crept into her dreams, turning into the wild screeching of the wind as it swept down on her making her shiver under the thin aeroplane blanket. The stewardess smiled benevolently as she handed Catherine her coat and hand luggage down from the overhead rack. Catherine let the woman help her put on the heavy full-length mink. It would probably be too hot, but easier to wear than carry, she thought, as she stepped outside of the plane and started walking through the little docking tunnel which connected the plane to the airport. The mink was a birthday present from the Japanese consortium to Miss Catheline, as they called her. A full-length black mink coat! Could they be any more ostentatious? She hoped no rabid European anti-fur people were in the Schipol transit lounge.

Catherine was pleased that neither Bob, nor her lawyers, had accompanied her. After two years Catherine was well aware that her role was still largely that of a figurehead, but she excelled at her job and had a wardrobe to prove it. She also carefully read anything before she signed it and made sure to find the right people to explain things to her. Lately she'd been striking out on her own every now and again and she liked it.

At the end of the tunnel a eager young man was standing next to a little electric cart. He welcomed her to the The Netherlands in a thick Dutch accent and whisked her down a series of long hallways to the transit lounge. Catherine felt a bit silly sitting like an empress on top of the little cart as they whizzed by economy class passengers struggling with overweight hand luggage and turbulent children. Then again, better them than me, she thought as she crossed her long legs, careful not to flash the tops of her stockings. She caught the young Dutchman throw a quick glance at her legs and then stare directly in front of him. Fool. Not for the first time she wished that tailored clothes were more comfortable. Why people thought that expensive trappings showed anything other than that the wearer had relatively good taste and enough money to indulge it, was beyond her. Still, she had to admit it worked. From airline employees to the CEO of multi-nationals, it was apparently difficult to resist the charm of a beautiful woman who was dressed to kill. The Japanese were particularly susceptible to designer labels and Catherine had made sure they were duly impressed on this trip, from the tips of her Manolo Blahnick heels to the hidden silk of her Christian Dior lingerie.

Catherine graced the young man with a smile and walked through the smoked glass doors of the VIP lounge. The room was softly lit out of respect for those whose bodies might be in another time zone. Plush armchairs and sofas were grouped around low tables, a full bar and luxury snacks were laid out on her left, while on her right a wide range of magazines and newspapers lay carefully stacked by language. She chose an empty armchair near the reading material. Catherine's flight to Schipol had bad connections to Paris so she had chartered a jet and had an hour to wait for clearance.

Catherine was looking forward to the next day's

meetings with some of the best perfume and cosmetic consultants in the world. It would be a respite from the norm. She was toying with the idea of creating her own line and was looking forward to hearing their suggestions. In the last two years she had become a minor public figure: popping up in the society pages, doing a photo shoot for *Vogue* on tycoons' daughters, getting on the best-dressed list; and she thought it might be fun to cash in on it.

The waiter came up and asked if she would like anything. On a whim Catherine asked if they had any jumbo shrimp, and when the waiter nodded, ordered a split of Veuve Cliquot to go with it.

Checking her watch and calculating the time in New York, Catherine picked up the phone on the table and dialled the Hampton number. Victor picked up after five rings.

"Your grandfather is well, Miss Catherine," said Victor, automatically recognising her. "He had a good night last night. He is resting now after his therapy."

"Thank you, Victor. I'm glad to hear it," Catherine said playing along. Her grandfather had barely regained consciousness since the stroke. Intense physiotherapy had fanned only the faintest spark of life. He was completely bed-ridden and incapacitated, his periods of resting and waking discernible only because his eyes were either open or closed. Officially he was in semi-retirement, having handed over the day-to-day business to his great-granddaughter, but still in control. The truth about his condition was a heavily guarded secret.

"Oh, and Miss Catherine," Victor said, "Margarita and I wish you a very happy birthday."

Catherine thanked him and hung up. Her birthday was not officially until tomorrow, but the champagne and shrimp was probably the only opportunity she would have to celebrate. The occasion was sure to be marked by a profusion of flowers and presents that Catherine didn't need and that she would send to some hospital or other. The Japanese had also given her a beautiful Noriyaki dinner set. It was winging its way across the world to New York's West Side and Catherine wished she had sent the coat along with it. It was a damn heavy thing to be lugging around. She had no idea what she would do with either present. Maybe she could use the dinner set the next time she needed a wedding present for someone. The coat could be turned into a bedspread if that wasn't so tacky.

Catherine started quickly scanning through a copy of the European edition of the *Wall Street Journal*. A big piece on page three caught her eye. It was a profile on some up and coming software whizzkid and was accompanied by the *Journal's* trademark pen and ink drawing. But it was the by-line which caught

Catherine's eye. It read: *Trevor Manning is a freelance writer living in New York.*

Catherine closed her eyes and took a long gulp from her champagne flute. The bubbles tickled her nose and the wine tasted wonderfully cool and golden with a nutty kick. It had been two years. Two years almost to the day since she had slapped Bob and walked back into the Tishman building, past Trevor, and up to her birthday guests. Their relationship had gone downhill fast after that night. Stupid fights, misunderstandings, words said in haste, too little time, had all contributed to it. They had drifted, unmoored and unsettled, until Catherine had cancelled one night too many and they had ended it lamely on the phone.

She had put away all thoughts of Trevor along with the peach chiffon dress and the red jewellery case. Little by little, with the help of a few drinks and a few pills, she had managed to bury any wayward thoughts about him, or about the nightmares she'd had, under a pile of work and meetings. The hurt had stayed with her longer than the missing. Then that too had faded behind a wall of indifference only slightly shaken by seeing his name in print. Well, he must be pleased with himself, thought Catherine, marvelling at how far away that time felt now. Could it have only been two years ago? She bet that he still had that atrocious haircut and terrible shirts.

Catherine had to admit that her love life left something to be desired these days. Everyone assumed that she was in some way hitched with Bob Stigeman and that was fine with her. She didn't have the time for anything like a relationship.

Bob had actually made a half-hearted attempt to seduce her. One fumbling, totally unsatisfying encounter had convinced both of them that there was no chemistry there. He escorted her everywhere and dropped her at her apartment afterwards, only coming in for coffee if they had business to discuss. Her social schedule these days was so full that she had very little time for personal socialising. Most nights off she was so tired that the thought of staying in was far more appealing than going out on the town. And sometimes, usually on a business trip, she surprised herself by picking up a total stranger and going to bed with him.

"Excuse me. You're Catherine Richardson, aren't you? We met at the Hungtinton's in London last spring. I'm Ralph Thomas. Remember?"

Catherine looked up to see a man standing beside her. He was pulling up an armchair. "Do you mind if I join you?"

Catherine nodded. He was a handsome man in his fifties, with dashing white hair and a great tan. Not her type at all. He wore all the right trappings but he had sleaze-ball written all over him. His traditional blue blazer and grey flannels were well cut, and a gold, not too large, Rolex hung at his wrist. Catherine glanced down and saw the requisite tassel loafers. His way of announcing that he was not only rich, but also a fun guy, was a pink Ralph Lauren button-down shirt. Catherine remembered that he was a pretentious, nouveau riche, snob who fancied himself a playboy, and whose accent was as fake as his Rolex was real. Definitely not one-night-stand material. Anyway they had a common friend so it was out of the question.

She couldn't remember what he did, however, so she nodded politely as he ordered a full bottle of Veuve Cliquot.

"Great choice. It's my favourite! Vastly superior to the Moët et Chandon everyone seems to be serving these days. Every damn party in London is afloat in the bloody stuff," he said, laughing at his own joke. Property development. That was it – he was a property developer. Good, that meant she did not have to talk to him. He was totally unimportant. Catherine decided to get rid of him as soon as possible.

"So tell me, what is the beautiful Catherine Richardson doing all alone in Schipol airport?" he asked with the suggestion of a leer.

"Waiting for a plane and celebrating my birthday," she answered flippantly, fully aware of the effect she had on him as she shook her hair out of her eyes.

"Then you must have dinner with me!" he announced like a warrior grabbing a well-deserved prize.

"I'm afraid I can't," said Catherine firmly.

"Nonsense!" he exclaimed. "It is my duty."

"Thank you very much, but no."

Ralph dropped his voice and looked straight into her eyes. "I'm a man. You are a woman. And here we are adrift in transit together. Isn't it just perfect?" he said with a wide seductive smile.

Catherine threw back her head and laughed. "I don't think so," she said, still laughing as she rose out of her seat. "Now if you'll excuse me."

She walked purposefully into the ladies' room and collapsed laughing on the sink. Wow, she didn't think they made them that way any more. Still, you had to give the guy points for trying. Catherine rummaged around in her bag until she found her little oblong pill box. Flipping the lid she surveyed the contents as she worked out time zones in her head.

"One pill, two pill, red pill, blue pill," she recited softly to herself. Definitely not a blue pill – that would knock her out. Catherine chose a small twist of paper and emptied the contents on to the lid's mirrored top. A little line of coke should do the trick. It would help keep her awake until Paris but not keep her up all night. And it would make Mr Playboy's company much more bearable, she thought, trying hard not to laugh

as she quickly snorted the line with a little silver straw she kept in the box. She was still giggling as she came back into the room, and nearly tripped over a beautifully tooled leather rucksack lying on the floor.

Its owner was a young French Art student with long black hair and the body of a rich kid who snowboards in the winter and surfs in the summer. His name was Jean-François. He was stuck in transit for five hours because his flight to Paris had been delayed.

By the time he had picked up his bag and joined her table, Catherine had offered him a lift on the jet. She was delighted to notice that Ralph Thomas seemed most annoyed. Watching the two men politely squabble for her attention was more fun than she'd expected in an airport lounge.

"*Bonne anniversaire, Catherine,*" said Jean-François toasting her with big liquid brown eyes. "I must find some way to thank you."

Yes, thought Catherine, he was much more like it.

"*Merci, Jean François,*" she smiled adding. "I'm sure we'll think of something." She was delighted to hear Ralph Thomas have a discreet, but persistent, coughing fit.

Two days later she was back in New York feeling terrific. Paris had been great. Jean-François turned out to be a more than adequate birthday present. He was attentive, had impeccable manners, and his lack of stimulating conversation was compensated by his qualities as a lover. Best of all, she never had to see him again. He had hung around the Ritz-Carlton with her, watching TV in bed while she went out to meetings. Catherine spent a delightful couple of hours each day smelling perfumes, choosing palettes of colours, and being fawned over by the wildly flattering French consultants; before joining Jean-François back in her suite. When they said their goodbyes, neither meant it when they promised to keep in touch.

Catherine decided to go down to the main office and check up on things. She had set up her own office in the West Side apartment, turning the library into a high-tech hub complete with video conferencing. She was taking her cues from her grandfather who had also worked away from the hustle and bustle of the main offices, appearing only when it was necessary, remaining charming but elusive to the employees. But today she thought an unannounced personal appearance was in order, so she had asked Fiona to meet her there. It would keep everyone on their toes to know she was back.

"You look wonderful, darling," said Fiona, handing her a stack of letters that needed her attention. "You must tell me all about the Paris trip. I think having your own perfume is a marvellous idea. I'll just pop out and get you a coffee and the appointment book."

Catherine had offered Fiona a job as soon as she had returned from her brother's funeral in London. In the panicky first days of life in the corporate business world Fiona was someone she could trust, someone who knew her needs. Fiona had risen remarkably to the challenge. Her official title was that of Personal Assistant but unofficially she was known as the Dragon Lady. Catherine had gained a valuable helper but somewhere along the line she knew she had lost a friend. They still kept up the easy banter, the informal attitude, but it was a far cry from the days when they used to slump together on the sofa, eating ice cream and sharing secrets. Catherine no longer confided in her and Fiona had subtly changed her manner to that of someone who was paid large amounts of money to make another person's life run smoothly.

Catherine just put it down to the price one paid for growing up. The old gang that used to hang out on 57th street had each gone their separate ways. Ramon and Scott had broken up. Scott had gone home to Idaho and joined the family business. Rumour had it that he was dating a debutante and would soon be announcing his engagement. She still saw a lot of Ramon, especially since she had become the primary investor in his new restaurant in Tribeca. It was wildly successful and

Ramon was nursing his broken heart by being the belle of the ball at all times. They often met at high profile events and Catherine always used the restaurant for any entertaining in New York. She had been amused to meet Sheree there a few weeks before. Sheree was on the fast track to becoming a supermodel and was appropriately hanging off the arm of a minor rock star. They had commiserated sincerely about poor Valerie. After being diagnosed as schizophrenic she had spent several months in a luxury loony-bin in Massachusetts. The medication seemed to be working well and Valerie was allowed to return home for a short holiday. She had seemed on her way back to recovery. The news of her suicide had been a shock. Apparently she had flushed all her pills down the toilet the minute she got to the airport. Valerie had hung herself in her parents' garage between the red Porsche and the vintage Bentley.

Fiona sat herself down across from Catherine and efficiently went through the next few days' appointments, and social schedule. Today was pretty easy with a luncheon in aid of the Lincoln Center and dinner with Bob and the legal team. They would be flying in from meetings on the West Coast in the evening and go straight to Tribeca. In between Catherine had time to go home and catch up on her jet-lag.

Fiona picked through the pink phone messages as she talked, selecting the ones she would deal with herself and passing the ones that needed personal attention to Catherine. She waved the last one enticingly.

"You'll never believe who called out of the blue," she said raising her right eyebrow. "Trevor Manning. He's requested an interview. It seems he's doing a series of trendy business profiles for the Wall Street Journal."

"I hope you told him to fuck off," Catherine said.

"That's what I thought you'd say so I told him that you were in Paris and were unavailable for an interview for quite a while. However, you might want to recon-sider. It could be a good PR op."

"Yeah right – for him." said Catherine, turning to the letters on her desk.

"You're the boss!" Fiona sang cheerily as she ripped up the pink slip and threw it in the trash.

By the time Catherine had come back from lunch, Trevor had called twice, faxed once and sent a courier over with a hand-written personal note.

Fiona had refused politely, firmly, and assertively, but Trevor would not take no for an answer. As Fiona said, "impossible doesn't seem to be in that bloody Australian's vocabulary". Catherine decided to ignore the whole thing and suggested that Fiona just hang up if he called again. She was too tired to deal with a blast from the past. The jet lag was creeping up on her. She decided to go home and take a nap before the evening meeting.

The phone was ringing as she walked into the apartment. It was her private line so Catherine waved Maria, her house maid, away and went to pick it up herself. It was either Fiona, or Bob, with some last-minute change; or it could be Victor with some news of her granddad. No one else had that number. Catherine answered the phone as she sat into a big leather wingchair, shucking off her heels with relief.

"Hello?" she said.

"G'day, Cat! I'm sure glad I caught you at home. You do seem to whizz around these days," said Trevor happily on the other end of the phone.

"This is a private line," said Catherine so surprised that she could not think of anything else to say.

"I know," Trevor said proudly.

"How did you get it?" Catherine asked still stunned.

"Ah now, you wouldn't expect me to reveal a source, would you? But you know what they say: anybody is only five telephone calls away from the President of the United States. For a journo of my calibre tracking you down was a piece of cake. It only took three phone calls. Which links me nicely to the subject at hand: will you do the interview?"

"I've already declined," Cat snapped.

"Let me just talk to you. Let me just explain the angle

of the series to you face to face. If you still don't want it to do it after you've heard me, that's OK."

The guy was incredible! Maybe a short succinct answer would work.

"Go away. I'm busy," she said as if swatting a fly.

"Just hear me out. It won't take a minute. I could meet you anytime that's convenient. I'll tell you what: I'll come over right now."

"I'll tell the doorman to throw you out," Catherine said impatiently.

"Fair enough. I'll wait. Just lean out and give me a wave when you're ready."

"What are you talking about?" Catherine exclaimed, caught off guard yet again.

"Look out the window," Trevor ordered. Cat went to the window and looked out. The street was sunny, the big trees still covered in their summer greenery but starting to show that Fall was not far off. What was she looking for anyway?

"Other window," said Trevor. "The one on the far right."

Catherine nearly dropped the phone. He was watching her? Still, she was intrigued. She stretched the phone line to the far window and peered out. Trevor was sitting on a park bench waving energetically back up at her.

"How do you like my new mobile phone? Neat, isn't

it?" Trevor turned up towards the window and waved the phone at her. Catherine tried to stifle a giggle. It looked like he'd finally found a hairdresser and she was mildly impressed by the cut of his burgundy jacket. He reached below the bench and pulled out a brown paper bag, holding it up for her to see.

"Look. I know you're busy," he said, "But not to worry. I've got a book and a late lunch. I'll wait a while. Take your time."

"Fuck off," she said and turned away from the window. The impertinent, arrogant, dickhead, she thought trying not to smile. Let him rot out there.

Catherine pottered around the big apartment trying to keep her mind on other things. A nap was out of the question now. She was too agitated to go to sleep. No matter how much she tried to forget him, her thoughts kept straying to that hard-headed Aussie on the bench. She peeped out a few times to check if he had gone, but he was still there two hours later. Once he caught her watching and gave her a thumbs up and a big smile.

He sat there all afternoon. Cat was damned if she was going to let him catch her looking out the window again. To stop herself from peeking out she decided to get ready for the evening early. A long hot shower and a change of clothes would have to do in place of the nap.

Feeling somewhat refreshed, Catherine, dressed but not yet made up, padded into the living-room and fixed herself a vodka and tonic. She wanted to keep a level head for the meeting, but one early drink would do no harm. Swirling the ice in the tall glass, Catherine slid up to the window and peered out. Her heart sank. The park bench was empty. Catherine could see the brown paper bag sticking out of the trashcan.

He's gone, she thought miserably. He wanted an interview, he didn't get it, and he's gone. The rat. But what did she expect? He was from another planet. They were two different lifeforms now. He saw her as he saw all of her kind – the dreaded "Them". The ones who never rode on a bus, or struggled to pay the rent.

And for all his lofty "holier-than-thou" attitude, thought Catherine, he was just one of the little people eager to get up the ladder and join the big boys, and prepared to do whatever it takes to get there. The fact that they had once been madly in love made no difference in the real world.

Twenty minutes later, she was pouring herself another vodka when the phone rang.

"Yes?" she said, rushing to the window. He was back on the bench, looking up, and waving.

"I got a bit peckish, so I went off to get us some yummy munchies," he said pointing to a large bag beside him. "I got coffee and brownies. Hazelnut for the java, and both the chocolate and butterscotch for the brownies. Have you got any spare sugar? I think they forgot to put some in. Oh, and Cat, take a jumper – it's getting a bit nippy out here."

Catherine was riding down the caged elevator before she realised she was still in her slippers. What did it matter anyway? She was just going to march out there and tell him to get the hell away from her.

He watched her as she waited for a bus to pass before crossing the street. A smile played on his face as if he was wildly amused. Catherine strained to keep her face closed and angry.

He did not get up when she stood in front of the bench. He just looked up with his bright blue eyes and gave her a warm welcoming smile. Despite herself Catherine felt an answering smile creep up. She turned it into a smirk and was about to berate him when Trevor held up his hand to silence her. He rummaged around in the big white bakery box and presented her with a tiny miniature version tied up with a little gold bow.

"Happy Birthday, Cat. I know it's a few days late but what the hell," he said handing her the tiny box. "It isn't much. They do a special Birthday Brownie Box as party favours. It's kinda cute, don't you think?" he said, laughing to cover up the fact that he was blushing.

"I see you can still blush despite having turned into a journalistic predator," said Catherine sitting down.

"Absolutely! It's an integral part of my boyish charm," he quipped.

Catherine sat and looked at the small box in her hand and said nothing. Few people called her Cat these days. Even Fiona called her Catherine around the office. She thought that she should get this over with. It would soon be time to leave for her meeting.

"So how are you doing these days?" Trevor asked breaking her thoughts. His voice was polite, a bit too bright.

"Great," said Catherine nodding at the box. "It's been great."

A wave of sadness welled up unannounced and hovered over her. It had been a hard two years. Hard, and scary, and most of all lonely.

"I'm doing just great," she said, turning to face him. His eyes tried to look into hers, probing, asking questions. She locked him out until he broke away for a second.

"Are you happy?" he asked looking at her again, not probing this time, just gauging her reaction.

"On or off the record?" she answered, regaining her composure. If there was one thing she was good at, it was putting her feelings aside behind a steel facade.

"Off, I guess," he said reluctantly.

"No comment." Catherine smiled, knowing she had won.

Trevor nodded, duly chastised. Then he plunged ahead again. "Will you do the interview? My editor thinks the series would be incomplete without you. And it would be great for you as well."

"My great-grandfather only ever did one interview in his life – and that was to a trade magazine back in 1959. It never did him any harm," she said, enjoying Trevor's struggle.

"But times have changed, Cat. I think this is an opportunity for both of us." He stammered slightly, running out of arguments.

"Cut the crap, Trevor. This is primarily about you. If you get me to agree, you land the big fish. It will do you more good than me," she snapped pushing him to beg. If he so much as mentioned their past relationship, she would have a barring order against him in the morning. Trevor looked momentarily hurt and Cat felt the sting of her words still lingering on her tongue. He hung his head and nodded.

"You're right," he said, measuring his words carefully. "It is a big break for me. But I promise to respect your privacy and take up as little of your time as possible."

Catherine did not know what to say. He left himself completely open as he waited for her answer. She glanced at her watch. It was time to go.

"I'm sorry. I have a meeting in thirty minutes. Thanks

for the present," she said sincerely. Trevor reached out and took her hand. She felt a shock of recognition at his touch. She willed herself to give it only a quick squeeze.

"Will you think about it?" he said, reluctantly letting her go. "Can I call you tomorrow?"

Catherine nodded, too confused to speak. Trevor broke into a loud whoop as Catherine shook her head and sighed, waving him away as he tried to thank her. She was just starting up the steps when he yelled across the street.

"Hey, Cat! I forgot to tell you how drop-dead gorgeous you look! I especially like the slippers! Very sexy!"

"Yeah, yeah," she answered over her shoulder, not turning so he wouldn't see the big smile on her face.

She was still laughing as she rode the elevator back to her big empty apartment. Well, she thought, wiggling her toes and giggling, it looked like she was going to do the interview whether she liked it or not.

Chapter Fourteen

•◆•

Even though it was a weekday night, the restaurant was packed. Catherine knew that you had to book two months in advance to hope to get a table at *Ramon's*. More for a Saturday night. In a little over a year the restaurant had become the place to eat and be seen. Ramon had managed to create a mix of old-world elegance and new-world informality that appealed to both his upwardly mobile patrons, as well as the more established New York set. The food was scrumptious, mainly Spanish cuisine but with a lighter, more American, touch that was the subject of rave reviews. Catherine was secretly very proud of the place. It was her first personal investment, and though the money was peanuts compared to a major business venture, the restaurant's success was a measure of her sound judgement.

Ramon saw her the minute she stepped through the wide glass doors. He swept through the tables exclaiming wildly, his arms outstretched yards before he was anywhere near her. There were more exclamations and wild air-kissing as they met, then Ramon swiftly led her to her personal booth. It was perfectly placed, well out of the way, but with a commanding view of the room.

"Fiona will be here in a few minutes," Ramon whispered in a heavy conspiratorial tone. "She ees caught in traffic." Success had made Ramon's accent even stronger and the camp gestures even more dramatic. As Fiona said, he was in danger of turning into Carmen Miranda. Pretty soon he wouldn't even need the pineapple on his head.

Her two main lawyers were already there, huddled deep in discussion with Bob. Pat O'Neil was a sandy-haired New York Irishman, while Jeffrey Jackson was a caramel-coloured African American from Atlanta. Though they looked totally unlike each other they dressed, spoke, and moved in such a similar manner that Catherine always thought of them as Tweedledum and Tweedledee. They were also both totally devoid of anything even vaguely resembling a sense of humour. Then again, she didn't pay them to be funny.

All three men stood up as Ramon led her to the table.

CATCH THE MAGPIE

A large bottle of San Pellegrino mineral water sat in the middle of the table. Catherine ordered a double vodka tonic and was pleased to see that Bob couldn't help a smirk. She often felt like sticking her tongue out at him – sometimes he was so stiff it looked like he had a palmtree stuck up his arse.

"Shall I make dat two wodkas?" Ramon asked. He gestured behind him to Fiona who was just making her way to the booth, leather-bound diary in hand. Catherine nodded as he turned to the men with a leer.

"And for you gentleman? *Mas agua?* Shall I get another bottle of water and a couple of snorkels?"

Catherine laughed and waved away the menu Ramon had produced with a swirl. She had to hand it to him, he always knew who the most important person at the table was. He literally enjoyed poking fun at everyone else. If he didn't outright ignore them – which was far worse. In fact, being insulted by Ramon was a much sought after prize in certain circles.

"Will you order for us, Ramon?" said Catherine, gesturing to the others who all nodded their approval. "Surprise me."

"*No problema*, darling," Ramon said with a swish of his long pony-tail.

Fiona quickly brought her up to date on the afternoon's calls.

"Trevor Manning never called back," she said,

241

sipping her V & T gratefully. "Who would have thought he'd give up so easily?"

Catherine just smiled. Somehow she didn't feel like telling anyone about Trevor just yet.

The two lawyers sipped their mineral water as Cat outlined the plans she had for the new cosmetics and perfume line. They listened politely and made a few suggestions but Cat knew they were just humouring her. Bob was barely listening. She was annoyed at the way they all toyed with her. She could read their minds too clearly: let her go off and spend a few million of her own money to amuse herself, if that's what she wants.

Catherine knew they never would have dared to act that way with her great-grandfather. The fact that these four people were the only ones who knew how bad his condition was gave them an edge over her she did not like. But there was very little she could do about it. Her great-grandfather's empire extended over so many different areas, in so many different countries, that it was very hard for her to get a handle on it, even two years after she had taken over. After the First World War, her great-grandfather had taken the family's already considerable wealth and increased it a hundred-fold, ploughing into the lucrative burgeoning markets of the twentieth century. He moved from land to oil, from heavy industry to banking and financial services, from retail outlets to computer chips.

The lawyers took her through the West Coast business developments as Catherine nibbled on the delicious selection of *tapas* that Ramon sent over: roast peppers in olive oil, fresh olives in garlic and herbs, tiny plates of fried fish, and chunks of cold Spanish omelette. The lawyers did not pause to eat as they talked. It was the same old thing: mostly tax hedges, like mink farms, and resort development deals that promised a high yield. Catherine was bored. She knew she paid them enough to ensure that her interests were their main concern. They were billing her even as they sat around her table, in her restaurant, drinking her overpriced Italian mineral water. Catherine's mind drifted as she tried to keep her face looking attentive. She wondered if they could produce a list of exactly what she owned. She wondered how many pages it would be?

"So that just about rounds things off," said Bob brightly, bringing the report to a close.

"What about the venture capital people," Catherine asked mildly. "You know, the two guys I asked you to look up," she added. Catherine had read an article on two young LA computer nerds who were looking for venture capital and had suggested that Bob look them up.

"I did call them, as you suggested, but I don't think we should pursue it any further," Bob said firmly.

"It is a money-losing venture for sure," said Tweedledum.

"With no tax incentive in sight," echoed Tweedledee.

"Well, *I* think we should pursue it," said Catherine, smiling at the waiter as he cleared the little plates of *tapas* away. "I'd like to look into it personally."

The table all stopped and looked at her. Bob opened his mouth and then shut it again. Even Fiona arched an eyebrow.

"OK," Bob said slowly. "We'll send the file over to you tomorrow."

"Great. I'm glad that's settled," said Cat as Ramon came up.

"No more talking about business now!" he admonished. "Not when you are eating my food. No business! It spoils the palette."

"Now look! *Mira lo que te traigo mi amor,*" he said, lovingly placing a steaming earthenware dish in front of Catherine. The smell was gorgeous.

Catherine watched as the lawyers tried to hide their discomfort at the slick white parcels swimming in a thick black sauce.

"I went to the market to pick them myself," said Ramon. "They are the tiniest little baby ones I could find."

"Ramon, you are a genius," said Catherine playing the game.

"They certainly look different," said Bob heartily. "What are they?"

"Baby squid in a sauce made from their own ink," Fiona explained in her clipped British accent. "Thoroughly delicious, except that they stain your teeth black."

"That's right!" said Catherine tucking in.

Bob nibbled on a little piece and the unlikely twins followed suit. All three nodded their approval.

"So you like them?" asked Catherine. The three men smiled bravely, their teeth blackened by the ink. Catherine laughed out loud, pleased at the surprised look on their faces as she stuck her black tongue out at Bob.

Ramon had produced two bottles of Banda Azul Gran Reserva to go with the wonderful meal that he had personally served. Fiona was watching her weight and the three men only had a glass each, so Catherine had finished the wine herself. As she let herself into her apartment she had to admit that she felt wonderful. Catherine shucked off her suit jacket, dropping it on a chair in the hall, and gratefully undid the top button of her skirt. She let it fall on the floor and stepped out of it. Groaning with satisfaction she kicked off one high heel, then the other, as she walked down the hall to her room. She had told Maria not to wait up for her, and she was glad to be alone. Most of all she was relieved to be finally happy on her own.

When she had first moved into the West Side apartment she had often felt a sense of unease alone at night. Even the knowledge that her maid slept down the hall did nothing to soothe her as the old building creaked and whispered to her. She was scared to go to sleep and often stayed up late at her computer, with the TV on. Maria would find her slumped at her desk and gently help her to bed. In the morning Catherine would wake up groggy and ill-tempered, haunted by images on the edges of her memory, surprised to find that she had gone through an entire bottle of vodka.

After a few months she decided to face the problem head on. First an army of decorators had been called in to completely revamp the place. Except for the reception rooms and the library, all the old furniture and clothes had been shipped out to the Hamptons to be stored in the east wing. She was going to make the place *her* home. Catherine had knocked down walls and created a suite of rooms for herself full of gleaming glass and chrome, including a bathroom the size of most New York apartments. Then she had privately gone to seek counselling. The therapist was kind and understanding. She had explained that the recurring nightmares and anxiety were normal. Catherine had been under a lot of stress. It was only natural. Best of all she had prescribed some wonderful pills: the yellow ones kept any anxiety at bay during the day, while the blue ones ensured Catherine had a restful dreamless night.

Catherine walked around shedding articles of clothing, as she nibbled on a few grapes from the fruit basket. Maria had turned down the covers of her huge double bed, and laid out a silk night-gown on the pillow. The hidden stereo system was softly tuned to a late-night jazz station.

Catherine stood at the big bay window and gazed across the dark park to the brightly lit buildings on Fifth Avenue. She was giddy from the skyline and filled with a sense of satisfaction and well-being. She had commanded respect at dinner and watched as Tweedledum and Tweedledee backed off and carried out her wishes. Even Bob had put up with her jokes and digs. Catherine opened her arms wide and spun around the room until she fell giggling on the bed. She could take them on. She could even handle Trevor Manning. She'd show him who was in charge!

Slipping on the cool silk night-gown, Catherine glanced at her night table and was pleased to see that a tall pitcher of ice water and a crystal goblet were laid out with care. Next to them was a bone china plate that held a single blue pill. She poured herself a glass of water and took a long refreshing gulp. Yup, she thought, she was on the top of the world and she liked it. It was amazing what some redecorating, a little counselling, a little drugs, a lot of alcohol and loads of work can do. She gazed at the little blue pill and shook her head. She didn't need it.

"All gone," she sang to herself. "All the bad vibes are gone."

Cat snuggled down in her huge bed and sighed, content. The last thing she thought about was her call from Trevor the next day. She smiled, remembering his stubbornness. He had won this battle, but she would win the war. She'd show him.

It started as soon as she closed her eyes.

Valerie sat on her bed looking down at Catherine strapped to the hospital gurney. Catherine could feel the rough material chafing her wrists as she strained against the restraints.

"You've been in my dreams," Valerie said. In her lap she held the red jewellery box. "But why the birds? Why do you keep sending me birds?"

Catherine's heart was banging in her chest as she strained to lift herself up. Valerie was handing her the box, but Catherine could not reach it. Trevor looked down at her sadly and shook his head, as Fiona and Ramon turned away. She twisted her head and saw her grandfather smiling at her, Margarita and Victor at his side. She could feel the cool pillow against her cheek. She smelt the cut flowers in the vase by her bed. The sound of music drifted into her mind and she felt a flood of relief. She was in her room lying safe among her white linen pillows.

Catherine fought to wake up and banish the dream. Her head was so heavy she could barely lift it as she tried to scan the familiar surroundings. Her eyes had trouble adjusting to the dark. Her heart froze as she heard the sound of scratching. She immediately felt a presence somewhere near the window. A soft fluttering. She opened her eyes wide trying to make out the shadows by the open curtains. A fluttering again. A flash of white. Magpies! There were several birds pecking along the draperies. Catherine felt a scream rise in her throat as one of them jumped onto a side table and was silhouetted in the dark window.

She woke with a start. The lights were still blazing. The music was still softly playing. She was huddled under her bedclothes, her hands desperately clutching the crisp linen sheets. She groped blindly for the little china plate, knocking the crystal goblet on the floor. After what seemed like an eternity her fingers finally found the little pill. She swallowed quickly, afraid that she might drop it, afraid to open her eyes again. Then she huddled back under the covers and listened to her beating heart. Slowly, she felt her grip on the sheets relax. Sleep would come soon and with it the relief of knowing that she would remember none of it in the morning.

Their conflicting schedules had only made it possible to set up the initial interview ten days later. Trevor had sent a small bunch of colourful anemones with a note: *Thanks. T.* Apart from that, he not called except to confirm the night before. Trevor had been businesslike and polite on the phone.

Catherine sat at her long polished desk and glanced at the small bunch of flowers, marvelling at how beautifully the pinks, purples, and reds looked together. She fingered the short note and felt a sharp pang, remembering how formal Trevor had been. Wasn't that what she wanted? What was wrong with her anyway? She was glad she had decided to meet him at the office downtown. It was her power base. There would be lots of other people around. People who all worked for her. It would set the right tone for an interview, as would the bright red Valentino power-suit she wore. Catherine knew she looked both beautiful and intimidating.

Fiona hid her surprise when Catherine told her to cancel all calls between eleven and twelve. She merely raised one eyebrow and said nothing as she led Trevor into Catherine's office with its imposing view of the twin Trade towers.

Trevor hesitated for a moment, clearly taken by the view, but he made no comment. This was going to be strictly business. Trevor nodded his thanks to Fiona and busied himself setting up a little tape recorder on the wide expanse of the desk. Catherine watched him, poised and ready, but she could not help feeling uncomfortable in her tailored jacket and pencil-thin skirt. Trevor barely glanced at her except to ask if he could take a seat. After checking the sound level, he flipped open his notebook and plunged straight into the interview.

"I thought I should start by just checking through some background. I know you're very busy so I'll try and keep it short," he said, consulting his notes. "Hopefully we'll get most of it done today. Then perhaps we could meet again in a few days to add your personal input into the general picture."

Catherine nodded and sat back in her big leather armchair. Trevor was well-informed and she found that she had to stay sharp to keep up with him. He seemed to know as much about the Richardson empire as she did herself. More than once she had to say that she would have to check to see if his information was correct. But on the whole it went well. She could handle it.

Catherine was just starting to relax, feeling confident that she was conveying the right balance of calm and power, when the intercom button flashed.

"Excuse me," she said, interrupting Trevor's question about their expanding Asian presence. Catherine pressed the little button and was surprised to hear Fiona ask for her.

"Sorry to interrupt, Catherine."

"I thought I told you to screen all calls."

"I'm terribly sorry. It's Bob Stigeman. He insists that he needs to talk to you now."

"Tell him to hold," Catherine snapped. Who the hell did he think she was, she thought angrily. She wasn't a dog who came when it was called. "No, better yet – tell him I'll call him back."

"Sorry. But he's not on the phone. He's right here with me. He says it will only take a minute."

Catherine was about to yell, but thought better of it. Trevor sat, pretending not to listen, engrossed in his notes. It would not look good to have him hear her throw a temper tantrum.

"Excuse me," she said again. "It seems something important has come up which demands my attention. I'll be right back. Get yourself something from the bar while you're waiting. Or shall I have Fiona get you a coffee or tea?"

"I'm fine, thanks," said Trevor.

Catherine calmly walked out of the room as if nothing out of the ordinary was happening, but she was seething inside. This better be damn good, she thought. Something better have blown up, or she would.

Bob was standing in the reception area outside her office. He seemed totally unafraid. In fact he looked ready for a fight.

"I specifically told Fiona that I was not to be interrupted," Catherine said as she walked up to him, loud enough for the employees milling around to hear. Bob signalled her over to a corner.

"This better be damn important," she started.

Bob cut her off. "What do you think you're doing?" he said, his voice hard and low.

Catherine was momentarily taken aback by his tone.

"Why wasn't I told? You agree to a major interview with an international newspaper and you don't tell anyone? And then you proceed to meet the man alone, with no one to monitor? Are you out of your mind?"

"I can do exactly what I like," Catherine hissed. "It's my company, my life and I don't have to ask you for permission."

"Oh, it's your company all right and I guess that gives you the right to be as stupid and naive as you damn well please," snapped Bob. "Though it would be hard to beat giving an exclusive interview to some rookie journalist who just happens to be your ex-lover."

Catherine's anger flared through her. Her hands were trembling and she had to pause for a breath so as not to strike him. Bob stood his ground defiantly, oblivious to the glances of those behind them. Catherine steeled herself, feeling the ball of anger come together in a powerful whirlwind just below her heart.

"He's just using you, Catherine. He . . ."

Bob started to speak again, but she hushed him with a flashing look as she pointed a long red fingernail at his face and looked directly into his eyes. She was pleased to see him flinch and take a small step back.

"You are totally out of order," she said very softly. "I'm very busy right now. I will deal with you later." Then she turned on her high heels and walked back to her office without giving anyone a second glance, making sure not to slam the door.

Once inside she found she could not control her trembling. Catherine went over to the bar and pretended to choose a soda while she calmed down. She dared not look at Trevor.

"Is something up?" he asked casually. "Is that wanker getting on your case about me?"

"I thought you liked Bob," said Catherine, still not facing him.

"Naw. He's not my type. Tell you what," Trevor added softly, "I've pretty much wrapped this baby up for today and you seem very busy. Why don't we call it quits and meet again? At your convenience, of course."

"That would be great," Catherine said gratefully. Her breathing had returned to normal and she found she could face Trevor and smile.

"How about same time tomorrow? At my place?" she asked. "We could finish up with lunch."

"That would be peachy!" said Trevor, eyeing her carefully. "But are you sure it's all right? I don't want to get you into trouble," he added, breaking into a sly smile.

"I'm the boss remember? I'm not the one who's in trouble."

Chapter Fifteen

•—◆—•

The fight with Bob had upset her more than she cared
to admit. She had left the office immediately after
Trevor, telling Fiona not to expect her back in. She
would work from home and needed no assistance. In
fact she was thinking of taking a few days off. Maybe
she'd go out to visit with her granddad. Fiona had
nodded dutifully not responding to the sharpness in
Catherine's voice.

Catherine had decided that the best way to deal with
Bob was to ignore him. Make him realise how unimportant he was. She had refused to take his calls and
had not called him back. She had gone home, told
Maria to fix her something simple for dinner, and read
a book all evening. She made sure to take the yellow
pill the minute she got home and the blue pill before

she got into bed. She wasn't going to let anything, or anyone upset her. She'd tell them all to go to hell if she wanted. Right now she just needed some space.

As usual Trevor was right on time. Catherine heard the door buzz as she stepped out of the shower. She decided to slip on a pair of jeans and a simple T-shirt. She just wasn't in the mood to dress up. Catherine hummed a little tune to herself, feeling a nervousness in the pit of her stomach. She knew what she was doing, she assured herself. She was in control.

Trevor was waiting for her in the library.

He smiled quickly and nodded as Catherine gestured to a big armchair. They shuffled around, like children warily circling each other in a playground. He bumped into her and Catherine jumped away as if she had been burned. They laughed to hide their embarrassment and then watched in silence as Maria brought in a tray with coffee all laid out. Then they both watched as she left, closing the big door behind her. The click of the hinge seemed incredibly loud in the panelled silence of the library.

He too was dressed informally and Catherine couldn't help noticing that his build had improved considerably. She could make out the outline of pecs that had not been there two years before. He must have been working out, she thought. Trevor caught her looking and blushed. She would have liked to make a joke but she found that her mouth was dry and she could not think of anything to say.

She cleared her throat to try and cover the awkward pause.

He did not look up as he fiddled with his notebook and chatted about the weather while she paced the room. Yesterday it had been easier to keep up the pretence of a business meeting. They had been in an office building surrounded by people. Now they were alone and Catherine knew that he was as uneasy as she was at their sudden closeness.

She tried to avoid looking at him as he started checking back on where they had left off. Guiltily she wondered if Bob hadn't been right. Maybe she couldn't handle it. He'd called her stupid and naive, which pretty much summed up the way she felt as she stood at the window trying to keep her attention focused on the clouds outside. Had she been naive to think that she could erase the past? That she could forget the way Trevor smelt, or how his nose crinkled up when he was concentrating? Stupid! She really was stupid, she thought. The nervousness in her stomach had increased, making her tingle uncomfortably. She wondered if she should excuse herself and go take a yellow pill. Oh God, she was pathetic! Catherine felt tears prick the back of her eyes.

"So, I thought we might just quickly run through your

education, if you don't mind," he said, addressing his comments to the back of her head.

"Sure. Whatever," said Catherine hastily. This was not going at all the way she planned. She'd better get it over with quickly. "Actually, something's come up. I don't think I can make lunch," she blurted out.

Trevor's head snapped up and he looked straight at her, his eyes squinting against the light.

"That's too bad, Cat," he said, a shadow of pain dulling the brightness of his blue eyes. Catherine felt them reach out to her. "I was really looking forward to that."

"So was I," Catherine said slowly. She knew she had to look away. If not he would read her need for him. He would see how lonely she'd been without him. Catherine dropped her gaze. "I'm sorry Trev, but I just don't think it was a good idea to see you again."

He was out of his seat before she had finished her sentence and crossed the room in two strides. Before she knew what was happening he took her in his arms and kissed her hard. Catherine kissed him back despite herself. She wanted to pull away but her arms went around his neck and her body pressed against his. She could feel their passion rising with all the longing of lovers kept apart too long.

Her fingers ran through his hair as her mouth kissed him hungrily. Trevor groaned and pushed her up against the wall, grinding his hips against her until she was swooning, held up only by his embrace.

"Jesus woman, I have missed you so much," he said, his voice husky and deep. Catherine felt the ache in her belly like a rocket that was going to explode. Her body shuddered, straining against all the voices in her head telling her this was wrong.

She willed herself to put her hands firmly on his shoulders and push him away. Trevor would not let go. One hand caressed her breast while the other ran up and down her back. Using all her strength, Catherine shoved him hard. His eyes flashed, bewildered, as he lost his balance and stumbled. Catherine turned her back on him, hanging on to the big armchair for support as she tried to catch her breath.

"Oh God, Cat, I'm sorry," he said reaching out for her again. "I didn't mean to grope you like that."

"Go away."

"Please, Cat."

"Go away. Just go away and leave me alone," she said, trying hard not to cry.

Trevor circled the room so he could face her. He tried to put his hand on her shoulder but she stopped him.

"Look, I'll leave now if you want me to but I'm buggered if I'm going to lose you again."

"This is wrong," she whispered. "All wrong."

"I want you Cat and I know you want me. I felt it when you kissed me. How can that be wrong? What's wrong with loving you?"

"I can't do this, it was a mistake," she said, standing up straight. "I should never have agreed to an interview."

"Fuck the interview! We're talking about us."

"There is no us. I don't know how I could have thought I could trust you. You're just using me," she said, the words just spilling from her mouth. "You're just like the rest of them, just using me to get ahead."

Trevor's face contorted with a mix of hurt and rage. He clenched his fists tightly at his sides until the knuckles were white. Catherine felt her heart sink as she watched him take a deep breath and look at her in total disgust.

"I don't know what they've done to you, Cat, but don't like it one bit," he said coldly. "If you can't tell the difference between someone who loves you and someone who's using you, then you're damn right – there is no us. I don't care about the damn interview, all I care about is you."

He hung his head as if deep in thought. Then he turned on his heel and started across the room. At the door he stopped. His eyes were sad and weary.

"If I could, I'd take you away from here. Away from all this – this, stuff," he said softly as if speaking to himself. "We'd go to a place where we could just be happy. But I can't, because you're too damn stubborn to come with me."

Catherine watched as he opened the big door, willing him to come back. She stuffed her hands in her pockets to stop them from shaking. Trevor hesitated and looked back, waiting for her to speak. But she said nothing.

"Look," he sighed finally. "I'm still living in the same flat. I've still got the same number. Hell, you're still my landlord so you've got a key. Just show up. If you want me, you know where to find me."

Then he slipped out of the room and was gone.

Catherine stared blindly at the wood-panelled door. She didn't need him. She'd been fine without him. How dare he think he could just come back into her life and take up where they had left off? She crawled into the armchair and curled up, pulling her knees up to her chin. Something fluttered to the floor and she bent down to pick it up. It was Trevor's notebook. Catherine scanned the doodles and notes. His writing was terrible. She could barely make out the words. It didn't help that her hand was shaking and her vision was blurred. Catherine rubbed her eyes with the back of her hand and found that her face was wet with tears. At the bottom of the last page was a big wobbly heart crossed with a crude arrow. In the middle he had written *I love u* in big flowery script.

Cat held the notebook up to her cheek and let the tears take over. She cried without restraint, letting the gulping sobs wrack her body as she rocked back and forth like a child hanging on to her teddy bear, alone and frightened in the big empty house. She spent most of the afternoon crying in the library, refusing to come out when Maria knocked softly on the door to ask if she wanted lunch. She reached for the phone and then stopped, knowing that there was no one to call. She was alone. There was no one left to talk to. No one to confide in. In the last two years she had built a high wall around herself, insulated by little pills and dreamless nights, her loneliness camouflaged with paid employees, one night stands, and an endless round of empty social functions. All she knew was that no other man had made her more than blink in all that time. Trevor, with his stocky body and freckles was the only one who turned her on. In his arms she was someone else. No – not someone else, rather really herself.

But she could not just fall back into the comfort of his embrace, the laughter of his company. He too had changed. Two years as a journalist in New York would change anyone. How could she ever trust him?

It was late afternoon. Catherine looked at the pile of little tissues littering the library floor. She couldn't just sit here and cry forever. Catherine picked up the phone and dialled the loft. She hung up the minute she heard the recorded message click in. Just as she had hoped, Trevor wasn't home.

Catherine held her breath as she let herself into the loft. Trevor's aftershave and the smell of oriental stir-fry still lingered, stabbing her with a sense of guilt. She wasn't proud of sneaking behind his back, but she knew it was the right thing to do. She had to either trust him completely or not at all.

She didn't really know what she was doing here. What was she looking for? She just knew that she had to put her mind at ease.

Catherine's heart raced as she slipped silently into the loft space. She'd called the number again from the shop downstairs just to make sure that Trevor was still out. Though she knew she was alone she was still scared.

The loft space was clean, but unused. Her old canvases were stacked neatly in one corner alongside pots of paint. The only improvement was a mini-foot game in the middle of the room. Catherine smiled as she went over and gave one of the little men a spin.

The door to the flat was ajar and Catherine peeked inside before stepping in – just in case he was asleep in there. The afternoon light was fading but she didn't want to turn on a light and attract attention. Then again, if Trevor did catch her it would be better if she weren't standing alone in the dark. Catherine switched on the light.

The futon was opened and messy, the Bart Simpson sheets tangled in a heap in the middle of the bed. The room had acquired new bits and pieces: a night table, some shelves, a desk and computer in the corner, a TV and a stereo. The most dominant new feature hung above the bed. Taking pride of place was her painting of the sunflower. Catherine stood back and looked at it, letting the memories of those early days with him flood back, filling her with a mixture of joy and sadness.

Feeling herself relax, she started pottering around, picking up a magazine here, a book there. She was careful to put things back exactly where she found them. There was a voyeuristic thrill in being there alone, looking through his closet, opening his night-table drawer. She smiled as she recognised his atrocious jacket hanging alongside some new clothes. They were more Gap than Armani, but not heinous. The man has developed a modicum of taste, she thought to herself. The night-table drawer held a packet of condoms, which gave Cat a nasty feeling. Then again, she hadn't expected him to be celibate, had she? Still, she was pleased to see that the packet was unopened and seemed to have been knocking around the drawer for some time.

In contrast to the room, the tiny kitchenette was spotless and filled with shiny gadgets: a Darth Vader phone, a high-tech juicer, and an impressive collection of knives and woks. Two pictures were thumbtacked to the wall. One was a landscape postcard of what could only be the Australian outback. The other was a picture of her, head thrown back and laughing. Catherine searched her memory, trying to remember where it had been taken. It was an extreme close-up. Catherine took it off the wall but neither the background nor what she was wearing was visible to give her any clues.

A large wicker basket caught her eye as she peered at the photograph. It was overflowing with papers and envelopes. It must be Trevor's mail – would she stoop so low as to read his mail? Her moral dilemma was swept aside as she read her name on a note sitting on the top of the pile. It was a short memo to Trevor. After *Subject* it read: *Catherine Richardson Profile*. Catherine stood over the basket not daring to touch it as she read.

Memo: To Trevor Manning
Subject: Catherine Richardson Profile.

Glad to hear you are making progress. Don't forget to focus on the old man. If you can get confirmation that he is truly incapacitated – we've got a scoop! I have every confidence that your past "friendship"

will work in your favour now that you have your foot in the door! Go for it!

Albest, E.

Catherine ran back to the bedroom. She savagely switched on the computer, cursing its slowness to boot up. She opened a dozen files before she found it:

"Catherine Richardson/Little rich girl grows up? Angle? Fairy tale princess maybe?

At the age of twenty-five, and with no previous experience of running anything more than her busy social schedule, Catherine Richardson found herself at the helm of one the world's largest family owned conglomerates after her great-grandfather, James Richardson Sr, suddenly went into retirement two years ago (check date in file). Medical condition? Background on great-granddad? (see file) Bob the Wanker really in charge?

Cat's eyes were smarting as she tried to hold back tears of rage. Check file? What file? She had only found one document with her name in the computer. She looked wildly around the little desk. On the floor was a pile of black ring binders. Catherine pushed them over, spreading them out like dominoes on the carpet. The thickest one had *Cat* scrawled on it in black magic marker. Squatting down, Catherine opened it. The first item was a group picture taken at the meeting in Tokyo. It had been in all the Japanese newspapers but had not made it into the American press. Trembling, Cat flicked through the file. More photos, clippings, copies of documents and what looked like cancelled checks flew through her fingers. She was too upset to register anything more than the pictures. She had to get out of there. Catherine rearranged the pile into a stack, keeping her file aside.

As she stood up her heart froze. The door in the loft was opening! She could hear someone coming in! In a blind panic Catherine tried to switch off the computer. It was taking too long! She scrambled under the table and pulled the plug out. Grabbing the file she tried to stuff it into her bag, but it was too big.

"Hello! Anybody home!" Trevor sang merrily through the doorway. "Nobody? Guess I forgot the lights again!"

Catherine quickly put the bulky file back on the top of the stack and turned to face Trevor as he came through the door. He meandered in holding a pile of envelopes and junk mail and stood sorting through them.

"Hi, Trevor!" Catherine said, keeping her voice as calm as she could.

Trevor looked up and his face registered shock before breaking into a huge smile. The envelopes fell fluttering to the floor as he opened his arms wide and shook his head.

"I can't fucking believe it! There I was crying into my beer and you were here all the time!" He staggered slightly as he walked up to her with his arms outstretched. Catherine could smell the drink off him. He reached for her and then stopped and giggled.

"No! No groping! I promise," he said slapping himself on the wrist with a throaty laugh. "However, it is my duty to inform you that I am incredibly drunk *and* incredibly horny. Though seeing the former the latter could just be an illusion."

Catherine felt her confidence grow. He was drunk. He would be easy to handle. If she knew Trevor he would be passing out soon.

"So how much did you have to drink?" she asked, smiling seductively.

"I dunno. Lots of beer, little vodka, *un poco de tequila* just to keep the spirits up, ya know? Started, oh, five, maybe six hours ago. After I left you."

His face suddenly crumpled and he looked as if he was about to cry.

"I miss you, Cat," he said, pouting. "I miss you *sooo* much."

Catherine steeled herself against his puppy-dog eyes. He was a low-down piece of scum and she was going to make sure he burned in hell. She smiled warmly and

CRISTINA PISCO

put her arms on his shoulders, looking deep into his eyes until she felt she had him trapped. Then she leaned over and kissed him on the forehead.

"And I miss you too," she whispered, leading him to the bed.

Drunk as he was, Trevor still managed a few fumbling caresses before falling asleep in her arms. Cat untangled herself from his embrace and slipped soundlessly out of bed. Carrying her shoes in one hand, and the big binder in the other she crept down the stairs and out into the street.

Chapter Sixteen

◆

It was one o'clock in the morning before Catherine had read through the entire file, scrutinising every photograph, examining every document. She had sat in the corner of an all-night diner, drinking endless cups of bad coffee, ordering food and not eating it, stopping strange men from talking to her with one glance. She was wired, her head exploding from too much caffeine, too many questions, too many deceptions.

Catherine shook her packet of cigarettes and found it was empty. Carrying the binder under her arm, she walked up to the vending machine and fed it coins, hearing the satisfying clunk as they went down the slot, the noisy clatter as the fresh pack fell into the tray.

"Ya want some more coffee, honey?" said the waitress, eyeing her as she sat back down in the little red booth. Catherine nodded and then shook her head. Her mouth felt dry and her stomach was churning.

"No, thanks. I'll have a coke."

Catherine watched as the waitress sashayed over to the soda fountain, marvelling at the pink rayon uniform, heavy make-up and platinum blonde hair. *Rose* was embroidered over the large expanse of her right breast pocket. The harsh neon light was not kind. It only accentuated the fact that Rose had seen better days. Catherine wondered if she had once been pretty?

"More caffeine. That's not good for you," Rose said as she brought the glass of coke over. She pointed to the binder. "You studying? That's great. I would have loved to get an education."

Catherine nodded, both wishing that Rose would go away and grateful for the distraction. What she had read in the file had numbed her beyond her power to think straight. She offered the woman a cigarette.

"No thanks, sweetheart. I gave up fifteen years ago – thank God. My husband smoked sixty a day. That's what killed him. Though I should be grateful," she added with a dry laugh. "He was a real jerk."

Catherine smiled and reached for the coke. It tasted flat and too sweet. She opened the binder again to indicate that the chit-chat was over. The waitress shrugged and turned away.

"Don't work too hard," she said over her shoulder.

"A pretty girl like you should have a little fun. You're only young once!"

Cat looked out the window. A light rain had fallen, making the street slick and glistening in the lamplight. She watched an old man shuffle by, oblivious to anything but the forward motion of his own two feet. She was invisible sitting there, safe in her little booth. She wished she could stay in the diner forever. Cat let out a short sharp laugh. She would never have to go anywhere, or do anything. Rose would take care of her, providing endless cups of coffee and mountains of greasy food.

Cat lit a cigarette and checked her watch again, postponing the moment when she would have to make a decision.

The anger and disgust she had felt at Trevor's betrayal had been beaten down by one blow after another, as she went through the information he had accumulated on her. The binder had separate sections: one for her, another for Bob, a big one on her grandfather and the Richardson empire. There was even a small file labelled *Friends*: reviews of Ramon's, an obit on Valerie, a section on Fiona.

The one on Cat started with the picture she had seen in his kitchen. It had been taken at a charity ball. Trevor must have found the photographer and had him blow it up and crop it close for him. There were clippings of every mention of her in any newspaper or magazine that had ever appeared, including one from the East Hampton local paper when she had won a spelling bee in the 5th grade. Cat flipped the pages and watched as her life flicked past her in chronological order.

The section on Bob was more sinister and shocking. Someone had been following him around. Catherine wondered if Trevor had done the dirty deed himself, or if he had hired someone to do it for him. Whoever it was had got some excellent shots of Bob Stigeman that would be worth a pretty penny if they got into the wrong hands. If the pictures were anything to go by, Bob had a taste for the seedier side of New York, especially gay peep shows featuring pretty boys in bondage. He also seemed partial to cruising the streets and picking up young men. Not that it really mattered to Cat – she couldn't care less what turned him on. Much more shocking was the fact that Bob Stigeman was probably robbing her blind. Trevor had proof that Bob had travelled to the Cayman Islands at least six times in the last year alone. She doubted it was for a short weekend break. He was more than likely setting up numbered accounts to siphon off funds. But that did not hurt as much as the checks he had made out to Fiona. Catherine had no doubt in her mind that they were payment for spying on her.

When she thought she had seen the worse, Catherine

had found a long brown envelope attached to the binder.

She opened it again now and carefully picked out the documents inside, feeling the old yellowed paper, crumbly to the touch. Like a tarot reader, she spread them out in a semi-circle on the little Formica table.

The first was a copy of a birth certificate:

Catherine Kelly, born on September 9, 1966.
Central Maternity Hospital, Dublin.
Mother: Anne Kelly. Father: Unknown.

Catherine looked at the piece of paper and shook her head. It didn't make sense. Her father was James Richardson III, her mother was from Philadelphia, and she was not born in Dublin.

It was followed by a series of old newspaper clippings: mainly society page gossip. Each one had been highlighted in one section or another:

Annie Richardson was the Belle of the Spring ball . . . also attending was Anne Richardson . . . in a wonderful creation by French designer Givenchy, Anne Richardson . . . which Merry Widow got arrested in her flashy red sports car last weekend? We're not telling!

Catherine let her gaze drift through them all, delaying the moment when she would have to face the last piece of paper. Bracing herself, she picked up the small official-looking document.

It stated that Anne Kelly, born in Ireland in 1950,

was to be committed to the Mayfair Institute, Connecticut, for her own safety. It was signed by the presiding doctor, a judge, and her grandfather. It was a committal order made out to the name of her mother.

And it was dated November 1969.

But if her mother had died in a drowning accident in the Hamptons right before her third birthday, how could she have been committed to an institution in Connecticut two months later?

Catherine looked at her watch again and lit another cigarette, oblivious to the fact that she still had one smouldering in the ashtray. If she left now she could be in Connecticut in four hours. She was dead tired, but it was nothing that a quick line of coke couldn't solve. Her head was pounding. She would stop by the 24-hour drugstore near the garage where she kept her car and pick up some Tylenol. They'd have food and drink as well. Diet pills to keep awake. She'd need them all to drive. The Interstate 95 should be pretty easy going at this time of night. She could get a map once she got to the State border. Hell, if she made good time, she'd get there way before the Institute was open. Maybe she could even grab a few hours sleep in a nearby motel.

Catherine stood up and stubbed out both cigarettes. She carefully put the documents back in the envelope and picked up the binder. Rose waved as she headed for the door.

"You calling it quits for tonight, honey?" she called out. Catherine nodded. "That's good. You look like you could use some sleep. But remember what I said — don't work too hard! You're only young once!"

Catherine hesitated, her hand on the door. She didn't want to leave Rose and her never-ending stream of comforting coffee and platitudes. She was scared to walk out into the great unknown. She was scared of what she might find. Maybe she should just go home and forget about it. Burn the file, take a bath, and go to bed.

"You OK, honey? You want something else?"

Cat didn't bother to answer. She pushed the door and slipped out into the street. The air tasted damp and metallic. The rain was slick and oily, and Cat shivered as she willed her feet to hit the pavement. Up a block she saw a cab slowly cruising the street, its lights reflected in the black pools on the road.

Cat stepped out into the road and waved it down, hugging the black binder to her chest.

Chapter Seventeen

• • •

"The doctor will see you as soon as he has finished his rounds." The nurse eyed her suspiciously as she led Catherine into a sparsely furnished office. "You can wait here. He won't be long."

Catherine looked around. A solid plain desk and a huge old swivel-chair dominated the room. The walls were painted a dull beige, only a shade lighter than the worn grey linoleum. Someone had made an attempt at decoration and hung a small framed postcard which looked lost on the wide blank wall. The colours were fading, melting into blues and greens. It showed a man in lederhosen in front of a wooden chalet. On the balcony a young Fraulein in pigtails and a checked gingham dress was reaching up to ring an enormous cow-bell hanging from the rafters. Switzerland circa

1960, thought Cat, immediately calculating. Her mother had been ten. It was six years before her own birth. Cat's hand flew up and covered her mouth as she gasped. Her mother had been sixteen when she was born!

Dublin. Father: unknown. Mother: Anne Kelly.

Two straight-backed chairs sat in front of the desk. Catherine chose the one on the right and sat down. She wondered if she could get a cup of coffee anywhere, but the intimidating squeak of the nurse's crepe-sole shoes were already fading in the distance.

Cat had made good time from New York, arriving dazed and glassy-eyed in front of the big iron gates of the Institute before dawn. She could make out a gravel drive across an expanse of lawn. It led up to a large two-story red-brick building. Around the back she saw a few modern pre-fab buildings. Her head was still buzzing with the mantra that had pursued her as she drove through the night, cutting in and out of her consciousness but always buzzing somewhere in the back of her mind: *Dublin. Father: Unknown. Who was arrested? For her own safety. In a wonderful creation by French designer Givenchy. Central Maternity Hospital. Mother: Anne Kelly. Committed. Born in Dublin. November 1969.*

Too tired to go looking for a motel, she pulled around the corner and went to sleep in her car. Dates floated back and forth in her mind. She saw the woman beckoning her while Trevor stood behind her. A magpie landed on the hood of the car and winked. She sorted through the red jewellery box and put on the old necklace. The jewellery jingle-jangled.

She woke to sound of clinking. Lifting her head, she saw a large milk truck turn the corner and stop in front of the Institute gates. It was eight o'clock. Her neck hurt, her head was groggy and her mouth tasted like an ashtray. Cat caught a glance of her blood-shot eyes in the rear-view mirror. Better find a place to clean up, she thought.

The only thing open on the one-street town of Burton, Connecticut was a small diner. *Sol's place! Home of Sol's famous Pickle Pie!* blinked on and off at her as she pulled up between two pick-up trucks. She'd ordered the "Farm-hand Breakfast", but when it was served she found she could hardly bear to look at it, much less eat it. Cat forced herself to eat as much of the pancakes as she could, pushing the eggs and bacon to the edge of the plate in disgust. She washed up in the tiny toilet, and made herself more or less presentable. She wished she'd thought of a change of clothes before dashing off into the night. Thank God she had some makeup and eye-drops in her bag. Her white T-shirt looked a bit shoddy, but she had a suede jacket she kept in the car which would cover it up. She took out her little pill box. Two yellows and one blue pill nestled in the twist of paper that contained the last of her coke. She threw the pills into the toilet and flushed. So what if the nightmares might come back? She wasn't planning on sleeping.

A door slammed somewhere above her and Cat jumped. Not for the first time she wondered if she had any idea what she was getting herself into. It was hard to think straight. Other thoughts kept distracting her. The bright sun streaming through the window made the night before seem like a bad dream. But the black binder sitting on her lap was very real, as was the small committal order she now placed on the desk in front of her. Cat blinked hard, trying to wake up some more. It was almost eleven o'clock in the morning and the line of coke she'd snorted in the diner was starting to fade, leaving a nasty lingering buzz. She was wired and sleepy at the same time. She'd told her story three times so far. Once to the receptionist and twice to the suspicious nurse.

I want to know about Anne Kelly who was committed to this institution in 1969. I am Catherine Richardson, her daughter. She saw no reason to lie.

Steps were echoing down the hall towards her. Catherine's heart jumped a beat as the door swung open and a tall, man in a white coat swept into the room.

"I must say that this is rather unusual. But I have no problem with it," he said as he leafed through a large box file. "You are Miss Richardson, I presume? Anne Kelly is the maiden name, of course. Unusual that, but not unheard of," he added, looking over his glasses at her. Cat nodded. He had incredibly big hands with long elegant fingers. She wondered if he played the piano.

"I'm Dr Jacobs. All this goes back a while, now. Long before my time, though I know the case well. November 1969. Funny that," he said looking up and smiling, "that's the year I qualified."

She watched his hands as he turned the pages. There was something terrible about the way his long fingers caressed the paper. Something was terribly, terribly wrong and this kindly-looking older gentleman didn't know it. He didn't care, because he couldn't. He'd never learnt how.

"As I said it is highly unusual but as you are her daughter you have every right to see her," he said, putting down the file and smiling politely.

"See her? What do you mean see her?"

Alive? She was alive? It had never occurred to her that her mother was still alive. *Central Maternity Hospital, Dublin. For her own safety.*

Cat felt a trembling start in the pit of her belly. She looked down, sure that her legs were shaking.

How can she still be alive?

"You may visit if you wish, though you may want to reconsider. It could be a shock."

Cat looked up at him wildly not understanding at first, hearing the words with a slight delay, as if his mouth was not in sync with his voice. Her hands were trembling so much that she slipped them under her legs. The binder fell on the floor with a clatter breaking through the whirring noise in her ears. She hastily bent down to pick it up, taking a deep gulp of air.

"A shock?" she snorted. Cat laughed. It sounded hollow and brassy and out of place.

Not half the shock of finding out that she's still alive. Guess what? Your mother didn't drown – she was locked up in a loony bin. And she's still there! She isn't dead! She's still alive!

Cat felt peals of high-pitched laughter bubbling up inside her. She bit her lip and forced them away. The laughter in her ears stopped.

"Your mother is not well," he said lowering his voice and bending his long frame down towards her. "As you know, she has been here a long, long, time. You may not recognise her."

She waited a few seconds, looking the doctor full in the face. He stood smiling benevolently, his eyes behind his glasses reassuring her to take her time. He had the type of kind features that had laughed a lot. But they were the wrinkles of too many forced smiles. Hundreds of smiles, smiled benevolently at hundreds of different people as he announced horrible things. Terrible things. He was a little man who spent his life pretending he had a big heart, but was more worried that the proper procedure had been followed than anything else.

"I was told that my mother had died when I was three," she said coldly.

"Oh, dear. This is indeed unusual. But then again her committal to this institution is of public record, as you know," he said pointing to the paper on the desk.

That's right, you coward. Make it perfectly clear that it has nothing to do with you.

Cat suddenly thought of Trevor. "Has anyone come to visit her recently?" she asked.

If she had found this place Trevor certainly could. *How long would it take him to miss the file? Did he know Anne Kelly was alive?* No way. There was no way he knew that her mother was alive. He could not have kept that from her. *Or was he going to use that information?*

"Well, let me see," said the doctor, pleased to have something official to do. He placed the box-file on the desk and opened it again. He ran a long index finger across a few pages and closed the file coughing discreetly. "No. Not recently. Actually, you are the first visitor she has ever had."

Cat felt stuck to her seat. Her mouth formed a perfect O, but only a hissing sound escaped her lips. All thoughts of Trevor vanished.

Since 1969. Alone. All alone.

"She does receive a large fruit basket twice a year, on her birthday and at Christmas and over the years there have been a number of generous donations made in her name. Very generous indeed. Though not recently, I may add."

Prick. Is that the best you can do to soften the blow?

The doctor was clearly becoming agitated. His smile faded. His eyes took on a look that said this meeting was coming to a close. Cat bet he'd just figured out that whoever had lied to her must be the same one footing the bill all these years.

Not very quick, are we?

"Look, Miss Richardson, I know it sounds trite but sometimes one *does* have to be cruel to be kind. I'm sure that whoever told you that your mother had died felt it was the best thing for you."

"They told me she was dead," Cat repeated bluntly. "I was three years old and they told me my mother was dead." She watched the long fingers flutter aimlessly until they landed on his glasses. He took them off and coughed again.

"Before she came to us your mother had some very disruptive behaviour. Disturbing even. That must have been very upsetting for one so young." He put the glasses back on his nose and folded his arms, imprisoning the long fingers. "You were only three years old. You did not need to know."

"I do now," she said, not taking her eyes off him.

"Really, Miss, I'm not sure this is healthy." The fingers had escaped. They described circular patterns in the air. "You've had a serious shock already. It is perhaps enough for one day. Would you like a glass of water?"

"Tell me about my mother," she commanded.

The doctor looked at Cat for a few seconds and then shrugged.

"In the years before your mother came to us she had a few little problems, though her behaviour at first was considered just reckless. Your mother had quite a taste for parties, expensive dresses, fast cars, and such. She was stopped several times and finally arrested for drunk driving. When her licence was revoked she continued to drive. There was a serious alcohol problem. We had to wait until she dried out to see the extent of her syndrome truly appear. She was brought to us after a suicide attempt."

He paused and fidgeted. Cat said nothing, willing him to go on.

"She drank a bottle of scotch and walked into the sea. Someone saw her and dragged her out. She was very violent at the time. She had to be restrained."

The doctor sighed deeply and leaned on the desk. He seemed to take a silent decision. When he spoke again his voice was without emotion, as if he were reading out the phone book.

"Her mental condition deteriorated rapidly into dementia. She had recurring themes. Intense bouts of mania and paranoia. In her manic phases she would draw on anything with anything. She would not sleep until we took away the drawing materials. One night we found she had cut her finger and drawn on her walls in blood. She suffered intense paranoia. At its most severe only heavy sedation could give her relief. Both phases were coloured by very vivid Catholic imagery. The devil had her soul, that sort of thing. Rote praying for hours on end. She was delusional in the extreme."

"Was? Why do you say was?"

"We have made great progress over the last twenty years in Psychiatry. We are better able to manage patients with your mother's condition. Her life is far more comfortable now. We cannot treat the cause but we can make the symptoms less likely to appear. In the last ten years she has settled in. Her medication is quite strong. We regularly try to adjust it, but she can still become agitated at times. We try to screen her television viewing. It seems to help. But she has very limited contact with others. As the saying goes: she lives in a world of her own. We hope we have made it a less frightening place to be."

Catherine looked at his shoes. They were highly polished. Good solid brogues that had cost a lot but had already lasted a long time. She saw him sitting on the edge of the bed in his pyjamas holding up a shoe to the light as he polished it with long straight sweeps of the brush.

"This isn't your office," Cat said softly to herself.

"You are very perceptive. I only use this office very rarely. Mainly when admitting a new patient."

"You live alone."

"Yes!" he said, jerking his head. "But how could you tell?"

"Your shoes," she answered disregarding his look of surprise. He must think she was crazy. Maybe she was. *Delusional in the extreme. In a world of her own. She would draw on anything with anything. Intense paranoia.*

Cat leaned forward and opened the box-file. "Are any of her drawings in here?" she asked.

A look of alarm crossed the doctor's face. He quickly

replaced it with one of stern concern. "I'm not sure you should be reading –"

"Look, let me get one thing perfectly clear," she said cutting him off. "I am her daughter. More importantly, my great-grandfather, who put her in here in the first place and who has been paying the bills ever since, is out of the picture. He has been hooked up to a machine for the last two years. He can't talk, much less write. OK? So basically, I'm the one signing the checks and sending the fruit baskets."

Cat started laying the contents on the desk. She looked up at the doctor who was hovering, but who seemed to have accepted the change of command.

"I'm sure you are a very busy man. I would hate to take up any more of your time. Why don't you send someone to fetch me in about twenty minutes. Then they can take me to see her."

Cat did not look up as he left. She found what she wanted quickly. With trembling hands she took out a pile of loose-leaf pages, handling them gingerly as if they could burn her fingers. She didn't look as she smoothed out the crinkly paper. She knew it had been crumpled up and thrown away once, long ago. Finally steeling herself she looked down and gagged.

The entire page was covered in black and red. Who-ever had drawn this was very, very, angry. The rage still lifted off the page. Drawings of devils, crosses, words, and gross depictions of babies. Babies with horns. Babies consumed by flames. In some places the pictures and words had been so savagely crossed out that the pencil had punched a hole in the paper.

Every available space between the drawings was filled with tiny writing. Cat peered at the scribblings. Most were prayers written out in full. Others were lists of prayers like a discarded spiritual shopping list:

3 Hail Marys. 2 Our Fathers. 3 Hail Marys. Holy Mother of God help me. Jesus her Son, help me.

She would not cry. She could not cry now. Maybe later, but not now. Cat carefully put everything back in the box file and closed the lid. Then she sat back in her chair and waited.

They sent a different nurse to get her. She was a big, black woman with a happy round face which shone on the backdrop of her crisp white uniform. She chatted all the way down the long central corridor, out a side entrance and across the lawn to a low prefab building with big windows which overlooked the grounds. Cat could see old people shuffling around in bathrobes while others sat in small groups.

"Your mama is in the day room. She seems to like to sit there for a few hours in the morning," said the nurse as they walked into the building. "I heard your story. It must be a shock for you, honey."

Cat nodded and looked away. The nurse seemed

disappointed that Cat was not going to feed her curiosity.

"She spends most of the day in Geriatrics, though she is not officially in that part of the Institute. She still sleeps in a secure ward," the nurse rattled on, suddenly stopping as if she might have said too much. She stole a quick glance at Cat. "It's better for her, honey. There are more staff on duty at night in case she needs something."

Cat nodded again and the nurse smiled broadly, relieved not to be at fault. Their footsteps echoed down the corridor as she followed the slow swing of the nurse's wide hips, their rhythm in sync with the squeak of her shoes. Cat saw her walking down the aisles of a late-night supermarket pushing a cart piled high with groceries.

The rooms along the corridor all had glass walls. They came to one where a solitary figure sat facing the big window. The nurse stopped in front of the door. Cat followed the nurse's eyes. Cat could only see a few wispy grey locks above the back of the wheelchair.

Is that her? She's so very small. She looks shrunken into her chair.

Cat reached out to open the door. The nurse put her big paw out to stop her. Cat pulled away, surprised by the heavy, warm, hand. It felt like soft bread dough.

Is that my mother? Why can't I see my mother?

The nurse was looking at her kindly, her big brown eyes soft with compassion. The nurse's lips were moving but Cat couldn't hear her.

Snap out of it!

"Are you all right?"

"I'm fine now," said Cat, her voice still unsteady.

Snap out of it now!

"You have to be strong now. Your mama spends her days staring out the window. She doesn't really talk much. In fact, I've been here six years and she has never recognised me yet." Cat let the nurse open the door and walk ahead of her. "What's your name, dear?" the nurse whispered.

"Catherine," Cat whispered back hoarsely. She followed the nurse as if she were wading through syrup, holding back a few steps as the nurse bent down over the shrivelled frame.

"Annie? Sweetie? We have a visitor today. Catherine came all the way to see you. Isn't that just great?"

The nurse gently turned the chair so that it would face the room. The old woman looked up, confused at the change in the view. She looked blankly at the nurse and then at Cat. Her face was soft as silk and crisscrossed with fine lines. Cat tried to recognise something in her features but could only focus on the woman's eyes. They were a very light blue, but no spark shone in them. They looked blankly around the room for a few seconds. Then they settled on a cup that lay on a small side table and stared at it.

"Would you like some more tea? Maybe Cathy here would like some too."

The woman stared at the cup.

Anne Kelly. My mother's name is Anne Kelly.

This stranger was Anne Kelly. Cat felt nothing. No love. No pain. Nothing. If that woman there had been her mother it was a long time ago. All that was left was a hollow husk.

"It's your daughter, Annie. It's Cathy? Katie? Your daughter?"

There was a faint stirring like the rustling of dead leaves. Cat's heart beat faster. The light blue eyes flashed for a second and then dulled. A whirring sound droned in Cat's ears. The tiny wrinkled hands lifted and then dropped back in her lap. This slight movement did not go unnoticed by the nurse.

"It's Katie. Your daughter," she repeated as she gently pushed Cat towards the wheelchair.

Cat's legs were made of lead. Her temples were throbbing.

The woman they said was her mother looked up at her. Cat reached a hand out and laid it on a bony shoulder, unable to speak. She flinched as she felt the skin under the thin robe.

The blue eyes locked with hers in a flash of recognition. Cat recoiled from the hate she saw reflected in those suddenly bright blue irises. The eyes grew wider, wilder. The corners of her mouth turned down before pursing up and spitting.

"Annie! Now that isn't very nice, is it? Why you want to do that to your little girl?" said the nurse fussing with the blanket that covered the old woman's lap. The nurse jumped back with a shriek as Anne Kelly slapped her hard and pushed her away. The wheelchair flew backwards with the force of the blow.

"*Hoor!*" Annie Kelly was pointing a long white finger at Cat. "A hoor like your mother and her mother, and her mother before her. All hoors! Devil's spawn. All the hoors are burning in hell." Her voice was hoarse and cracked, but something about it echoed in Cat's memory. The accent was coarse and harsh and very Irish. It chilled Cat's soul to hear it.

She was starting to pray now. "*Hail Mary full of grace, the Lord is with thee . . .*" The words tumbled out through tightly pursed lips, rolling over and over until they filled the room with a tangled web. Cat felt them spread out like tentacles grabbing her, wrapping her up tight. She couldn't move. She couldn't breathe. Cat tried to cover her ears but still she could hear her.

The nurse grabbed the wheelchair and turned it around. She wheeled it back over to the window.

Slowly the web loosened its grip. Annie was still praying but her eyes had become blank again as she looked out to the gardens.

"Oh dear," said the nurse, smoothing her uniform, "I'd better get the head nurse. Will you stay here, honey?" But Cat did not hear her. She was already out the door before the nurse turned to face her.

She managed to walk until she left the building. Then she broke into a run across the lawn.

Margarita was sitting in the main living-room, sipping a coffee and enjoying the sea view. Her housework was all done. The old man was comfortable. The day nurse had left early to do some shopping and the night nurse was not due for another hour. There was nothing to do until supper time. She was making *adobo*, a Filipino pork and chicken stew, for herself and Victor, but that wouldn't take long. The meat had been marinating all day. She only needed to boil it up and make some rice. Maybe she would have a little siesta right here on this comfortable sofa. After so many years of service, she deserved a small nap.

The sound of wheels screeching over the gravel made her jump up. A car door slammed. Who could that be? Someone was banging on the big front door. Margarita looked at her flowered house-dress and Chinese slippers. She had no time to change into her uniform. She just hoped it wasn't anyone important.

"Senorita Catherine! You should have called," cried Margarita, trying to hide her dress behind the big door. Cat did not notice her. She pushed her way in and headed for the central staircase.

"Would you like a coffee? Your grandfather is having his nap now, but he should be awake soon." Cat started up the stairs taking them two at a time. Margarita noticed that her hair looked dirty. There were dark circles under her eyes. "Senorita? Are you all right?"

Cat stopped in the middle of the staircase and turned around as if she'd only just noticed Margarita standing there, still holding the door. Cat's eyes darted around taking in the casual house-dress, the cup of coffee left on the hall table. Margarita squirmed under the probing gaze.

"Were you there the night my mother drowned?" she asked suddenly. The question caught Margarita by surprise. Her hand flew over her mouth and she shook her head vigorously.

"No, senorita," Margarita answered, shocked and confused. "We were not married then. I only came stateside in 1972."

Cat paused as if thinking hard about something. "But Victor was. Wasn't he? He was here the night my mother drowned."

Margarita nodded and dropped her eyes. She rummaged around in the big pockets of her house-dress and took out a hanky.

"Did he tell you what happened?"

"No!" Margarita insisted plaintively. Her fingers twisted the handkerchief round and round.

"Don't lie to me," hissed Cat.

Margarita sniffed loudly and blew her nose. She was scared. Where was Victor? Miss Catherine was staring at her fiercely.

"She went swimming," she recited, shooting quick furtive glances at Cat. "Victor tried to pull her out but he could not reach her. They never found the body. That is why we have the memorial in the garden."

"Is that what he told you? Is it?" Cat barked. She heard the shrillness in her voice, saw Margarita shiver with the sharpness of it. Margarita opened her mouth and closed it again several times before speaking.

"Please, *senorita,*" she whimpered. "I have been good to you. It was a long time ago. Your mother is happy now. She is in heaven."

"Don't lie to me! I just saw my mother. She's alive. She's only in her forties and she looks like she's my grandmother! She's not in heaven – she's been locked up in an insane asylum for years in her own private hell!"

Margarita was crying. She didn't understand what Miss Catherine was saying. Her round black eyes disappeared behind her cheeks as her face scrunched up. She was holding the hanky out in a melodramatic gesture and babbling something in her native Tagalog.

"Tell me what you know, or you're fired," hissed Cat.

Margarita's round black eyes shot open. She blew her nose loudly. The tears stopped. She hung her head and sighed.

"Victor said she was always acting crazy, always drinking, running away. They had to lock her up in her room. She got out and went down to the sea. Victor pulled her out of the water but she kept fighting. She was screaming and biting, senorita." Margarita started crying again. "She bit Victor on the arm. He still has the scar. The ambulance took her. She never came back. She was dead. They said she was dead."

Cat knew she was telling the truth. Victor and Margarita had no part in the sordid little secret. It was her grandfather alone who was responsible.

A discreet cough made Cat look up to the end of the long hall. Victor was standing in a doorway. He was wearing his dress pants and a net singlet. He hadn't been expecting visitors either. Cat saw his shirt and tie hanging on a kitchen chair. Victor stared at his wife. He was angry, fuming at Margarita for having told her, but he had nothing more to reveal. Cat knew more than Victor knew. Only one other person in the house knew more. Her grandfather had signed the committal order. He had told everyone Anne Kelly Richardson was dead.

Cat started back up the stairs. Behind her she heard Victor and Margarita arguing in Tagalog. The clipped harsh consonants mimicked the click of her boots as she ran up the stairs.

Cat stopped on the landing. She paused for a minute, disoriented to find herself at the top of the house. Where was she going? Her grandfather was on the ground floor of the west wing. They had turned the place into a luxury hospital room. If she was going to see her grandfather, why did she run up the stairs? She could hear Victor and Margarita pause in their argument, and listen to what she was doing. Cat started walking to get out of view.

She had driven all the way down from Connecticut in a daze. She just managed to keep her mind clear enough to watch the road. She could think of little else. She drove with a terrible purpose. Foot jammed on the accelerator so that she could get there sooner. Time suspended until she felt the crunch of the gravel on the drive. Then she would jump out of the car, up to the big oak door, get into the house, and run up the stairs. The image of herself running up the stairs kept her going mile after mile. It was as if the moment when she would get home and run up the stairs was her final destination as she followed the long black strip of road.

But where was she running *to*? She had imagined she was going to see her grandfather. Had rehearsed speeches. Had she totally forgotten he could barely make eye contact?

Cat came to a stop at the end of the corridor. She was at the top of the east wing. She turned the corner and shivered. A cold blast of air blew through her. Cat leaned heavily against the wall. Her head ached. She was exhausted. It dawned on her that she had been here before. Something had made her return. She saw herself run up the stairs, down the east wing hall and into that room. She knew she would go down this corridor again. Down to the room. She stalled, delaying the moment.

Cat hugged herself, crossing her arms around the suede jacket, and took a step forward. She remembered the last time she'd been up here. The soft sound of running footsteps, the shadow darting behind the door, the magpie turning its head to look at her. Cat did not want to go back there but her feet continued to walk down the hall.

She stopped apprehensively in front of the room, as if testing the air. This was not like the last time. She was not afraid this time. Somehow she felt she was no longer afraid of anything. Somewhere faraway she heard the echo of a lullaby. It was sweet and sad but Cat could not make out the words, though she knew the tune. She closed her eyes and hummed along, feeling her breathing slow down, her features relax. She felt a stab pinch her heart as she suddenly remembered the smell of her mother's perfume as she bent over her bed and sang her to sleep. But behind the pain a voice told her to let go. To stop resisting. To let herself remember.

Cat took a deep breath. Emptiness surrounded her like a bubble and cushioned her emotions. She let herself remember the sound of her mother's laughter as they made faces at each other, the feel of her hand holding Cat's as they ran into the sea, her mother catching her by the arms and swinging her around and around.

She was not afraid, and she did not feel alone. But she was sad. Infinitely sad with a sadness that has no tears. Only empty blankness. She heard faraway voices. They were so faint she could not tell if it was just a distortion of her own rapid breathing, or maybe a trick of the wind and the sea heard through the window. Voices were shouting. She could hear her mother yelling. Doors slamming.

She reached out and opened the door, smelling the scent of lavender.

The woman stood by the chimney. She smiled. She seemed happy and relaxed. Cat could clearly see her face. The light blue eyes sparkled with love and concern. But this was not her mother. Cat blinked and she was gone. The echo of voices receded.

Cat opened her eyes and sighed with relief. It was an ordinary, normal, spare room. There was no ghostly fire in the grate this time. No magpies. The shutters were open and the golden late afternoon sunlight shone brightly on the overblown chintz roses of the furnishings.

There were boxes stacked in the corner. Cat realised they must have stored some of the things from the West Side apartment. She opened the first one knowing perfectly well what she would find. The red jewellery box was near the top, carefully wrapped in tissue paper. She took it out, feeling the depth of her tiredness like a heavy chain around her shoulders. She hadn't changed her clothes in two days. She'd slept in her car. She'd had enough shocks in the last forty-eight hours to last a lifetime. She was probably off her head. No wonder she couldn't think straight.

Cat's gaze drifted across the room. It came to rest at the foot of the four-poster bed. A great feeling of calm swept over her. She lay the jewellery box at her feet and crossed the room. On her knees she lifted the silky Persian carpet. The dark oak floorboards shone from years of waxing. Cat started tapping the floor, running her fingers across the grooves. Just behind the ball and claw foot of the bed was a smallish section which seemed loose. Cat got down on the floor. The section lifted off easily Her fingers immediately brushed something hard. It felt like a book. Cat twisted her wrist painfully trying to get it out. It was a notebook, or ledger, covered in red fake leather. Cat knew at once that it had belonged to her mother.

Cat opened it and a photograph fell out. She held it up to the light. She had never seen a picture of her parents together before. But there was no denying that the two lovers smiling at the camera were her parents. Both of them. Anne Kelly and James Richardson III. Behind them the spires of a church rose into the cloudless skies. There was horse-drawn cart to the left of them, and a little ratty-looking kid in the background. They looked so happy, so young. Cat felt a surge of violent anger like a wave rearing up, threatening to crest, and then slowly subsiding.

She turned the photograph over. *Christchurch* was scrawled in bold blue ink right across the back. Below was added: *Dublin, 1966.*

She felt the rage threatening again. She had to leave. She had to get away. Cat put the picture back into the notebook. She opened the jewellery box and emptied it into chair, taking the old necklace and the thimble and leaving the rest.

*   *   *

Victor was waiting at the bottom of the stairs. He had changed into his uniform. "Will you be staying for dinner?" he asked politely as if nothing unusual had happened.

"No," said Cat running down the last few steps. "In fact, I am going away for a while. I just needed to pick up something. Please call Maria and tell her to lock up the West Side apartment. She can have a little holiday. I'll call before I return."

"Yes, Miss Catherine," said Victor, nodding slightly to indicate he had understood her instructions. "Margarita has gone to see if your grandfather is awake. Will you visit with him before you leave?"

"No," said Cat with such disgust that she saw Victor's impeccable facade crumple into a look of surprise.

Cat tore up the driveway, the squeal of the tyres making a satisfying release for her anger. Visit with him? If she saw her grandfather she would screech with rage. She would howl questions. Scream until his eyes grew wide. Until he finally connected. It would probably kill him. If he weren't already half-dead she'd turn the car around and hunt him down. But he was no use to her now. Neither for answers nor for revenge.

A flock of magpies flew off. Black and white. Blue green flash of feathers underneath. How apropos! thought Cat. She counted them: *one, for sorrow, two for joy, three for a girl, four for a boy*. She could not remember the rest. Did not remember but just knew her mother had taught her. Counting games. *"One two buckle my shoe . . ."* she sang loudly as she drove out onto the main road.

Cat stifled a giggle and felt a shiver run up her spine. She knew that if she started laughing she might never stop. She had to get a grip. She had to get away. Had to get some space. Have some time to think. She had too much to think about. She had to get away.

Cat forced herself to breathe slowly until she felt her racing pulse calm down. She checked her watch. If the traffic wasn't too bad she could make JFK by six o'clock.

Chapter Eighteen

◆━◆

The traffic was bad. The parking was worse. The pounding in her head worst of all. The neon lighting glared, shoving needles into her eyes. Crowds of people swayed through the huge departure hall, bumping suitcases into her shins, shoving hard shoulders against her back. The noise was appalling. Babies crying. PA's screeching static. The clang of a thousand trolleys protesting at being wheeled through this chaos.

Cat forced herself up to a free counter. To try and act normal.

Get a grip. Get a grip.

"May I help you, Miss?"

Long skinny guy. White shirt. Fake smile.

"I want to catch the next plane to London."

Get on the other side of the ocean. London is a hub.

You can go anywhere from there. You can wait and take the time to think. Just get away from here.

"I'm afraid you've missed the British Airways flights and the American Airlines overnight is fully booked. The best I can do is tomorrow morning."

Long skinny guy smiling at the screen. Not even looking at her.

Cat went blank.

For one fraction of a heartbeat everything just blanked out. As if someone had pulled a plug on her senses. Then the panic started.

I have to get out. I HAVE to get out! I HAVE TO GET OUT!

"I have to get out of here! I have to get out as soon as possible!"

Cat jumped at the sound of her own voice. It was hoarse and cracked, as if she hadn't spoken in years.

Oh my God, you're really losing it now.

Long skinny guy's head snapped up from the keyboard and looked at her suspiciously. Cat was suddenly aware of her rumpled clothes, her unbrushed hair. No luggage, just a plastic bag she had picked up at a gas station. Inside were the black binder and the diary.

Long skinny guy thinks you're a nutcase. Deep breath. Get a grip.

"To London," she blurted. "I have to get to London by tomorrow."

Long skinny guy shrugged and fiddled at the keyboard, still pursing his lips as he looked at her.

"I have to get to my family as soon as possible," Cat added quickly. "There's been an accident. My brother died, and my mom really needs me."

"I'm sorry to hear that. Let me see what we can do." Skinny Guy's voice soft and comforting.

Better, that's better.

"What about through Paris? Or even Rome?"

Cities flashed through her mind: the Pont-Neuf bridge, the roar of traffic in a Piazza. Mind racing.

It doesn't matter where! Just get me out!

"Wait a minute!" Skinny Guy is happy. His fingers racing across the keyboard. *Nice hands.* Hope.

"I have an Aer Lingus leaving for Dublin in two hours. I have seats available in Economy. There's a stopover in Shannon, then a quick hop to Dublin. You get in at six o'clock local time and you have a connecting flight to London at eight."

Dublin? Dublin? Cat stifled a giggle. *Why the hell not?*

"Great. Thanks," she said, pulling out her credit card.

Waiting for the printout. Sign the tab. Take the ticket.

Cat forced a smile and turned back into the crowd.

Dublin?

She could get off the plane there. No one would find her in Dublin.

CATCH THE MAGPIE

And then what, Cat?

Cat stood in the middle of the big hall. People streamed off the escalator. They flooded through the automatic glass doors. Up the stairs. Out of the elevators. Walking fast. Speeding up. Beelines criss-crossing the hall.

Then what?

The floodgates of her mind started slowly to open. Cat could feel thoughts, ideas, images, plans, pain, all crowding to get out. The woman in the wheelchair screamed. Trevor turned in his sleep and nuzzled her neck. She could feel his breath on her skin. Feel the soft stubble on his chin.

Stop!

Her grandfather lay in a silent room. His mouth was open, eyes glassy as he stared at the beeping monitor by his side.

Stop it.

Bob. Fiona. Valerie. The doctor shrugged his shoulders and sighed.

Stop it!

Cat shuddered as she tried to keep the thoughts from tumbling out and rushing through her. If she let them, they would tear at her hair. They would run through this big hall screaming.

A soft hand squeezed her arm.

She snapped around and gasped. The black-haired

309

woman was standing right next to her, softly reassuring, patting her shoulder. The noisy airport melted away as Cat looked at the bare feet, the worn brown dress, the long black hair and bright, bright blue eyes.

She felt a sense of peace blow through her. It made her choke back the tears she could feel pooling behind her eyes. Cat wiped her eyes.

The woman was gone.

Cat stood quietly, breathing deeply as the bustling scene around her came back into focus. She straightened up and looked around.

She needed to stay awake for a few more hours. Then she could collapse. She had to eat. Maybe have a few drinks to help her come down slowly instead of crashing. Buy some clothes. Toiletries.

But first there was some stuff she had to do.

"Hello, this is a message for Fiona from Catherine. Fiona. I'm calling from the airport. I'm going away for awhile. I need a break. Cancel all my appointments for the next three weeks. I'll call you before then. Bye."

Cat hung up and dialled again. Tweedledee picked up on the first ring.

Cat told him to fire Bob Stigeman first thing in the morning.

Four . . .

Chapter Nineteen

◆◆◆

"Miss, would you like some dinner?"

Cat woke with a start. She'd fallen asleep the minute she'd taken her seat in the plane.

"No, thank you. Just coffee, please."

Cat switched on the over-head lamp. She flipped down the little table. Everyone was watching the movie. She watched the coloured images flicker across the screen.

Cat took out the photograph and propped it up in front of her.

Christchurch, Dublin 1966.

She waited until she had her coffee before opening the diary. The pencil marks were faded and smudged after years of lying unopened. Cat traced the writing with her fingertips. It was a sprawling childlike scrawl.

Her mother had bought this notebook. Had sharpened the pencil. Had carefully rounded the letters in an effort of good penmanship.

She started to read.

Dublin
December 15, 1965

Happy Birthday to me! Sixteen today – except that everyone here thinks I'm eighteen. It makes things easier. I can't believe it. Two weeks ago I was ready to throw myself into the sea and here I am, in Dublin, with a job and my own room. No one to tell me what to do, no busybody Auntie Mary snooping around. No more yelling, no more beatings. No more bloody rosaries for hours on your knees (maybe I should go to confession for that!). I'm free.

The chipper is hard work but Mrs O'Brien is really nice. I don't like himself much, but he's not around much. I can eat for free and they take the rent straight out of my wages so I don't have to worry

*about a thing. I got paid today! £4! I went looking
at the shops but I just couldn't make my mind up.
Bought this, two pencils and a topper.*

*My room is just above the shop. I have a bed and
a chair and a little table. I even have my own gas
fire. I'm going to make the place more cosy. If I stick
my head out the window I can see the spire on Christchurch and a bit of Dublin Castle. I'm in Dublin!!*

*I wonder what the nasty old wasp would say if she
saw me now!*

Annie Kelly closed the little red notebook with pride.
It was the first thing she had ever bought for herself,
with her own money.

She'd walked all the way up Henry Street, feeling
the comforting weight of her wages jangle in her
pocket. The shops were so full of enticing things to
buy she could hardly keep from giggling with delight
and pointing. In the end she had been too over-
whelmed by the choice to make up her mind. Besides,
she had to be careful with money. She was going to
save up. And when she had enough she would get as
far away from this Godforsaken Island as her money
would take her. There was no turning back now. Wild
horses couldn't drag her back to Kilkeam and that tiny,
damp cottage with no electricity, no radio, no nothing
except the rantings of the old woman.

She hated that miserable piece of rock open to the wind and rain half of the time, shrouded in fog the rest. When the sun came out you could see the sea shining in Bantry Bay and the purple Kerry mountains miles away. It was so beautiful it made you want to cry. But that was once a year and the rest of the 364 days you had enough to cry about just living there with that demented mean old woman. She was sorry she'd had to steal to get out, but she wasn't sorry about who she'd stole it from.

But that was all over now. Dublin was a great place to plan her escape. Who cared if the holes in her shoes let the cold rain in, as she peered into the bright shop windows and drooled at the pastries all laid out in Bewley's? That old hag would never beat her again. Or force her to say the rosary for hours on end. There would be no more screaming that she was cursed. No more looking over her shoulder to see if the old bat was coming up behind her. No more hearing how grateful she should be for the little she had, how a less kind person would have turned her back on an unwanted child. "A right hoor your mother was, in her fancy clothes and make up, with a two-year-old child and not a husband in sight."

No more whispers behind her back. No more laughing giggles when she went to the village shop. No one in Dublin knew or cared a toss that her mother ran away to London, came back with a child, and ran away again. She was Anne Kelly and she had a job and a room of her own. On her way home Annie stopped off at the Pro-Cathedral. She lit a candle to the Virgin of Perpetual Succour and thanked her for having helped her this far. She spent almost as long looking into the shop window of an electrical appliance shop watching the telly. She'd never seen one before. Annie knew a lot of the pubs had a telly, but she was too scared to go in on her own. She promised to take herself to the pictures on her first day off.

Annie checked herself in the tiny mirror over the little basin that was hidden behind a faded curtain. She checked twice that the door was locked before going out. She daren't admit it, but being alone in Dublin scared her as much as it delighted her. She saw more people in one evening working at the chipper than she would have in a whole week in Kilkeam, bar Mass on Sunday. Going to Bantry market was a rare treat, and she had never even been up to Cork city before she stole the money in her Auntie's jam-jar and headed for the capital.

Her room was right above the chipper but she had to go back out to the street to get into the shop. A cold blast of icy rain pierced her thin blouse as she stepped outside. Dublin was a lot colder than home. No, she thought, this is home now. She should think about buying a proper coat.

It was hot in the shop. On cold days the shop-front window would get steamed up, blurring the view of the street. Annie got stuck into it right away. She was soon up to her elbows mixing up the batter for the fish and batter burgers in a huge vat. She was working with Jeannie who usually worked the night shift. Jeannie was an older woman with bleached-blonde hair piled on the top of her head and a fringe. She wore masses of make-up and had a different outfit every day under her apron. She was a native of the city. "Dublin born, bred and buttered," she declared in her thick Dub accent to anyone who cared to hear. Jeannie was always cracking jokes about the customers, her cackle of a laugh filling the tiny shop. Annie really enjoyed her company though some of the stories about the late night-shift scared her senseless. She didn't know how Jeannie could just laugh at what some of the men said or did. The mouth on that woman was a shock.

"Oy, Annie," Jeannie hissed in a loud whisper, "Look at wha' just walked in. Santy's come early."

Annie looked up to see a tall young man with longer than usual black hair. He was wearing a paint-splattered shirt and trousers under his black donkey jacket. He looked straight at her and smiled.

Annie was rooted to the spot, mesmerised by the

strong line of his jaw, the dark blue (almost purple) of his eyes which sparkled as if he was remembering a funny incident as he looked at her.

Jeannie prodded her in the back, whispering. "G'wan. Or I'll take him for meself."

Annie blushed as she took his order and was thankful to be able to turn away as she prepared it. Jeannie kept up a constant barrage of questions, flirting outrageously. The young man answered cheerfully, taking Jeannie's remarks on the cuff and coming back with witty retorts while all the time keeping his eyes on Annie as she worked.

By the time she'd dipped the cod into the batter and carefully slid it into the boiling oil she knew he was an American. By the time she shook out the chips, fried to a golden perfection, she knew he was a student at Trinity on a study abroad scheme. By the time she handed him the carefully wrapped up fish and chips ("No vinegar, please. Lots of salt, thank you.") and dropped his 1s3d into the till she knew she was in love.

"I think that wan fancies you," said Jeannie dead pleased with her matchmaking skills. "You'll hafta get some new clothes now, girl. He's a real catch. I can tell."

Annie blushed and made a quick silent prayer that Jeannie was right.

CRISTINA PISCO

December 20, 1965

*I bought a radio. Jeannie calls it a tranny. I am
so thrilled to have it. Even second-hand it cost me
half my wages, but it was worth it. I love to listen to
the radio in the evening. When the gas fire is going
and I'm safely locked inside my room I feel so happy
I could cry. I also bought a skirt, some shoes and a
new jumper. It's soft and fuzzy and pink and I love
it to bits (Jeannie thinks I should buy some pink
lipstick to match but I'm not sure about that yet.). It
looks like something Twiggy would wear. I read all
about her in the magazine Jeannie gave me. She
buys loads of magazines and gives them to me after
she's finished. She also pushed me to buy the jumper
– bless her! The very first time I wore it James came
in (that's his name – James Richardson. From New
York!) and asked me when I got off work and if I
wanted to go for a walk!*

*He's been coming in every day this week for his
fish and chips. He has a studio where he paints just
across the road. When he told me he painted I
thought he was a house-painter, like. I felt a right
eejit when he told Jeannie he paints pictures. He said
he'd love to paint me! Fancy that!*

*We took a little walk around Christchurch
Cathedral. I hardly said anything at all. Not to worry,
James can talk up a storm. He knows everything*

*about everything. I swear he's like a walking book.
I could just sit and listen to him for hours on end.*

*I can't help thinking about him all the time. I'd
love him to be here now, sitting there by the fire. We
could just sit together and listen to the radio. And if
he tried to kiss me – I'd let him.*

Annie looked over to the little chair by the fire and
sighed with pleasure. Her eyes took on a glassy stare
as she imagined him sitting there. He would reach out
and lay a soft hand on her cheek. Maybe he'd brush a
lock of hair from her face before kissing her. Annie
sighed and shuddered with delight. Then she laughed.

"You are a sad eejit, Annie Kelly," she said out loud.
But she could not erase the smile on her face, nor could
she silence the thrill running through her each time she
thought of how James had taken her hand as if it was
the most natural thing in the world.

Jeannie had helped her set the new tranny to "the
best pirate radio station in the world: Radio Caroline."

It played a type of music Annie had never heard
before. Then again, what music have you ever heard,
Annie Kelly? she asked herself. Old sad songs that go
on and on for twenty verses, and hymns. The music
on Radio Caroline was happy and light. All the songs
were about being young and in love. Jeannie had it on
all the time in the chipper. Annie had listened wide-

eyed as Jeannie told her about the brave radio pirates who were out in the middle of the sea. James listened to it too! Annie loved all the popular songs, got to know all the DJ's, laughed at the jokes and sang along with the adverts. And now she could listen to it in the evening as well, on her own tranny.

The rain was lashing down outside, banging on her little window so hard that she had to put up the volume. Annie wondered if the same gale was blowing out wherever Radio Caroline was transmitting from. She listened to the music and thought of the lonely DJ sitting on his boat alone in the middle of the night. Annie thought the idea of a pirate radio was wildly romantic. She imagined James and herself, stranded on a little boat, madly in love as they sailed away together.

The voice of the DJ interrupted her reverie. The mention of Ireland jogged her back to her room above the chipper.

"And now a request from Ireland. And he's got to be really hung up on this girl 'cos it came in over the ship-to-shore radio here! It's from James to Annie in Christchurch, Dublin. So especially for two Dublin love-birds, the Searchers: with one of my fave hits: Here we go: NEEDLES AND PINS!"

Annie jumped up and down whooping and yelling, till the floorboards shook and she was sure they would hear her downstairs. She couldn't believe what she'd just heard! She knew the song well. Her heart was beating wildly as the first chords started playing.

"*I saw her today.*
I saw her face.
It was a face I loved."

She started to move like she'd seen Jeannie sway along to the music as she worked. Picking up the tranny she put the volume to maximum and held it close to her heart. She heard shouts in the street outside. The pubs must be closing and the night rush starting downstairs. But for the first time the harsh voices did not scare her. Annie closed her eyes and danced in the little space in front of her fire, singing her heart out as she clutched the radio.

"*Needles and pins.*
Needles and pins.
Needles and pins."

The next day Jeannie could talk of nothing else. She'd heard the dedication on Radio Caroline at home the night before, and she told every customer that came in the whole story, embellishing it with every telling.

The chipper was packed with the lunch crowd and Jeannie and Annie were working flat out. Annie looked up and saw James slip in.

"There he is, lads. He's the one I was telling you

about," said Jeannie, pointing at James with a packet of fish and chips she'd just wrapped in paper. "That's the Romeo who dedicated a song to this Juliet over here."

The crowd of men applauded and whistled. James looked startled, but he quickly took in the scene and made a sweeping bow. Annie blushed furiously as the men clapped again.

Annie's eyes were sparkling as she asked James what his order was.

"I'm not having anything," he said, smiling. "I just dropped in to say Merry Christmas, a little early." His brow clouded for an instant before he smiled again. "I'm invited to visit with some friends of my parents for the holidays."

Jeannie cut in before Annie could answer. "G'wan. Take a break. I can handle this lot with one arm tied behind my back."

Annie ignored the men's lewd comments as she followed James out of the shop. The wind was bitterly cold after the sweatshop of the chipper. Annie shivered as they sheltered in a doorway.

"That *was* you then? On the radio? Jaysus, I can't believe you did that," she said.

James chuckled. "It took some doing," he said slyly. "But I managed to place a call to Radio Caroline."

"That must have cost a fortune!" exclaimed Annie

her hand flying up to cover her mouth. "Where'd ya find a phone?"

James just shrugged and shook his head. He pointed to a window on the top floor of the building across the little lane.

"See? That's my studio. I can see you when you go in and out to work. That's why I went into the chipper in the first place. I just had to meet you."

"You came in just because of me?" said Annie, her mouth dropping open again.

"I don't even like fish and chips," he said, laughing.

"You ate fish and chips and you don't even like them?" Annie laughed. She was entranced by the colour of his eyes. She couldn't stop looking at him.

"I didn't eat them!" he snorted in disgust. "No offence to your culinary skills, but at first I just threw them in the trash. Now, I give them to that kid on the street. You know the skinny one that's always begging on the corner of Dame Street. He's really rooting for this romance!"

Anne tried to answer but the combination of chattering teeth, wild giggles, and the flip-flop her stomach made at the mention of "this romance" made it impossible to speak. She hit him playfully instead and laughed, which set her teeth chattering even harder. James's eyes softened and Annie thought she might faint. He opened his coat and drew it around the two of them.

"I'm really sorry I have to go," he said, wrapping his arms around her. "I'll be back soon. I'll probably be bored stiff, but my parents would kill me if I didn't go. Dad and this guy go back a long way. Since before Harvard. And Mom thinks they're just wonderful, especially since he was appointed Ambassador over here. There's some big Embassy thing I have to go to with them, then we're out to the country for Christmas. There's no way I can get out of it. It was either that or go home, and I'm not going home a minute before I have to."

Annie didn't have a clue what he was going on about but she didn't care. She lay her cheek on his chest and shyly put her arms around his waist. The smell of him made her swoon.

"I'll call in as soon as I get back to Dublin," he said, cupping her chin. Then he kissed her softly.

Annie could still feel the tingle on her lips as she went back to work. She almost dipped a portion of chips in batter by mistake. It was a good while before the magic of his kiss wore off.

Then it hit her. He was gone! She wanted to run out into the street after him. She fought back the tears stinging her eyes and pretended to be busy under the counter.

He said he'd be back. In a few days, he'll be back, she thought. She calmed her aching heart and settled into reliving the ecstasy of that kiss. That's what she would do. She would daydream about kissing James until he came back. The days would pass so fast that before she knew it she would be back in his arms.

Except that a few days turned into a week, and a week into two weeks.

By the third week Annie had stopped crying herself to sleep, but even Jeannie's jokes couldn't raise a smile on her.

December 31, 1965–1966

I can't believe that bollocks is making me work tonight. I'm dead tired from the day shift as it is. I haven't written since J left. I haven't done much except work and sleep. Jeannie is down with the flu and Mrs O'Brien isn't well so I'm supposed to work the night shift tonight. I can't bloody well believe it! New Year's Eve no less. The night when every drunken bollocks can do as he pleases. Mr O'B promised to help but Jeannie's told me about him. He goes off for a couple, and promises to be back before the pubs close, but sometimes he doesn't make it. And Jeannie has said to watch him if he has a few jars in him. What will I do if he tries anything with me? Happy New Year, my arse.

Annie could think of nothing else to write. She closed the notebook and pushed it aside. She watched the hands of the clock ticking. It was nearly closing time and there was still no sign of Mr O'Brien who had slipped out "for a quick one" saying, "There's a good girl, you mind the shop. I'll be back before the rush to give ya a hand."

There was still ten minutes before closing but Annie was getting worried. She'd heard singing and roaring on the street most of the night. The few customers she'd served so far all looked pretty well-locked already. She hated to think what the crowd would be like that was going to throng through those doors in less than ten minutes.

She had everything ready. The batter was glistening in the big vat. The fish was laid out ready to be dipped. The chips had already been blanched in the big galvanised tub and she'd carefully stacked a larger than usual pile of paper for swift wrapping.

Annie stood hugging herself behind the counter listening to the street, jumping at every drunken yell. She tried to concentrate on Radio Caroline playing softly behind her. She had her back turned when the door burst open, letting in a bitterly cold blast of air.

She turned and faced her worst nightmare. Four lads swayed in each other arms. Four big drunken lads. One of them had a cut over one eye, but he was grinning like an eejit. Whatever had happened to him, he was past caring.

The four stood smiling stupidly as they read the menu above Annie's head. Then one by one they looked down and noticed her standing there. Their smiles got wider, showing their teeth. They did nothing to hide the fact that they were leering at her from head to foot.

"There's just one thing a man wants," echoed through Annie's mind. The old woman lay in her bed near the fire, her long stringy grey hair shining on the pillow as Annie brushed it. "And if he thinks there's any chance he'll get it – he'll just take it! You'd do well to keep away from them all together like I have or you'll end up a hoor, and burn in hell like your mother."

Annie shuddered and held her arms crossed tightly across her chest. She tried to put on a brave smile but failed miserably. Instead she took a step forward and asked them timidly what they were having. The men exploded into raucous laughter which made Annie jump back.

"Isn't she a pretty little thing?" asked one pointing an unsteady finger at Annie. Then he belched loudly, making them all laugh again.

"Up from the country, are ya?" leered a second. "What you need is a good Dublin man to show ya around. Teach ya the ropes."

The one with the cut found that hilariously funny. He was bent over giggling, but he kept his eyes locked on her.

She checked the clock. Five minutes to go. Maybe more. It was New Year's Eve after all, and the pubs would take a while to clear. She prayed desperately that someone would come in. Anyone.

Annie thought of Jeannie, the way she handled troublemakers with one swift glance. Annie uncrossed her arms and put her hands on her hips as she'd seen Jeannie do.

"Now so," she said trying to control the quiver in her voice. "What is it you want?"

The first man was behind the counter before Annie could get out. He moved fast for a man who probably had well over ten pints in him. He grabbed at Annie and pulled her up close to him. Annie heard the sound of her apron ripping as she strained away. She could smell his beery breath as he pulled her close.

"How's about a New Year's kiss?" he said pursing his lips grotesquely. The three others clapped and hooted as Annie struggled to avoid his mouth. No one noticed the door open and close.

"Excuse me," said a clipped American accent, "but can I get some service here? I know it's New Year's Eve but I'm starving!"

The man turned to face James who was looking

straight at him. He had a big friendly grin but he stood
with his feet apart and his eyes had a cold angry glint
in them. The other three men dropped back to watch
them. Annie held her breath for what must have only
been seconds but which felt like an eternity. Then the
man laughed and let her go. He walked around and
slapped the counter.

"Four chips then!" he shouted happily.

Annie plucked at her blouse trying to readjust her
clothes. Her fingers found a broken apron-string and
stared at it blankly. She looked up and stared at James,
not understanding what he was doing there. Not understanding anything.

"Get the order, Annie," James said softly, catching
her eyes and willing her to get on with it. Annie quickly
fried up the chips. She was wrapping them when Mr
O'Brien burst in singing "The Ol' Triangle". He always
sang when he'd had a few jars.

"Are ya right, lads?" he asked jovially. "It'll be the
New Year soon. 1966!"

James signalled Annie to join him. She slipped
quickly from behind the counter. James discreetly took
her hand.

"Happy New Year to you, sir," James said, patting
Mr O'Brien on the back. "Annie's leaving early. She's
had a scare on her own tonight. Thanks for coming
back."

And before Mr O'Brien could protest James had pushed past the people starting to come in and led Annie out of the shop. Behind her Annie could hear Mr O'Brien braying over the orders being shouted from the crowd filling up the chip shop.

"Right lads, now. One at a time, lads. One at a time."

The studio had no electricity. James lit a few candles which cast long shadows over the high ceiling. Big panes of glass in the roof let in the yellow lamplight. Shouts drifted up from the street below. Far off someone was singing "Auld Lang Syne."

Annie couldn't stop shaking. She could still feel the harsh grip of the man's fingers as he bruised her shoulder. She could still smell his beery breath. She clung to James, barely aware that she was safe. That he was back.

What would that man have done if James hadn't come in? Annie had no doubt about his intentions. Her Aunty was right, she thought. Men were bad. They only wanted one thing.

But what about James? Wonderful James who had come in and rescued her like a Prince in a fairytale, who now held her close and softly stroked her hair, kissing the top of her head as if comforting a child.

"I managed to get back early by telling them I was

going to a big New Year's ball at Trinity," he said. "I'm so sorry I couldn't get back sooner."

"Is there really a ball at Trinity?" she asked breathlessly. She wanted to sink into his arms and melt away the sadness and fear. To never be scared again.

"Yeah, but it's going to be boring. I wanted to see you. I've thought of nothing else. I hate thinking of you alone, working in there."

James held her close and nuzzled her neck. Annie felt a thrill run from her neck to her toes.

"I'm in love with you, Annie," he breathed as his mouth searched for hers. His lips were soft and warm, so different from the harsh mouth that had pressed against her roughly. She could smell the drink off James as well, but it did not disgust her. She let the malt warmth replace the sharp sour smell of hops from the man in the chipper.

They sank down together as they kissed. James pulled her close until they lay side by side. Annie could feel something hard pushing up against her thigh which both excited and repulsed her.

Annie pulled away and then stopped. James was looking at her with a hurt and embarrassed expression on his face. But he could not disguise the hunger in his eyes.

He was the same as the rest and not the same. He

would never hurt her. He said he was in love with her. And she loved him more fiercely than anything she had ever loved before in her life. Annie steeled herself and made a decision. She sat up and pulled her pink jumper off.

"Are you sure?" James asked, his voice soft and gruff. Annie nodded. She was trembling as he pulled her down back into his arms.

Annie wasn't going to let some man on the street just reach out and grab her. She was going to choose who to give herself to. Better to choose than to have some man just take it. And as for choosing to end up like that sad old woman in her bed in Kilkeam.

Well, thought Annie, she'd rather burn in hell.

The next morning at work Annie couldn't look anyone in the eye. She felt ashamed of what they had done. She was sure everyone could tell by just looking at her. Jeannie teased her about her "Romeo" and Annie felt the shame burn inside her and rise to her cheeks. She knew that even Jeannie would be disgusted if she knew what they had done. Annie felt so guilty she had said an extra rosary at night.

Annie had no doubt that she was madly in love. She saw him every day and really enjoyed his company. She was only happy when she was with James, but she shied away when he tried to put his arm around her. James said nothing, though Annie saw his eyes cloud over as she pulled away. It was a week before they found themselves alone in the studio again.

Annie tried to calm her rising panic as they started to kiss. James was gentle and patient. He kissed her softly until he felt her relax in his arms. Then he slipped his hand in her blouse. Annie stiffened.

"What's the matter, Annie?" James asked, sounding hurt. Annie started to cry.

"Don't cry, Annie," James said. "I love you, baby. Don't cry. Whatever it is we'll do something about it. It can't be that bad."

Annie cried even harder.

"What is it? You can tell me."

"I can't," she sobbed, "We can't, you know, do that again. It's a sin."

"A sin? Who says two people loving each other is a sin?"

"I went to confession today. He said what we did was a sin. I'm doing penance. The priest said we must not do that anymore. I'm doing penance," she repeated. "One extra rosary a night."

James jumped up and started pacing. His face was grim, his mouth drawn in a tight thin line. He held his fists clenched at his sides as if to stop them striking out. Annie had never seen him so angry. He stomped around cursing and swearing.

"James, you're scaring me," Annie whimpered.

James stopped and looked at her. His face softened and he reached out for her again.

"I'm sorry. I never want to scare you. It just makes me so angry that anybody could make you feel ashamed of our love. What we did is natural. Love between a man and a woman is the most natural, beautiful thing in the world."

Annie shook her head. She could not look at him. "It's wrong, James. We're not married. It's wrong if we're not married. If you love me you'll understand."

"Is that it?" he said holding her at arms' length. She felt his arms trembling as his fingers gripped her shoulders tightly. "Is that what it takes, Annie? Well fine, I'll prove that I love you. Come on."

James grabbed her by the hand and dragged her outside. His face was determined as he scanned the cars. Then he was running into the street, pulling her along, to flag down the first taxi he saw turn the corner from Patrick Street.

"Where are we going?" Annie asked breathlessly as James guided her through the traffic to the waiting cab.

"We're taking the next ferry to Scotland. We're going to Gretna Green. We're going to get married."

Dublin, February 7, 1966.

I can't believe it's been a month since I last wrote in my diary. What a month!! I don't know where to start. Well, to begin with I am now Mrs James Richardson! I can't believe it! I'm so happy I feel like I've died and gone to heaven. James made me hand in my notice at the chipper and came with me because I was so scared. But everything turned out just fine when everyone heard that we'd just got married. Mr O'B took us all out for a drink to celebrate and James took pictures. Jeannie took a lovely one of us together outside Christchurch.

We're living in a lovely boarding-house just off Parnell Square. We have a bedroom and even a little sitting-room. It's run by Mrs Barry, who is a widow from Cork. She's been a bit nosy about my people but I've managed to put her off so far. The last thing I want to talk about is that miserable place, with its curses and lies. She's got a good heart, so she doesn't push – and she makes the best scones I've ever tasted. Who's cursed now? I'm living in the lap of luxury with the most wonderful husband in the world in a lovely place where even the walls have flowers on them!

James takes me shopping every day after he gets off from class. And every evening we go out to dinner and dancing. He says that now that I'm his wife I deserve only the best. I've more clothes now than I've had in my entire life! Coats with matching scarves and gloves, piles of shoes, and even trousers!

At first I was scared going into the fancy shops on Grafton Street, but James made it easy. I even got my hair done in a salon! It's cut in a short bob and the girl also helped me try some make-up for my new "look".

Sometimes I worry about how much this is costing, but James won't hear of it He says his parents have more money than sense. I keep asking him when he is going to tell them about us, but he says that they don't deserve to know. I'm scared when he talks like that. He seems so angry. He says his mother is only interested in parties and his father is only interested in money. The only person he has ever talked of kindly is his grandfather. He says he doesn't care what his parents think but that he does not want to disappoint his grandfather. All I can think is how wonderful it must be to have a family – even if you hate them.

A knock interrupted her as she wrote. Mrs Barry's soft Cork accent called to her from the hallway.

"Annie, pet? Will you come downstairs? I've something to show you."

She put away the diary and checked her reflection

in the mirror before opening the door. As every time she looked at herself these days, she could hardly believe what she saw. Her black hair bounced in a sleek straight line at her jaw in a way that made the frosted pink of her lipstick even shinier. Annie smoothed the skirt of her mini-dress. It was covered in pink, green, yellow and orange swirls, with a high collar and tight sleeves that flared out at the wrist. Annie loved it. They'd bought it the day before along with smart plastic boots that came up to her knees.

At the front door Mrs Barry told her to close her eyes.

"Don't open them until I lead you outside. It's a surprise," she said, hardly containing her excitement.

Annie opened her eyes on Mrs Barry's cue and shrieked. James was sitting proudly on a bright red scooter, grinning from ear to ear.

"Like the wheels, babe?" he asked patting the seat behind him.

Annie whooped in delight and ran down. She jumped on, hugging him close. They went around Parnell Place twice before zipping into O'Connell Street. Annie found it easy to move with him as he bobbed in and out of the traffic. This was heaven. She loved holding him, feeling the ripples of his muscles in his back. Why couldn't it be just like this always? she thought. James was patient and rarely made demands on her. He said that she would get used to it, that one day she would feel the same pleasure in their love-making as he did. But Annie doubted it. As soon as she saw that look in James' eyes that said she was not going to be able to put him off, she just blanked out her mind and hoped he'd get it over as soon as possible. She would steel herself and try to blank out the memories of farm animals mating in the fields as James shuddered on top of her. The thought that Mrs Barry might know what they got up to in their room made her blush bright red.

But it was easy to forget. Especially when you were young and free and speeding down O'Connell Street passing all the cars and buses. James jumped the light and they sped across the bridge way ahead of any other traffic. Annie looked down the river to the Halfpenny Bridge. The sharp spring sun bounced off the rooftops around her making even the shabbiest building look like a palace. It was a beautiful day and all of Dublin was out to enjoy it.

Annie felt everyone on the street watch them with envy as they zoomed by: the bright red scooter, the handsome young man with his fashionably long hair, and the mini-skirted young woman perched on the back, her short bob bouncing in the wind. Annie felt like she was living in one of those pop songs she loved so much.

James had bought a record player and they spent

hours listening to music in their room. James teased her about her musical tastes and tried to get her to listen to more "serious" music like that song "Universal Soldier", which he played over and over again. He could get quite worked up about it all. He could talk all night about War and the Establishment, and Dropping Out. Annie just smiled. She was happy just to sit back and listen to him talk. She didn't see what any of it had to do with them.

James slowed the scooter as they came into Stephen's Green. He cut the engine and wheeled it into the park to the nearest bench. As they sat down he produced a double-size chocolate bar. He knew Annie's passion for chocolate. She grabbed it greedily. Annie had also been eating more than ever before in the last month. Some of her new skirts and trousers were getting a bit tight.

"I just love the scooter," she said happily between bites of chocolate.

"Yeah, so do I," James said, shaking his head sadly. "It's too bad I've got to give it back to the garage."

Annie finished the bar and looked at him. He looked miserable.

"It's all right. I don't mind if you give it back," she said cheerfully. "It was great just to go for a spin."

James only looked more miserable. He was staring straight ahead like a man who had just heard of a death in the family. He didn't even turn to her as he started to speak.

"I got a letter from my parents. They say I'm spending too much money. We have to be more careful," he said, biting his lip. He looked so forlorn that Annie's heart leapt out to him. She took his hand and held it up to her cheek.

"James, I only have two feet and seven pairs of shoes," she said looking into his deep dark eyes and loving him even more for the sadness she saw there. "I don't need anything. Just you."

James swept her into his arms and kissed her hard.

"Oh, baby, you are the sweetest thing in the entire Universe," he said finally releasing her. "I want to buy you all the pairs of shoes in the world. And some day I will. But we have to be careful. My parents can be very spiteful. If they find out about you the wrong way they could cut me off entirely."

Annie didn't understand. She didn't really care. Sure, as long as they had each other wouldn't they'd manage? They could both get a job. They could start by moving to cheaper lodgings. She could imagine the fun they'd have looking for a flat. The sound of James's voice cut through her daydreaming like knife. It was cold and resigned.

"They want me to come home."

"But you can't!" Annie blurted out. "You can't leave me. We're married now."

"I know, baby, I know," he said grimly, as if he were talking to himself.

"But I can't just write them about it. It's not something you write in a letter or announce on the phone, you know: Hey, Mom and Dad, by the way – while you thought I was studying I ran off and got married to some girl I met in the chipper."

James's words cut Annie to the quick, though she didn't understand why. He took no notice of her as he talked.

"I'll just have to go back and face the music. I'll just have to walk straight in and tell them face to face that we're in love, and that we're married, and that if they don't like it – well then tough shit!"

"Oh James, I love you so much. I don't care if they cut you off. We'll manage. I just can't stand the idea of being without you." Annie started to cry softly. "Please don't leave me."

James looked at her and forced a smile. He took her in his arms again and she felt herself melt. She never wanted this moment to end.

"I'll be back for you," he said rocking her gently. "And in the meantime Mrs Barry will take care of you. It's better this way. It's just a little while and then we'll have a lifetime to be together."

"I don't care about money," Annie whimpered softly, sniffing back her tears.

"*Money can't buy me love!*" sang James tickling her under the chin. Annie laughed and joined in. They sang "Can't Buy me Love" as loud as they could causing the passerbys to smile at the lovely young couple on the bench, who looked like they did not have a care in the world and seemed so very much in love.

February 20, 1966

I've been feeling terrible since James left. He sent me a postcard from Shannon but I haven't heard from him since. I can't seem to keep anything down. Mrs Barry tried to persuade me to go see a doctor. I thought I was just pining for James, but when I fainted dead away at breakfast yesterday Mrs Barry would not take no for an answer. So I went to a doctor that she recommended. He says I'm going to have a baby. I don't know how I feel about that. I should be happy, but with James gone everything just seems like a dream. Thank God he's calling me tomorrow. He said that a week would be enough to sort things out with his parents. I can't wait to hear his voice again and tell him about the baby.

Annie got to the GPO an hour before her phone call was due, to be sure that she wouldn't miss it. She nibbled on a chocolate bar and watched the hands tick across the great clock in the middle of the hall. Her name was called almost immediately after the clock struck four.

"Annie? Is that you?" James's voice sounded miles away but there was no mistaking him.

"James? Oh James, darling, I miss you so much. Can you speak up? I can hardly hear you."

"I'm calling from the library. My parents have gone out but I don't want the servants hearing me," he whispered. "I can't talk for long. This is costing a packet. They've put me on a really tight budget. If they find out I'm calling Ireland they'll have a fit."

"James? Can you hear me?" Annie yelled down the phone. "Have you told them? What did they say?"

"Not yet. I haven't found the right moment. There's been some delays."

"Delays? What delays? When are you coming back?" Annie felt the panic creep into her voice.

"I can't come back just yet. You're going to have to make do for a while on your own. I'm really sorry, Annie. They'll cut me off. I can't go into the details right now. I'll write you explaining it all. I've got to go now. Goodbye, Annie."

Annie stared at the big black receiver. She put it back up to her ear but James was gone. She stumbled out the big doors of the GPO and into the confusion of

O'Connell Street. People bumped into her and apologised. Brakes screeched and drivers hooted as she blindly crossed the road. She kept walking until her feet bumped into an obstacle. She looked up at Horatio Nelson towering two hundred feet above her head. She leaned against the cold stone and replayed the conversation in her head. What did he mean that she had to make do? Why did he say goodbye like that? She felt herself starting to cry. He hadn't said that he loved her, not once. He'd talked about money, about not coming back, and before she knew it he was gone. She hadn't even had the time to tell him about the baby.

Annie stayed in bed for three days, reassuring Mrs Barry that she just had a touch of the flu. She lay in bed staring at the ceiling clutching her rosary, reciting reams of prayers that had lost all meaning. On the fourth day Mrs Barry demanded she come down to the dining-room.

Mrs Barry forced her to accept a cup of tea and some freshly baked scones. She watched Annie like a hawk until she had finished the last crumb. Then she cleared her throat and straightened her shoulders.

"Now I don't want to be prying into your business but I'm afraid that this week's rent is due and I need to know if you will be keeping the room any further," she said as curtly as she could manage.

Annie stared at her hands as Mrs Barry's words slowly sunk in. Two tears slowly crossed her cheeks. Mrs Barry handed her a handkerchief. "Maybe you could give me something towards it and we can settle up when James comes back," she added kindly.

"He's not coming back just yet," Annie whispered. "He says he can't come back just yet. He doesn't know about the baby. I've written to him. I'm sure he'll be back soon."

"I'm sure he will, pet," said Mrs Barry but she sounded worried.

"In the meantime maybe I could find cheaper lodgings. I'll pay you what's due and leave in the morning. I'll look for a new place to stay. And find a job. I'd best find a job," Annie said, talking to herself.

Mrs Barry looked at her sadly and shook her head.

"Listen pet, I'm sure he'll be back for you soon. But you can't be traipsing around the city looking for a job and living on yer own in your condition. You'll be showing soon. Nobody's going to give a pregnant woman a job. You have to go back to your own people. They'll take care of you. I'll forward any post. You have to go back home."

Annie sat dumbly and watched as the lovely world where the flowers on the walls always matched those of the curtains came crashing down around her.

*　　　*　　　*

347

The old woman said nothing when Annie came back. It was as if she had never left. She watched in silence as Annie dragged in her cases and carried them up the rickety stairs to her little room beneath the eaves. Annie had stuffed as much as she could carry into two suitcases. The rest she had sold to scrape together the bus fare to Bantry.

Aunty Mary looked her slowly up and down. Annie knew she was taking in the short hair, the new clothes; but still she said nothing. Annie was dripping wet. It had been raining ever since she left Dublin and she had walked all the way up from the village dragging the suitcases. She was exhausted.

"I'm going to lock up the chickens," said Aunty Mary. "You could make a start on the spuds. But first you'd best get out of those wet clothes."

The old woman crossed the room. At the door she turned and looked at Annie, her mouth turning down at the corners. She spit on the doorstep.

"*Devil's hoor*," Annie heard her hiss before she stepped outside.

The days ran into one another until Annie could not tell how long it had been since she had returned. The rain poured down relentlessly day after day. Sometimes it was a fine mist that seeped into your very bones, sometimes it lashed down in great cold sheets of water that made you gasp for breath the minute you stepped outside and soaked you to the bone in seconds. But it was always present, always there, until the drip-drip-drip of water became the backdrop to every waking moment, every tortured dream.

Her only respite was in the morning, when she would wake and think that maybe today she would see the postman pushing his bike up the boreen. For that small moment between sleeping and waking she would hope against hope that this day would bring some news from James. That tiny flicker would carry her through another day of dripping cold rain. Then Aunty Mary would call her in to make the supper and Annie would realise that the postman would not be calling today. And her heart and mind would go blank.

Aunty Mary said little except to bark orders. She seemed so uninterested in her that Annie wondered if she'd even noticed that she had been away. But sometimes in the evening she would catch the old woman giving her a long hard look and she knew that the old bitch was just biding her time. Making her wait.

One morning, as Annie bent over to collect eggs in the hen house, she felt the old woman come up silently behind her. Annie stiffened. She tried to straighten up, but she had to reach out for support. She was definitely getting heavier. That night as they sat drinking tea by the fire the old woman spoke.

"When is the brat due?" she asked.

"In September," Annie answered, looking into the fire. "But he'll come for me before then," she added to herself. "Surely he'll come for me soon."

Aunty Mary sucked in air between her toothless gums making a sharp hissing sound. She raised herself painfully out of the chair and went to the press. Annie was surprised to see her take out the bottle of poitín the old woman kept for medicinal purposes only: colds, stomach upsets, or to rub on a sprained muscle, or a sick dog.

She poured a big measure into her teacup and drank it down in one gulp before pouring herself another. She sat sipping, lost in thought. The wind howled around the little cottage as if it was going to rip the roof from the rafters, whistling down the chimney and making the flames leap in the hearth. The bottle clinked against the teacup as she filled it up again. Annie stared into the fire and tried not to think of anything except that James would soon come for her. She watched the flames as they jumped and swirled. The embers made grotesque faces, mocking her. She was startled by the sound of Aunty Mary's voice. It was slow and cruel and slightly slurred.

"Here, this is yours," she said, holding out a chain that shone as it swung in the firelight. She gave it to Annie with disgust, as if she had just handed her a turd.

"It was your mother's, and her mother's mother's before that."

Annnie turned it over. It was a necklace with a T-bar. She undid the clasp and put it on. The metal felt cold and heavy against her skin. She turned to ask about it but the old woman cut her off, waving the bottle before pouring herself another measure.

"So it starts again," she snickered. "And who will raise this one? I'm not getting any younger. Sixty years old and no one left to carry the burden of this curse. All gone. Every last one of 'em. Gone like your mother and your grandmother before her. Cursed – the lot of 'em."

Annie felt her anger rise. How dare she speak of her baby and utter curses in the same breath? It had nothing to do with her. They had nothing to do with a bitter old woman's superstitions. Not Annie, not James, not this baby.

Annie looked hard at Aunty Mary: the old wool skirt, the black wool stockings, the worn-out jumper and moth-eaten shawl. There was no way this woman was going to ruin her baby's life with old wives' tales and imagined sins that existed only in her warped sick mind. Aunty Mary flinched as Annie lashed out at her.

"Get away from us, you witch! You have no need to worry about who will raise it. It's no concern of yours. Sure, haven't I heard it a thousand times that we're not blood! I still don't know why you raised me, except for the pleasure you took in having someone to beat. I'll not leave this baby. Her father is coming for me. I'm just waiting for him to fetch me. You won't ever see this baby. I'd rather die than let you fill her head with your talk."

Annie voice rose in passion until the old woman eyes opened wide at the unaccustomed tone of her voice. She waited until Annie had finished then she took a sip and started to laugh. She laughed so hard she had to set the cup down so it would not spill. Tears of mirth ran down her cheeks and she slapped her thighs as peals of laughter shook her shapeless body. She laughed until all you could see of her face were the two yellow and broken stumps she had left in the gaping blackness of her mouth. Annie wanted to scream. She wanted to cover her eyes and ears to block out the horror of Aunty Mary's laughing.

"*You* call me a witch! Maeve's bastard brat!" she laughed, shaking her head and wiping her face with a corner of the shawl. She pointed a gnarled finger at Annie and narrowed her eyes. "You think you know it all, don't you?" she said, her voice still shaking. "There's more to it than you know, girleen. There's a lot more. You think you have a choice? You carry Maeve's curse with you. And that child in your belly will carry it too. Your mother wasn't the first. Nor was your grandmother. They had no choice. *I* had no choice. None at all! I *had* to raise you. I was cursed to raise you. And when I'm gone who will carry that bond? Huh, girl? Who? What will happen when there is no one to carry Maeve's bond? We are linked by stronger stuff than blood, you and I and that bastard child you're carrying."

"It is not a bastard!" Annie screeched, jumping out of her chair. "We were married. He is coming for me soon. You'll see! I will not sit here and listen to the stupid rantings of a demented old woman!"

Then she fled up the stairs and fell into her bed sobbing.

The night was filled with strange noises that kept Annie tossing and turning under the thin blanket. Flames leapt up and licked the rafters, dry timbers crackling as the fire spread. She woke, cold and shivering, only to hear the sound of the fire turn into the screech of the wind. She fell back into a black sleep and heard a woman's keen, her wails riding down the crest of the hill to the valley below. The rain dripped steadily as she waited by the window and watched James walk up the hill, but the longer he walked the further away he got. She called to him but he just got smaller and smaller until he was gone.

The warmth of the sun woke her the next morning. The storm had blown itself out. Wild chatterings came in from the courtyard. Annie looked out through the dirty pane of glass set low in the stone wall. A group of magpies danced in the sunlight, squabbling for a scrap. They flew at each other, squawking loudly, their feathers flashing as they lifted off the ground and dived back down at each other. Annie counted them: *One for sorrow, two for joy, three for a girl, four a boy, five for silver, six for gold, seven for the secret that's never been told.* With a great cry one of them seized the scrap in its sharp black beak and flew straight up in the air followed by two others. Annie watched as the three birds flew over the shed and up the hill.

Annie could hear Aunty Mary moving around downstairs. She seemed to be bumping into things, cursing and yelling.

"Out! Get out. Annie!" she called through the floorboards. "Get this thing out! Out!"

Annie ran downstairs to find Aunty Mary cowering in the corner, waving a broom in front of her. She pointed to the middle of the room. A large magpie walked up and down quite calmly in front of the hearth, as if inspecting it. The bird hopped onto the back of the chair and turned its head to look at Annie with one shining black eye.

"It's bad luck to have it in the house," yelled Aunty Mary. "A sure sign of death. Get it out!"

Annie opened the window and shooed the bird off the chair. The magpie jumped onto the ledge and gave them one last look before it swooped out the window and up the hill cawing loudly as it flew. Annie watched it disappear into a small copse of trees.

"Something bad is going to happen for sure," mumbled Aunty Mary. "A death in the house." She grabbed her rosary and fell to her knees, motioning for Annie to join her. But Annie was having no more of her incantations. She ran off, slamming the door behind her. She spent all day outside the house returning only when all the chores were done and the dusk was beginning to fall.

She found Aunty Mary sitting at the table. She had lit a candle and was holding a piece of paper up to the light. As Annie came in she looked up with a smug smile. She slipped the paper into an envelope and held it out to her.

Annie started to tremble as she caught sight of the thick creamy paper, the embossed address in the left hand corner, the flowery penmanship, the expensive blue-black ink. She knew instantly that it was not James who had written it. Long tapered fingers with manicured nails had written that letter. Long white fingers that reached out over the sea like a cold vice around her heart.

"So he's coming to fetch you, is he?" the old woman sneered. "Did you think you could shrug off who you are so easily? Don't you know everything you touch is cursed?"

Annie's blood froze in her veins. She saw the magpie looking at her. She saw James disappear into the distance in her dream.

"Oh my God James!" Annie whispered. "He's dead. They're writing to tell me he's dead!"

"Not dead," the old woman laughed. "Though you might wish he were."

Annie reached out and snatched the letter from her hand. She tried to still her trembling as she read it:

Dear Miss Kelly,

I am writing you on behalf of my son James Richardson III. Though we were sorry to hear of your predicament it is of no concern to James . . .

Annie felt a scream rising in her throat.

He is a young man with responsibilities which you cannot begin to grasp. He has his whole life before him. I'm not sure what it is you want to achieve, but if you think you can use some cheap trick for you and your bastard child to lay claim to any of the Richardson fortune you are sorely mistaken. I know your kind. The type that preys on the honour and sensibilities of young men such as James, and I will

*not let you destroy him. He will be sent away by his
father to where you cannot reach him . . .*

Annie's vision was blurring. A whooshing sound was
pounding in her temples, making her dizzy. She swallowed and tasted the bile in her mouth.

*Because I am a Christian woman and I feel sorry
for your situation, no matter whom the father may
be, I have enclosed a check for $500 to help you in
your time of need. Be advised, however, that should
you try to make contact with James or any other
member of our family, you will be hearing from our
lawyers. Blackmail is a very ugly thing, Miss Kelly. I
suggest you take the money and consider yourself
lucky,*

    Mrs James Richardson Jr

Annie stumbled to the door. Faraway she heard herself cry out in pain. The old woman laughed. She was
pointing at Annie, her eyes full of glee. Annie ran across
the courtyard and up into the back field. Gasping and
sobbing she ran up the hill. Her legs strained as she
ran but she relished the pain, so sharp, so much more
bearable than the pain in her heart.

She ran until she could run no more. She ran until her
knees buckled and she sank into the wet grass. She was

at the top of the hill, near the blackened ruins of a small building. A fire had wiped out an entire family there long, long ago and as a child she had believed the place was haunted. She leaned on an old bit of wall, holding her side painfully, and prayed that whatever evil slept there would come and take her away for good.

The clouds were a dark grey canopy overhead. Between them and the black silhouettes of the hills the sun set the horizon on fire. The land was streaked red and pink. High above her the black round disk of a new moon hung like a bad omen in the crimson blaze. Annie wished that the fire would come again and strike her dead, burning her; burning everyone and everything around her, until all that was left was black and charred and would never grow again.

The clouds raced across the sky and Annie felt the cold slap of rain. She sank moaning into the mud and crawled through a break in the wall. Something was shining in the mud. She dug her fingers into the cold slimy soil and picked out a small metal object. It was a thimble. She dug some more and felt a sharp pain in her hand. She had cut herself on something. Glass, it was a sharp piece of glass. She picked it up and saw the red streaks of her blood smeared across the shiny surface of a mirror. She felt a wail rise from deep inside her as she saw the reflection of her eyes staring back at her, wild with despair.

She clutched the letter and shook it at the black moon. Desolation stirred deep within her, rising up into her throat until she found herself howling like a wounded animal. Her long wailing cry echoed from the hill. She could feel the poison pouring out of her soul. She watched it grow until it shattered her heart. She cursed the old woman who laughed in the cottage below. She cursed the other woman who wrote with such a flowery hand. She cursed the father who was taking his son away from her. Most of all, she cursed James for tricking her into loving him.

She cursed them all and wished them dead, tasting the bitter poison as the curses filled her mouth. Her hand grasped her neck as the poison trickled down her throat. She felt the heavy gold chain and wrapped her fingers around it, clutching the T-bar.

Annie lay back in the mud and stared at the black moon. She was bad. She was evil. She deserved to die. She swallowed hard, letting the poison run through her veins. She sunk into the muck and welcomed death. They should all be dead. There would be no more pain. Dark clouds covered the moon as the rain lashed down on her. The poison seeped through her, chilling her limbs until they were numb. It flowed out from every pore, enveloping her in a dark mist that swirled around her belly. Then it stopped.

Annie's body shuddered violently. She was wracked

with nausea as something inside her fought back. She felt a warm glowing spark of life that did not want to die. She doubled up in pain. Retching and gasping, she forced herself to sit up. It was the child. The child wanted to live. The child would not let her die.

Clutching her stomach, Annie struggled to her feet. She looked blindly into the darkness, the rain and her tears blurring her vision. She thought she saw a shadow pass in front of her. The wind carried a warm breeze from the sea that lifted her feet over the low stone wall. The current pushed her up past the ruins to a small copse of trees. Gentle hands made her lie down on the soft, dry, moss. They smoothed her brow. Sweet lips kissed her as she fell asleep.

Annie woke only once. The branches were rustling. She opened her eyes and saw a figure slip out from under the trees. It was a woman dressed in a long brown dress, her feet bare and muddy, her black hair gleaming as it fell the length of her back. In her arms she cradled a small baby as she walked slowly down the hill to the cottage, carefully choosing her path lest she stumble and disturb the sleeping child.

Annie's lids were heavy. She could not keep her eyes open. Three sharp knocks echoed in the night. She struggled to keep awake but could not fight back sleep. In the distance she heard a high piercing scream and she knew the old woman was dead.

CATCH THE MAGPIE

Dublin Central Maternity Hospital
  September 9, 1966.
  My darling Katie is born. She is the most beautiful child in the world. How could anybody think I would give her up? That smiling doctor and evil nurses kept talking about putting her up for adoption but I would hear nothing of the kind. I still have a good bit of money left. It will last us a good bit if I'm careful. And after that we'll manage somehow. Tomorrow I can take you home, Katie, and we can start a new life. We'll manage and we'll forget.

Annie stood waiting at the bus stop, the newborn baby wrapped in a blanket in her arms. At her feet was a small suitcase. She looked up the street, searching for the bus. A long black Mercedes pulled out of the line of traffic and stopped in front of her.

The door opened and a hand beckoned her. Annie looked in and saw a handsome older man in an elegant dark suit. His grey hair was slicked back from his broad forehead and he wore a navy silk bow tie. He smiled at Annie and she felt the shock of recognition. He looked just like James except that he was much, much, older.

"My name is James Richardson Senior," he said gently. His eyes filled with tears as he looked at the child in her arms. "I've been searching for you for three

months, but I see that I have found you just in time."
He patted the plush seat and Annie slipped in beside
him. The smell of the leather filled her head as she
sank gratefully into its soft embrace.

"What have you called the child?" he asked, never
taking his eyes off the sleeping baby.

"Catherine," she whispered. "I call her Katie."

"Catherine," he repeated nodding. "Catherine
Richardson. It's a lovely name."

"I have some very sad news," he said gently. Annie
nodded but she could not speak. Tears choked her
throat and ran down her cheeks. She knew that James
was dead. She knew his parents were also dead. Just
like the old woman was dead. She'd cursed them all
and they were all dead.

The baby stirred and the old man laid a gentle finger
on her fat rosy cheek. Annie looked fearfully down at
her perfect baby. She had wished them all dead: James,
his parents, Aunty Mary, and most of all herself. But
the child had wanted to live. The child would not let
her die.

"I've come to take you and little Catherine home,
Annie," he said. "You are all I have left. Will you come
with me? You will never want for anything. It would
make a sad old man very happy."

James Richardson laid a soft hand on her shoulder
and handed her a crisp linen handkerchief to dry her

tears. The tiny baby stirred and opened her eyes. They were dark blue, almost purple and they fixed Annie with a deep and knowing gaze. The big car slid back into the traffic as Annie hid her face in the sweet smelling handkerchief to hide the fear she felt growing inside her.

Cat closed the diary.

The stewardess tapped her gently on the shoulder. Cat saw the concern in her eyes.

"Are you all right Miss?" she said. "We'll be serving breakfast soon. We'll be landing in Shannon in about an hour."

Cat smiled through her tears and sniffed. "I'm fine," she said.

"Breakfast sounds great. Thank you."

The stewardess took one more look at her and then turned her attention to the passengers sleeping across the aisle.

Cat could read no more. She knew the rest of the pages must be filled with growing references to curses, to death and evil. Her hands still held the little notebook. As she slipped the photograph inside the back cover her fingers felt a rough tear in the binding. A scrap of paper was wedged there. Cat recognised the childish scrawl as she read: Kilkeambeg, Kilkeam, Bantry, County Cork.

Cat pulled out the in-flight magazine from the pocket in front of her. She found County Cork on the big map of Ireland. She found Bantry. She could not find Kilkeam but she knew it was too small to figure on the map. It didn't matter. Once she got to Bantry it would be easy to find.

Five . . .

Chapter Twenty

◆

Cat slowed the car and pulled over onto the soft shoulder. She stepped out and stretched, casting her gaze back in the direction she had come. Below her the valley was veiled in fog.

She'd driven halfway across Ireland since she'd landed that morning but she'd seen very little of it. The country had been shrouded throughout. She'd had a coffee and a processed muffin in Killarney before driving off up the mountains through more mist and fog. She could only see a dozen feet in front of her. She had driven along, vaguely aware of the drop on the other side of the road as the car hugged the sheer rock-face. The map she had been given at the car rental told her she was close to 3000 feet above sea level. But only the popping in her ears told her the road was rising. The only living thing she'd passed were shaggy white sheep who did not even glance in her direction as she battled with the unfamiliar gear shift and tried to keep on the left-hand side of the road. Then she sensed she was dropping down, down, twisting around hairpin bends, until she practically ran into Kenmare. A few miles later she was shocked to discover the sea. She had followed the coast road until she found herself in a large square in Bantry town. As she pulled in to park, Cat finally acknowledged that she had no idea what to do next. Rows of houses and shops beckoned and confused her. She walked twice around the streets, letting her feet decide which way to go until she found herself staring at a shiny brass plaque. It read: *McCarthy, O'Reilly and Associates, Solicitors.*

A door opened and a kind-faced woman in a business suit asked her if she needed any help. Having nothing to lose Cat followed her into the building. After a quick chat she was ushered into an office where a tall young man reached out and shook her hand vigorously. He was a startling strawberry blond, with freckles, and glasses, and a big wide smile that flashed white teeth as he introduced himself with a hearty laugh. He seemed delighted at the interruption.

"My name is Seamus O'Reilly. Margaret tells me you've just landed on our shores! Welcome to Ireland! Did you drive all the way from Shannon? My God, you must be exhausted. Jet lag is terrible. I was over in your part of the world last year and it took me a week to recover. Did you drive over the Reeks? It's beautiful, isn't it? Then again you can't have seen much in this weather! What a shame! You must go back up and have a look when it's sunny. It's truly magnificent. Then again you could be waiting until spring! Ha ha!"

Cat blinked, feeling thrown off balance by this out-pouring from a total stranger.

"So, what can I do for you?" he asked peering over his glasses with a look as if nothing would please him more than to help her.

To her surprise and disgust Cat burst into tears. The big man's smile did not waver as she cried. He gestured her not to worry as he pushed over a large box of tissues. Cat started apologising profusely for her lack of composure, but he just waved her apologies away.

"Why don't you start at the beginning?" he prompted. Before she could stop herself she poured out how her mother had died when she was a child, how she had only just discovered that her mother, Annie Kelly, had come from these parts, of how she had come looking for Kilkeam, or rather a cottage somewhere called Kilkeambeg, and how she had no idea how to go about it, or whether it even existed.

Cat could see the cogs of his mind turning as he listened. She could not help noticing how his eyes sparkled. She blew her nose and apologised again for wasting his time, but he silenced her as if hushing a child. After a pause he held up his index finger and winked at her, giving a little shake of his head.

"This is most extraordinary," he said, his voice quivering with excitement. Then he reached out and dialled the phone.

"Margaret?" he yelled into the big black receiver. "What are you still doing in the office? It's Friday, for God's sake! Listen, since you insist on working, be a dear and get me the file for that place Maggie Stewart stays in. You'll never believe who just walked in! It's only amazing!" He turned to Cat, shaking his head. "This is really an amazing stroke of luck. What possessed you to come in here?"

Cat shrugged, not understanding what was happening, but intrigued all the same. Seamus was literally dancing in his seat.

"Amazing really. Divine providence I call it. This is no simple coincidence," he continued, clearly having trouble containing himself. "I actually know the place quite well," he added with a swagger.

The door opened and the woman Cat had met came in with a file and handed it over with a questioning look. Seamus was still shaking his head happily as he smoothed it out. Then he paused and looked at Cat before beginning again at a rapid pace.

"Do you realise that we've been looking for you, or rather your mother and her descendants, for close on thirty years? It's extraordinary. That is what I love about the law. People think it's boring, but so many exciting things happen. Last year we closed an inheritance case after fifteen years when a fella out in Australia sent a local genealogist a pair of boots belonging to his grandfather! He was trying to trace his roots with a pair of boots! Ha Ha!"

Seamus paused again to let his audience express the appropriate measure of surprise. Then he cleared his throat. Cat found that she was smiling despite herself. She felt a tingling buzz of excitement as he opened the file and started scanning it.

"Let me see: a certain Mary Kelly died in 1966. She had never married and had no descendants. She did, however, have a will which left her property to an Annie Kelly. There's an odd note here. She did not actually bequeath it as such. The will claimed that the property should revert to its rightful owner. That is to say, Annie Kelly. Not to worry – it's all above board." Seamus stabbed happily at the file with his long index finger. "If you can prove you are her daughter then you have not just found your roots, Missy, you've got yourself a little piece of Ireland to boot. One cottage and a few sheds, and five acres of scrub, including a hill with a bit of a folklore attached to it as well. Isn't that just a wonderful bit of luck that you walked in here today?"

Cat was speechless. Voices clamoured in her head demanding to be heard, but she pushed them away. Seamus rambled on.

"It's said to be haunted. You Americans like that sort of thing, don't you? At the moment it is occupied by a real live tenant, however. About fifteen years ago we came to a sort of agreement with a lovely woman to rent the place off and on. Also an American. Maggie Stewart is her name. Don't worry, she's only there a few months of the year. And you will of course receive the accumulated rent. It's all above board. When she enquired about it I decided to let her use it. That's why I said I knew the property well. I hope you don't mind. Then again she has saved the place from falling into complete disrepair. Improved it, in fact. Put in the electrics and indoor plumbing. She doesn't mind the ghosts. That's what brought her there in the first place. She's a folklorist. Collects stories. Lectures all over the world. You'll have to sort things out with her – though I don't see that there will be any problem. She's a lovely woman. Very intelligent. Very well read. Great company. I've loads of time for her. You'll love her to bits."

Now standing by the car on the road above Bantry Bay, Cat stared into the mist, bewildered at the chain of extraordinary events which had led her to this spot just a short drive from where her mother had grown up. Forty-eight hours earlier she had been crossing Manhattan to go to Trevor's apartment. Cat remembered the cab crawling through the heavy mid-town traffic and now, here she stood, in the middle of nowhere, entirely alone. She wondered how far away the closest human being was: half a mile away? Two miles? Five?

Below her Bantry Bay was shrouded in fog but above her the sun was shining on the hills. Looking out over the edge of the cliff all she could see was thick grey cloud. There was no sign of the town, nor of the sea, nor of the valley she knew she must have driven through before starting to climb again. Everything around her had seemed to melt into varying shades of grey: the winding road, the low stone walls, and the craggy rocks that reared out from the fog like menacing beasts poised to strike. Here and there a burst of colour only heightened the monochrome palette, as if some mad artist had dipped into his pots and added a touch of bright green moss, a splash of tiny pink flowers, or a patch of blue high up on the horizon to an otherwise black and white print.

The air was as still and heavy as a goose-down quilt, enveloping her senses along with the landscape in its soft embrace. Cat resisted the pull of that soft grey mass that seemed to promise the comfort of oblivion if only she took a few steps and let herself fall.

Cat felt a shiver run up her spine despite the thick sweater she had bought in Killarney. She must be coming down with something. She was feeling feverish and all her joints ached. She knew she would have to stop and rest soon or she would get ill and collapse. She had not had a real night's sleep for two days and very little to eat. She had come a long, long way. She was almost there. Cat took a few deep breaths to clear her head, tasting the sweet, clean air. She'd better get a move on. It would soon be dark.

She took out the piece of paper the solicitor had given her and checked her bearings. Up ahead she saw a sharp turn. A white and black signpost indicated a road to the right, though from where she stood it looked as if it was pointing straight at a wall. Cat couldn't read it but she knew it must say Kilkeam.

Sitting back in the car, Cat reread the directions, again hearing the young solicitor's delighted laugh as he took his time writing it all down. She felt somebody watching her and looked up. Sitting in the puny branches of a stunted tree was a fat magpie. It blinked at Cat as their eyes met.

"Go away and leave me alone," she shouted, rolling down the window and shooing the bird. It took off in a graceful curve rising a few feet before swooping down over the edge and disappearing into the fog.

"*One in flight is worth two in sight,*" she recited, wondering what hidden pocket of memory that had popped out from. She knew her mother had taught her that but she could not remember when.

She swung out into the road, keeping the window down. She was past being tired. Everything about this road spoke to her: every bend, every steep drop. The roll of the valley below. The outline of the mountains she knew instinctively were far off on her right; and behind her, the waters of Bantry Bay.

Cat took the sharp turn to the right and followed a steep climb as it cut into the mountain. The fog vanished as the road rose, revealing tight green fields that got smaller as she climbed. It twisted and turned until it came to a bend. Tucked into the curve was a crossroads with a few houses, a tiny shop, and a pub. The place looked deserted. Further down on a knoll Cat could see a small church. In a field next to the church a large group of people were standing, watching some sort of football game.

Cat stared at the crossroads and wondered which one to take. She read the instructions again and chose the road which continued up a hill to her right. The light was starting to fade below her while above her the last of the sun's rays spotlighted the road ahead. The road forked and Cat again went to the right.

After a hundred yards the road became rutted and muddy. Cat hesitated as she drove slowly over the green grass growing in the middle of what had become a track. This looked as if went nowhere, she thought. Stopping the car she looked down and saw the tops of the houses in the village below. Cat turned the car in a small lay-by and started back down.

A sudden movement made her slam on the brakes. Up ahead a large fox sprang from the hedge and stopped in the middle of the road. Cat held her breath as she saw its quick black eyes, its pointy face and long bushy red tail tipped with a white tuft. The beautiful animal stared back at the car, seemingly unperturbed. Then the fox turned and slowly loped down the road, its tail enticing her to follow. After a few yards Cat saw him dart to the right, down a road she had missed on the way up. The fox stopped and looked back as it came to another crossroads. Cat followed. The left looked like it would lead her back down to the village. The right led straight up again. The fox ran up the hill a short way and then disappeared over a wall. Cat turned right.

The road rose steeply, undulating over a series of successive inclines like an exotic dancer's belly. The moss-covered stone walls on either side of it started off running parallel to the green stripe of grass in the middle, yet all three lines converged in a single point

somewhere above. To her right Cat could see the dark
shadow of a hill backlit in fiery hues by the setting sun.

It was as she peered up the hill that she first caught
sight of the house. A flash of blue peeping through the
greenery in the corner of her eye. It was a pale blue,
washed almost grey by years of rain and wind. Cat
drove along a high fuchsia hedge until she came
to an entrance. She parked and got out, smelling
the woodsmoke. The trees on either side had grown
together forming a green archway. Looking up she saw
a tiny plume drifting above them. She passed under
the arch and up the path, slipping and sliding in the
shiny mud. It was dark in the shadows and Cat moved
slowly, careful not to lose her footing.

The rays of the setting sun were blinding as she
stepped out from under the trees. She shaded her eyes
and found she was in a tiny yard. Late flowers bloomed
in hanging baskets on the front of a small cottage. A
large ginger cat slept curled on a low bench framed by
the creeping branches of a climbing rose. Cat's heart
seemed to pause and fill with ease. Here was somewhere you could raise a few chickens, or take a break
from your morning chores and sit on a bench in the
spring sunshine. She peered through the slits of her
shaded eyes and felt herself sitting there, looking up
into the sun to see who it was that had just emerged
into the yard, and saw herself looking back at her mirror

image. Cat blinked, confused and disoriented. For a split second she did not know which one she was: the woman sitting on the bench, or the one looking down on her?

She was startled by a voice hailing her from across the yard. Looking up she felt the clouds start to spin. For one nauseating moment the sunset, dark sky, and pink clouds swirled over her head. Up was down and down was up. Her head felt faint and she felt her knees start to buckle under her. Then a strong arm grabbed her by the elbow and held her up.

"Whoa there," said a warm and friendly voice. "You looked like you were going to pass out. Come inside and sit down."

The world stopped spinning as Cat made an effort to focus on the silhouette of a woman. She felt the woman's strength flow through her as she helped her walk a few paces. Her vision cleared and she found herself held by a tall woman. The woman waited patiently for Cat to get her bearings, all the while looking at her as if measuring her up. Cat did the same. The woman's face was wide open. Laugh lines ran all over her features, showing the passing of time, but her eyes had the sparkle and amusement of childhood. She was dressed in layers: boots over socks over leggings. Over that went a long flowered dress which she wore under an enormous bright blue sweater. Her hair was wild, and long, and curly; the natural auburn run through with grey. Then the woman smiled and Cat felt herself returning the warmth despite still feeling feverish and light-headed.

"I'm Maggie. You must be Catherine. Seamus called to tell me you were coming. Isn't he just a darling?" Not waiting for an answer, Maggie struck out her hand. "I'm very pleased to meet you." It was nut-brown and seemed to have done a lot of manual work, but Cat found that it was as soft as it was strong. "We were just getting ready to make dinner," said Maggie as she gently led Cat to the door. "You'll join us, won't you?"

Cat felt her stomach rumble. She was ravenous. The thought of eating a meal this woman had cooked made her very happy. In fact, though she felt like shit, Cat found herself relaxing. This was safe. This was good. This felt like home.

Maggie led her into a room with a low ceiling. One entire wall was taken up by a big hearth that crackled with a wood fire. On the rafters were hung an assortment of things: various hats, bunches of drying herbs, and a collection of masks. Old sofas and comfortable armchairs flanked the fire. The low windows let in very little light and it took a few seconds for Cat to realise there were other people in the room.

"This is the famous person I was telling you all

about," Maggie declared, still holding on firmly to Catherine's arm. "The return of the prodigal daughter!"

"Catherine, this is Spider," she added pointing at a thin, long guy lounging on the sofa. Cat couldn't decide if the name was in honour of his physique or rather because of the bush of dreadlocks at the top of his head.

"Wicked!" pronounced Spider, his wide grin revealing a large gap in his front teeth.

"Sit down. Sit down," Maggie ordered, pushing Cat towards a big armchair. "Catherine had a bit of a turn out there. Let me get you something to drink. Do you like wine?"

Cat nodded. A figure rose from the sofa and extended a fat pink hand. Cat was surprised to hear the voice of a woman. With her elaborate mohawk, nose rings, and lumpy clothes, Cat had assumed she was a man.

"Hi there, Cath. Name's Stubbs. Me dad called me that because he said I reminded him of the Stubbs safe in the back of the shop where he worked. Short and stout. He was a right 'ol bastard, he was." Stubbs laughed loudly and the others in the room all joined in.

Maggie came in with a bottle and introduced the last two as Sean and Lizzie. Like the others they wore a colourful jumble of clothes that had an ethnic clown side to it. They all smiled happily at Cat, except for the one called Lizzie who just stared aimlessly into the fire.

The wine was surprising. Cat had thought it a Rosé because of its colour, but it tasted intensely of strawberries and had a real punch behind the sweetness.

"Do you like it?" asked Maggie. "I made it myself. I grow a couple of things over the summer. This year was a strawberry bonanza!"

Cat murmured her appreciation. Cat sipped slowly, tasting the ripe fruit. She was suddenly so tired that she could barely speak. She certainly didn't feel like moving.

Cat watched as Maggie lit candles, and thought she should say something about the extraordinary circumstances that had brought her to this place. But she didn't know where to start. The others sat around talking quietly, laughing out loud, their faces reflecting the firelight. No one seemed to notice her silence. No one asked her any questions. They acted as if it was the most natural thing in the world for a perfect stranger to walk in and collapse in a chair. Soon big bowls of steaming stew were passed around. It was highly spiced with curry and chillies; and thick with vegetables and a variety of beans. The pungent odours steamed up to her and Cat fell upon the food with relish.

Cat ate two bowls along with fresh brown bread still warm from the oven, and a salad composed of a variety of things she had never eaten before. Maggie surprised her by naming all the ingredients: "Sorrel, dandelion stalks, wild cress and wild spinach." She was even more astounded when Maggie explained she had picked most of it on the surrounding land.

Cat found her eyelids drooping. She thought that she should get up and find her way back to Bantry for the night, but her body refused to budge. As the homemade wine and the meal lulled her body, her brain finally caved in. The thousands of questions, images, secrets and lies, that had buzzed through her mind like a swarm of locusts for the last three days finally flew off and left her in peace. Cold shivers ran up and down her body and she gladly accepted a shawl from Maggie and the offer to sit by the fire. Hot flushes followed and she felt a trickle of sweat run between her breasts. Her legs and arms ached and there was a terrible throbbing pain at the base of her neck. But above the leadened weight of her limbs, her mind drifted light as a feather, passing in and out of consciousness as Maggie held court in the candlelight.

"It's all about meaning. How you actually describe it – what name you give it, matters little," Maggie was saying emphatically. "What is important is that the underlying thing, or feeling, or *meaning* that you are trying to grasp is the same in every culture."

Cat let the words drift over her and caress her brain.

Spider answered something but Cat couldn't make out what he said.

"I don't agree, Spider." Maggie's voice cut through her dreamy state loud and clear as a bell. "Any object can be sacred. What about cargo cults? They manage to find the sacred in a broken radio. Or a plastic toy! It's all about the underlying *meaning*."

She fell asleep to the sound of Maggie's voice as it droned on, more comforting than any lullaby.

Much later that night, Cat woke up still wrapped in the shawl but with an extra blanket thrown over her. The fire had died down to glowing red embers. Cat heard a sigh and realised that two people lay entwined, asleep in the sofa. Someone else seemed to be lying in a sleeping bag on the floor and she could see the shadow of someone warming themselves by the fire. Cat sat up to see who it was. She caught a faint whiff of lavender. Her heart stopped.

Clearly illuminated by the fire was the barefoot woman she had seen before. She was half turned and bent over so that Cat could not see her face, only the black hair that fell thickly like a heavy veil over her shoulders. She wore the same brown dress as before, but this time Cat could see a thin shawl crossed over her chest. The woman swayed back and forth and Cat realised that she was rocking a cradle. Cat was wracked with nausea as a black despair welled up from her belly. She tried to cry out but she made no sound. Her hands gripped the blanket tightly but her arms refused to move. Then all was blackness and Cat passed out.

Fever gripped her. She was vaguely aware of being led to a bedroom and being undressed. A heavy duvet was wrapped around her. Several times in the night she woke screaming from her nightmares and strong hands helped her up and gave her cool water to drink, or a warm tea which smelt funny. Cat could not tell where her dreams began nor when her nightmares ended. She would sink into a deep sleep until the chills would wake her and she would find herself clutching the sheets in fear. Flames were leaping from the walls, curling up the rafters. Voices screamed, babies wailed. She turned and touched Trevor's strong shoulder. She pressed her cheek to his chest and cried. She reached out only to find an empty space. Her pillow was wet with tears. The aches and pains had disappeared leaving her clammy and numb. She snuggled back into the safety of Trevor's arms, feeling his warmth and love finally conquer her restless wanderings

Chapter Twenty-One

✦

The morning sun shone through the low window, casting slanting shafts of light along the wooden floor. Cat lifted herself up and looked around the small room. The bed was tucked under one of the eaves, which were so low Cat could not have stood up under them. There were books everywhere: cluttering several shelves, arranged around the baseboards, propped between huge grey stones, and in little stacks around the bed. Under the other eave, was a computer sitting on a small desk piled high with papers. A big *yin* and *yang* poster was stapled on the door. Scarves and throws seemed to be draped everywhere, giving the room an air of a Turkish bazaar.

"I've died and woken up in the Sixties," thought Cat. She smiled as she pulled the duvet up to her nose. The room was cold and her breath blew little plumes of smoke. The night's terrors seemed faraway and unreal in this comfy safe haven under the roof. She was wearing an oversized T-shirt. Her clothes lay folded on a three-legged stool. Her boots and bag stood beside it. Laid on top were the necklace and the thimble.

Cat reached out to pick them up as a soft knock came through the door. Maggie came in carrying a tray whose sweet smells made Cat's stomach growl.

"Well, you look much better this morning." said Maggie, placing the tray on the foot of the bed. "Or should I say this afternoon!"

Cat smiled gratefully and started to thank her.

"Nonsense," said Maggie, waving her big hand as if swatting a fly. "It's your house after all. You are welcome to stay, entitled to stay rather, as long as you like. In fact I should be thanking you for your hospitality. Besides you were one sick puppy last night. You weren't going anywhere."

"What time is it?" Cat asked. "I feel like I've been asleep all day."

"Almost – it's coming up to four. Are you hungry? I made you some pancakes for breakfast. I bring the maple syrup over myself. It costs an arm and a leg over here. Thought you might like some coffee as well."

Cat nodded and then realised that first she had to deal with a more pressing natural urge. Maggie directed her downstairs to a tiny toilet off the kitchen, which was in a glass extension to the cottage. Cat felt light-headed and wobbly as she climbed down the creaky stairs. The others seemed to have left.

When she came back up, Maggie was looking at the necklace and thimble.

"These fell out of your jacket when I was hanging it up. They're lovely. Are they a family heirloom?"

Cat nodded, tucking into the light pancakes smothered in syrup. "They were my mother's." She could feel strength flowing back into her. "I've never seen a necklace like that," she added.

"It's a T-bar. Quite common over here. See this little bar. It was the piece that hooked a man's pocket-watch chain to his waistcoat. Often a child might be given the pocket-watch and another the chain and T-bar. Women wear them around here. Of course they're made straight into a necklace these days. But this one looks like the real McCoy. Do you know how old it is?"

Cat shook her head, still intent on savouring her breakfast.

"I'd say it's pretty old. And the thimble looks even older. It's a beauty. You know, thimbles have always been very potent symbols. And again, like the pocket-watch, it was often the only thing of any value a family might have around these parts."

Cat pushed away the tray and cupped her hands

around the rough pottery mug filled with hot coffee. "Thank you very much. That was delicious."

"Glad you like my cooking." Maggie sat back and smiled. Cat felt slightly awkward, uncomfortable with the silence. It seemed to expect something heavier than easy banter. But Cat wasn't ready for that yet.

"So how long have you been here?" Cat asked brightly to dispel the moment.

"I came through here about fifteen years ago. I was collecting data, stories, for a book. I kind of specialise in woman's folk stories and legends. I teach a class called "Feminine Myths and Legends", though some have called it "Feminist Mist and Lies", she laughed. "Anyway. There's a rather famous witch associated with this place. Well, actually not precisely this house. It's up the hill. Her name was Maeve Cleary, or Maeve Ní Laoghaire depending on the account. She was said to have lived about a hundred years ago. The next summer when I was looking for a quiet place to write I remembered this place and contacted Seamus. I've been coming off and on since then. After a few years going totally rustic, no electricity or running water, I made some basic improvements. But even though it had been uninhabited for quite a while it was still very sound. The basic structure of this cottage was very well built and maintained. There must have been some money back there somewhere. If I can manage it in my schedule, I try to be here from about May to September, sometimes October, depending on the weather. I'll be leaving soon."

"Was the witch the reason Seamus said this place was haunted?" Cat asked. Something jostled at her memory. A name, a story.

"Oh yes. She's quite famous – infamous – around here. They say she walks the hill above. She is often described as holding a baby. Presumably to steal it away and do something awful," added Maggie, her nose scrunching up in distaste. "That's what attracted me to her in the first place. Maeve practised witchcraft. She killed children, including her own. She whipped horses, and cursed the church. She is said to have been banished and cursed, whereupon she burst into flames. Or sometimes the story goes that she was sprinkled with holy water and turned into a large stone. For what it's worth she cursed her accusers before her death, saying she would get them back. She had all the stereotypical traits associated with a 'bad woman or witch'." Maggie hooked both forefingers in the air as if encasing her words in apostrophes. Cat had already noticed the night before that Maggie was one of those people who spoke in italics and apostrophes. She liked that about her. That and the way she seemed not to expect anything but just to enjoy your company. And her wide, soft body, and her long, wild hair. Yes, thought Cat, she liked this woman very much.

"I'm interested in women who were cast out as witches," Maggie continued. "They often were healers, or women of independent means. Though I also suspect there was a fair share of women we would now consider as suffering from hysteria or schizophrenia. But in many cases the witch was someone who did not conform to the norm. Women who did not correspond to what the times considered was acceptable womanly behaviour. Also she was close enough to our times to try and research her. To find if there was ever a *real* woman behind the myth."

"Did you find anything?"

"Not really. There is no mention of her in the parish records. No baptism or burial. There is, however, a baptismal record dating back to the late 1880s for a child born to a Maeve Ní Laoghaire who shares her name and has no father accounted for. I'm pretty sure that's her. But the trail stops there. The rest is only hearsay and legend. Though around here, people talk about her as if she really walks the hill. They even say that she came back and killed the woman who used to live here and that that's why nobody wanted the place. Until I came along that is!"

Cat shuddered. Maggie made a clicking sound with her tongue. She laid a warm hand on her arm.

"I'm so sorry. That was very callous of me. I forgot that you have a less mythical link to this place. Besides, I checked: Mary Kelly, the one who gave this place to your mother, died of natural causes. She was sixty-three when she died. Don't worry. I've come here for fifteen years and I've never seen her."

Cat had a nasty taste in her mouth. She swallowed hard to get rid of it and smiled at Maggie hoping she hadn't noticed her unease. But Maggie was off and running with another story. "I once had a rather drunk guest try to convince me he could hear a woman wailing on the hill, though all I could hear was the keening of the wind. And another time, a friend on holiday swore she saw a woman downstairs by the fire."

"But I've never got to see her," Maggie added with something close to regret. "My friend said she saw a woman standing by the fire rocking a baby in a cradle. She also said that she was not so much scared as sad. Very, very sad. In fact she was crying when she told me about it."

Cat forced a smile and said nothing, though her heart was pounding. She desperately wanted to confide in this woman, but she dared not. She might think she was nuts. And anyway, she wanted to enjoy the respite from it all a little bit longer. Something deep inside her told her she needed it. She yawned heavily. It was still too soon to try and make sense of it all. She just wanted to sleep and forget. Just sleep and then wake to hear more of Maggie's stories until either the horrible thoughts had gone away, or she felt strong enough to face them.

"I think you should sleep some more," Maggie said kindly. "In fact, you should stay in bed until tomorrow. It's probably just a bad flu compounded by jet-lag. But it's better to take it easy so that it doesn't turn into something worse. Let the body have the time to heal itself. Another day in bed and you'll be right as rain. I'll bring you up some paper and pencils in case you're bored. There's plenty of books around. I'm afraid I don't have a TV, but I could bring you up a radio."

"No thanks," said Cat sinking back under the covers. "It's so quiet here compared to the city."

Maggie patted her on the arm and slipped out without another word.

Cat closed her eyes and listened to a bird singing outside and the wind rustling through the trees. Far off in the distance she could hear the rumbling of an engine and thought it must be a truck or a tractor miles away. She sank deeper into the bed and drifted gratefully into a sleep disturbed by no dreams other than those filled with birdsong, and whistling wind.

*   *   *

Maggie joined her again in the evening, plugging in a little two-bar electric fire to keep out the chill. Cat sat up in bed and ate the soup and bread Maggie had brought in. When she'd finished Maggie lit some candles and burned some sweet-smelling oil in a burner. The room was cosy and warm and Cat felt safer than she had been for a long, long while. Maggie got an elaborately carved box from a shelf.

"Do you mind if smoke some grass?" she asked politely.

"Not at all," said Cat. "I wouldn't mind some myself, though actually I'm dying for a cigarette."

"Well, I'm afraid the only thing I have to offer is home-grown." Maggie opened the box and started rolling a joint with quick precise movements. "I gave up the devil tobacco ten years ago. It was harder than giving up most men I've known and I've certainly missed it more than any," she added, laughing again.

Cat laughed with her. "I have some in my bag," she said, pulling out a packet and lighting one. The nicotine hit her system immediately. Cat smiled. Maggie picked up the packet lovingly and turned it in her hand.

"Luckies. They're toasted!" she read, shaking her head sadly. "After all these years I still love that logo. That used to be my brand. And you've got a crush pack? How could fate be so cruel? When I was a teenager I used to go around with a pack of these stuck in my back pocket." She lit up her joint and winked. "I was *really cool* as a teenager." Taking a deep drag and laughing at the same time made Maggie choke. She sputtered and coughed, laughing through it all.

"And now I'm just an *old fool*," she added taking another, slower drag. She held the smoke for a few seconds and then exhaled slowly through her nose as she passed the joint to Cat.

"Well, I don't agree," said Cat, smoking. The grass smelled sweet and tasted oddly like spinach. She paused and looked at Maggie straight in the eyes. She stared back, amusement dancing unchecked on her face. Nothing was hidden, nothing concealed, or closed. "I think you're wonderful."

Maggie's face relaxed into a goofy sort of smile. "You do?"

"I don't think I've ever met anyone like you before," she said.

"You've been in New York City way too long, honey," Maggie guffawed, taking the joint back. Cat picked up the sketch pad and started to draw.

"You could be right," said Cat measuring up the space between Maggie's eyes as she held the pencil up in front of her.

Maggie giggled and Cat caught the curve of her lip as it curled up.

"Please don't make me pose. There is no way I'm

going to keep still. I go all jiggly when I get stoned."
Maggie made a face and laughed infectiously, her big,
soft frame heaving with giggles. "See what I mean?"
she said, falling into another cascade of giggles.

Cat sketched quickly. "You don't have to stop
moving. Just keep talking. Tell me about yourself."

"I'm basically an army brat. My Dad was stationed
all around the world so I grew up following my family
from one country to the next. I guess that's why I find
it hard to stay in one place."

Cat nodded, encouraging her to go on. She had just
about got the glint in Maggie's eyes right. She added a
few shadows and held the sketch out.

"There!"

Maggie looked at it and broke into peals of laughter
"Oh my God! This is terrific. You've really captured me.
Anyone who knows me would know I was out of my
tree. You're really very good! Do you paint?"

"I used to," said Cat, picking up the pad again. The
smell of turpentine briefly passed her thoughts. It made
her think of Trevor. She shut that door quickly. "So
how did you get interested in witches?" Cat asked to
get her mind back to the present company.

"I'm not interested in witches as such. I'm interested
in women's myths. The archetypes passed down from
the beginning of time. The Harlot, the Saint, the Good

Mother, the Witch. They go back as far as Adam and Eve. Or Adam and Lillith, I should say."

Cat sketched aimlessly. She let the pencil mark the paper as if it had its own free will, not directing it. Just overseeing its general progress, correcting here, erasing there.

"Adam and Lillith?" she asked, her mind only half on the conversation. She drew a figure standing in a three-quarters pose. It was definitely a woman, with slender wrists and ankles, well-defined hips and broad shoulders.

"Lilith was Adam's first wife."

"I didn't know he'd had more than one," said Cat, shading in long hair, high cheekbones.

"Oh, he did. Lillith is mentioned in a number of different accounts. The Jewish tradition is perhaps the most well known, but she is mentioned by Moslems as well. She is the "wind-spirit" in Assyrian-Babylonian mythology. You see, first God created Adam and Lilith, either as Siamese twins or both moulded from the earth. Either way, Lilith was equal to Adam. Which is, of course, why she's so dear to feminists, and to the whole revisionist view of women and witchcraft," said Maggie, wiggling her eyebrows.

Maggie tried to peep at the drawing but Cat pulled it away, shaking her head. She concentrated on the face, sketching wide eyes under heavy lids, a full mouth and a small but strong nose. She looked at the face and realised she was drawing Annie as she was in the photograph.

"Presumably, Lilith and Adam led a happy enough life until they got horny," Maggie continued, her voice relishing the story as if it was a piece of juicy gossip. "Adam was upset that Lilith wouldn't 'get under him' – in other words assume the missionary position. She wanted to be on top! Adam refused. When he tried to force himself on her, she walked out. You can almost hear the women in the audience cheering 'You Go, Girl!'" Maggie declared triumphantly. She paused to put out her joint in the ashtray. Cat's cigarette had turned into a long tube of ash where she'd forgotten it while she sketched.

"Lillith then becomes, like, the first witch," Maggie continued, her hands flying around as she talked. "You know: the demon woman who kills children and comes to men in their sleep and has sex with them and then kills them too. The original succubus. She's in cahoots with the devil. She spawns legions of demons. She is really bad news!"

"So what happened to Adam?" asked Cat, catching herself thinking how much Trevor would have liked this story. The drawing was almost finished. A few strokes to fill in the dress, a few lines to suggest a room.

"Well, Lillith wouldn't come back and Adam kept

whining about how lonely he was, so God took Adam's rib and made Eve. And we know what sort of trouble that got us into!"

Cat added one last stroke and then put the sketch face-down on the bed without looking at it.

Maggie gave a quick glance, but did not ask to see it. "But enough about me!" she said, clapping her hands together. "What about you? How long are you on holiday?"

Cat shrugged. She felt very tired again. The wind had changed direction and picked up speed. Cat heard it come up from the valley and spill over the hill creating whirlwinds and eddies. No other noise cut through its shriek. It wasn't buried under the constant drone of traffic. Maybe Maggie was right, she thought. Maybe she'd been in the city too long. It was time to take time out.

"I don't really have a date in mind," Cat said. "I'm sort of on sabbatical."

Maggie nodded, as if silently agreeing to something Cat had not said. She did not ask what Cat was taking a sabbatical from. She just smiled and flicked her hair away from her eyes.

"Well, as I said, you can stay here as long as you like. It's yours after all."

Cat took the drawing materials off the bed and put

them on the stool. The drawing fell out and swooped to the floor. Maggie passed it back to Cat.

"May I?" she asked, nodding at the drawing.

"Sure," said Cat softly.

Maggie held it out and asked, "Who is it?"

Cat bit her lip. She was about to say it was her mother when a name came to her unbidden as if answering Maggie's question.

"It's Maeve," Cat said, astounded to hear her mouth utter it. Yet she knew that it was absolutely right. She recognised the long black hair, the worn brown dress. And she knew that it was Maeve. It was Maeve at the *toque*. It was Maeve in the east wing. It was Maeve rocking the cradle by the fire. It had always been Maeve, calling her, bringing her here to this place. But far from scaring her, it made her feel right and secure. It was simply Maeve. As simply as the sun and the moon just are and always will be.

"That is extraordinary!" said Maggie. "She is exactly as my friend described her to me." Maggie looked at it closely.

"Yeah, I guess I was influenced by your story," Cat answered, her mind still whirring with new possibilities.

"But you've got the dress and the hair. You've even got the shawl, and I know I never said anything about that. How on earth did you do it?"

"I don't know," Cat said, her face expressionless.

Maggie lowered her gaze. "Have you ever been tested for ESP?" she asked.

"No," said Cat, forcing a laugh. "I don't think so."

"Well, you could be the lucky one in twenty that seems to possess something, a "knack", a charm, whatever you want to call it." Maggie looked at the drawing one last time and set it aside. She stretched and the moment passed. She got up. "By the way, do you want me to get in touch with anyone and tell them you're OK. Is there anyone you need to call?"

Cat shook her head. She remembered the dream of lying in Trevor's arms. She wondered what he was doing. She suddenly realised that he was the one person she would love to talk to about it all. She ached to lie in his arms and let it all pour out, see his eyebrows crinkle up as he listened, hear his measured response make sense of things that didn't make any sense at all. Except that she couldn't. Not anymore. Maggie gave her one of her silent questioning looks, but said nothing.

"Thanks, but no," said Cat firmly. "No one knows I'm here."

Chapter Twenty-Two

✦━◆━✦

Trevor listened to the phone ring until it stopped and the answering service kicked in again. He sighed and hung up. It was three o'clock in the morning and no one was home. Not even the maid. Trevor felt a flicker of unease which he quickly brushed aside. It was Saturday night. Cat was probably out and she'd given the maid the night off. Maybe she'd gone away for the weekend. She could be down at the Hamptons. He hadn't thought of the Hamptons! Maybe that's where she was. He thought he would try calling the Hampton number in the morning, pushing aside the question of why she hadn't rung him.

He had been trying to reach her for two days. He had woken up alone in his bed with no sign of Cat and a wicked hangover. He'd forgotten to set his alarm and the little glowing numbers told him he was already an hour late for the press briefing at the UN. He had a pounding headache as he jumped in the shower and tried to beat his hangover with the weak pulse of warm water.

"Shit, shit, shit," he mumbled as he pulled on a fresh shirt and some trousers. He was going to have to find someone to fill him in on the briefing. His editor at the wire service in Sydney would have his ass on a stick if he didn't file in time.

"Except that you're already late you, wanker!" he said out loud as he rummaged through the kitchen for some aspirin. He hoped to find a cheery note tacked on the fridge, but there wasn't one. Cat's picture smiled down from the wall and he tried to remember what had happened the night before. It would be so much easier if she'd left a note. She always used to leave a note: "*Didn't want to wake u. I luv u. Cat.*" Something like that.

Had they made love? He didn't think so. Had they made up? Was everything OK between them again? He couldn't remember anything much past the surprise and delight of finding her standing there, her arms open wide to welcome him.

He made a mental note to call her the minute he got in the office. As he stood looking at her picture he dropped his gaze and noticed the memo from his New

York editor about the interview. A little warning bell went off in the pit of his stomach. He hoped she hadn't seen it. It occurred to him that he didn't know what he was going to tell the paper. He couldn't possibly write an objective article now. He'd fallen in love with her all over again.

"Right, like as if you ever fell out of love!" he muttered under his breath. Trevor tore up the memo and chucked it in the bin. He'd worry about the article later. First he had to get going on today. Find some excuse for not filing on time. He'd call Cat as soon as he got to work.

The day had gone into high gear the moment he'd walked into the busy press centre. The glaring lights and yelling voices had pounded at his brain and he'd had to beg some pain-killers from a secretary just to get through the afternoon. His editor screaming long distance over the phone didn't help. He vowed never to bloody-well drink again. It was very late before he got around to calling Cat. The office was closed. Trevor tried her apartment, but got no reply. He left messages at the office and twice on the answering service.

"This is Trevor Manning for Catherine Richardson. Could you please call me ASAP?"

"Hey Cat! It's Trev. Sorry I missed you this morning. Call me."

The next day he'd tried again but with no success.

Fiona wasn't taking any calls and the receptionist didn't know when Cat would be back in the office. The apartment was still not answering. She must have left early, creeping out so as not to wake him, thought Trevor. He wished he could remember more. He was sure they'd fallen asleep in each others' arms. He remembered the sweetness of kissing her again, surely that meant something? He didn't want to blow it this time. Play it cool or she'll bolt, he told himself. But not too cool, or she'll think you don't care. He called her private line, knowing that no one would answer but trying it all the same.

"Hey Cat. It's Trevor again. I'd really like to see you. Call me when you get the chance."

No one answered at the big house in the Hamptons until late Sunday afternoon. Margarita picked up after five rings.

"I am sorry but Miss Catherine has gone away. No, I don't know where. She came by to pick up a few things and told Victor to close down the apartment in New York. I do not know where she is, sir. I will tell her you called."

Trevor thanked her and hung up. He had a strange, uneasy feeling that something wasn't right. Cat hadn't mentioned going away. Or maybe he had been too drunk to remember. Maybe he'd forgotten something really important. He picked up the phone and dialled again.

Margarita picked up on the first ring.

"Sorry there, Margarita, Trevor again. Did you say she came over?"

"Oh yes, sir. She ran into the house and left after a few minutes upstairs. She was in a big, big hurry. She did not even visit with her grandfather. She just came in and told Victor to close down the apartment and then she left. Maria said she did not go home."

"When was that?"

"Thursday. She was here on Thursday."

Trevor thanked her. The next day? She had driven all the way out there, stayed what sounded like only a few minutes and left again? What the hell was that about?

Trevor felt his frustration growing. There was nothing more he could do just now. He tried to think about the week ahead. One feature was due, he should be setting up interviews for the next one after that, and of course the wire service still had to be fed every day. If he screwed up just one more time, he'd probably lose the string. Trevor looked at the computer on his desk and tried to will himself to sit down and work.

"Fuck it," he said out loud. Then he walked out and went down to the bar on the corner, hoping to find company in the misery of the other losers and broken hearts who had nowhere better to go on a Sunday night.

He was on the phone to Cat's office first thing Monday morning from the press centre. He would not take no for an answer and demanded to talk to Fiona.

After being left on hold for a full ten minutes, Fiona finally answered the phone. Her voice was weary behind her usual efficient manner.

"I'm sorry but Catherine has gone away for a few weeks. I suggest you don't call back until the middle of next month. I'll be sure to tell her you called," she said, not even waiting for Trevor to speak.

"Listen Fiona," Trevor said, his frustration breaking through. "Don't bullshit me. We were together all night. Then she upped and left without saying anything. She's closed down her apartment and nobody can tell me how to reach her. What's going on?"

Fiona did not answer right away. Trevor could imagine her pursing her lips on the other end.

"Well then, you know as much as I do," she said curtly.

"Cut the crap, Fi. Did she tell you not to let me through? Is she avoiding me?"

"Don't flatter yourself," Fiona said coldly. "Though, of course, if she had, I doubt I would tell you anything. As it is, I can be perfectly honest. Catherine left for a few weeks' break before the weekend. She left a message on my answering machine Thursday night. She said to cancel everything for the next three weeks and that she would get in touch."

"She left? What, like she's left the country?"

"I have no clue. Now if you'll excuse me, you aren't the only one she's left in the lurch."

"If she calls, will you please tell her to ring me?"

"I'll put you on the list of a dozen or more people who have requested that this morning, shall I? Goodbye, Trevor."

Trevor tried to concentrate on writing his piece for the wire service that day but he could not focus. It was totally useless. He closed down his lap-top and got himself a coffee from the vending machine. What was he going to do? It wasn't like Cat to leave everyone hanging. He felt the warning bells go off again. He didn't know what to do but he knew what he couldn't do. There was no way he could work.

Trevor hung around the press centre talking to people, but by four o'clock he knew it was no use. He had watched the big clock tick past his scheduled time to call the wire service and done nothing. Trevor called the papers for whom he had deadlines coming up and said he was sick. No one was particularly supportive and he found himself promising to try and get the articles written though he knew there was no chance of it. He had a flaming long-distance row with the wire service about his second missed deadline and decided to go home. He needed to be alone.

Trevor walked down his street deep in thought. A bum called out to him, but Trevor just walked on. He had enough problems of his own without having to try and deal with the dregs of humanity as well.

"Hey man, just take a minute. I only want something to help me get a coffee. I haven't eaten all day," the bum yelled at him as he passed.

Something made Trevor stop in his tracks. Wrong, this was all wrong. How could he just walk blindly past another human being? The bum on the street was just what he needed right now. It was time to take things in hand and change his luck. Trevor turned around and walked back to where the bum was sitting on a small blanket which had once been blue but now was the indeterminate colour of the sidewalk. He had a huge trolley piled high with black plastic bags parked next to him. His clothes were filthy but under a dirty woollen cap, Trevor saw two bright eyes looking at him.

"Hey, like I didn't mean no offence, OK?" said the bum, worried at Trevor turning back. "I just could really use a cup of coffee."

Trevor looked at him carefully, seeing the man

beneath the bum. He searched his pocket and pulled out a bill.

"Here get yourself that coffee and something to eat as well."

The man bit his lip and looked down. "Thanks, man. Thanks."

"Don't mention it," said Trevor walking away. I should be thanking you, he thought, I should be thanking you.

He was still thinking about the bum as he went into his building. He knew he was getting immune to the city and he didn't like it. Maybe he should think about getting out. Then again, maybe he'd already blown it. If he worked really hard and seriously kissed ass, he might catch up on the fuck-ups of the last few days. But he didn't know if he cared enough to try. The light wasn't working in the hall. The bulb must have gone out. Shit, Trevor thought, he'd have to remember to get a new one. It was just one more thing to do that he hadn't the energy for. Trevor made his way carefully up the stairs, waiting for his eyes to adjust to the light. His mind was racing. Where could she be? How could he even start looking when she had apparently disappeared without a trace?

A sharp pain shot through his wrist. Before he knew what was happening his face was smashed up against the door and his arm was straining not to move.

Someone had him in an armlock – if he moved, he knew his wrist would break.

"Open the door," said a gruff voice. Trevor tried to place it. It was mean and maybe drunk, but he'd heard it before.

"Give me the keys!" barked the man. The pain in his wrist shot up his arm as his attacker changed his grip and started going through his jacket pockets. He found the keys easily and unlocked the door. Trevor was pushed into the loft. He stumbled and fell, landing painfully on the floor. Trevor heard the door close and then he was blinded by the lights. He lay catching his breath, biding his time until he got his bearings.

Shading his eyes, he looked up.

"What the fuck do you think you're doing?" screamed Bob Stigeman. "Where is the bitch?" His mouth was contorted in fury. His Italian suit was impeccably cut but his tie was askew and one shirt tail was hanging out. Trevor sized him up quickly. He was taller, but Trevor was probably heavier. He'd most certainly been drinking.

"I don't know what the fuck you're talking about," said Trevor standing up and brushing himself off slowly and casually. "What the fuck do *you* think you're doing? And if you mean Cat, I'd like to ask you the same question."

"Don't play games with me, bush-boy," Bob

screamed his voice rising into high-pitched squeals. "What did you tell her? What lies did you tell her?"

"What the fuck are you talking about?" asked Trevor. The little warning bells were ringing like mad in his head. He thought with distaste about the dirt he'd collected on Bob. He remembered the file lying in his room. The sense of unease he had felt ever since he'd woken to find Cat gone was growing like a black balloon inside him.

"She fired me! The fucking bitch fired me! She didn't even have the decency to tell me herself. She got her messenger boy to do it and then she just fucked off. What the fuck did you tell her!"

Trevor took a step forward and grabbed Bob by the lapels, shoving him up against the wall. The satisfaction of feeling him cringe barely contained the empty black-ness that burst as Bob's words hit home. She knew about the file. She must have known. He had to check. First he had to get rid of this fucker. Then he had to check the file.

"Listen, you slimeball. You deserved whatever you got handed to you," he said hoarsely. His hands begged him to let them hit Bob. If he didn't control himself he would shove this bastard down the stairs and happily break his neck.

Bob's eyes opened wide with fear. "I'd be careful if I were you. I'm a black belt in judo," he said, but his voice was shaking. "Anyway, I know it was you. I know you had me followed. What's your game anyway? Blackmail?" he whined. "How much do you want?"

Trevor's fist shot out and he felt Bob's nose crunch under his knuckles.

"I didn't tell her anything, you arsehole," he snarled. "But I wish I had."

Then he grabbed him by the shoulders and kicked him out the door in one swift movement. "Judo, my ass," he gasped as he locked the door.

"You broke my fucking nose!" he heard Bob holler. "I'll get you for this!"

Trevor waited until he heard Bob making his way down the stairs. Then he ran into his room. His right hand was sore and swollen but he barely felt it as he desperately threw files around the floor. He went through them twice before he accepted that the one he was looking for was not there. He switched on the computer but it wouldn't boot. He got down on his hands and knees and crawled under the desk. The plug was pulled out of the socket. Trevor saw Cat standing next to the desk, a wry smile on her face as he walked in on her. Stupid drunk fool! He'd thought she was happy to see him.

He threw himself on the bed and groaned.

* * *

Trevor sat at the kitchen chair, nursing his aching hand with a bottle of tequila. He dialled madly around the city, calling anyone he could think of, taking a shot of tequila every few calls. He was getting nowhere. He tried to remember what was in the file. Anything that might give him a clue about where to start.

He'd started looking for Cat's mother because she'd asked him to. The birth cert had been easy to find, but he hadn't shown it to Cat, knowing it would upset her. He needed to know more first. Things were obviously not what Cat thought them to be. He'd found the committal order long after they'd broken up. He didn't know what to do with it, so he had just tucked it away with the birth certificate and the clippings. It was perverse, but he just kept looking. It was a way to keep her in his life. He knew he shouldn't have. He started collecting everything he could about her. It was like a hobby. It never became an obsession, but Trevor knew it had come damn close. Some bits made his heart ache. Others made him even more determined never to see her. He'd never really planned to do anything with it all. Answers just led to more questions until he accumulated enough information to fill a whole file.

Then the profile for the Wall Street Journal had come up and he'd jumped at the opportunity to see her again. The assignment also came with an expense account which would allow him to check if his suspicions about

Bob Stigeman were correct. He'd always thought that there was something fishy about him. He was too per-fect. Then Bob's name had come up and Trevor had been surprised to hear a gay colleague who had come out of the closet yonks ago react violently. He said he'd overheard Bob boasting in a bath-house about how much he was stashing away. He said Bob was a sordid little man who deserved to be outed except that he was the type who gave gays a bad name. It made Trevor yearn to learn more. After all, Trevor had always hated the bastard. The detective he hired had proved him more than right. But he had not mentioned any of it to his editor yet. He had kept the detective's photos and reports to himself in the file.

Trevor reached out for the bottle again and stopped in mid-air. Why hadn't he thought of it before? He quickly found the number and dialled. As always it picked up immediately.

"Loman's detective agency. Barney speaking."

"Barney, It's Trevor Manning. I've got another job for you"

"No problem. Same account?"

"Yeah. I'll file it in my expenses," Trevor said though he had no idea who the fuck was going to pay for it now that he wasn't doing the article. Man, if he kept screwing up like this he'd have to flee the country in the middle of night. Just like Cat did, he thought. Is that what she had done?

"You still there?" asked Barney. He sounded as if he was eating. Trevor had only actually met him once – all their business was conducted by phone and post. He was a small round man, who always seemed to be eating something.

"No problem. I'm still here."

"You want more pictures of pretty boy?"

"No, no. I'm trying to find someone who just upped and disappeared. I want to know where she went. Her name is Catherine Richardson."

"What, she like vanished into thin air and you want me to find her? Did she walk away, or did she just get on a broomstick and fly away?" Barney asked, still chewing. "Do you know if she left the country? Does she own a car? Anything I can go on?"

"She could have been driving," Trevor said thinking hard, clutching at straws. "I think she drove to the Hamptons on Thursday. She must have driven. But after that, who knows? She could have driven off to California – but I have a hunch that she's left the country."

Barney whistled through his teeth. "It's not much to go on. What sort of car does she drive?"

"I'm not sure. She used to have a Land Rover."

"Classy. And so no one's heard from her since Thursday?"

"No," said Trevor his voice betraying his despair. "Can you do anything?"

"You mean like work a miracle? Yeah, probably. Let me start with the airports. You never know. I'll call you back."

"Thank you. You're terrific."

"Hey kid, are you sure this is business? Don't worry, I don't care. I just do my job. I'll call you."

Trevor hung up and stared at the bottle. He screwed the cap back on and went to put it away. It was only when the phone rang, making him jump, that he realised that he'd just been sitting there, staring blankly out the window with the bottle in his lap.

"Bingo! First time lucky. Your hunch was right. Her car, which is by the way still a Land Rover, is parked in the long-term carpark at JFK. So your bird has most certainly flown the coop. Unless she's really smart and left her car there to put people off. Who is she hiding from?"

"I don't know that she *is* hiding. I just have to find her."

"By the way you failed to mention that this isn't just any old Catherine Richardson. This is *the* Catherine Richardson of Richardson-fucking-Corporation and Conglomerates. Not that it matters – except that these people never just disappear. You sure no one bumped her off, or kidnapped her?"

Trevor did not answer. He wouldn't consider that. No, he knew that Cat had left of her own free will.

"So that's it," he said finally. "Her car is at JFK but she could be in Kathmandu for all we know."

"There is one more thing I could do but it will cost. I could run a credit-card check on her."

"Is that legal?"

"I said it would cost, didn't I?"

"Go for it."

By the end of the day Barney had found out that a Catherine Richardson had bought a one-way ticket to London. She had got cash out of an ATM at Shannon airport, very early on Friday morning before flying on to London. It was a substantial amount.

"This lady was all over the place on Thursday," said Barney chewing again. "She got gas in Connecticut and Long Island. Bought some stuff at a store in East Hampton and then got a load of stuff at the airport. And she made two phone calls. One to her office number, the other to her lawyer."

"What was she doing in Shannon? Isn't that in Ireland?"

"Yeah. Her ticket was with Aer Lingus to London through Dublin. There's a stopover in Shannon. She then travelled on to London. If you know any of her friends there, her favourite hotels, restaurants – whatever it'd be a start."

"Thanks," said Trevor, feeling deflated. London was big. Very, very big. She could be anywhere.

"If you want I can keep an eye on her credit-card transactions, but it could take a while. Some of the foreign ones don't come through automatically, ya know. You have to wait until the end of the month. Sometimes more. Can you believe they're still using slips of paper over there? In this day and age? I hope she hasn't taken off to Asia, it could be months before her bills come through. Hey, she might be back by then, you never know! So, you want me to keep checking?"

"Yes. Please," said Trevor. "Do whatever you can."

Chapter Twenty-Three

◆—◆

Cat followed Maggie from stall to stall. The market on the big square sold everything from vegetables to shoes, jewellery to oilcloths. Cat had plenty of time to browse. Maggie seemed to know everyone. Cat had accompanied her shopping before, and going into town always seemed to take three times longer than it should as Maggie stopped every few yards to say hi. It was taking even longer today. Maggie would be leaving soon and was taking the opportunity to say goodbye to everyone she met. She had already spent five minutes buying some bread from a woman and it looked like it might take about ten more. Cat moved away as the woman started telling Maggie about her mother-in-law's recent heart attack in detail. Cat wandered off along the stalls. She bought herself a big hand-knit fuzzy sweater in a bright jumble of colours, two pairs of cheap baggy jeans, and a stout pair of rubber boots. The laneway up to the cottage turned into a stream whenever it rained. Cat accumulated half a ton of mud around her ankles just getting to her car. She decided to keep the boots in her car and take them off at the door under the little roof that jutted out for shelter. They could be her laneway boots, she thought, delighted with her purchases. She stopped in front of a stall that sold workmen's overalls.

"Is it fer yerself?" asked the man behind the stall, eyeing her and then checking the navy overalls flapping in the breeze behind him. "I've only three sizes. The small might still be a bit big on ye, but ye could roll up the bottoms."

Cat shook her head and laughed out loud. "Thanks, but I think I'll pass today."

She walked away smiling, thinking of what she'd look like in the oversized overalls – with the big black rubber boots and colourful fuzzy sweater. She thought about the rows of business suits hanging in her closets in New York. The racks of shoes. All those heels, and flats; all the pairs of loafers and dress shoes would be completely useless to her here. How many suits did she have anyway? How many cream silk blouses? Black knit tops? Cat looked at the packages she was carrying and laughed again. I wonder what they'd say if they could see me now, she thought to herself.

A little black cloud of panic passed her by as she briefly visualised New York and all that she had left behind. But she refused to let it cast a shadow on her mood. After recovering from her bout of flu and near madness under Maggie's gentle care, Cat realised just how close to losing it she had come. She needed time to get her head together before tackling the problems that had almost driven her over the edge. She was going to take it easy and get strong. Though her life had been turned upside down, there was nothing urgent to attend to. Nothing that couldn't wait until she was good and ready. She was on holiday. Maybe she'd send them a telegram: *Have extended my vacation. Wish you were here!* Cat giggled. She couldn't care less if all hell was breaking loose across the Atlantic. And as for Trevor, she hoped he was miserable. Still, though she hated to admit it, she would have liked to see the look on his face if he could see her now.

Cat strolled around the Square, peering into every shop window whether it sold clothes, souvenirs, or pots and pans. Many of the smaller shops seemed to sell a little of everything, and their windows were a jumble of articles piled one on top of another and hand-written signs urgently declaring: *Farm Fresh eggs! Kerr's Pinks! Hand Knitted Hats!*

One shop was fancier than the rest and Cat spent a while gazing at the watches, rings, and brooches. No item was more than a few hundred pounds and most of it was worthless trinkets. A young couple came up and peered at the display. Cat watched them as they pointed excitedly at the rings. Cat knew they'd be saving up for the ring they chose. The girl blushed as she caught Cat's gaze and then smiled. Cat saw the light in her eyes. She imagined the same light years later, as she showed the ring to a small child and told the story of its purchase. Cat felt a stab of guilt at having looked at the jewellery and considered it worthless. Why? Because she could just walk in and pay for it in cash? What determined its value? She knew it was more than money. Maggie was right. It had to do with meaning.

Cat moved on to a long display of T-bar necklaces. Some were heavy braids, others just a light chain. Cat thought about her necklace. She wondered who had bought it. For whom?

Cat strolled around the square. She bought a pair of earrings and a brooch from Lizzie who was tending a stall with Sean. They were made of bronze and inspired by Celtic designs with delicately engraved knot-work.

"You coming for a pint?" asked Sean, starting to pack up.

"Are you closing up already?" asked Cat.

422

"Yeah. We made enough money for today!" laughed Sean. "It's time to have a pint!"

"Have you seen Maggie?" asked Cat.

"She just went down the street a few minutes ago," answered Sean.

"Great. I'll find her and join you."

"Nice one!" Sean waved.

Cat waved back as she walked away. She realised that she was walking down the street with a great, big, open smile on her face.

How long had it been since she'd walked that way? She certainly remembered walking like that as a child. Probably the last time had been with Trevor when they used to run around Central Park. Cat sat on a bench to ponder the changes she'd been going through since she'd arrived up on the hill. As the weeks passed Cat had felt herself relax and grow. It was as if she had shed a tight restricting skin and was starting to fill out and stretch her new body. Maggie's cooking and days of walking the hills, or helping out in the garden, had increased Cat's appetite. She was getting stronger too. She had built up muscles different to those when she worked out at the gym. And as she grew stronger, she found that she could sit still for longer periods of time. The days were clearly broken into bursts of intense activity for a purpose, or complete relaxation. Cat silently thanked Maggie for the space she had given her. The solitude and the silence. Especially the silence.

As the days went by Cat became aware that the silence around her had become whole. The intense buzzing that she had carried around in her head since she had first found the file had disappeared. In her relief Cat realised that she had been carrying that constant buzz not for a few days, but for many years. It had been with her as far back as she could remember: the drone of traffic, the whisper of voices, the stereo, the television, the litany of rules, of things unsaid, of things not done. And under it all, the muffled crying hidden deep under layers of brightly coloured distractions. Cat had felt the layers stripped away one by one until she had finally found, and then embraced, the silence.

Cat looked out at a little fishing boat in the bay, it's bright red hull bobbing on the turquoise waves under an impossibly big sky. Clouds bigger than the biggest skyscrapers drifted placidly over the bay, dwarfing everything except the outline of the mountains high up on the horizon. She was constantly astounded by the landscape. After a week of rotten weather summer had made a curtain call, suddenly revealing miles more to the surrounding hills, and fields, and sea. It could have been the middle of July except that the air was heavy with the smell of leaf mould and earth. Cat wondered what it would smell like in the spring, when everything would start growing again.

Cat saw Maggie chatting by a garden stall and went over to join her. The stall sold bulbs and shrubs. Cat picked up a packet of daffodils.

"Wouldn't these look great up the lane?" she asked Maggie.

"I've always thought they would. But I won't be around to see them. If you plant them now they'll be up in late February. I really hate to leave this year. I should have gone last week but the weather has been so great."

"It's been wonderful," Cat agreed. "I hope you haven't delayed your schedule because of me. You've been most kind."

"Nonsense. I always like to keep things flexible – *just in case*. I only really have to get back to Arizona before Halloween. I'll be lecturing there for a few months. After that I have to work on a new series of lectures. I'm not really sure *what* I'm doing for Christmas," Maggie said. Then she cocked her head and looked at Cat. "What about you?"

"I don't know really," Cat answered slowly shaking her head. "I like it here."

"Well, if you're still around, then maybe I'll come back. If you'll have me that is! I've never had Christmas in Ireland. I hear it's great fun except that the weather is really foul!"

Cat smiled. She had a vision of herself battling across the yard in a heavy gale, the wind whipping her hair, the rain pouring off the little roof. She'd take off her muddy boots and fight the door open, feeling the blast of warmth as she slipped into the little room with its low ceiling and roaring fire. She liked that idea.

Cat signalled the stall owner and bought a packet of daffs and a packet of narcissus.

Maggie raised an eyebrow. "So you're staying?"

Cat shrugged.

"I don't know yet. I can always plant them. I don't know if I'll be around to watch them bloom, but I'll plant them anyway. I like that. It's like those incredible gardeners who planted things which they would never see because it would take three hundred years for the garden to be complete."

"Sounds good to me," said Maggie, flinging her arm around Cat's shoulder and giving her a squeeze as they walked to the car.

Cat and Maggie were putting their heavy bags into the trunk, when Spider came up leading a large sheepdog and a puppy. They both had long bits of string tied around their necks. Cat bent down to pet them.

"Nice-looking dogs," she commented.

"They're not mine," said Spider looking a bit lost. "Me mate's had to go back to England. He gave me the dogs to find a new home for them. I'd love to keep 'em, but I can't. I brought them down to the market, but nobody wants 'em."

The big sheepdog jumped up and licked Cat's hand. The puppy was overexcited and kept straining at the bit of string, running in circles and biting it until he was completely tied up. Cat laughed and bent down to help him get unravelled. The puppy jumped up and licked her nose as his mother looked on approvingly.

"They like you," said Spider smiling broadly, showing the gap in his front teeth. "Don't you two ladies want a dog? You'd need one up there. The place isn't really right without a dog. The big one's the mother and the little one's her pup. She had seven, this one's the only one still left from the litter."

"I'd love to take them," said Maggie rubbing the big dog's neck. "But I'm afraid I'm leaving."

Cat looked down at the mother. She could swear the dog was reading her mind. The big brown eyes seemed to be saying, "Go on! We could be happy for a little while."

"OK," said Cat, still looking at the dog who seemed positively delighted with her decision. "I can take them off your hands for now. At least until we find a permanent home for them. I'll still be around for a little while."

"Great!" said Spider, much relieved. The dogs caught his excitement and started wagging their tails and jumping on Cat. "They like you – that's for sure. The Mum's name is Sheba. The pup hasn't got a name yet."

"He looks like a Ralph to me," said Maggie.

Cat crouched down and let the dogs lick her. The puppy jumped straight into her arms. It was black and white and brown, and at that teenage stage: all lanky and leggy but still with a round puppy belly.

"Ralph it is," said Cat taking the string leads from Spider.

"By the way they're vegetarians. They love peanut butter and bananas."

Cat led the way to the pub, the two dogs trotting happily by her side. The first thing she was going to do was buy them collars, she thought. Then she was going to the butcher's for some steak.

The pub was dark after the bright sunshine in the square. It was a large room with metal tables and chairs all along the walls, and a rounded counter at one end. Only a few men stood at the bar. They all turned and looked as Cat came in with Spider and settled down at Sean and Lizzie's table. The dogs immediately curled up near her feet. Spider called the orders and went up to the bar to fetch the glistening black pints of stout when they were ready.

He came back with a young man in a tweed cap and dirty overalls. As soon as he settled in, the young man ignored the rest of the table and concentrated on Cat. He took a long slow pull off his pint and then took a good long look at her.

"So you're the one living up there with Maggie," he said, licking the foam off his upper lip. "Where is she? I thought I saw her on the square."

"She was coming with us but she stopped to say goodbye to another fifty people," said Cat laughing.

"She's leaving, is she?" asked the young man peering over the rim of his glass. "And are ye staying on yer own then? Aren't ye afraid?"

"Should I be?" Cat asked defensively.

"Well, I tell ye," he said shaking his head, "I wouldn't stay up there on my own for love or money." Then he leaned in closer and gave her a flirtatious wink. "But if you were around I might not be as frightened," he added to the general amusement of the patrons of the pub who all laughed.

"I gotta say it's kinda spooky up on the hill at night," said Spider, "but that's probably because I've heard all the stories about Maeve and the cursed hill and all that. I've stayed there loads of times and I've never seen anything. It's probably all just stories they used to tell to scare little kids."

"Bollocks, boy," said the young man shaking his

head again. "Maeve is real all right. She really lived up there, and before she died she cursed some people and said she would get them from beyond the grave. And she did! And their descendants too. Here, just ask Gerry over there," he added, waving one of the older men over to their table. "He knows that hill well. He grew up there. Come over here, Gerry! Tell these lads about Maeve's hill."

The old man shuffled up to them and nodded.

"Now so, Gerry," started the young man, "This lovely girl here is living up in Kilkeambeg." He turned to face Cat with a seductive smile. "What's your name? I didn't catch it."

"Catherine."

"Right, so." He turned back to the old man. "As I was saying Catherine here is. . ."

But the old man held up his hand and cut him off. He looked intently at Cat, his bony finger pointed in the air. His eyes were clouded as if someone had spilt milk into a blue china saucer and Cat shivered as he paused, took a long whistling breath, and then pointed at her.

"I don't care what you say your name is. You're the spit of Anne Kelly, you are. It makes my skin crawl to see ye. I was there the day they found poor Mary. And I knew that Annie was back, parading around with her fancy ways. They said poor Mary died of natural causes. But no one ever saw Annie again, and anyone who saw poor Mary's face as she lay stone cold dead on her own doorstep will tell you that there was nothing natural about her passing. You don't need me to tell you anything about that cursed hill. You know all there is to know."

Then he shuffled back to the bar and turned his back to the room.

Cat drove out of town and up the mountain in silence. She was grateful that Maggie didn't seem to mind her lack of conversation. Even the dogs respected her mood and curled up quietly on the back seat. That old guy had spooked her. She couldn't wait to get out of the pub. He seemed to be glaring at her though he kept his back turned the whole time.

Cat pulled up alongside the cottage. Before they got out she stopped and took a last look back at the valley. She had fallen into the habit of doing that whenever she drove back to the cottage. Maggie murmured appreciatively as they both looked back at the winding road, the green fields, and the bright glare of the sea on the horizon. Then she snapped her hand up to her brow and executed a military salute. Cat gave her an inquisitive look which Maggie answered by pointing out the window.

"A magpie crossed the road. It's a habit I picked up over here. You know? You've heard the rhyme about magpies?" Maggie explained as they got out of the car and unloaded their shopping.

Cat nodded. Maggie started to recite as they walked up the laneway. Cat found herself silently reciting along with her. *"One for sorrow. Two for joy. Three for a girl. Four for a boy. Five for silver. Six for gold. And seven for the secret that's never been told."*

"Saluting a single magpie is one way to ward off the bad stuff," Maggie continued. "Magpies are messengers. They can carry curses, or bring bad news. Sometimes good news. But they're not very powerful. Their curse can easily be countered. You know: *One in flight is worth two in sight?* So all you have to do is make it fly away. If one flies by and you salute it, that will also counter the *evil eye* – or whatever you want to call it. There are lots of stories relating to magpies. Apparently not so long ago, seeing a magpie before setting off on a journey would be enough to make someone turn around and go home. Even today I've often heard people here say things will turn out well because they saw two magpies. You know: *Two for joy.*"

The dogs bounded up in front of them, happy to be freed from their bits of string. *One for sorrow. Two for joy.* The verse rang through Cat's head.

Three for a girl. Four for a boy. What did they mean? *Five for silver. Six for gold.* What were they trying to tell her?

"But of course the worse magpie encounter is if one is chattering at you, or at your door, or *worse yet* – comes into the house. It means bad news. A death generally."

Cat stopped in her tracks. They had come to the door and Maggie had dropped her bags on the step and had sunk gratefully on the little bench to soak up the sunshine. The dogs snuffled around the yard, their noses pressed to the ground. Cat heard the echo of birds screeching in the little yard. The flap of wings beating against the curtains as it tried to get out of the room. A flash of black and white feathers swooping over the sheds and up the hill. The time had come to talk. To face the horrors she had been avoiding. She knew it but did not welcome it.

"A magpie came into the house the day that Mary Kelly died," Cat said suddenly. "My mother told me," Cat added softly as if to herself.

Maggie looked up, shading her eyes. She cocked her head and paused, as if acknowledging that something had changed. But when she spoke, her voice was casual.

"Was Mary Kelly your grandmother, or your great-aunt? "

"No, she wasn't my grandmother," answered Cat, sitting down next to Maggie and lighting a cigarette. "And I don't think she was an aunt, though my mother called her Auntie Mary. I don't think she was a relation at all."

Maeve's brat. She'd called Annie Maeve's brat.

Maggie said nothing as if she knew that Cat had more to say more.

"There was an old man in the pub before you arrived," Cat said, pulling hard on her cigarette. "The old man said something about my mother. He said I looked just like her. And then he implied that she had something to do with Mary Kelly's death. And all that stuff about a curse on the hill."

"There are a lot of stories that go around about this hill," Maggie said slowly. "Maybe I should have told you myself, but I figured you'd end up hearing them anyway."

"Like what stories?"

"Oh, like there's a black dog that sits at the bottom of the road. A weeping woman – a sort of banshee – up at the stream. There's a "fairy fort" up at the very top of the hill – you should go up there – it's really pretty. And of course the stories I've told you already about Maeve: walking up on the hill. That she's the one who killed Mary Kelly. They say she came back to get Mary Kelly because of some old curse that Maeve brought on the Kellys when she died."

"And what about my mother?"

Maggie paused. When she spoke she used a light voice, downplaying the story.

"I've heard a lot of stories about Mary Kelly's death. Some say that Mary Kelly was frightened to death. Some attribute it to Maeve. Others hint at the fact that her niece, who had been visiting, disappeared the day Mary Kelly's body was found. I assume that would be your mother. And people kinda give you a *nudge, wink* kind of look. But Mary Kelly died of natural causes. There was nothing strange in the official record, and as far as I know no one went looking for the niece. It's probably all lies anyway. Or half-truths that get distorted over time."

Cat sat back and watched the dogs play in the only spot of sun left in the yard. Her mind was racing as Maggie continued her explanations. Cat instinctively picked her way through the images and stories which flashed past her as if she was searching through a rolodex. Some thoughts she discarded as irrelevant, others she set aside. Somehow she knew that Annie Kelly wasn't what this was all about. Whatever *that* was. It was about Maeve. Annie Kelly had just got caught up in it like Cat had. And it had destroyed her.

"The stories about Maeve are like *supernatural* gossip," Maggie continued in her best lecture voice. "The story about your mother is *village* gossip. Both are distorted with time and retelling. Like the kid's game Chinese whispers. From old primitive creation myths, to more recent ghost stories, to urban myths about stealing kidneys – most of it is just all gossip really. I wouldn't put much credence in it."

Maggie took Cat's hand and patted it.

"You're not upset, are you? I bumped into Seamus and he says you should pop in when you get the chance. He has all the papers drawn up for the house. It's a great little place – don't let stupid gossip ruin it for you."

Cat nodded and turned to smile at Maggie. She was right. But she didn't know the whole story. The half-truths that had spun a web of lies, nor the lies that had taken root and grown strong until nothing could distinguish them from the truth. Maybe it was time to stop running away from the past, thought Cat, as she looked up to the dark silhouette of the hill above her. Maybe she was ready.

Cat reached out and lit a cigarette. She'd stayed up late on her own. Maggie had gone to bed early. It was going to be Maggie's last day and she didn't want to waste it. Cat spent the night leafing through the diary and file, sitting sketching, or just staring into space and thinking.

The snap of the fire and the steady rise and fall of the dogs' breathing as they slept lulled her, making her feel safe enough to let her mind roam free and slowly try and approach what she was going to do. She let her mind drift as she sketched.

She'd thought about Trevor a lot. His image seemed to come up unbidden, and she would pause and measure how she felt about him. She was surprised to still be able to see him in his old light. Could people change as much as he seemed to have? Maybe there was a reason for his deceit. Maybe she should let him explain. But she knew that something had been broken that would never be put together without showing the cracks.

She let herself think about her grandfather lying in his bed. Even though he had no idea that she hadn't called, Cat still felt a pang of guilt. He had his part to play in the charade of her childhood, and she imagined that it was not always the role of the hero, but she could not help loving him.

She felt no guilt about not calling the office. She'd closed that door in her mind for now. The whole thing ran quite smoothly without her. And as for Bob Stigeman, she couldn't care less if the earth opened up and swallowed him whole.

Most of all she let herself think about her mother: images of an old woman staring out the window alternating with Annie Kelly whizzing up a city street on the back of a red scooter. When the sadness threatened to overwhelm her she got up and put on some music. Then she would empty her mind and just draw, barely noticing the tears creeping down her cheeks.

She felt better for having started to face her fears. But she was no closer to understanding. Nor did she know what she was going to do or when? Cat looked around the room. She was curled up in the sofa covered in a duvet. The puppy slept snuggled up in the curve of her hip, while Sheba snored by the fire. The table in front of Cat was cluttered with the jumbled puzzle of her progress through the night: glasses and mugs of coffee, cigarettes and overflowing ashtrays, candles and plates of food. The file and the diary were stacked on one end, while all over the table lay pages ripped from the sketch pad.

Cat had drawn Maeve over and over again. On a New York street. In that room in the east wing. Walking down the hill. Sometimes she had put a magpie in the picture. One page was covered in magpies: one in flight, two pecking at the ground, another sitting on a branch, others in various poses.

Cat thought about the drawings her mother had made and flinched. Then she shook her head and stubbed out her cigarette. She wasn't going down that road. Not yet.

Cat rummaged in her bag and brought out the thimble and the necklace. She lay them next to a candle that was burning low on the table. The tiny flame flickered on the gold braid, making it shine. Cat stared at the flame, feeling her breathing slow and her heart-beat grow calm.

Sheba stirred and started whimpering. Cat snapped her head up and looked around, but the room was still and silent. The puppy was fast asleep. Then Sheba jumped up, nose in the air, and started to whine.

She slinked back to the sofa and sat in front of Cat. Cat reached out and rubbed Sheba's back. She could feel the dog trembling under her fingertips. Sheba was staring at one corner of the room. Cat looked intently at the dog. She did not want to turn her head in the direction of the dog's gaze because she knew what she would see. She could smell the lavender hanging heavy in the air. She took a final glance at the small pool of candle-light around the necklace and thimble. Then she took a deep breath and looked over.

Maeve was standing in the corner rocking the cradle. She was talking to someone out of sight. Cat could not hear what she was saying, but knew that she was distraught. She could feel the anger and the pain.

Maeve looked down at the baby in the cradle. Cat felt great love pouring out of her along with the blind fear of leaving her child. Maeve reached up and took off the T-bar necklace around her neck. She bent down and tucked it in the cradle, kissing the baby one last time. As she straightened up, she disappeared.

The cradle was still by the fire, but Maeve was at the

door now. She had another baby in her arms. She looked longingly at the cradle behind her and Cat knew that the child in her arms was not her own. Maeve was talking again. Harsh words spoken in anger. And under them Cat sensed a terrible fear. Maeve held out the baby as if showing it to someone.

Cat felt a screaming panic rise in her throat.

Maeve was trembling as she turned to open the door. If she stepped outside something terrible would happen. Somebody had to warn her! Why didn't anyone warn her? Maeve turned back one last time. Her eyes were wet with tears as she blew a kiss to the little cradle. Then she was gone.

Cat sprang to her feet. She ran to the door yelling, the dogs barking and jumping alongside her. She yanked the door open and looked up the hill. She could just make out a slight figure going up the goat path.

Cat screamed for her to stop. Already she could smell the smoke curling around the sleeping house. But the figure just kept walking up the hill towards the fire which glowed red in the dark night.

Maggie was shaking her. Cat stood on the doorstep still screaming for Maeve to stop. Maggie put her arm around Cat's shoulder and led her back inside, whispering comforting words in her ear. She sat Cat back on the sofa and poured her a drink. Cat drank in silence, still overwhelmed by her experience. Maggie got another bottle and her stash box. She tidied the table and then sat on the big pillow facing Cat. She watched Cat as she rolled a joint. She lit it and took a long pull, holding the smoke for a few seconds before letting it slowly slip out her lips.

"Right," she sighed, her eyes squinting up as she peered up at Cat through the blue haze over her head. "What the hell is this all about?"

Chapter Twenty-Four

—◆—

Cat told her everything in a jumbled spurt of mixed up thoughts and events. Then Maggie made her go through it all again, starting with when she first thought she saw the black-haired woman at the *Santeria toque*. When she had finished, Cat felt calm again. The drink and grass had cushioned her as she came down. The bottle was half empty and the ashtray was topped with the tiny roaches Maggie used. Now that her fright was over, she felt stupid and slightly embarrassed by the whole episode and she wished she hadn't dragged Maggie into it.

"Now that is one helluva story," said Maggie making a clucking sound with her tongue. "Wow! I don't even know *where* to start to try and figure it out."

"I don't know if I want to start at all," said Cat. "I've

had quite enough really. I just want it to all go away."

But Maggie wasn't listening. Her eyes sparkled with excitement. "I wish I didn't have to leave now. This is extraordinary. If we can somehow find a link, then we could at least start with that."

Maggie stopped to think for a minute, her brow furrowed in concentration. Cat yawned, she was exhausted. She didn't feel up to another of Maggie's lectures.

"I guess we could start with what you saw tonight. And that other night. These types of phenomena generally fall into one of three categories: run of the mill ghosts, poltergeists, and recordings. Ghosts are what you would expect – spirit beings who you can interact with; poltergeists actually physically move things around a room, make things fall through the ceiling, that sort of thing; and the recording just replays some past event on a sort of cosmic loop."

"You don't understand," said Cat, irritably. She was tired of the whole damn thing. "I don't want to know! I just want it all to go away. I don't care what it is – I don't want it."

"Look, whether you want it or not – it seems to want you. You've tried hoping it would just go away, and that didn't work. Maybe it *is* just in your head. But you might as well find out. What have you got to lose?"

"My sanity! That's what!" Cat snapped back. Sheba looked up, surprised at Cat's tone of voice.

"I'm sorry, but this isn't some sort of game," Cat apologised. "My mother went crazy. She's been locked inside her own world for almost thirty years. And I think it was because she was convinced that she and I were cursed. I'm scared of what that means for me. What if I'm predisposed to madness. I don't want to go there."

"Nobody does," said Maggie gently "But going into denial is the best way to madness."

"I know this sounds funny, but let's say I'm the sane one here. OK?" Maggie continued, smiling at Cat. "And as the sane one I'm saying that you're not going crazy. Look, I don't want to push anything. I'm just trying to put some *order* here. Tidy up our thinking a bit." Maggie looked to Cat, who nodded slowly.

"Good. Let's start with tonight. OK? First of all you thought you saw a ghost."

"No," said Cat, remembering the woman rocking the cradle. "It wasn't a ghost."

"What do you mean?"

"You know what you said about ghosts and poltergeists? This wasn't like meeting a ghost, it was more like watching a recording."

"But you said you've seen this ghost – or vision – before. In New York? Was it the same woman?"

"Yes, but this was different. In New York *she* was looking for *me*. She was more like a ghost then. Tonight

444

was like I conjured her up. Like I hit a replay button in time. She wasn't really there. Except that it all *felt* so real."

"OK," said Maggie holding up her hand to slow Cat down. "You saw something which feels like a re-enactment. Are you sure it was Maeve? You said she had your necklace and was giving it to a baby. Could it have been your mother?"

"No. She was not my mother. This woman was stronger, more sure of herself. And older. This woman was older. Very motherly."

"She wasn't your mother but she was motherly," Maggie repeated.

"Yes," said Cat letting herself relive her experience without the fear. "There was a deep feeling of connection with her. I'd never really looked at her before. When I saw her in New York I was too scared. But this time she wasn't really there. So I could watch. I wasn't scared of her."

"You weren't scared? Then why did you scream? You seemed terrified. You kept screaming: No! Stop!"

"I was scared *for* her. She was in terrible danger. The baby was in terrible danger. I don't know why, but I didn't want her to go back up that hill. It was horrible. She was walking back up to a house on the hill. I was trying to stop her."

"There used to be a house up there," Maggie said. "The place is in ruins but you can still see it."

Cat suddenly knew there had been a fire up there. There had been a terrible fire, and the house had burned down with Maeve and the other woman's baby inside. Maeve's baby was safe, here in the cottage, sleeping in the cradle with the necklace tucked in her blanket. Maeve's baby was saved, but Maeve had died a horrible death. Cat closed her eyes to try and blot out the flames licking the gable end. Maggie sensed her distress and gave her a quick pat on the arm.

"You've had a rough night. I say we hit the sack."

"I second that," said Cat wearily. "In fact I'm so tired I don't have the energy to go upstairs. I'm going to sleep right here." She squeezed Maggie's hand, relishing the strength and warmth. "I'm sorry I woke you up. Thanks. For everything."

"Hey, it's nothing," she answered. "Though I've got to say you scared me shitless. But it was worth it! What a story! By the way – what's it feel like to be that rich?" she added winking broadly.

"The same as being poor, I guess," Cat smiled back, "except with money."

"You're going to be just fine," Maggie said as she rose to her full height and stretched, her hands pulled high over her head.

"I'll tell you what. Why don't you come and visit my

friend Ciara with me tomorrow. I have to pop in and say goodbye. She's a witch in her own right. She has a family tradition that goes way back."

"That's last thing I want to do," said Cat, drawing the duvet back around her. "Consulting a witch doesn't sound very like a very rational way of dealing with this."

Maggie threw back her head and laughed.

"What's so rational about seeing a woman who's been dead for a hundred years standing on Lexington Avenue? Being rational sometimes means taking reality with a grain of salt. Being irrational as it were. Stretch your mind! If you had warts, and I told you this woman could cure them, and you went to see her, and your warts disappeared – you'd be happy! Where's the problem? Anyway, the fact that Ciara is a witch just makes it more interesting. That's not why I think we should visit."

"It isn't?" Cat asked, confused.

"No. The reason we should visit is that she's got the best hot tub in the whole of West Cork," Maggie said wincing as she tried to stretch her lower back. "My back is killing me and you certainly need to relax and just chill."

Cat found that she was smiling. She snuggled into the duvet and made a space for the puppy to cuddle into. Just chill – that sounded good, she thought.

"Does she really cure warts?" Cat asked as Maggie started up the stairs.

"She is one hundred percent effective. And she has no idea how she does it!"

Cat listened as Maggie creaked up the stairs. When she reached the landing she called down again.

"Cat?"

"Yeah?" she answered closing her eyes.

"Are you really Catherine Richardson of the Richardson Corporation?"

"Yeah."

"Well, fair fucks to ye, as they say over here!"

Cat slept until the sun woke her. The dogs were whining to go out. Cat got up and opened the door, standing wrapped in the duvet as they sniffed around the yard. The sun was a pale yellow glow behind the early morning clouds, but the air held a gust of warmth from the coast that smelt of seaweed and salt spray. The dogs stretched their legs and then started chasing the ginger cat. They ran around in circles until they veered off after a bird and chased it out of the yard. The puppy bounded up the rise but Sheba held back and looked at Cat over her shoulder, her tail wagging as if to invite her out.

"OK. I'll go for a walk," Cat said dropping the duvet

on the floor and grabbing the big fuzzy sweater she had bought at Bantry market.

There was a cold chill in the air. Mist hung in wispy plumes about a foot off the ground, but though the dew was freezing against her bare feet, the pale sun held the promise of warmth to come.

Her nostrils were tingling. Everything smelt fresh and slightly damp, as if the whole landscape had been sprayed with a fine perfumed shower. Cat stood very still and listened. A bird was singing in a copse of trees up on the hill. Cat heard another bird answer from a tree in the lane. Under the bird calls she made out other sounds: the rustling of leaves in the breeze and, beyond that, the sound of running water.

The puppy was dashing around, running ahead a few yards before turning back and charging at Cat and Sheba as they walked up the hill. Sheba was pacing herself to Cat, stopping at Cat's heels every time she stopped. They followed a rough path of white stones that meandered up the hill in a vague sort of line. Water trickled down the tiny gully made by the path, tripping over stones and collecting in ice-cold little pools.

There must be a stream up there, she thought. There was a copse of trees above her and Cat headed in that direction with a vague feeling of deja vu. The dogs bounded up ahead towards an overgrown outcropping. The puppy reached it first. He sniffed around and then let out a yelp and ran back to his mother.

Cat saw that what she had thought was a bunch of rocks was in fact the outline of a house. Only a low portion of the walls remained, black and greasy-looking. Her heart skipped a beat as she realised where she was. No wonder it felt familiar. Annie had written about walking up here. Annie had laid down here and wanted to die. This was the house. Maeve's house. Cat let her gaze drift across the black stones, overgrown here and there with dark ivy. The hearth was still visible, though the chimney had tumbled down into the house's belly long ago. Up close Cat could see it was a more substantial cottage than the one below. Cat crossed the wall and stood in the middle of the house, carefully picking her way through the deep mud and matted grass. She idly looked around trying to fend off the terrible feeling of desolation. Who had lived here? Loved here? Died here? Her attention was caught by something shiny lying in the muck. Bending down she saw that it was a piece of glass. Cat picked it up and wiped it off, noticing the silver flecks still clinging to it. It must be a piece from an old mirror, she thought suddenly feeling an intense pang. Someone had once looked into this mirror, perhaps brushing her hair, perhaps checking her reflection.

The dogs had got bored with her and had taken off

after something. They were now chasing each other up the hill. Cat left the mirror on the wall and followed them up to the trees.

Sheba stopped at the treeline and waited for her. The puppy looked at his mother barely able to contain his excitement as he nipped at her legs. As soon as Cat caught up with them, they dashed into the undergrowth barking wildly.

The copse of trees seemed to explode. Cat was over-whelmed by the mad rustle all around her as the dogs flushed out birds from the trees, rabbits from the under-growth and other small animals whose frantic scut-terrings turned the dense ivy and ferns into a trembling carpet. A flock of starlings lifted off the branches as one, and sailed away like a giant swarm of bees. Everything around her shivered and shook. Then all grew still again. The silence was deafening after the bursts of barks, and squawks, and rustling of leaves and snap-ping of branches.

Cat giggled and felt her heart pounding wildly in her chest. The sun peered timidly through the branches, spotlighting patches of the undergrowth in its golden light. The land rose very steeply under the trees and Cat was delighted to discover the stream she had heard. It cascaded over rocks, no more than a foot wide, but perfect in its lively descent. Cat crossed it and walked through the tiny wood. She was surprised to see a wall appear. It was camouflaged in moss and ferns, but you could still clearly make out the rounded stones piled one on top of the other. It looked very old and had a narrow ditch running along its base. Cat followed the wall and realised that it went around in a circle. After a few yards she found an opening. The dogs ran in and disappeared.

Cat followed them through what must once have been a small stone arch and was astounded to find herself standing in a round walled area, no bigger than the length of three cars. Six beech trees grew in the middle, equally spaced between each other. They were small and gnarled, no taller than herself, and covered in a bright green moss which gave their bare branches a soft velvety appearance. Another tree grew on its own, on a little rise close to the wall's edge. It looked as if it still had some foliage on it which fluttered in the breeze. On closer inspection, Cat discovered that it had little strips of cloth tied to its branches. The little rags were grey and rotted. At the foot of the tree was a large round moss-covered stone with a hollow in the middle. Cat dipped her hand in the cold water that had collected there, somehow knowing that others had made the same gesture many times before.

Behind the rag-tree, the wall rose to over six feet and a little rock ledge jutted out under a square opening. Cat scrambled up the ledge and looked out. The opening and little ledge were not put there by accident, she thought, marvelling at the ingenuity of whoever built this tiny fort. From where she sat, Cat had a command-ing view of the surrounding hills. As her eyes grew accustomed to the horizon, Cat found with delight that she could actually see the sea far away like a thin blue line on the horizon. It was the perfect look-out post. Cat leaned back and imagined someone sitting in her place, scanning the sea for the outline of a sail, the black spike of a mast. Her gaze fell naturally on a hill across the valley and she knew instinctively that up there she would find another ruined wall, perhaps with its own lookout.

Cat sat and marvelled at the stillness. She found she could selectively experience each sense one by one. The light wind as it rippled through her hair, the taste of the sea that it carried, the smell of the wet grass, the cold hard stones under her.

The dogs were getting restless again. Cat rose to leave, stopping once more at the little tree. On impulse she dug into her jeans and ripped out the light cotton pocket. Then she leaned down and tied the bit of material on an empty branch. She had no idea why it felt so right, but the sight of that little piece of white cotton fluttering in the breeze made her feel very happy.

The sun was fully up as she left the trees and started

walking back down the hill. In front of her she could make out the purple outline of the mountains. All around her the land rose and fell in a succession of little green fields held captive by their low grey walls. It looked like a crazy jigsaw left behind by a gargantuan child, the green and grey only relieved here and there by the flashy splash of yellow gorse.

Cat stopped at the ruins of the house. A great sadness hung over it like a small dark cloud. Cat saw the piece of mirror she had found. She picked it up and started walking down to the cottage. Maggie must be up, she thought as she saw a thin plume of smoke coming from the chimney. Cat could smell the peat burning in the fire, and carried faintly in the breeze, the smell of breakfast cooking,

She would stay here for a while longer, she thought. She would stay and think, and take long walks, and think some more. Cat decided that before visiting Maggie's friend she would stop in Bantry and hand in her rental car. She'd get some money out of the bank and buy a cheap second-hand one. She'd have to get some shopping as well. There were things she needed if she was going to stay on her own in the cottage. She wasn't ready to leave yet.

Chapter Twenty-Five

Cat sank deeper into the hot water and groaned. She had to admit that Maggie was right. The hot tub was just what she needed.

"Isn't this just pure magic?" asked Maggie as she floated, her toes peeking out like a row of pink cocktail sausages. The water was scalding hot and it had taken five minutes of dipping and hesitating, until they felt comfortable enough to ease themselves into the big round tub. Cat submerged herself completely, blowing bubbles through her nose as she resurfaced. The essential oils in the water seemed to seep into every pore, both relaxing and refreshing her. Ciara had listened to Maggie's explanations and thought a few moments before deciding that what Cat need was a combination of rosemary, bergamot, and a dash of orange. The tub was big enough to fit three people comfortably. Ciara looked on approvingly as Cat let her whole body float on the surface.

"You just lie there and relax," she said, her voice like the purr of a contented cat.

"If I get any more relaxed I'm going to fall asleep," Cat murmured lazily.

"You can do that too," said Ciara laughing. "Just listen to your body."

Ciara was older than Cat had thought when she first caught sight of her, closer to fifty than thirty. She had stood, waving madly, as Maggie and Cat had trudged through the marshy land that led to Ciara's place. Her flowing dress whipped in the wind and her long braided hair extensions and slight figure belonged to a woman half her age.

It had taken over an hour to get there, driving down a long finger of land which extended into the sea until they reached the Head. Cat had hung on to her seat as Maggie followed a dirt track which hung just a few feet from the edge of a sheer drop into the dark blue water. She hadn't dared to ask what one did if a car arrived in the opposite direction. After about a mile, the track ended at a farm gate. Cat and Maggie climbed over and then walked for another half mile or so, until they saw Ciara's silhouette waving up ahead. Cat was so taken by the enormity of the landscape that she did not speak at all. The sky above her was huge, the cliffs black and rugged. All around her the sea roared. Waves swept in and crashed on the black rocks in bright spumes of foam, three stories high, and Cat caught the taste of salt on her tongue.

Ciara had built a tiny construction perched up on the rock overlooking the sea. It hugged the cliff so closely that it blended in perfectly with the landscape. If you didn't know it was there, you wouldn't see it at all. Inside was a tiny kitchen, one wall just the bare rock of the cliff, and a small bedroom which seemed to jut out over the ocean. Cat peered down and saw the water swirling wildly below. A seagull flew right by the window looking as surprised to see Cat as Cat was to see it. The land all around was wild and scrubby except where it fell away from the little house and rolled into a long meadow. In the top corner stood a Japanese gazebo that housed the hot tub.

"When it gets too hot, just run out and jump into the lagoon. It's freshwater and ice cold," Ciara said, pointing out the door of the gazebo, to a calm expense of black water about fifty yards from the tub. A little stream ran into it on the left and a row of black rocks formed a barrier between the lagoon and the crashing sea.

Cat sank back into the water and looked out to the Atlantic Ocean. On the horizon hung the faint outline of little islands suspended in the low fluffy clouds.

"I think I'm just about ready," said Ciara lifting herself out of the tub. "Here goes!" she yelled giving her entire body a little shake, her wet hair extensions swinging out in a wide circle and spraying the room. Then she let out a loud war whoop and ran out the door. Cat and Maggie laughed as they watched her run across the meadow with the wild abandon of a five-year-old. Her body was bright pink from the heat of the tub. Her hair was flying. Her breasts were bobbing and her hips were swaying as she ran giggling in pure delight. Then she turned and started running back to the lagoon. Ciara jumped high in the air before splashing into the cold water, screeching at the top of her lungs.

"*Sweet Mother of Christ, that's cold!*' she yelled as she resurfaced. She got out, water streaming down her body and lay on a flat rock facing the sea. "It's wonderful! You have to try it!"

"Aren't you freezing?" Cat yelled down to her.

"Nope. The heat is still in me from the tub. You've really got to try this."

"She's quite something," said Cat turning to Maggie who was still floating languidly.

"Isn't she just? We've been friends for about ten years and she never ceases to amaze me."

"How did she end up here?"

"You're not going to believe it but she was in the

rag trade for twenty years. Seventh Avenue garment district. She was a big time PR consultant. Made her way up the ladder from the shop floor."

"You're kidding?" Cat looked at the deeply tanned woman lying naked on a rock. It was hard to imagine her in a power suit yelling down the phone.

"It's absolutely true. After fifteen years she got sick of it. She bought this place, worked for another five years saving and investing her money, and then she just quit. That was about ten years ago. She owns about two hundred acres. It's all just wilderness really except for this tub and the house."

Maggie heaved her large frame out of the water.

"Shall we?" she asked Cat, nodding towards the lagoon.

"I guess," said Cat, pulling herself out of the tub.

Two women looked at each other and smiled. They stopped at the door feeling the wind flowing over their bodies like a caress. Then they joined hands and ran screaming down the little rise. They both jumped as they reached the lagoon, splashing into the water together, screeching and giggling, laughing and gasping for breath.

The water was so cold it made Cat's heart stop. But it tasted so sweet and clear that she wanted to open her mouth and take great big gulps of it. She pulled herself out of the water and lay down next to Ciara as

Maggie started swimming through the lagoon with a slow majestic breast stroke.

The sun had warmed the rock and Cat hugged the stone, feeling her own inner heat from the hot tub rise slowly to the surface of her skin, and sighed.

"This is the business, isn't it?" asked Ciara.

Cat murmured in agreement. She sat up and felt the wind as it swept off the sea. It was extraordinary, she thought. Here she was, sitting naked on a rock, with the wind whipping past her, and a light rain starting to fall, and she did not feel the cold.

"Maggie was telling me about your problems with Maeve," Ciara said, casually broaching the subject.

"Do you know about her?" asked Cat. For the first time she really wanted to know. "Do you think she was a real witch?"

"I've heard of her, of course," Ciara answered pulling a long stalk of grass and chewing it out of the corner of her mouth. "She's pretty well known around here. As to whether she was a real witch – I don't know. The witch hunt craze never hit Ireland as violently as the rest of Europe but women were still often falsely accused of witchcraft up until the late nineteenth century. Have you ever heard of Bridgit Cleary?"

"No. Was she a witch?"

"I don't think so. Not in the conventional sense by any means. Bridgit Cleary was burned to death by her husband and neighbours in 1894 in Clonmel. Her husband, Michael Cleary, accused his wife of having changed. He said she had grown two inches taller, and acted more refined. She liked to take long walks on her own and she was said to visit the local fairy fort. Michael Cleary suspected foul play by the fairies. Michael confronted Bridgit and accused her of being a changeling. She denied it, so with the help of Bridgit's own family and neighbours, Michael Cleary began to torture Bridgit. When that did not change her story, they held her over the fire to chase the evil out. The whole lot of them were sent to trial for manslaughter. Michael Cleary got twenty years of hard labour, but he was still convinced his wife had been bewitched."

Cat lay back and pondered the story. Was it a coincidence that Ciara had chosen to tell her about a woman who had been burned to death? How could she know?

"So what about you?" Cat asked. "Are you really a witch?"

"What do you think?" Ciara answered turning to face her. Cat looked at her closely, not knowing what she was looking for behind the light green sparkle of her eyes.

"I don't know," Cat said, suddenly unsure of herself. "I can't read you."

"But you can read other people, can't you?" asked Ciara, her pupils widening ever so slightly.

Cat nodded slowly. She'd always known that she could read people. Since she was a little girl she'd known if they were sad, or angry. She also knew how to catch their attention and get them to do what she wanted as if they had thought of it themselves. Sometimes she just knew something about them – that they had great pain in their past, or something really stupid, like that they loved chocolate. She had just never really admitted it before.

"Can you read people?" Cat asked.

"Most people," Ciara said spitting out her grass stalk and pulling out another one.

"Can you read me?"

"Not really. Not unless you let me."

Cat said nothing as she let that sink in. She knew what Ciara was talking about, but she didn't understand it.

"How does that work?" she asked as if talking to herself. "How can I do that?"

Ciara shrugged and shook her head, her long extensions flying around her before settling back on her shoulders. She waved at Maggie who was climbing out of the lagoon.

"I don't really know," she said laughing. "Some of us have it and some of us don't. All I know is that if you do have it you can recognise others who do, because you can't read them."

Cat watched Maggie as she stood in front of the sea and stretched her arms high in the air.

"Maggie doesn't have it," Cat said suddenly. Maggie was like a cool stream. Cat could see right through her.

"No. Maggie doesn't have it," Ciara said smiling. Then she took Cat's hand, turning it palm up to face her. Cat felt a shiver run up her spine.

"But you do," Ciara said tracing the lines with her finger. "It's there inside you. You just have to trust yourself."

"So how are we getting on?" Maggie asked as she sauntered up to the rock. Ciara patted Cat's hand and smiled.

"We're grand," she said, nodding at Cat. "Just grand."

The effects of meeting Ciara and lounging in the tub were still with her as she waved goodbye to Maggie the next day. Cat had slept like a baby. It was as if she had left all the stress and the worry that plagued her behind in the water.

It had taken three false starts before Maggie was truly off, waving back at Cat as she drove down the hill, shouting promises of an early return out the window. Cat looked at the beat-up Toyota parked in the laneway and smiled. It was a far cry from her Land Rover but it would do just fine. The cottage was stacked with food and fuel. She had no need to go anywhere. No one knew she was there. No one would come looking for her. Cat had composed a short note saying that she was booking into a holistic retreat for two weeks and gave it to Maggie to send to her lawyers once she got to Arizona.

She found she could think about New York without the sour taste of panic rising in her throat. She had all the time in the world to think about it. One step at a time. First she was going to make sure that she never spent another night plagued by visions of burning houses. She wasn't sure how, but she knew she would do it that night.

Cat spent the day wandering around the house deep in thought. Occasionally she picked something up and placed it on the low table in front of the sofa. The light was starting to fade and Cat thought she might take the dogs for a walk up the hill before nightfall. She looked down at the table and started picking through things. She discarded Trevor's binder, but kept her mother's diary, propping up the photograph against it. The binder had nothing to do with this, she thought. The necklace and the thimble were in the middle surrounded by candles as they had been the last time she'd seen Maeve. On impulse, she opened her sketchbook and placed a few drawings on the table. It looked like a little altar she thought, with a laugh. What did she think she was doing? It was like walking blindly through a tunnel that twisted and turned in the dark, hoping that one more step would bring you into the light.

Cat picked up the cheap hardback notebook she had bought that day in town. It was too thin and too large for her taste but they had nothing else in the discount shop. She should have gone to a stationary store and bought a proper diary.

Cat thought of her first diary. She must have been ten or eleven. She had just read *The Diary of Anne Frank* and was very impressed. She'd asked for a diary with a lock and was given a lovely red patent leather one. It was shiny and had *My Diary* embossed in gold letters. Cat remembered that she had named it Kitty. Or was that the name of AF's diary? She couldn't remember. How could she forget, she wondered? What happens to the things that we forget? Where do they go?

She was really proud of that diary. It was so shiny and red. It had a heart-shaped lock and two little golden keys (shades of Alice in Wonderland – *Eat me!*). She'd lost the little keys but found that the heart-shaped lock could be opened with a twisted bobby pin. It was even better than a key. More secret somehow.

She poured her heart out to it. It was like finding a friend. Over the years she'd filled a stack of diaries and piles of hard-backed notebooks. Some of them were covered in silk. Some had beautiful paintings on them. She'd kept it up in boarding-school. She couldn't remember when she stopped altogether, nor where her diaries were now. Probably in a box somewhere in the Hamptons.

She'd bought the notebook because she'd thought that she should write it all down. By hand in a note-book. She didn't want to write on the computer, though Maggie had said that Cat was free to use it. She didn't want the alienation of the keyboard. She wanted some-thing more immediate. To press the pen to the paper and break the silence around her with tiny scratchings. She thought of her mother sitting alone in her little top-floor room in Christchurch. She too had felt the cool whiteness of the paper on the back of her hand.

Cat looked around the cottage. The whole house was smaller than the nursery when she was a kid. Mr Jiffy's head would probably touch the ceiling! There was stuff everywhere, just like in the good old days when she'd lived with Fiona. I've reverted to my post-adolescent mess living alone here, she thought. Or maybe it's just the absence of a housekeeper. Perhaps her inherent sluttishness was carefully concealed by a long line of domestics, only to appear in full glory as soon as she had no one to pick up after her.

Cat had never lived completely alone. This would be

her first time. She guessed that if she got too lonely she could always talk to the dogs.

Cat wasn't really worried about going crazy anymore. She even wondered if she might not welcome it. After all it seemed to run the family, she thought with a smirk.

Sheba sat at her feet looking up at her, expectantly wagging her tail.

"OK. OK. I'll go for a walk," Cat said, laying the notebook back on the table. She'd start writing in it as soon as she got home, she thought, giving a last look at the funny little altar on the table. Something was missing.

Cat reached over to the window-sill and picked up the broken piece of mirror from where she had left it the day before. She bent down and placed it with the necklace and the thimble. There – that looked right.

Then she went outside and started walking after the dogs who were already bounding up the hill.

Six . . .

Chapter Twenty-Six

•◆•

Cat stirred in her sleep. The wind whipped around the cottage. High on the hill she heard a keening wail. Cat knew that she was dreaming. She tried to open her eyes but her lids were too heavy.

Maeve was talking to a woman.

The woman was scared of Maeve. But under her fear she was consumed with hatred. She hated her life of toil and pain which had turned her into an old woman before her time. She hated the man who had chained her to this place, had burdened her with his children. Most of all she hated Maeve. She hated her strong gaze, and her straight back, her clear commanding voice and her ringing laugh. She hated her beauty which had every man in the village bewitched, including her wretched husband, who had never uttered a kind word in his life, but who dropped what he was doing and ran the minute he saw Maeve coming down the hill to fetch water.

"I will leave her here," Maeve said. "You will keep her safe. If you hear them coming you'll warn me. I'll come for her first thing in the morning and we will leave this place forever. In return I'll give you the cottage and the land."

"How do I know you're not lying?" asked the woman. "Why should I go out and try and stop a pack of drunken fools for the likes of ye?"

Maeve held out a piece of paper. "This gives you claim to the house and the land."

She folded the piece of paper and handed it to her. The woman shrugged and tucked it in her bodice. She couldn't read anyway.

Maeve walked up to the cradle and took her necklace off.

Cat shifted in her sleep. A bell was ringing somewhere. Cat struggled to block out the sound but it just kept on ringing. It was a phone. Why didn't someone pick up the God-damn phone?

"Sorry to call you so late. I just got in and have I got some news for you! You're not going to believe this, but she never went to London. She got off the plane in Shannon. It bothered me that she took so much money out of the ATM at the airport. Why would she get Irish money when she was going to England, I said to myself? But I just figured she was just rich and eccentric. Maybe she likes carrying cash? I don't know. So nothing's happening on the card for weeks. Then she goes into a bank to get some money. This is in Bantry – that's some little town in the South. I guess she needed more cash.

But here's the good part. When she got off in Shannon she rented a car! And the same day she goes to the bank she hands the car back – paid on the card! So I figure it's a little town – maybe they remember her. I just called the rental office. A lovely girl answered. A real chatterbox. She sounded like the leprechaun in the Lucky Charms commercial. She remembers your friend real well. Says she's been around for weeks living up some mountain in a cottage. She said she thinks your friend is staying for a while. She bought a second-hand car. The kid in the office knew that, because she recommended her cousin who has a Used Car dealership. I've got the name of the place where she's living but I'm going to have to spell it for you. I sure as hell can't pronounce it!"

Trevor searched frantically for a pen along the kitchen counter. Finding one he quickly wrote down the letters as Barney called them out.

"Kilkeambeg," Trevor said mouthing the name slowly. "And this is near Bantry in Ireland?"

"Yeah, Bantry in County Cork. My little friend at the car rental tells me it's gorgeous over there. She made me promise to go and visit some time."

"Thanks, Barney. You've been great," said Trevor. Then he hung up and immediately started to pack.

Bob Stigeman paced his bedroom. He'd spent most of the last few weeks pacing rooms, trying to figure out where he had gone wrong. What the fuck was he going to do now? He knew he should probably have already left the country. He had a substantial amount stashed away. And one day someone would come looking for it.

It was a tidy sum, but nowhere near the prize he had worked so hard to achieve. He had come so close. So close – and then he'd blown it. Stupid. Maybe he'd been too greedy. Maybe he should have waited a little longer. In time he may have persuaded that stuck-up spoilt bitch to marry him. Then he would be riding high. More money than he could have ever dreamed of. His nest-egg in the Cayman Islands was peanuts compared to what he could have had.

Bob looked at the pile of pornographic videos stacked on the floor and wondered idly how he would spend the evening. Stupid stuck-up bitch! He would have liked to show her a few of the things he kept in his closet for entertainment. But he'd gone at it too fast and he hadn't even been able to get it up when he had his chance. Stupid stuck-up spoilt bitch!

Maybe he could get her for blackmail? How much would she pay for him to keep quiet about the old man?

Bob discarded the thought as he picked up the phone and dialled a number by heart. He was getting too boring. It was time for a little fun. All work and no play makes Jack a dull boy, he said to himself, as he poured a large tumbler of Scotch.

When the woman answered, Bob put in his order briefly. He wanted something to get his mind off his worries. They knew his tastes and had never disappointed him. It was time for a little fun. He would deal with the bitch later.

Bob crossed the room and opened the closet. Then he stood sipping his drink as he surveyed the black leather belts and heavy metal chains.

The night nurse came in and tucked the covers up to the old woman's chin. She looked so peaceful when she slept. The nurse picked up the chart and read it, nodding approvingly. The old woman would sleep well tonight. Then she quietly left the room and squeaked her way down the hall . . .

*   *   *

Maeve held out a piece of paper and handed it to a large short woman. The woman shrugged and tucked it in her bodice. She couldn't read anyway.

"I don't trust you, Bridgit Kelly. I'm taking your baby and leaving mine. Like that I know that you'll warn me. You'll have to warn me. I'll be back by first light."

Maeve was trembling as she turned to open the door. She turned back one last time. Her eyes were wet with tears as she blew a kiss to the little cradle.

"You'll keep my child safe. Promise me that you'll keep her safe."

The woman shrugged.

"You'll keep her safe! If anything happens to me, you'll keep her safe or so help me God I will come back from the grave and curse you and yours forever."

The woman's eyes grew wide as Maeve's voice rose.

"I'll keep her safe."

Maeve turned and left, carrying the woman's baby in her arms.

"Curse you, Maeve Ní Laoghaire," the woman hissed under her breath. "Curse you and that brat of yours."

The sound of shouts and yells echoed up from the valley, but the woman paid no heed. She was too scared to go for help, or to tell anyone about what had happened that night. Too scared to go out and face the men. Too scared of the beating that she'd get from her husband who was sure to be leading the pack, his belly full of whiskey and his eyes full of lust for that hoor up the hill. She stood at the window and watched as Maeve walked up the hill to her house . . .

"Tell her!" Cat yelled. "Tell her they're coming! Warn her! You said you'd warn her!"

Chapter Twenty-Seven

◆—◆—◆

Cat woke with a start. The dream had rattled her. She could only remember snatches. She knew she'd dreamt of Maeve. And of Fiona. And something about Valerie and Ramon. All the old crowd. She'd clearly dreamt of Fiona and Trevor. The thought of Trevor made her pause. It occurred to her that he was looking for her. And what about Bob? There was some very weird stuff about Bob.

Cat reached down and picked up the open notebook lying on the table. She read what she had written before falling asleep

Kilkeambeg
  I took the dogs for a walk this evening. We went to the top of her hill. At the very top I climbed the

gate and the dogs jumped up on to the wall with me. The sun had just dipped below the horizon and the hills looked like they were on fire, glowing pink to blood red. I knew that to my left was the sea and to my right, far away, were the Kerry mountains, but I could see nothing through the scarlet glare except for the round flat disk of the new moon, like a black hole sucking in the landscape.

And somewhere, out there, thousands of miles away was New York. I heard a loud chattering coming from the copse of trees where I'd found the fairy fort. I looked over and saw a group of magpies take off and fly down into the valley. I counted them under my breath: one, two, three, four, five, six, seven:

We must have looked like cut-out silhouettes up there on that wall, me and my dogs. I bet you could see us for miles around. The evening chill seeped in under what was left of the afternoon's summer breeze and I shivered under my thin T-shirt. By the time we got home the night had come, making shapes out of shadows.

What an odd way to start, thought Cat closing the notebook and throwing it back on the table.

Cat checked her watch. It was coming up to midnight. She looked at the objects she had carefully assembled on the table: piece of broken mirror, thimble, and necklace. Her mother's diary, the picture of her parents. The candles had all burned down low. They flickered faintly in glistening pools of wax. Ciara had said to trust herself. That the answer lay somewhere inside. So Cat had assembled the objects and waited. She'd thought about calling out to Maeve, or humming a mantra, but had rejected it as silly.

In the end she had just fallen asleep and had some weirdly vivid dreams of which she could only remember scraps, like tatters of tiny ribbons flitting in the breeze. She felt a bit stupid really. And tired. She was very tired.

Cat started blowing out the candles and thought about the dreams she'd had. Her mind kept going back to the dreams about Maeve. To the baby in the cradle. She picked up the sketches of Maeve and stacked them on the table. The one with all the magpies lay on top. Who was the woman with Maeve?

Cat was leaning over to reach a candle when she was attracted to something flickering. It was a reflection in the piece of mirror. Cat peered at it and gasped. It looked like an eye looking back at her. A small round eye. Cat held the mirror further away. She could see a bird reflected in the mirror as if it was peering down at her from the rafters. Cat looked up knowing perfectly well there was no bird there, but looking all the same. The room was quiet, the dogs were asleep. The fire was low, just red glowing embers. No cradle stood in the corner. But when Cat looked into the mirror again she clearly saw Maeve taking her necklace off and tucking it into the cradle.

A movement caught her eye at the window. A woman was peering out of the window as if watching for someone outside.

Cat's heart started to pound. Down the road she could hear voices. Angry voices. They were coming! They were coming to get her. Cat looked into the mirror and saw Maeve walking up the hill towards the black outline of the house, its windows casting yellow light into the dark night. High above her hung a black moon.

Cat ran to the door, only vaguely aware that she had run straight through the woman at the window. She had to warn Maeve. Maybe if she caught up before Maeve reached the house she could stop her going in. Cat scanned the hill but saw nothing.

She stood bewildered, feeling the wind rushing past her. It rose from the valley carrying the sound of yells and curses. Cat strained to hear but she could barely make out the words. She ran down the laneway, slipping in the cold mud and falling. As she pulled herself up she could hear that they were much nearer.

Cat cringed as she saw the bright light of the torches

coming up the road. A man in a long black robe was standing in front of the mob. He seemed to be address-ing them, but the mob kept moving, pushing him aside. A large man in a cap took the lead. He raised his torch and yelled something to the crowd who in turn waved their flaming torches, yelling and hooting.

Cat turned and ran back into the yard. At the window she could still see the woman peering out. The woman wasn't going to warn Maeve. She was so filled with hate and fear, and lies and pain that she would do nothing to save Maeve. She would forget her child up in that house. She would forget and no one would ever know. She would have the house and the land. She set her face in grim determination, her lips turned down as if she had smelt something bad. She was going to stand there and watch the witch burn.

Cat looked up and saw Maeve walking up the hill. Or was she walking down it? Cat was disoriented. Time seemed to have lost its familiar shape. Behind her she heard the mob's frenzy rise, while above her the house was already in flames. One man was yelling loudly, egging them on.

Cat ran as fast as she could. She could see the house clearly. The windows glowed with candlelight. It seemed very comfortable inside, with high draperies framing the windows, and pictures hung on the walls.

A figure slipped out of the shadows. It was the big

man in the tweed cap. On the other side of the house Cat could hear the angry mob yelling, she could smell the blood-lust in the air. But this man was alone. He held a flaming torch aloft and jammed a big rock against the door. Then he bent down and lit some dried grass. It crackled and spit as the flames took hold.

The man stopped at the window. Cat looked over his shoulder and saw Maeve standing in front of a mirror. She was brushing her long hair. Maeve looked at the man for a second. Then she spat on the ground and turned back to face the mirror. Cat banged on the window. The man disappeared but Maeve just kept on brushing her hair.

Cat looked up in horror and saw flames licking the roof.

She struggled to open the door, shoving the big stone away. Black smoke poured out, making her cough. The curtains and all the furnishings were on fire.

Maeve seemed oblivious to the flames. She stood very still. She was talking to the mirror. She mouthed silent curses as the flames danced in the reflection of her eyes.

The heat was oppressive. Cat tried to grab Maeve's shawl but her hand swept right through it. Cat was frantic. She could not stay in the house much longer. Already the flames were swirling up the banister.

She stood behind Maeve and looked into the mirror.

She felt the reflection of their eyes lock. Then Maeve's face seemed to melt and Cat found she was looking only at herself.

Time stood still as she felt a rush of thoughts, and images, and feelings tumble into her mind like carnival streamers. She was mesmerised by their colour and brilliance. Then, quite suddenly, she was back in the house again, looking at her reflection. Only it was different. A door had opened to a new world. She knew everything Maeve knew. Felt everything she had felt. She knew the man at the door was Mick Kelly and that he was crazy with lust for the woman he thought was a witch. He had roused the others to banish her, had cursed her for laughing at him. His wife would not stop him, locked as she was in her prison of fear and hatred of the witch. Mary Kelly hated Annie because she was Maeve's brat. Maeve's brat.

Cat stood perfectly still overwhelmed by the feelings running through her. She was Maeve's brat. Cat and her mother, and her mother's mother all went back to that child left in the cradle. All went back to Maeve whom she could feel inside her as she stretched out and filled Cat's body. She could feel Maeve rediscovering the material world and she had to resist the temptation of letting Maeve lose herself in the sensations.

A loud crack made her jump. The staircase was

crumbling. Cat looked around and saw the flames running up the carpet towards her. She forced her will to override Maeve's and headed for the door. As she stumbled out, the windows shattered with the heat. Cat threw herself to the ground, covering her head with her arms. When she looked up again the house was engulfed in flames. Over the roar of the fire she could still hear the men laughing and jeering.

Cat ran up the hill, her feet barely touching the ground, her mind blank except for the need to get away. She ran into the shelter of the trees until she reached the stream and came to an abrupt stop. The water tripped over the black stones and into little whirlpools that reflected the starlight shining in through the trees. Something was stopping her from clearing the stream. Though she still shivered with fear at the sounds behind her, she could not seem to put a foot forward into the water. Maeve was stopping her. Maeve was scared. But Cat knew that they had to cross. Only if they crossed would they be safe.

Taking a few steps backwards, Cat made a huge effort of will, took a running start and sailed over the little stream. She landed on the other side with a thud and fell to the ground, winded. When she had caught her breath enough to look up she saw Maeve's shimmering outline beckoning her up into the fairy fort. Cat followed, amazed to find herself alone in her own body again. Her step was as light as her head. They were safe now.

Cat found Maeve sitting at the little lookout post. Next to her, on a little rock ledge, sat an old mirror. It looked like the one she had seen at the house, except that this one was shattered and had a big piece missing. Cat reached out for it and realised she was still holding the piece of mirror she had carried from the cottage. It fitted perfectly.

Cat held out the mirror seeing herself reflected in the faint light. Maeve stood behind her. As she watched the mirror seemed to mend, its pieces melting into one another, until she held a glowing frame in her hand.

Cat looked in the mirror and saw Trevor, asleep in what looked like an armchair. A magazine was open on his chest and tiny earphones dangled from under his tousled hair. He's on a plane, she thought. He's on his way here! The thought shocked her so much that she looked away.

But the glow pulled her back again. Looking in, she was disappointed that she could see very little. It was dark except for a few small blinking lights. A shape in the middle looked like it could be a figure lying in a bed. Cat peered more closely, willing herself to see more clearly and found herself actually in the room she was looking at. She was standing next to a high bed which she immediately recognised as her grandfather's sick bed. He was sleeping peacefully, his mouth open. Cat bent down and hugged him, feeling his heartbeat, slow but strong. There was still life burning there. All it needed was a bellows. She kissed his cheek and wished him well, willing that tiny spark she had felt to grow.

The scene dissolved around her and Cat felt confused until she realised that she was in another room. It was much smaller than the last, with high windows that had iron bars on them. The small woman looked tiny in the large hospital bed. Her eyes flashed open suddenly with a small gasp of surprise. They smiled when they saw Cat.

"Katie? How are you, pet? I worry so much about you, you know."

"I know," Cat whispered, her voice catching in her throat.

"So, are ye well?" the woman asked her eyes full of love and concern.

Cat could only nod. She tried to smile back, but her face was crunched up with the tears that she felt coursing down her cheeks.

"Don't cry, pet," she said softly. "Let me see ye smile."

Cat swallowed her tears and watched the woman sigh happily.

"That's good. That's all I have to know. As long as you're well, I'm happy."

Cat reached out to her but the room was dissolving again. She cried out to stop it but it was too late.

Cat looked up and was surprised to find herself still standing holding the mirror. Maeve sat peacefully beside her. Cat knew she was losing her. Already the sky was not as dark, and Maeve's figure seemed to have paled with the night. Cat saw that the mirror too was losing its glow.

She felt an urgency to look in it again. To use its power. At first she only saw her own reflection, with Maeve sitting behind her. Then their two figures changed until Cat was looking at two people sitting at a table. It was covered in fine cutlery and a crisp white linen tablecloth.

Fiona hung her head as she wept. Ramon stroked her hair and offered her a tissue.

"I don't know where she is. No one does."

"I'm sure she is fine. Maybe she met a man – God knows she could use one. Maybe she needed a break. She's been very stressed out lately."

"Lately?" said Fiona, shaking her head. "It's been longer than just lately. The woman has become absolutely driven. But I still can't believe she hasn't even rung me."

"Look, when she gets back why don't you just talk to her? It'll be all right."

"No," said Fiona sadly. "There's no use talking to

her. I'm afraid it's worse than you think. At best she'll just fire me. Not that I care. You know that she fired Bob."

"And I say good riddance! I never liked that *cabron*."

"Neither did I. I hate the bastard," said Fiona spitting out her words.

"That sonofabitch is the reason I'll never be friends with Cat again."

"What are you talking about Fiona? You're not making sense."

Fiona looked stricken. Then she collapsed into another flood of tears. When she started talking again it was in a rush of words too long suppressed. "I don't know how it happened. It just seemed like one of Bob's sick jokes and then before I knew it I was caught. And Cat was so distant and cold I figured she'd believe him rather than me."

Ramon shrugged his shoulders, not understanding. Fiona took a deep breath and started again.

"When I was living with Cat I accepted some money from her grandfather. I was broke and he offered to help. I didn't want Cat to know. Stupid really, but I was always very, I don't know, proud that I couldn't give a hoot whether she was rich or not. I just love Cat.

"Anyway Bob came across the checks and he joked that the old man had paid me to spy on Cat. Then he started hinting that he wanted to continue the business deal. He would pay me to keep tabs on Cat. He never came out and said it. Not right away, but he always alluded to it. How it could really be worth my while and such rubbish. Then one day when I refused to show him the appointment book he said that I might as well keep it up. That I was in too deep to pull out! That if he went to Cat now, she would throw me in jail. I told him to fuck off! I didn't know what he was talking about. Then he started laughing. And cool as you please, he tells me to stop pretending. He had all the proof he needed. 'Stop making believe this never happened, Fiona', he said. And he showed me cashed checks: 'for services rendered'. And dates and false rendezvous! I didn't know what to do. I should have gone to Cat immediately but we just didn't seem as close anymore. I didn't know if she'd believe me." Fiona took a long gulp from her glass of wine. "I don't care about the job. But I do care about Cat. She's so alone. If she thought I had betrayed her she'd be terribly hurt."

"And you think she knows?" Ramon asked softly.

"Yes, I do. She fired Bob. I'm sure it has something to do with it. And I don't know where she is, so I can't explain. Why doesn't she call me? Maybe she's so disgusted that she just can't bring herself to talk to me," she said, hanging her head again.

"So what are you going to do?"

"I'm going to wait for her to come home. Then I'm going to quit this stupid job and see if I can get my best friend back."

Cat was seething. The reflection in the mirror swirled in crazy spirals, red, orange and yellow. The anger she had been repressing for weeks, years, reared up inside her and focused on one point: *Bob Stigeman.*

Bob Stigeman, the bastard who had conned her grandfather into trusting him, had stolen her money, and blackmailed her friends. What else was he capable of? Firing him was too good for him. She would get his ass and get it good.

Cat saw his standard-issue good looks smiling leeringly at his reflection as he strutted around in black leather chaps. She could see him as if she was sitting behind a one-way mirror. The image repulsed her but it did not dampen her anger. In the corner of the room Cat could make out a figure sitting on a chair that seemed to be bound and gagged. She could not tell if it was a man or a woman. She scanned the figure for fear or pain, but registered only boredom. So *this* is how you get your rocks off, you creep, she thought.

Bob pranced in front of the mirror, clearly aroused. Cat's anger rose to a red blinding fury. She willed Bob to look deep into the mirror feeling his eyes lock with hers. His expression changed from pleasure to surprise as he watched his hand reach out for a long black belt and tie it around his neck. Then he stepped into the closet and lashed it onto a big shiny hook, throwing a horrified look over his shoulder at his reflection.

Cat looked away, frightened of what she thought she had seen. Her anger dissipated in her fear. She stole a quick glance back at the mirror and was relieved to see that it was dark except for the faint radiance of dawn reflected from the sky.

The dawn was rising! She looked around for Maeve, but she was gone. The window at the look-out post was deserted.

Cat felt the mirror fading in her hands. She held it up once more catching the red glow of the sunrise in her reflection. Then she clearly saw Maeve standing behind her. Only this time she wasn't alone. Maeve stepped aside and Cat saw Annie Kelly take her place and smile. Behind her was another woman who raised her hand in welcome, and behind her was another, and behind her yet another. Maeve walked back a few yards and stepped into a space in the long line of figures that Cat now saw extended far over the hills. A long line of women, linking hands over the fields, over the mountains and across the oceans until they reached the mouth of a cave.

As the sun rose over the hill, blazing a trail in the sky with its rays, Cat saw a woman step out from the cave. She was naked. Her long hair fell in waves down her back and over her breasts. In her hands she held the mirror, the reflection of that long line of women extending from its surface to Cat and back again, until they criss-crossed to infinity and Cat no longer knew which reflection she was looking at. *"Lillith,"* whispered a voice in her head.

Then one by one the women turned and walked into the cave as the sun fully lit up the sky. Maeve stood aside and waited until Annie caught up. Annie hesitated, giving Cat a longing glance, turning only when Maeve and the naked woman put their arms around her and led her in.

Cat strained to see but the sun's glare blinded her. She blinked and was surprised to find herself holding the piece of broken glass she had picked up in the ruins. Little flecks of silver stuck to it, reflecting the landscape like a weird kaleidoscope.

The birds were singing all around her. It was a new day.

Cat started walking back out of the little wood. With each step she took she knew that her mind was absorbing the events of the night, forgetting some, recording others. She worried that by the time she got to the cottage she would have forgotten it all. But she felt confident that some bits would remain. She would remember as much as she could handle. They were, after all, things she had always known but had been unaware of.

She felt a flood of relief knowing that Maeve was at peace now. She no longer had to stand cursing those who had failed to warn her, had murdered her in her own house. She would never walk the hills again, nor haunt the cottage, or the blackened ruins which Cat now walked past without a second glance. She was quite content to sit at the lookout post searching the horizon.

Cat heard the cackle of birds fighting over a scrap. A group of magpies bobbed and darted in the grass. *Seven for a secret that has never been told,* Cat said to herself as she shooed the magpies away. Well, she would have to tell it someday. In her own time, she would unravel it all.

Cat stopped and looked down the valley, shading her eyes against the sun. The world was bright and fresh. She looked around and felt a sharp new focus to her gaze. The world was the same and yet slightly different. The landscape shimmered with possibilities like a lake that held hidden meanings under its still waters. She listened to the birds singing, to her soft even breathing, as she looked inward with her new found sight. She knew that Trevor was on his way. And that her mother had gone in peace. And that Bob had gone in pain. And that her grandfather was not ready to go yet.

She whistled for the dogs and smiled as she heard their answering bark. Already she could see Sheba bounding up the hill to greet her. She would go in and cook a big breakfast. Then she would tidy up and maybe have a nap. When she woke up, it would be just about time to go sit on the wall and wait for Trevor to come up the road. She didn't know how she knew it – she just did.

Cat stopped in the doorway and thought about him driving down to Bantry, getting directions, maybe a bite to eat; and then slowly going up the mountain. She knew that he would be taken by the beauty of the landscape. She knew that he would stop at the signpost and consult his map. She knew that he was tired, and a little frightened, and very much in love with her. She knew all of that, and yet she had no idea how she'd feel when she saw him again.

Cat smiled to herself as she stepped into the cottage. She'd just have to wait and see.

Seven . . .

Chapter Twenty-Eight

·•·

The night nurse stopped and listened at the door. She thought she heard voices coming from the room. Trying to make as little noise as possible with her big bunch of keys, she carefully opened the door. The nurse was surprised to see her charge sitting up in bed, a small lamp lit beside her. The woman turned and smiled as the nurse came in.

"You've curled your hair," said the woman.

"Why yes, I have," said the nurse even more surprised. In fact she was positively flabbergasted, as she would recount to the day nurse when they switched shift later that morning. In the five years that she had been working at the institution she did not remember ever having had a conversation with this particular patient.

"Can I get you something?" she asked, caught off guard. She wondered if she should ring the doctor on duty. Though, frankly, she had never seen the patient looking so well.

"Well, to tell you the truth, I am feeling a bit hungry," said the woman smiling mischievously.

"I could fix you a sandwich if you like?"

"That would be lovely," she answered in a light lilting accent.

The nurse stopped and took a long look at the woman.

"Are you sure you're all right?" she asked.

"Oh yes," she answered, sighing deeply. "All is right with the world."

When the nurse came back with the tray, the old lady had nodded off. Her eyes were closed and her face had a peaceful smile. The little light was still on. The nurse lay the tray on the night table and bent down to turn it off when she noticed something not right about the old lady's breathing. She reached for the woman's wrist, feeling for a pulse, but finding none.

"Well, I'll be damned," said the nurse shaking her head. Then she pulled the sheet over the woman's face and stood back to say a little prayer for her soul, as she always did whenever one of the residents passed on.